OCEAN
OF TEARS

OCEAN
OF TEARS

A Novel

STEWART WIECK

cds
BOOKS

NEW YORK

For information please address:
CDS Books
425 Madison Avenue
New York, NY 10017

ISBN: 1-59315-029-6

Orders, inquiries, and correspondence should be addressed to:
CDS Books
425 Madison Avenue
New York, NY 10017
(212) 223-2969 FAX (212) 223-1504

Design by Holly Johnson

Printed in the United States of America

10 9 8 7 6 5 4 3 2 1

For Doug and Melinda Wieck—
who allowed me to pursue my dreams.

ACKNOWLEDGMENTS

Thanks to Dan Enright of SOE for years of EQ assistance and Kurt Hausheer (author of *Plane of Hate* for the EQrpg) for some of the dark elven lore referenced herein.

OCEAN
OF TEARS

PROLOGUE

THE OATH OF AATALTAAL

THE TALL, LITHE FIGURE STOOD SILENTLY IN the shadows of the great oaks. He was dark-skinned, like the enormous trees, but there the similarities ended. Where the trees were gnarled and ancient, the elf was smooth as polished ebony and . . . far, far older.

Though it was midday and though the landscape—as well as the huge trees themselves—was devastated by fire, no sunlight penetrated to the forest's floor. Shadow-Wood Keep had been built hundreds of feet above the ground and woven into the very fabric of the ancient oaks, though they still dwarfed it. Their vast, yawning canopies had seemed beyond reach of time or pillaging orc, and the dense foliage at the uppermost branches had actually proven to be beyond the touch of the bonfires that had blossomed here only days before.

The scent of charred flesh and a sprinkling of glowing orange ornaments that were the embers of those fires attested to this recent umbrage.

The elf shook his head, only slightly, but distinctly: a terrible display of emotion from one so inured to pain and suffering that the goriest of battlefields had come to give him no pause. Of course, his soul cried out on those occasions, too, but he'd confronted so much tragedy in his centuries that he could no longer afford to acknowledge it, to truly confront it. His own personal failures weighed too heavily upon him to take on the burdens of others also crushed by the entropy of history, the disassembly of empire over which he'd too often presided.

First Takish-Hiz—*always* Takish-Hiz, the original home of those dedicated to the worship of the goddess Tunare, dedicated for the simple reason that they were elves and she'd created them. The ruinous exodus eastward across the Ocean of Tears that gave that seemingly limitless body its name only made that destruction loom larger in the elf's mind. His head sank, the chin dropping to his slender chest. His eyes, for so many hours clear of tears, nevertheless fluttered and wept a thin rivulet. The tears glistened upon his dark skin; the slight luminance of the region around Shadow-Wood Keep was just enough to cause them to shine. They streamed down his cheeks, but as they dripped from his face, the elf's eyes suddenly blinked open. His gaze remained focused downward and, as if hypnotized, he watched as the tears splattered on the limbs of the tree in which he perched. He intently studied their motion and became strangely serene, almost hopeful, as if the elven life of Shadow-Wood Keep—the men, women, and children who had teemed through these branches, who created here the seeds of a new elven kingdom, who lived life within the shadows of the Faydark Forest but beyond the gloom of the fate of Takish-Hiz—would somehow spring back to life.

Aataltaal's magical powers were prodigious, but this vision was wishful thinking, and he knew it. An old adage held that it was easier to destroy than to build, and tears would not recreate the greatest glories of the past. Indeed, the elf remained baffled how, in the face of opposition from the gods themselves, civilization existed at all. If such social orders did not suit the purpose of the gods, then why should they people this world of Norrath with races intent on empire?

It made Aataltaal almost uncontrollably angry, which meant that he clenched his eyes shut again and swallowed hard, choking back a millennia worth of frustration. The gods had surely had many countless years to determine what they desired; that their ill-conceived plans should find fruition in elves, dwarves, humans, halflings, and even trolls, ogres, iksar, and more amounted to an almost unconscionable act of ego and stupidity.

It all served to convince the elf that the gods were in truth not worthy of worship, even though their power was truly terrible and surely worthy of respect. They put ambitions in the minds of those races of Norrath, but denied them the means to see those ambitions through. Or at least they were so disorganized in their own pursuits and so opposed in their own ambitions that they put these races at odds with one another. Such dissention was for children, not beings of grandiose and incalculable power.

Yet Aataltaal also feared the people of Norrath were more than mere pawns. Knowingly or not, the gods had put too many tools in their hands. Stymied in their ambitions on Norrath itself, these people were bound to threaten the gods directly again and again, going so far as the extra-dimensional planes where the gods lived. How long would the gods allow it?

Hopefully at least once! For Aataltaal himself hoped to reassemble Tarton's Wheel and access the true homes of the gods. Not just the realms in which their shadows lived, such as Innoruuk's Plane of Hate, but the *true* homes where the gods' own immortal souls dwelled.

The elf clenched a fist and swore an oath upon the battleground before him—the ground where his fellows had so recently died. The small handful of elves here had been survivors of Takish-Hiz. They had dedicated their lives to sublime pursuits, or else they might have possessed Aataltaal's power—and therefore the capability to repulse the entire orc offensive without further support. But despite the horrendous past, despite the cruelty of the events that stripped them of their king and queen and brought glorious Takish-Hiz to ruins, these elves did not discern the essential paradox of the gods. Or perhaps they refused to admit it as Aataltaal had done, for to accept the frivolity of the gods was perhaps to find existence itself a laughable fraud.

Nevertheless, the elf's oath. He vowed that ere the gods realized the threat their creations could pose to them directly, he would succeed where the armies of the war god Rallos Zek had not: Aataltaal would undo the handiwork of the gods. The Prince of Hate, evil Innoruuk himself, was the architect whose monoliths of despair would first tumble.

Failing that, Aataltaal would slay that god and damn him alongside the perversions he created.

The fervor of his internal dialogue faded, and Aataltaal steeled himself once again to dispassionately observe the scene. Shadow-Wood Keep was lost, but he would see to it that elves lived once more within the trees of this great forest. Takish-Hiz had died because the forest around the empire withered and turned to dust. Here only elves themselves were lost. So long as this ancient forest remained, then elves would find and fashion a home here.

But before he could attend to such work, there was a matter of even greater need. He did not truly seek vengeance for this or other past acts of deceit—even in his quarrel against Innoruuk, that was not Aataltaal's real goal—but the lives lost here added to the tally that demanded redemption. The dead could not be reclaimed, but the release of those perverted by evil was yet possible. As grotesque as it seemed on the face of it, their deaths provided the excuse he required, in fact, so perfectly that he wondered if he wasn't somehow responsible for this attack. Aataltaal wove a vast tapestry of plans; some threads left unattended had a way of gaining a life of their own. Perhaps one of those resulted in this?

He shook the thought from his mind. Surely he would never allow *this* to pass, even if in the end it would lead to the redemption he sought for his race.

Though they were unaware of it, the orcs who executed this attack would now play a part in the great drama Aataltaal penned. The destruction of Shadow-Wood Keep, while tragic for the lives lost and the promises of the gods broken yet again, at least provided ample rationale for the next step in Aataltaal's great game. It meant the lives lost here were not lost in vain but rather as part of the war to recover a stolen heritage. That offered scant succor, but Aataltaal dwelt in the twilight of passing epochs, not in the bright light of any single day.

Time had come to travel among the orcs. Fortunately, Aataltaal was nearly tireless and unbeknownst to even his nominal king of the moment—Emperor Tsaph Katta of the Combine Empire—Aataltaal lived a score of different lives and was prepared for this next step. Several of his guises would now be required. Personas developed for decades would soon realize the purpose for which they'd been crafted.

He feared his unseen enemies were prepared as well, but after two thousand years of waging clandestine war against Innoruuk, Aataltaal still lived, and that meant his enemies had never yet been quite prepared enough. Not that it had been easy and by no means did he evade them completely. He came oh so very, very close to death in

Narthex'Hiz, the heart of the dark elven empire buried deep in Bristlebane's realm of Underfoot. Even the traumatic *hejira* across the Ocean of Tears was a harried flight only a half-day ahead of the pursuit, but they had fled with strength enough to conquer Weille and gain time on their enemies.

The escapes for Narthex'Hiz and Weille came first to his mind not simply because of their importance, but of their conjunction in space. The harbor now inhabited by pirates but still known as Weille would surely figure prominently in Aataltaal's future designs. There the exodus began, and there, too, he would arrange to re-enter Narthex'Hiz—or perhaps even infiltrate the newer dark elven citadel of Neriak.

And that gave the orcs of the hills an important place in his plans now. Lessons from the animal kingdom applied equally when dealing with beasts that walked on two legs: do not enter the serpent's den without knowing another exit. Such an exit existed beneath the feet of the orcs ruled by the one known as Crush.

Now Katta would surely send a force against the orcs who had destroyed Shadow-Wood Keep. And not only did the impending attack of a Combine army give Aataltaal the perfect cover to infiltrate the orcs, but it also meant he could arrange for General Seru's absence during the Great Combine Summit when Aataltaal's plan for Emperor Katta to admit the Teir'Dal to membership of the empire would finally reach fruition.

That was why it seemed almost too convenient. And because he had not planned it, these events gave Aataltaal pause. Rarely did coincidence work in his favor unless he manipulated it to be so. If it did without his involvement, then it signaled the intervention of an opponent with as much guile as himself. And if in this instance their plans overlapped, then Aataltaal could be equally sure that the next time, their plans would not.

The elf knew he needed to complete his business among the orcs quickly and then return to advise Katta. A window seemed to be opening. Secure his foothold among the orcs, delay Seru, and admit the dark elves to the Combine Empire. The means to enter Neriak would thereby be assured. And once he was again among the dark-skinned Teir'Dal, his plans could proceed.

Aataltaal's thoughts were wide-ranging and far-reaching, but these plans passed through his consciousness in the time it took for leaves, disturbed by the winds, to settle again. Ever it was thus: confronting tragedy in the present with fleeting thoughts—hopes—of distant renewal.

"May you walk among trees," Aataltaal softly spoke when the wind next rustled. The leaves fluttered and his long white hair stirred with the words of the ancient elven blessing. The Koada'Dal blessing was poison to most of those with purple lips, but Aataltaal's case was unique and he uttered the words with impunity and fervor.

Now that more of his ancient contemporaries had died, slaughtered by the orcs in their homes of Shadow-Wood Keep, who would ever believe that this youthful-seeming elf was in fact the author of that blessing? Written among the great oaks that once surrounded the elvish capitol of Takish-Hiz, where now blew only dust and sand, and strode the apparitions of all that Aataltaal sought to mend, the proverb, like its author, found a new home in this great woodland.

The elf reached overhead and plucked two acorns from a branch brimming with the seeds. One resting in each of his palms, he held them aloft in front of his face. Phrases that would tie human tongues in knots came

melodiously from his lips, and the acorns slowly blossomed with light. Dim at first, the illumination grew so
bright that a viewer a league hence might mistake the
lights for twin will-o-wisps some short distance into the
wood.

Aataltaal stretched out a single hand and turned it
over. One acorn dropped, the brilliant light leaving a
trail through the forest half-light as it fell. The elf watched
its descent. A full four-count before it hit the ground
and bounded to the feet of the nearby oaks, blackened
in the middle. It rolled to a stop and the light faded.

The other acorn's glow subsided simultaneously, and
this one Aataltaal placed in a small pouch hanging from a
silver cord around his neck. The seed rattled against another such memento and the elf moved on, his work beginning again. He stepped from his perch, but strangely
did not plummet as had the acorn. Instead he drifted
down like a leaf.

As ever, Aataltaal chose his direction, but the winds
could still alter his exact destination.

1

THE FORTRESS OF CRUSHBONE

THE TWO HUMANOIDS GLOWERED AT ONE another. The lower incisors of one were so long and sharp that he was called Sabertooth, though such beasts lived a continent away in Kunark, far to the south of Faydwer. Both figures had powerful, angular features. Their arms rippled with muscles, and the cords of their necks stood out against the dull, mottled gray and green of their skin. Their heads were bald and their foreheads sloped back from heavy brows that shadowed malicious eyes.

One crouched, its sword in hand and freshly released from a crude leather scabbard. The other hand scratched through the dirt behind him where lay what he could not see and dared not glance for: a gossamer cloak just beyond his reach.

The other, Sabertooth, loomed nearby. His strong legs set wide, he stood on the balls of his feet, ready to pounce, ready to lunge with the spear he gripped with both hands. The tip of the spear was steel—surpassingly unusual among these creatures—and a tiny triangle of the gossamer fabric hung from the flared edge of the blade.

Sabertooth had failed to snare the cloak, but he'd managed to tear it from the neck of Marrowsucker, the current owner.

Thus two orcs prepared to battle over the bounty of their recent success. This despite the fact that the spoils were supposedly already divided.

Sabertooth growled, brandishing the point of the spear in Marrowsucker's direction. The small piece of elven cloak fluttered from the weapon and wafted leaflike to the ground.

Marrowsucker did not budge. He was at the disadvantage and, recognizing that, he stopped feeling for the missing garment. He said, "The cloak is mine by right."

The other orc said, "Your claim is no good. My blood earned that prize." His voice had an undercurrent of perpetual hissing pitch as the sound worked its way around his enormous lower canines.

Marrowsucker chuckled: a raw sound, like a pig rummaging for truffles. He said, "My group scaled the trees and gutted the first of the elves. I *did* earn the prize."

Sabertooth's eyed narrowed. "Cheat! Lie! You moved your group to the gap ahead of where my warriors drew the elvish arrows. You may as well have made a ladder of the corpses of my soldiers for your climb!"

"Of course I did this."

Sabertooth's eyes opened wide and gleamed. "You admit it!"

Marrowsucker took this brief moment of his foe's celebration to stand. He nodded his head as he did so, but he dared not retreat. That would incite the other orc to lunge. So he still stood within Sabertooth's range, but unfortunately just beyond the reach of his own sword. Then Marrowsucker smiled. It was ingratiating and even Sabertooth realized it. But Marrowsucker said, "Here, then."

The orc held his breath as he turned. He paused,

waiting for the strike, but it did not come. Sabertooth was already celebrating, smiling to the crowd that gathered, nodding his head. Before Sabertooth knew it, Marrowsucker whirled, retreating beyond the range of a spear-lunge and at the same time whisking the cloak off the ground.

"Of course I admit it, fool. You grew teeth instead of brains. My attack won us the day. You were brave but dumb; I, brave and smart. The cloak is *mine*." He roared the final word, startling the orcs near him. Then he feigned a charge by taking two hard, fast steps toward Sabertooth.

The crowd of orcs, nearly fifty of them now, surged to life as well. Cheers and encouragement rang out just as quickly as the two orcs readied their weapons.

The massively muscled orc bellowed in response and lunged. But Marrowsucker had already pulled up short of the orc's reach, and that left Sabertooth overextended. He stumbled forward, falling to one knee, and only caught himself because the point of his spear drove into the ground.

At that, Marrowsucker leapt into the air and came down with both feet on the shaft of the spear. It shattered.

The roar of the crowd sounded like the fields of a human farmer, echoing with grunts and groans of every animal flavor. A few youngsters, with ears tall and pointed and nearly adult-sized though their heads were still those of youths, pushed their way to the front.

Marrowsucker bounded again, swinging his sword and slashing Sabertooth across the tricep. That orc's lips quivered, baring even further his namesake fangs. But as Marrowsucker stepped in again, this time to deliver a blow to Sabertooth's torso, the wounded orc lashed out wildly with his shattered spear. The fragment of a shaft that he still clutched clipped Marrowsucker on the temple and sent him reeling backward. His hands went limp, and while his warrior determination let him keep his hold on the sword, the cloak again fell from his possession.

Neither combatant noticed the fervor of the crowd begin to subside. One side of the circle that formed the arena of orcs fell silent completely, and the spectators parted as if a leper sought passage.

Sabertooth regained his balance and moved his short staff to the hand of his uninjured arm. Marrowsucker's brow oozed blood through the fingers he pressed against it. Meanwhile, he stood and pivoted so that his sword arm faced his foe.

"Rallos Zek shall eat your craven hearts."

Instantly, the entirety of the orcish assembly fell silent. This was no leper, but someone equally untouchable. They called him the Ashen One now, for his features were pale and gray, though otherwise identical to before, when he'd been known as Lifedrinker. The whole of the orc community hung on his every word to learn whatever this elderly shaman had done to earn the favor of the gods. Many of them had seen him fall in the battle against the elves, one arrow in his gut and another, ominously, in his heart, the organ he most often identified in his threats.

Left among the fallen when the orcs retreated after destroying Shadow-Wood Keep, the Ashen One somehow not only survived, but escaped the wrath of the handful of elves that pushed the orcs back from their destroyed city. Returned from the dead, though with flesh tinted of the ghostlands he'd walked—and whereon he must have encountered their lord and master, Rallos Zek, god of war—the shaman had shuffled back to this Hill days after the victorious army returned.

At first, no one spoke to him, for they thought him

truly a ghost. The other shamans, including two once considered Lifedrinker's superiors, pronounced him the Ashen One, returned to be the mouthpiece of Rallos Zek animated among them. Most of the tribe wholeheartedly believed this.

And while the shaman's nature and mission were subject to argument, some things were indisputable, including the fact that the Warlord claimed the soul of the most senior of the shamans the night following the Ashen One's return to the orcs of the Hill. That next morning, the Second Shaman, who now found himself promoted to First, instead demoted himself upon seeing the corpse of his former master. He withdrew the beads of his station and laid them at the feet of the Ashen One, who first accepted those and then entered the tent of the dead First Shaman. The Ashen One exited a moment later with that elder's beads as well.

Now the ghostly First Shaman stepped between the battling orcs. Both of them were stunned by his sudden appearance and each retreated a step. Accounts later would claim that they also shuddered, though elaborations explained that Marrowsucker shook in fear and Sabertooth in anger. Meanwhile the shaman scooped up the fallen cloak. He stuffed it within the dirty clothing he wore: a tunic stained with the blood of his deathwounds and punctured by the holes left by the arrows that had killed him.

The Ashen One extended his arms straight out to his sides. He raised his face to the sky and his eyelids fluttered shut. Many of the orcs cast glances back and forth among themselves and to the shaman who stood in their midst. A few nervously knelt while watching the shaman intently. Like an applause that's halting at first but quickly grows, all the others followed suit. Soon, a great circle of kneeling orcs surrounded the Ashen One.

Except for the combatants themselves. Perhaps still stunned at being called out by the shaman, they now stood out even more. Marrowsucker looked rapidly around him, then he, too, fell to his knees. He shook blood from his fingers and then pressed the hem of his tunic to the wound to staunch the flow further.

Sabertooth was not as willing. He looked about him and, though he did not utter a word, his eyes said to the assembled orcs, "You are weak." He gritted his teeth, which pressed his large canines hard against his upper lip, and tightly gripped the length of broken spear shaft.

His eyes still closed, the shaman addressed the heavens, "The elves and their Combine masters march upon us, great Warlord, yet we struggle over trifles, over elven baubles. Bring our enemies to our Hill so that we may fight a battle with meaning!"

Many of the surrounding orcs had their eyes closed as well—or their heads bowed—so many missed what happened next, but enough were watchful that the whole of the story was told many times.

Bursting with anger, Sabertooth exploded at the shaman. He wound his arms fully back, the staff in his hands like a club. He took one long stride toward the Ashen One and swung. The air whistled from the speed and fury of the attack aimed at the shaman's face.

But suddenly, the shaman was not there. Perhaps Rallos Zek granted him the foresight to avoid this craven assault. Or perhaps he truly was a ghost and the staff passed right through him. Whatever the explanation, the blow did not land and Sabertooth was once again thrown off balance. Several of the obeisant orcs scattered as Sabertooth careened toward them. He stumbled to the ground and threw up a great cloud of dust.

Everyone was watching now as the Ashen One stood patiently in the same place as before and calmly turned one leg so that the toe of his sandal slid beneath the steel spear point that remained fixed in the ground. With a deft flip of his foot, the weapon came free, spinning end over end straight up into the air. The shaman gracefully caught it by the fragmented wooden shaft and he threw it in the same motion—not straight like a spear, but like a dagger, so it spun again just as it had the moment before.

Sabertooth realized his danger only as the weapon flew in his direction. He bellowed only "Gods!" before the steel point imbedded in his face, crushing into his skull through the softer area surrounding the nose. He fell back, dead instantly.

Then the shaman turned to Marrowsucker. Like only a few others, that orc remained bowed. He paled considerably when the Ashen One regarded him, and a tremor of fear shook his body again as the shaman stepped toward him. However, the warrior's instinct told him this was not a foe he could defeat by violent action, so he steadied himself. It was to good effect, for when the Ashen One reached Marrowsucker, the shaman merely reached a hand toward the orc's injured head.

A brief incantation lathered from the shaman's lips, but even this simple spell that many orcs had seen Life-drinker perform countless times seemed suddenly difficult for the shaman. Still, an angry red glow encircled the shaman's hand and this he pressed to Marrowsucker. It was healing magic, but the orc still yelped in pain, for his wound healed, yes, but seared shut as well. Marrow-sucker's eyes rolled back in his head and he crumpled, the sharp pain overwhelming him and knocking him senseless.

The assembled orcs murmured in awe. This was the final proof they required. Only a true shaman of Rallos Zek could inflict pain even as he restored the Warlord's army.

The shaman then turned back to the corpse of Saber-tooth. He pointed forcefully at the ground on which the orc lay, and everyone understood him to mean that the corpse was not to be disturbed. For good measure, the orcs nearest it shuffled several steps away from the body. Then the Ashen One slowly strode away, and no one gave a moment's thought to the elven cloak that precipitated the entire event. Save perhaps Marrow-sucker, but that orc was too canny to draw any further attention to himself—or to the cloak.

AATALTAAL HAD HOPED TO FIND ONE AMONG the orcs who would pass the simple test. His plan required an accomplice—one among this tribe who possessed wits enough to both lead and to recognize an opportunity, but not so bull-headed that he would later decide to go his own way.

What would be partnership in the lifetime of this orc would have to later pass into legend among his descendents. Those later orcs would need to fulfill the obligation of an ancestor if Aataltaal were to have the means to escape Neriak.

Sitting in the guise of the First Shaman known as Lifedrinker, Aataltaal cast a glance at the dried meat hanging on racks around him. After several days without food, he felt the slight tug of desire for repast, but he refused to touch this stuff. Not only was it inexpertly prepared, but it was the flesh of his kin. Some of the dead dragged from the treetops of Shadow-Wood Keep now hung on this wooden housing. He wanted to cast it out. Not only would that remark upon Lifedrinker's passage from living to a state beyond death, but it would be Aataltaal's own repudiation of the craven attack upon the elves. But in the end, he thought it more poetic that the conquest of these orcs be planned in the shadow of the dead of Shadow-Wood Keep. If the shades of those dead yet lingered, they would care little to see him allying with any orc, but when they saw it meant an elf would have a hand in commanding this orc nation, then perhaps they would rest easier.

But in matters of the dead, Aataltaal had less than perfect knowledge. He'd long shunned the use of necromantic skills, but he realized they were required for some disguises—some like this—and somewhat to his chagrin he found that he excelled at the practice. On the other hand, healing talents did not come easily to him; thus mending the wound of the injured orc had nearly gone awry. Fortunately, the ignorant orcs interpreted that near-failure as another sign of the Ashen One's divine favor.

In fact, the difficulty had come because Aataltaal's faith in the gods was nearly extinguished. What narrow sliver of hope he held that they might yet rise to their divine potential hardly amounted to enough to be called "faith," and faith was required of the best priests and the miracles of healing they dispensed.

Still, the orc he'd assisted, the one called Marrow-sucker, seemed a likely candidate for his needs, so the healing was required. He suspected this orc possessed the requisite wiles, but whether he possessed the courage and grit required revelation.

For that, he would have to wait. Just not too bloody long, he hoped.

THE SHAMAN WAS NEXT SEEN THE FOLLOWING morning. He sat impatiently outside the smokehouse that he'd commandeered shortly after his return to the Hill. No one knew why he chose this location; certainly not for the food, as no one had seen him eat or drink these past days.

The cause for the Ashen One's impatience was plain, but none of the orcs was quite certain what to do. When the orcs of the Hill rose that morning, they found Sabertooth's corpse still in its prior location and position, but now surrounded by an oval of tokens and coins. The tokens bore the symbol of Rallos Zek, and they were very intricately carved. No one could explain when the Ashen One created them or from whence they came if not created by his hands. Made of wood and bone, each token featured the likeness in wood of a closed helm within a wooden band. Piercing this band on the top and the bottom and hooking through the back of the helm was a small piece of bone carved as the favored weapon of Rallos Zek, the bastard sword.

The coins were easier yet to recognize for they shone with solid gold of the kind minted by the dwarves who lived in the mountains far to the west. Still, the orcs could not explain the origin of such a trove.

Stranger yet, this circle of tokens and coins around the body of Sabertooth extended into a line that stretched from the corpse all the way to the smokehouse where the shaman impatiently waited. The path stretched several hundred feet, which meant there was a fortune for the taking just lying there on the ground.

But no one dared touch it!

The entire length of the course was plainly visible to the Ashen One. That and his obvious annoyance made most of the orcs uneasy. Eventually, though, one among them was bound to try, and finally one did. His name was Throatslasher. He was cunning in the woods, for it was he who ambushed two key elven guards in the attack on Shadow-Wood Keep.

But, as it turned out, Throatslasher was not wise in the ways of the gods.

"The shaman just wants someone to haul this corpse to him," Throatslasher explained to any who would listen. Meanwhile, he did just that. He clenched Sabertooth's arm and, with one great shrug, he slung the orc over his shoulder.

"And here's my compensation!" Pleased with himself, Throatslasher made a great show of scooping the coins and holy tokens into a pouch he untied from Sabertooth's waist.

Most of the other orcs regretted their timidity. There was nothing ominous about this at all! They were too careful, and now Throatslasher would collect the treasure that would surely make him the wealthiest orc of the Hill, excepting of course Crush himself.

Even so, none of them interfered. Glancing toward the Ashen One, the orcs feared the shaman would punish their initial cowardice if they dared now to undermine Throatslasher's bravery.

By the time Throatslasher was halfway to the old smokehouse, he was walking with difficulty. He plodded under the weight of Sabertooth as well as the strain of squatting and rising every few paces along the way in order to retrieve the tokens and coins. With so large a crowd, the orc felt compelled to finish the journey as he'd begun it, though, and so resting or proceeding by different means would open himself to ridicule.

On he struggled, so intent on stopping for the next batch of coins that he did not see the Ashen One rise. There was a slight intake of breath, though, that echoed through the crowd, and that alerted Throatslasher. He looked up, startled to see the Ashen One walking toward him beside the path of coins and holy symbols. Uncertain what to do, Throatslasher rearranged the corpse upon his shoulders, straightened to his full height, and awaited the arrival of the shaman.

As the Ashen One neared, Throatslasher beamed. More and more orcs arrived to watch. Everything in which the shaman participated was a spectacle—the best entertainment to be found in all of Crushbone—and those who had missed the action of the prior day would be anxious to see today's event for themselves.

They would not be disappointed.

Aataltaal made a show of walking slowly. It didn't matter to Throatslasher, who'd forgotten the weight of his burden and begun to wonder if he'd be allowed to collect the remainder of the coins.

In the guise of the shaman, Aataltaal was of average build for an orc and so did not measure up to the size of the warrior who bore the corpse, but he did not seem small in comparison to the other orc. His oversized ears, now so bulbous and gnarled at the top they could hardly be discerned as pointed, and his misshapen and yellowed teeth did not diminish him even though these traits in Lifedrinker had once seemed comical. None of this was an issue in light of the evidence of the wounds he bore and his pale, ghostly complexion. Even as his mouth began to open, silence swept across the throng of orcs.

His face impassive, without a hint of what was to come, the shaman said, "Allow me to save you the trouble."

In truth, Aataltaal did not want to waste time and needed to begin the test anew. As rewarding as Throatslasher's death was to the ghosts of Shadow-Keep, that was not the real reason he would strike down the orc.

Suddenly, a dark-handled dirk was in his hand. The black blade seemed to absorb what little light penetrated the thick foliage over the orc stronghold. Throatslasher had time only for a grotesque caricature of a reflexive attempt to evade the attack. No stranger to surprise attacks himself and among the most able warriors of the orcish community, Throatslasher's best attempt to save his life looked feeble and even pathetic in comparison to the force of divine retribution that seemed to guide the shaman's attack.

Almost before the assembled orcs realized the Ashen One attacked Throatslasher, the larger orc collapsed, his throat slashed wide open. By the time the orc struck the ground, throwing up a great cloud of dust and scattering gold coins and the symbols of Rallos Zek in a semicircle around him, the shaman again stood still and impassive.

Blood poured from Throatslasher's rent flesh. The shaman looked down at him. "Weakness can be followed only by death," said the Ashen One, intoning one of the guiding principles of Rallos Zek.

Then he turned, and again motioned dramatically that the corpse—now *corpses*—should not be disturbed. Then he slowly returned to the smokehouse. Not a single orc moved or made a sound during that entire progression. The Ashen One did not resume his position outside the smokehouse. This time—in apparent disgust, for he shook his head sorrowfully—he entered the largish building.

The orcs slowly milled about and soon wandered back to the duties and chores from which they'd been drawn. Quietly at first came the whispered retellings of the events, but soon this rose to merriment, laughter, and applause. Of course, no one approached Throatslasher's corpse.

Not at first, anyway.

As the crowd dispersed, one figure was gradually revealed. He waited motionlessly and patiently for at least the bulk of his fellows to depart. Like most orcs, he was proud, often boastful, and he would be quite content for throngs of them to witness his victory as they had the day before. But he was careful as well. And this instance called for care, as well as for cunning, something very few orcs possessed in his abundance.

It was a familiar figure that soon stepped toward Throatslasher's bloodied form. Marrowsucker glared at the fallen orc with the same disgust the Ashen One exhibited. In the warrior's case, though, the repugnance was at the fallen orc's lack of wits. Marrowsucker had thought he knew the answer to the shaman's simple riddle even prior to Throatslasher's imbecilic effort, but he had reckoned it better to risk missing this opportunity than to fail and be punished in the same tragic manner as the dead orc. Marrowsucker's first-row vantage of the Ashen One's prowess the prior day caused the warrior to predict precisely this penalty for failure.

And now that he'd seen failure, Marrowsucker was certain his earlier suspicions were correct. Before some other dimwit stumbled onto the solution by pure chance, Marrowsucker decided he'd best make his move, even if the shaman was not in position in front of the smokehouse as before, and even though he'd motioned for this corpse, too, not to be moved.

The warrior grasped Sabertooth by the ankle and hauled him forward about ten feet. He did the same with Throatslasher's corpse. Then he backtracked and stooped to collect some of the items upon the ground. However, Marrowsucker ignored the gold—a lure for fools! He selected only the tokens that bore the symbol of Rallos Zek. It was the Warlord's task that Marrowsucker performed now, and it was fit that only the god be honored.

Marrowsucker repeated this process a dozen times

over and soon dragged the lifeless remains of both Sabertooth and Throatslasher to the door of the smokehouse. He turned and collected the last half-dozen tokens. Then he returned to the building and rapped on the door. By this time, a small crowd had gathered. While Marrowsucker preferred that this occur privately, his growing reputation and connection to the Ashen One could only serve him well in the longer term, so he made no attempt to disperse the audience. Besides, the fewer the witnesses, the more extravagant the exaggerations of the truth would be, in absence of naysayers.

"Shaman? Lifedrinker?" he said. "I have brought the corpses."

Then the warrior stepped back. As seconds passed, Marrowsucker realized he held his breath, so he purposefully inhaled deeply in order to calm and steady himself.

Seconds turned to minutes, yet Marrowsucker remained. He listened intently and felt certain he heard the sound of movement within the smokehouse. He resisted the temptation to repeat his announcement, for he was equally certain the Ashen One had heard him the first time. Besides, speaking again might only give insult—and Marrowsucker had witnessed two recent occasions when the shaman disagreed with the behavior of others.

More time, and still no response. More than that, Marrowsucker discerned no further movement within. The orc narrowed his eyes; a silent fury seethed behind them that, if made physical, would have knocked in the door. But he took a deep breath and waited.

And waited.

Eventually, the handful of the gathered orcs wandered away. Moments later, a larger exodus began, until soon only a few remained, these mostly elderly orcs who perhaps had no worthwhile tasks to perform and so had no cause to leave.

Several minutes later, Marrowsucker said to these, "Esteemed elders, did you not hear the words of the Ashen One yesterday? The elves march upon us, yet here you stand idle. Many are the arrows that I and the other warriors will require to fend off this attack."

The words found their mark and most of the remaining orcs departed.

After another ten minutes, even the most determined loiterers finally gave up.

Five minutes after *that*, the smokehouse door cracked open. At first Marrowsucker thought his eyes and ears deceived him, but it was true. He hesitated, glanced about him, and then strode quickly inside. He left the corpses outside but carried the symbols honoring Rallos Zek.

The interior of the smokehouse appeared virtually unchanged, except that all the furnishings and tools had been pushed to the walls. This included a few racks of meat, several with dried strips ready to be eaten, and another one and a half that had been in the process of being set when the Ashen One had claimed the building. Marrowsucker tried to determine whether or not the shaman had eaten any of the dried strips. Was the Ashen One a living being requiring sustenance or was he truly a ghost? But there was no way to be certain, so the warrior centered his attention squarely on the pale figure of the shaman.

"Place them there." The Ashen One pointed to indicate an earthen pot.

"The gold did not tempt me, shaman. I seek only to honor Rallos Zek."

"Of course you do."

Marrowsucker thought he detected some irony in that response, but he was little served to be angered by it. Besides, what he said was not entirely true anyway, so it seemed more likely to him that the shaman read his mind and heart.

As the warrior stepped to the pot, he said, "It's true that I was tempted by the gold. But . . . it was more important to me to pass what I thought might be a test." He removed the pot's lid and carefully dumped the wood and bone tokens within.

"It *was* only a test."

As the last token dripped from his palm, Marrowsucker turned to the Ashen One. "And I passed?"

The shaman smiled very slightly. "You live, do you not?"

"Is that the reward for passing? Survival?"

The shaman shook his head. "No, this is."

From a bundle of clothing, the Ashen One retrieved the elven cloak, wadded tightly into a ball. The shaman held it by the collar and shook it once. Instantly, the wrinkles disappeared and an almost magical sheen glistened upon its surface.

Marrowsucker's eyes lit equally. Losing control of himself for a moment, he took a step toward the cloak.

The shaman withdrew it and the warrior stopped in his tracks.

"But not yet," said the Ashen One. He rolled the cloak back into a ball and suddenly it again seemed tattered and plain. He stuffed it back into the nearby bundles.

"My waiting outside? Was that a test, too? Or was it secrecy?"

The Ashen One smiled wickedly at Marrowsucker. It unnerved the orc warrior, for there was something eternal in the twinkle of the shaman's eyes that Marrow-sucker could barely discern and scarcely comprehend.

"That is a question that only time will reveal whether or not I should answer."

Marrowsucker glowered, but he was careful to cast his face down so his frustration would not seem to be directed at the Ashen One. Nevertheless, the shaman may have seen it, for he continued.

"However, the mere fact that you asked bodes well for the answer."

Marrowsucker could not stifle a chuckle at that. He shook his head as if to clear cobwebs within it. "I had best go, while I have some few wits remaining. I'll be trapped in your riddles if I remain."

The shaman said nothing but, after a brief pause, he nodded and Marrowsucker prepared to leave.

The Ashen One said, "First drag those dead fools within. They may yet be of service to the Warlord. There is a small, smooth stone in the pocket of Throat-slasher. You may take it." When the Ashen One said "stone," he clenched his fist tight as if in simulation of a rock. Marrowsucker thought this curious, for the shaman otherwise remained very still when speaking, but he let it go as a gesture that simply emphasized the worth of the stone. The warrior imagined the stone might have some magical power. Perhaps it was partly the explanation for Throatslasher's well-regarded prowess.

Marrowsucker started to inquire about that, but the shaman turned away and closed his eyes, meditating. The orc warrior shrugged his shoulders and did as instructed.

2

THE ARMY OF COMBINE

A VETERAN OF A DOZEN CAMPAIGNS IN WHAT she, at least, considered the good name of the Combine Empire, Delailith usually slept easily, secure in the knowledge that her cause was just, the intent of her leaders true, and the enemy a blight that stood in the path of prosperity for the good races of Norrath. But this campaign was a little different. There was no doubting the cause, for this was not retaliation, it was justified vengeance. And the enemy was essentially beyond doubt, for the orcs were a ruinous race. The Combine had allowed them an opportunity to settle peacefully, but they had refused, and attacked their neighbors.

But the leader? About General Seru, Delailith had her doubts. He seemed less concerned with leading another campaign at the head of the Combine army and more about his absence from court a month from the Great Combine Summit.

That he'd served the Combine well was an understatement. General Seru's strategic and tactical brilliance had won victories the fledging empire required. Emperor Katta had then proselytized a more progressive outlook on the future of Norrath and its citizens. Provincial thought ruled the world then, and of course it would never entirely be eradicated, but the prejudice that grew from it was at the heart of what the Combine stood against—which was why Delailith fought in the name of the Combine Empire.

The elves who'd inhabited Shadow-Wood Keep, while not formally citizens of the Combine Empire, nevertheless fell under the protection of Emperor Katta, for he ruled it to be so. An injury done to them would be punished by the might of the Combine, an empire that from humble beginnings now governed much of known Norrath. It delivered prosperity to all the people who accepted its rule and delivered magical conveniences like the great spires of Norrath to all who would likewise donate their gifts for the good of others.

Of course, some dissented from this rule more seriously than had the proud elves of Shadow-Wood Keep. The little-understood iksar of the great southern continent Kunark resisted all intrusion. These reptiles had evidently once been yoked by a mysterious race of powerful wizards known as the shissar, who had grown so powerful that they either dared to confront the gods and so were punished, or else they had in fact ascended to godhood and thus left Norrath for good. Delailith was no scholar and could not say, though she suspected the iksar overthrew and murdered their former masters—for such is the fate of empires built by one race upon the backs of another.

It was in this way that the Combine Empire was to be different and why Emperor Katta sought to include so many of the other races, even the dark elves who dwelt below the surface of Norrath and supposedly sought the downfall of all who walked above them. The emperor proclaimed that no one was to be excluded unless it was their will not to join, and those who declined the opportunity to join the Combine would not be targets of conquest—unless they threw the first stone.

Art and magic—and the science of the gnomes—held great sway in the Combine Empire, but security was preeminent. A few races that sought to test this benevolence they saw as weakness quickly learned the extent of the Combine's strength.

Just so would the thuggish orcs of Clan Crushbone learn the lesson. However, Delailith guessed the orcs had little knowledge of the Combine Empire and scarcely cared whether the elves of Shadow-Wood Keep fell under its protection. Two emissaries sent to meet with Lord Crush did not return. Only because their disappearance could not be absolutely pinned on the orcs did the orcs not suffer this wrath already.

Now, scarcely a half year after they established residence on the edge of the Greater Faydark, the orcs would be annihilated. No less a personage than the greatest warrior of the Combine Empire, General Seru, marched with this army to make certain of that outcome. With him came the ancient crone Rashalla, reportedly his advisor in all matters of magic, and a flock of her fearsome black birds.

Delailith shook her head. All of this was quite ordinary for these extraordinary times. Even the presence of General Seru, though seemingly a case of overkill, was understandable. The Teir'Dal—the dark elves—were said to be considering joining the Combine Empire. However, General Seru was rumored to resist the inclusion of the elves. Popular thought among these rumormongers held that he'd simply fought them too many times to now accept them as allies. Therefore this "urgent" mission provided Emperor Katta with the perfect rationale to remove Seru from the heart of the empire while preparations were made to receive the Teir'Dal. In fact, the timing seemed awfully convenient to Delailith. And what—if anything—did that mean regarding the orcs' attack on Shadow-Wood Keep?

Delailith hated politics. Leave that to the politicians. And if General Seru would maintain an attitude such as hers, then her thoughts on this matter would not even be necessary! Her suspicions would be irrelevant . . .

Still, at this moment, it wasn't the presence of the great general that caused Delailith her sleepless fits. It was the never-ending copulations among the army's faerie-folk allies. The Combine army itself was nearly all male to remove just such distractions, and warriors such as Delailith, though attractive and capable of diverting many a man's attention, had a disposition that discouraged such advances. It didn't help, then, that high-pitched hijinks unfolded all around the men who slept in vast rows and columns. Dancing faeries kept such nocturnal thoughts in the simple male minds.

And the men were the most ridiculous peeping toms! Forget that the faerie maidens had nothing possibly of use to the humans, elves, and dwarves who marched with the army. Delailith watched with amusement as the soldiers in turn watched the tiny and often naked sprites flitter among the foliage of the great broadroot trees. Still, the sight of row upon row of pale faces in the virtually nonexistent light of the forest floor turning first this way then that in pursuit of a glimpse of luminescent and miniaturized female anatomy was more than Delailith could stand.

That a few of the clods even dared cast a glance in Delailith's direction caused the warrior to begin remembering faces. She was bound to be installed as a unit commander—most likely before they even reached the orc stronghold—and then the simpletons she marked would pull the most loathsome of duties.

In the end, it was the lost sleep she rued the most.

Even after a hard day of marching in lines that navigated the great trees of the Faydark like rows of ants returning to their nest, who could slumber with such antics? Well, who but her friend Nestor? The big man fell quickly asleep each night—after drinking the entire day. Delailith imagined that a man of such girth could only withstand the discomfort of such a march as theirs with the clouded sensation of alcohol, but of course his drinking bothered her, even as she envied him the rest it afforded him—and the respite from the blatant displays of the faerie folk.

The small faerie men had no restraint—or shame, it seemed—and bared their tiny apparatus regardless of who might be eavesdropping so long as the object of his fascination in turn would offer hers.

And being nearly immortal and nearly tireless beings, the faeries kept at this frolic for hours unimaginable to all but the most starry-eyed girls who had yet to be jilted by lovers who whispered sweet nothings and then indeed left nearly nothing of themselves in return for the misadventures they claimed.

Despite her general disgust, Delailith could not help but be amused by the outrageous behavior of her good friend, Troy. The man was a rogue of the highest caliber. Not in the sense of his occupation, though Troy's skills in that area were commendable as well, but rather in terms of his personality. He alone of all the soldiers had somehow convinced—or tricked, though it would be the same to his thinking—a twinkling faerie to descend from the night air onto the palm of his hand. She sat combing her hair, and Troy plied her with nonsense that Delailith thought could surely work only on tavern wenches. But here was a diaphanous being ten times the rogue's senior unwittingly or at least unashamedly displaying herself to the man.

Delailith could only shake her head.

That's when she saw that at least she was not alone in spectating the spectators. The bard-in-training Cadmus also watched the proceedings with interest. He was the fourth in the band of fellows she formed along with Nestor and Troy, and Delailith found comfort in the fact that some months hence, when they were all relaxing in some bar, the bard would help her recall this moment in a far more humorous light.

Either way, she was not yet a unit commander, and her only duty for now was to prepare herself. With a few deep, relaxing breaths, she dispelled the buzzing of faerie wings and blocked out the lilting voices that exclaimed intentions less than musical. As she drifted off to sleep, one final thought continued to nag her: why did General Seru permit this outrageous business?

IN THE GUISE OF THE SHAMAN NOW KNOWN AS the Ashen One, Aataltaal drew a crowd again the next evening. Shortly after sundown, when the orcs were more comfortable and out of the bright midday glare, a small troop of their leader's personal guard exited the wooden tower that stood atop the Hill and marched toward the old smokehouse.

Word spread rapidly. Was this to be the showdown between Crush and the Ashen One? Would the shaman submit to the guards or would he resist? A crowd of orcs hurried to see.

A prominent secondary thought that kept some away from the scene despite their own curiosity was that if the shaman did in fact resist, then what side would individual orcs take? Crush was anointed by Rallos Zek to lead the orcs of the Hill, but no one doubted that the Ashen One was favored by the Warlord as well.

When the orcish crowd arrived at the smokehouse, a collective gasp shuddered among them. Even a few of Crush's bodyguards, arriving at the same time, could not contain their surprise. Flanking the entrance to the smokehouse stood Throatslasher and Sabertooth. They stood awkwardly, with backs bent and arms hanging slack and long at their sides. Their eyes were sunken, and Sabertooth especially had the pallor of death on his features.

The shock of realization that these two warriors were *still* dead sent another murmur through the crowd. Such necromantic magic was well known to exist, but not among the orcs of the Hill, and certainly never before had Lifedrinker possessed it. His taste of death now gave him power over it! The orcs all shuffled back, exposing Crush's eight personal guards to the exclusive attention of the undead orc warriors.

The leader of the guards, a savage but obsequious creature known as Bloodfeast, hesitated. That caused the remainder of the guards to shift uneasily. Bloodfeast then glanced back over his shoulder. The crowd reflexively followed his gaze. There on the third-floor balcony of the Tower on the Hill stood the mighty Crush. His arms crossed at his chest, Crush did not budge, did not even return Bloodfeast's gaze, but instead continued to stare into the depths of the Faydark, perhaps in search of the elusive army the Ashen One foretold. By all appearances, Crush did not take notice of the proceedings below at all. Of course, all the orcs knew that he watched them, but among them all, the only one being judged at this very moment was Bloodfeast.

Bloodfeast knew it as well, so he instantly stepped forward, raising his longsword into defensive position as he did so.

Bloodfeast called out, "None are allowed private guards but Lord Crush himself, Lifedrinker."

Aataltaal knew it was a simple matter to deflect such criticism.

The voice of the Ashen One came from within the smokehouse, "None save Lord Crush and I seem to understand that an army will soon threaten us. The Warlord shall protect not the idle, but only those who prepare for battle."

Again the warning of an army approaching. The assembled orcs shifted uncomfortably as the words of the Ashen One judged their effort on behalf of Rallos Zek.

"Lord Crush would speak to you on this matter," Bloodfeast said.

Then realizing the delivery was not appropriate, Bloodfeast added, "He demands your audience to speak on this and other matters. You are the chief shaman of the Hill, and Lord Crush requires you to dispense the favor of the Warlord upon his plans of battle. For none shall take the Hill from Lord Crush, least of all some rabble army of elves and dwarves."

"And humans," said the Ashen One. The door to the smokehouse opened and Aataltaal emerged, dressed in the image of Rallos Zek. Mainly, this required that he wear a full-face helm, gigantic and decorated with enormous feathered plumes. The Ashen One's voice sounded somewhat muffled because the helm entirely encased his head, but this faceless appearance was symbolic of Rallos Zek. Some shamans, including the former First Shaman recently culled by Rallos Zek, did not emphasize this fact, preferring to help the orcs imagine themselves the favored of the Warlord's servants. Yet it was true that all known incarnations of Rallos Zek were fully helmed so as to disguise his race. Aataltaal wanted to frighten the orcs into believing the Warlord saw weakness in them and to remind them that the Warlord favored no race. Rallos Zek favored only the strong, the prepared.

The shaman said, "Never forget the humans."

The Ashen One also wore a great wolf-skin cloak and boots trimmed with smaller feathers to match the plumage of the helm. The feathers appeared to be those of the dreaded cockatrice—fortunately rare in the Faydark Forest—but no one knew this beast well enough to say for certain. The small shaman might typically look comical in the large helm, but the cloak and boots gave the impression of greater bulk, so no one was even remotely tempted to chortle.

Bloodfeast glanced uneasily at the undead guardians that stood at each hand of the shaman.

The Ashen One shook his head. "Do not be troubled by them. Perhaps in death they will fight with the courage they did not often enough show in life. They are here solely to safeguard my abode while I am away. I anticipated Crush's summons."

This was true; and the time had come to test Crush. Maybe Aataltaal would not require Marrowsucker, but he suspected otherwise or else he'd not have gone through the earlier process that brought that orc into his fold. Aataltaal suspected the current ruler of the orcs here would not suffice for his long-range plans. He imagined the orc was a brute of a warlord, and not truly a leader capable of commanding this region as a static stronghold.

Meanwhile, more murmuring swept through the crowd. The shaman had again turned the tables so that it

appeared as if he went to Crush not because the Lord of
the Hill demanded his attendance, but because this meet-
ing was part of some larger plan of the Warlord's.

In particular, Marrowsucker chuckled at the shaman's
guile. He knew he was among the few who could
clearly discern this tactic. For the others it left the intended impression without the revelation of the strategy
itself.

The Ashen One walked into the midst of the orc
guards, who then showed uncommon discipline and organization for orcs by turning in place and proceeding
to march back toward the Tower on the Hill. Aataltaal
walked slowly, though, so the guards slowed to accommodate his pace and then their march became a disorganized
muddle of discordant cadences, which caused Marrowsucker to grin again.

The shaman's smokehouse home stood to the north-
east of the central hill of the area claimed by the orcs less
than a year ago. A single river the orcs called the Bloodwine for its dark color cut through the region surrounding the Hill, briefly dividing into three separate channels,
some of which created short, interconnecting tributaries
as well. All told, the waterways created five separate
"islands," all contained within a great circular area more
than one thousand feet in diameter.

The Tower on the Hill, by far the most impressive
building the orcs constructed—and in fact the only one
other than the smokehouse and slave barracks that
amounted to more than a shanty—stood on the central-
most of these islands and nearly in the direct center of
the area. The enormous trees of the Faydark loomed
everywhere around. Only the Hill itself was clear-cut,
though enough trees had been felled on the northeastern
island to allow uninterrupted views across most of its
length.

It was to the southwest, toward the Hill, that the guards marched the Ashen One. They crossed a simple log-and-rope pontoon bridge that floated in the Bloodwine. The water sometimes flowed quickly and could make this crossing treacherous, but the orcs had positioned the bridge at the widest point where the current ran slowest, though at the time it had taken a good bit of convincing before some orcs could see the merits of this. Those orcs had understood only that a longer bridge meant more work.

Normally, no one but Lord Crush and his loyal guards—and whatever people they required for their entertainment, be they orcs or slaves—was allowed on this central island, so this was the shaman's first visit. Lifedrinker had been Third Shaman before his return, and only the First Shaman was ever invited to join Crush. Which of course the Ashen One now was, though summons of the other First Shaman were not typically delivered by an escort of warriors.

The Tower itself was a large wooden structure. The broadroot trees of the Faydark were not only difficult to fell, but the dense grain of the wood made them hard to cut. So the orcs took the shortcut of using largely uncut sections of the trees. Since the trunks were far too immense and certainly too heavy to lift to create the upper portions of the three-story tower, the orcs mainly used the trees' branches. Still covered with bark—and with ends still nearly green, they'd been so recently cut— these branches were set into a basic rectangular shape to form a log tower. The only special feature of the Tower was the third-story balcony. The broadest portion, where Lord Crush still stood, faced south, though a walkway circled the entire perimeter of the top floor.

The danger of soft ground beneath the Tower went unnoticed by the guards, who paid attention to the dangerous shaman or otherwise to nothing in particular. But the Ashen One noted it, as well as how the Tower, only recently completed, was already sinking into the soft earth. And different feet sank at varying rates, so the Tower seemed to lean slightly to the southeast, where there was lower ground on this central island.

The orcs didn't seem to mind that either.

As the group neared the base of the Tower, the guards on one side picked up their pace, and the other side slowed. That meant the four guards to the shaman's right arrived first at the steps that crisscrossed on the exterior of the Tower. The ones to the shaman's left fell into line behind the shaman and the entire group made their way up, with Bloodfeast trailing them all.

One guard from both the front and back foursomes remained at guard posts along the stairs at each of the three landings prior to the third floor. Therefore, the shaman was ushered into the chamber of Lord Crush in the company of four guards and Bloodfeast. Two of these remained at the top of the stairs, and the other two strode purposefully to their positions flanking the doorway to the balcony. Bloodfeast lingered in the center of the crudely adorned room that took up the entirety of the third floor. More in his element again, Bloodfeast regained the cocky posture and contemptuous sneer that had earned him intense dislike among the other orcs of the clan.

Only then did Lord Crush enter. He seemed briefly disconcerted by the shaman's odd appearance, but he soon recovered and, though obviously wary, simply accepted the garb as a warrior might accept a foe who fought with a strange style but with whom he nevertheless must cross blades.

A brutishly humungous creature, Lord Crush had no equal among the orcs of the Hill. He stood a full head taller than any of his guards, and with the exception of Bloodfeast—who purportedly possessed a sharp mind from which Crush extracted the tactics he required—these orcs were the largest and strongest of the clan. Both of Crush's ears were mangled from battle, and their stunted size made his head appear to be enormous. Beyond those and the dark, determined fire that burned in his eyes, he was much like any other orc, if one that stood nearly seven feet tall. His clothing was in slightly better condition, but was nothing one could regard as regal. His armor was another matter, though even that was in truth much less than first impressions of it. Crush wore a plate mail breastplate and plate greaves over harshly and poorly tanned leathers. The metal armor clearly showed dwarven manufacture, though both the chestplate and leggings were crudely cobbled together from several smaller pieces. That a well-placed blow could shatter either was evident to anyone with even a small degree of formal combat training. Few foes, though, could manage the combination of strength and accuracy required to do such damage, especially when confronted by a gigantic berserk orc wielding a two-handed sword.

Crush's voice boomed as well. It was a trait of his family, and clan lore suggested that any orc within ten miles could hear him speak if he desired to communicate with them. "So, this is Lifedrinker, returned from the dead," he rumbled.

The Ashen One responded only with a slight nod.

"What do you think of him, Bloodfeast?"

The smaller orc seemed caught off guard by the inquiry. He flushed pale again and stammered, "Ah well, Lord Crush—" He bit his words off and glanced warily back and forth between the two figures, one large and imposing, the other small but clearly dangerous.

Bloodfeast was canny enough to realize that there

were two orcs in the entire Hill whom he should not cross, and he was now in the predicament of being between them. So he tried to change the subject. He said, "My lord, I can say that he brings hitherto unknown magics that will surely make your armies even more powerful. He has made the dead walk again!" Bloodfeast's eyes sparkled. He'd managed to compliment them both while still acknowledging the superior position of the current leader, Crush.

"Let us see your face, 'Ashen One,' " said Crush.

The shaman replied, "Now is not the time for that, Lord Crush. Rallos Zek shall remain faceless to all but those whom he favors the most."

Crush's eyes narrowed, the wheels inside his head clearly spinning. But wariness won out over his sense that the Ashen One wished a private audience. The orc leader insisted, "Remove the helm now. Rallos Zek may be faceless, but his servants upon Norrath shall be known, especially to their mortal masters."

This time, the shaman complied immediately, though his motions were as slow and purposeful as if removing the helm were part of a ceremony. The enormous plumes on the helm scraped the ceiling rafters as the headpiece came free and then they did an unusual thing—they began to bend and weave as if of their own volition. Those dancing feathers distracted everyone's attention during the instant the shaman's face came clear of the helm.

"What treachery is this?" shouted Lord Crush. If legends were true, then every orc within ten miles heard *that* cry.

Bloodfeast hastily retreated even as Crush stretched his enormous paw into the rafters and withdrew the two-handed sword that was his sole family heirloom. He adopted a battle stance before his guards even managed to ready the weapons they already had on hand.

Beneath the helm of Rallos Zek was not the face of Lifedrinker, but of a Teir'Dal, a dark elf, a race as cunning and cruel as the orcs were savage and brutal. The dark elf's black eyes were reflectionless depths with a gaze that seemed to fall on everything surrounding him. The creature had ebony-black skin made all the richer by wisps of fine, pure-white hair. These features plus the Teir'Dal's narrow, angular head stood in sharp contrast to its thuggish orc build with black hair and pale flesh—so much so that the Teir'Dal head seemed a slick, demonic serpent that had squirmed from beneath a brutish rock. A pitiless smirk effectively communicated the extent of this dark elf's regard for orcs in general.

In a rasping voice unlike that of the shaman Lifedrinker but still unearthly, the dark elf said, "I suggested this remain between us, Lord Crush. Now . . ."

In the split-second of his hesitation, the Teir'Dal whirled toward Bloodfeast. The dark elf reached down and pulled hard on the edge of the animal furs that lined most of the floor in the center of the room. Bloodfeast lost his balance as much from fright as physics, and tumbled into a helpless pile. In an amazing display of strength, the dark elf yanked the furs, and Bloodfeast hurtled ten feet to where the Teir'Dal stood. From a space in the helm he cradled in his other arm, the dark elf withdrew a narrow black blade from where one of the large feathers was attached. Bloodfeast scrambled for safety, but his limbs caught in the folds on the furs. A quick, clean thrust through the orc's right eye brought the prone figure to a shuddering halt.

". . . I must . . ."

The Teir'Dal then dropped the helm at his feet and

withdrew a dagger and a longsword from Bloodfeast's belt. He gracefully pivoted on the ball of one foot and flicked both weapons toward the guards at the top of the stairs. Throwing two such off-sized weapons simultaneously would challenge most accomplished warriors, but the Teir'Dal's attack seemed effortless, completely fluid and natural. Both weapons pierced their targets through the throat; both guards collapsed without a whimper.

The dark elf turned back to Crush and completed his sentence: ". . . remove any witnesses."

The elf crouched, his ebony dirk low and in front of his body. Lord Crush seethed with fury, the flesh at the edges of his eyes quivered as if the orbs would blast from their sockets. The other two guards edged forward, simultaneously wary of the Teir'Dal and of their enraged leader.

Then the dark elf wormed his toes under the plumed helm and kicked it toward one of the guards. "Catch."

With no way to avoid the missile, the orc did just that. "*Stone*," said the dark elf in his own musically alien native tongue. In a process just slow enough to allow an expression of shock to register across his face, the orc turned to stone. His flesh, his hair, his clothing, his weapon—all transformed into gray stone with the sound of a collapsing gravel pile. The helm itself, though, was unaffected.

There was a pause then, because one of the vast plumes stretching from the helm fell across the shoulder of Lord Crush. The orc looked from the dark elf, to the feather, and then back again to the now-expressionless Teir'Dal. Gears turned inside Crush's head, and this time cunning won out.

With a mighty roar, Lord Crush raised his weapon. The dark elf did not flinch: by the leader's flexing muscles, the elf could discern the orc's intent. Crush spun, his great blade whistling as its serrated edges cut the air and, in one clean blow, clipped off the head of the remaining orc guard. A fountain of blood erupted from the orc's neck, and the body collapsed into a heap atop the decapitated head.

Then Crush jammed the dulled point of his weapon into the planks of the floor and he strode quickly to the doorway at the top of the stairs. Pounding feet announced the imminent arrival of more guards. Crush unceremoniously kicked the corpses of the two guards away from the open doorway as he shouted, "Do not enter." And he slammed shut a crude door that did not quite close completely because it ill fit the opening. But once he barred the door, it held fast and blocked both entrance and view.

Then the orc leader turned again to the intruder. His nostrils flared in surprise when he saw not a Teir'Dal but rather, once again, the ghostly shade of the shaman Lifedrinker.

Crush said, "You have killed five of my best warriors and worked magic that it seems has doomed a sixth. Your explanation had best be worth their lives."

"Of course it is, Lord Crush. Six warriors or one hundred and six warriors, your clan will not survive the month without my assistance. Besides, as Bloodfeast claimed and can now himself prove, the dead can fight as well as the living."

Crush asked, "Are you Lifedrinker or are you Teir'Dal?"

That Lord Crush asked such a question was answer enough for the shapechanger, but Aataltaal answered as if Lord Crush posed the question he should have asked. Again in the sibilant voice of a dark elf, though he wore the guise of an orc, Lifedrinker answered, "To all but yourself I shall remain the Ashen One or whatever name they choose to describe me. But in private, you may call me . . . D'vinn."

D'vinn smiled at Lord Crush, who was still too overwhelmed by recent discoveries to notice the predatory curl at the edges of the Teir'Dal's lips. The dark elf did not mind that Crush himself would not suffice for his plans. In fact, the orc leader's relative stupidity would actually make things much easier, for his plan relied upon Crush's apparent death. And despite all his amazing talents, the Teir'Dal could not truly return the dead to life, so the real thing would serve his purpose even better.

The other pieces were all in place. He just needed to prepare for whatever surprise his antagonist would offer. There was *always* a surprise.

Besides, this way meant one more dead orc, and the death of the orc leader would be a small additional vengeance in the name of Shadow-Wood Keep.

3

THE PASSAGE OF NERIAK

THE BATTLE UNFOLDED ESSENTIALLY AS AATAL-
taal had expected. Seldom did reality meet expecta-
tion, so seldom was his hope realized as it was this day.

The only thing he had not truly counted on was the
ravens' involvement in the battle itself. It could be counted
a good thing, actually, because the attack was otherwise sloppy, executed without any of Seru's well-known
strategy, and carried out by clearly exhausted troops.

The elf knew why: General Seru wanted to return
immediately to Emperor Katta's side. Even so, it was a
disgusting sight. Fortunately, he reflected, the humans
suffered the worst of it. Elves and faeries, assuming they
maintained their energy and health in general throughout
their long lives, were perfectly capable of overcoming lack
of sleep for days or even weeks: it would be as if a human
skipped a nap they might prefer, so disparate was the scale
of the lifespans of these beings. Even so, the elves had obviously tapped their reserves and some senselessly lost their
lives. Aataltaal hoped the army's junior officers would
report Seru's egregious behavior to Katta; even the most
popular generals could be demoted or quietly retired.

However, as he was not officially here himself, "Governor" Aataltaal could not make this report. Besides, a few lives, especially human lives, were of little concern.

Aataltaal did not want to make a target of himself, or really be noticed at all, so he remained on the ground when sprinting scouts delivered the news that the army of the Combine Empire approached. Amazingly, many of the orcs looked to their shaman when the news came, as if his prophecy of coming retribution came as a surprise to them. Shorter-lived than humans, orcs in turn amazed the shaman.

There was no division between the sexes here, at least when it came to defending their home. The women and children all participated. In fact, it was mainly females posted on the Tower and the half-completed battlements surrounding it. With the advantage of height and terrain, their crude bows would have nearly the same range as those wielded by the attackers, even the elves. In fact, Crush ordered them to hold fire until an elven arrow hit the first orc.

That occurred mere moments after growls and howls from the male orcs arrayed at the perimeter wall greeted the sighting of the Combine army. A high-pitched *zing* silenced the snarling orcs for a moment. No one was quite certain what happened, but then one of the orcish archers crumpled and fell from her place on the middle levels of the Tower. A volley of arrows from outside the wall followed, and then the orcs responded, filling the sky with clouds of arrows so dense they often collided. The battle was on.

Aataltaal took relatively little interest in the fight itself. Yes, there was the matter of vengeance, but that held little sway with him in the bigger scheme of things, and even less now that the event was under way. This one battle would not change anything, and he had dedicated his life to altering, or preferably undoing, tragedies, rather than equalizing them. A battle between murderous orcs and an exhausted army led by a general growing corrupt with power meant little to him except that it last long enough to delay Seru's return.

What truly concerned Aataltaal were the residences of the orcs on another of the islands surrounded by the Bloodwine River. Those sad lean-tos and the couple of sturdier structures—including the ex-smokehouse the shaman made his own—had been abandoned. The orcs could not hope to defend two locations, so they fortified the central island of the Tower and stocked their supplies therein. Aataltaal explained to Crush that this would not be a siege, but still the orcs had collected large stores of food and water.

The disguised elf was interested in the abandoned residences both because that's where the ravens congregated, and because that's where his true objective lay hidden. The entrance to a natural cave, the extent of which was scarcely expressible and assuredly far beyond belief, lay hidden beneath a thin layer of dirt and stone—and until recently the wooden floor of the orcish smokehouse.

That's what he needed to safeguard, and unless he missed his mark, it was what Rashalla—if indeed these ravens belonged to Seru's pet magic wielder—was intent upon discovering. Like so many humans before her, this Rashalla probably sought the secrets of immortality that she foolishly believed might be granted by beings such as dark elves. Immortality learned was inevitably a curse. Greedy wizards and priests throughout the centuries had proved that time and again. The kind of long life that humans yearned to attain was a gift of the elves alone—and even many of them did not fully understand how to live *within* that granted time and not just *through* it. For instance, many elves died of "old age" when they had attained not even half of Aataltaal's years.

Whatever the exact nature of the arcane knowledge she sought, Rashalla no doubt intended to breach an entry toward the Underfoot of Norrath. However Rashalla came by the information, she clearly knew that the caves below Crushbone could indeed transport her all the way to the dark-elven city of Neriak. The underground river was treacherous in many locations, and hence the dark elves themselves had explored only a fraction of it, but that simply made it an even more suitable means to secretly gain entrance to the city.

Which is exactly why Aataltaal needed to secure its safety, which meant keeping it safe from Rashalla. If she used it now, then when they detected her entry, the Teir'Dal would take steps to guard the river against outsiders. The shaman's eyes darkened. He did not need it yet, but he *would*. Someday.

So it had been necessary to transplant the entire orc village. Assuming Rashalla had spied the location as below the former smokehouse, then that was the landmark she would use to begin her search. Not finding it there would of course not keep her from the true location for long, but it would delay her. Aataltaal counted on the delay being long enough that General Seru, anxious to return to court, would march off with his army. That in turn would allow Aataltaal the opportunity for a magical battle with the old crone. Of course it would be helpful if some orc survivors returned to repopulate this godsforsaken settlement, and that was why the shaman required Crush's demise.

With all these expectations, the shaman-in-disguise felt scant surprise when dozens of ravens began to congregate throughout the village, away from the main battle.

A gruff voice said, "Ominous, is it not, Ashen One?"

The shaman turned, though he knew already he

would find Marrowsucker. The wily orc was under the shaman's instructions and managed to place himself in charge of a small group of orc warriors responsible for reinforcing any portion of Crushbone's defenses threatened with penetration. Considering the good favor the orc had gained from the old shaman recently, securing the position had been little trouble, especially considering he had few rivals for that duty. The orcs did not shirk from battle, but who wanted to rush headlong into the thickest fray without benefit of a prepared, defensible position?

The Ashen One nodded in reply. Beyond Marrowsucker stood his small group of eight other warriors. They looked around anxiously, most of them watching the storm of arrows that continued to pick off the female orcs on the platforms of the Tower.

All of a sudden, the clash of the battle grew much louder. The orcs' defensive wall was engaged on multiple fronts, and bloodthirsty war cries rang out on both sides. At the same time, a bent humanoid figure hobbled along the empty paths among the orc shacks and lean-tos.

Marrowsucker whistled in surprise as he scanned the perimeter of the orc fort. The enemy army had nearly breached in at least three locations. He asked, "What portion should we reinforce?"

The shaman heard him, but only dimly. His concentration followed Rashalla as she made her way toward the smokehouse. The ravens slowly gathered into a flock, apparently scouting ahead on the route the wizened woman followed. Her features were difficult to make out because she wore a voluminous, hooded robe. The material flapped in the wind, billowing out to vaguely resemble wings. Despite her evident age, she stepped lightly, appearing almost birdlike.

And it was a hole in the ground that she sought, thought the shaman, though not one left by a worm.

Without looking at Marrowsucker and without obvious examination of the battlefield, the Ashen One pointed a crooked orc finger toward one of the trouble spots along the wooden walls. "Go there, Marrowsucker."

Marrowsucker hesitated a half-second out of surprise for the shaman's apparent omniscience, but he turned toward his warriors. He opened his mouth to speak, but he stopped when the shaman tugged on the edge of the warrior's chain-mail shirt. Marrowsucker turned and ended face-to-face with the deadly gaze of the shaman.

Fire in his eyes and meaning heavy in his voice, the Ashen One added, "But live."

Then the shaman released Marrowsucker. The warrior was confused by the shaman's intention, but he shouted to his warriors. "This way. For Rallos Zek!" And they all charged in the direction the Ashen One had indicated.

DELAILITH'S UNIT FOUND ITSELF ON THE PERIPH-ery of the human portion of the Combine army. That fact carried little meaning and meant no difference to her, but she could see that it made her soldiers uncomfortable to fight, not alongside other men and women, but beside faeries instead.

Delailith wondered if her friend Troy had a hand in this, as the unit in which he was assigned was the only other non-faerie force tasked with attacking this particular portion of the crude wooden wall the orcs had erected in an obviously desperate gamble to preserve themselves. Of course, throughout the march to battle, Troy had fraternized the most successfully with the faeries. He was a smooth-talker with human females, too, but other than Delailith, few were pretty enough to warrant his talents—and she counted as more friend than lover. Thankfully, or else they'd not be friends, either.

The faeries' use of magic and their swift, darting movements made it difficult for most of their human cohorts to concentrate on fighting the orcs. Delailith understood the problem—it was hard to fight when a quick-moving shadow was always visible out of the corner of an eye—but she did not suffer from it. Her focus was unbreakable, and nearly so was her sword arm.

But all of this would really only become a problem once the attackers penetrated the defensive wall—a task made ridiculously easy because of the faeries, though that did little to ease the humans' tensions.

The small humanoids could all fly, and of course that made the wall of little use against them. Missile fire injured a few, but the faeries' quickness made them well-nigh impossible to target. The orcs tried to ignore them and concentrate their fire on the few humans, but the faeries' magic incapacitated so many orcs that the humans soon safely gained the foot of the walls.

Heavy-headed axes struck fast into the wooden wall made stairs of sorts for Troy and the other unit of humans. Delailith ordered her soldiers to use the more traditional ropes. They looped the top of the wall and scaled it slowly but surely. The long march left them with little energy to do anything quickly.

Delailith was among the first over. She leapt from the top and dropped fifteen feet onto the backs of two orcs grunting in frustration at an elusive faerie maiden. Other soldiers joined her and the battle became a great melee.

Meanwhile, the last soldiers over the top retrieved and coiled the ropes. When they joined Delailith and the others, Delailith gave the command to disengage, and the humans attempted just that. The faeries cast spells that, among other things, animated the roots of the great trees that until recent weeks had grown tall on this hill. Withered, but not yet dead, the roots obeyed the woodland creatures and burst from the ground to grapple at the legs and waists of the surprised orcs.

A few of the orcs trained bow and arrow on the attackers, but most had either dropped those weapons in lieu of swords and axes, or spent their efforts instead on escape attempts.

Delailith hurried with her soldiers behind a wave of faeries toward the large central tower within the orc fort. Small fires from blazing arrows lighted it, and smoke swirled across the battlefield as a result, but the wood was too fresh to burn well enough to topple the tower—hence the mission of the faeries and two human units.

A small band of orc reinforcements engaged the Combine force, with much the same result as before, though most of the faeries had spent their magical reserves and so only a couple of the orcs wrestled with roots. There were fewer than a dozen orcs, though, and the humans took them on.

Three of Delailith's soldiers sustained wounds before the brief struggle resolved. One of them was badly injured by an orc who snuck a surprise attack on the back of the soldier's neck, even though the orc was enmeshed in roots.

Delailith glared at the orc but did not waste time eliminating him. She relinquished authority of her unit to the other unit commander and immediately bandaged the most grievously injured solider. Five wounded men were soon in her care as the battle raged all around them and their uninjured fellows fought on toward the tower.

The woman did not allow the wounds of the soldiers to dominate her concentration, though, so she was on her feet with readied sword when a lone orc approached her. He moved slowly through the gauzy smoke and Delailith realized it was not a warrior, but rather an elderly orc. Feathers festooned the orc's body, and so Delailith prepared for an onslaught of shamanic magic.

Still, the orc's personal appearance worried her. Not only was his countenance one of barely contained anger, but he was pale, like a ghost.

AS MARROWSUCKER CHARGED TOWARD WHAT the Ashen One knew was as safe an assignment as possible, given the strategic interests of that attacking force, the shaman returned his attention to Rashalla. She drew near the smokehouse now, and though the ravens presaged her arrival, the orc was still surprised that she investigated the place so soon. He did not think it would make a difference, but whenever something was not as he predicted, Aataltaal took careful note.

The ravens hopped about everywhere, providing perspective into every shadowed position Rashalla came near. No ambush would surprise her; the Ashen One expected that much, so he had not bothered trying.

Evidently satisfied the area was secure, Rashalla made a sudden gesture and the ravens took to the air. Under the cover of their aerial reconnaissance, Rashalla backtracked. The Ashen One furled his brow, unsure of her intentions.

After walking about fifty feet from the renovated smokehouse, Rashalla stopped, drew in a deep breath, and began the complicated motions and incantations of what to the Ashen One's knowledgeable senses was a very powerful spell.

Nevertheless, when she unleashed it, the shaman was taken completely by surprise. The crone did not intend to use the tunnel at all. Rather, her goal was to seal it!

The final furious movements that the spell's execution demanded seemed almost beyond the frail capacity of Rashalla's bent and withered frame, but like an injured warrior able to forget his pains in the duress of battle, the sorceress for a time overcame her physical limitations. With a flourish, she ended the spell and stamped the palm of her left hand onto the ground before her.

Instantly, the ground shuddered as if hit by a weight a thousand times greater. In a moment the earth upon which the sorceress stood undulated so much that it seemed more like water than dirt and stone. Tiny ripples spread like waves in all directions from Rashalla, but this force primarily gathered in front of her and began to roll out in the direction she faced—toward the smokehouse.

It moved slowly at first, but gradually the magical force below the surface of the ground gathered power and momentum. Soon the earth cracked at its passage and then deep ruts and rents opened as the waves became a full-blown earthquake that tore gaping holes in the ground. By the time the attack reached Rashalla's target, it had gained its full strength, and the ground beneath the smokehouse heaved upward like a subterranean giant suddenly revealing itself. The flimsy orcish structure splintered and the ground exploded. Huge rocks vaulted into the air like a shower of hail, and the ground all around this spot collapsed upon itself.

The entrance to the underground river, had it actually been in that spot, would now be buried by incalculable tons of rock and dirt.

The Ashen One did not long dwell on this fortune that kept his caverns safe. Instead, he was furious at his own inexcusable error in failing to predict Rashalla's intentions. He thought she sought to uncover the entrance, not *cover* it! What other secrets did this old woman hide?

Whatever they might be, the shaman now needed Marrowsucker more than ever. The protective spells he cast on the orc should have spared him until now, but the Ashen One could not risk the orc warrior further. He turned and strode toward the site of the faeries' attack.

As if on cue, as the shaman turned, the great Tower on the Hill shuddered. Small fires flickered up and down its height. None of them had caught hold with much vigor, but a crew of humans at the base of the structure applied force in ample measure. They heaved on a handful of ropes looped around structural weak points in one leg of the Tower. A buzzing cloud of faeries protected the humans as they pulled in unison.

The Ashen One hesitated for just a moment because he could sense the Tower was on the verge of going down. He ran his gaze up the length of the stairs, and sure enough, near the top, and descending with all possible haste, came Crush himself. He took the stairs three or four or five at a time, but after a few bounds, the stairs folded up beneath him and the entire building collapsed.

Fuming with anger at his miscalculations of Rashalla's intentions, the shaman stalked toward Marrowsucker, and soon saw the orc had avoided death, but not capture. The orc seemed to be prisoner under the guard of a lone human woman, but then the shaman noted several other wounded humans and he understood she was watching them, not Marrowsucker. The orc warrior's face brightened with relief when the Ashen One gaze's fell upon him. On the other hand, the woman tensed. She drew her weapon and stepped to interpose herself between the shaman and the cluster of root-trussed orcs and injured humans.

The shaman found this circumstance frustrating. Easiest to simply kill them all, the humans and the orcs—all but Marrowsucker, of course. He could spare the unconscious humans, he supposed, but the woman and two wounded men who also drew weapons, though they were on their backs, would be unwanted witnesses.

But the woman was canny. She caught the looks between the shaman and Marrowsucker, and for an instant, the Ashen One feared she would strike the orc down. A spell rose instantly on his lips, but he let it fade, unrealized, when she stepped to the side, opening a path between the two orcs.

How can one punish a pet when it has done something it thinks is right? In this case, how could the Ashen One punish a woman who preferred an outcome where more lived than died?

Marrowsucker snarled in the orcish tongue, "Yes, yes, shaman. In the name of Rallos Zek, strike down the sun-loving humans!"

The Ashen One kept walking and replied in the same language, "We do not have the time for such inconvenience."

In the common tongue of the humans, the shaman said, "Both your destinies lie elsewhere, it seems." He stopped then, looking at the woman, gauging her reaction.

She said, "We have won this day, orc. A wise soldier understands when battle is no longer the best option. A wise shaman should know as much."

Behind the Ashen One, the roar of the battle peaked as the survivors of the collapsed tower fought the elves and dwarves who broke through the wall beyond. The shaman could hear Crush's battle cry above all the rest of the cacophony.

The Ashen One took a quick breath. With a flick of his hand, the magically animated roots that bound Marrowsucker and two other orcs relaxed their grips and receded back into the ground. The shaman's gaze followed them for a moment, watching as they disappeared into the earth like great worms, knowing their fate was now to wither and die on land these orcs would rule for a millennia that would begin a few days hence.

The woman, though startled by the orcs' freedom, spun into a better position between the four orcs and the wounded humans. She did not spare the instant for a glare of recrimination at the shaman, counting that as time that might mean the split-second between life and death.

Marrowsucker's weapon flashed at the woman and she moved to parry, but it wasn't necessary. The Ashen One hurled his dagger and it ricocheted off Marrowsucker's sword with enough force to turn the blow aside.

"Remain here and you die," the shaman said in orcish. "Run for the woods. Your leader shall rejoin you."

Marrowsucker flashed a look first of disappointment and then relief, as he and the others moved away from the humans. The Ashen One understood that he'd just issued permission to these four to survive the day without appearing cowardly.

The shaman then regarded the woman. Perhaps the worth of the human race ran deeper than simply a few exceptional individuals such as Katta.

"Remain so wise," he said to the woman. Then in orcish he shouted at the warriors who disengaged from the area, "Not you, Marrowsucker. We have a mission."

Then the shaman walked toward the collapsed tower. He distinctly heard Marrowsucker's pause, but in a moment the orc ran clear of the humans and joined the shaman.

"Are you mad?" Marrowsucker complained.

"No," said the shaman flatly, though with a grin heavy in meaning.

As the two orcs walked into a thickening cloud of smoke, the Ashen One cast a spell. Marrowsucker barely held his surprise in check when the shaman's left hand became glossy and semitransparent. The old orc then brushed his fingers gently against Marrowsucker's forearm, and that orc's arm faded from view as well. In a moment, along with what felt like a rush of cool air that raised goose bumps on their skin, the effect swept over both their entire bodies.

Marrowsucker stuttered to a stop. He could see the outlines of their bodies, but he could see right through the shaman. It was as if they were made of water.

"To others we are completely invisible," said the Ashen One. "Walk quietly and do not talk, and we will be safe for a few moments. The faeries might see us once the battle settles to a close, so we must be swift."

Marrowsucker squinted at the old orc. "What are we doing?"

The shaman smiled a gap-toothed grin. "Making certain you are dead." When the orc warrior clenched his brow in thought, the Ashen One enigmatically elaborated, "No, not exactly. Marrowsucker is already dead. Follow me."

The orc warrior scrunched his face in confusion, but the magic and the enemy that swarmed around him made him uncomfortable. His only option was to follow.

The Ashen One led the way through a scene of terrible carnage. All around the collapsed tower milled the Combine army, but in the midst of the victors lay the beaten and mangled corpses of orcs. The shaman pushed his way through all of this chaos and picked a path around the grounds littered with corpses. Finally, he found what he needed. To the Combine army the corpse he sought was an orc no different than any other, but Marrowsucker gasped when he saw the crushed body of Lord Crush. The huge orc's legs were pinned beneath some of the great timbers that formed the Tower, and claw marks showed where he'd attempted to pull his way clear, but to no avail. Three gruesome wounds on his head indicated the orc had little opportunity for escape, though the broken body of a dwarf that lay nearby indicated Crush had fought until the bitter end.

The orc shaman nodded to Marrowsucker and then motioned that it was time to leave.

SOME TIME LATER, WELL AWAY FROM THE battlefield, Marrowsucker felt much better. The death of Lord Crush, the annihilation of the orc army, and the destruction of Crushbone seemed so many anthills to surmount. Marrowsucker stood tall, taller than ever before, and flexed muscles that bristled with more strength than he had imagined possible.

"It's no wonder Crush swatted his rivals aside with such ease," said the warrior as he flexed his fingers.

" 'I,' " prompted the Ashen One.

The orc that seemed nearly a twin of the powerful but now deceased Lord Crush laughed. "Yes! 'I'!" He looked over his body and rippled his muscles wherever his eye fell. He'd been transformed to exactly resemble the dead Crush—though with one important difference. Like the resurrected Lifedrinker, Marrowsucker's Crush was no longer dark skinned, but instead ghostly pale.

"But there is a limitation," the shaman said.

The new Crush turned to the Ashen One. Greed rimmed his gaze.

The shaman continued, "The illusion with which I've cloaked you would normally fade within a few hours' time. But as my ally in this charade, you've finally earned this prize."

From a pouch that hung at his side, the Ashen One pulled forth the cloak of elven make that he'd promised Marrowsucker. "The enchantment of this cloak is naught but that it maintains other magics indefinitely. Put it on now and so long as you wish to remain Lord Crush, *do not ever remove it*. Not when you sleep, not when you piss, not when you tryst to sire an heir."

He held the cloak toward the new Crush, and the giant orc accepted it as if it were made of glass, fingering it delicately in a manner the true Crush could not have duplicated.

"So I have passed all your tests, then?"

The shaman nodded. "You are the most cunning of your clan, 'Crush,' and with my magic now the most puissant as well."

"You don't speak like an orc sometimes, Ashen One."

The shaman simply nodded again.

Crush eyed the shaman carefully, as if close inspection would somehow pierce the veil of magical illusion. "And if you can remake me in the manner of Lord Crush, then what—who—might you have originally been?"

The Ashen One answered carefully, his words heavy with the message between the lines, "I revealed myself to Lord Crush the day he summoned me to his tower."

Marrowsucker nodded, understanding the implication, but he pressed immediately, "But did Crush pass any of your other tests?"

"No."

A beat passed in silence.

His voice that of a crafty conspirator, Crush asked, "So it wasn't really the revelation of your identity that excluded him from your plans?"

The shaman smiled. "Very well, ambitious one. I have little time and must leave you before you return to your land at the Bloodwine. As we discussed, that is my only price—that you return and maintain Crushbone as your ancestral orcish home. Well, that and that some years hence your son, or your son's son, who shall carry on your name of Crush, shall welcome a dark elven ambassador named D'vinn and trust him implicitly."

As he spoke, Aataltaal let his orcish guise fall away again and stood revealed as a Teir'Dal. He flexed his fine limbs. It felt so much better to be in the body of an elf than an orc, particularly an aging one.

Marrowsucker laughed. "Of course this form could be a ruse as well, but your price is small and your gifts—an orcish empire included—are great." He chuckled again. "Besides, it seems I shall be dead by the time you call in your favor."

With a few words, Aataltaal's form melted into the thick semblance of the old orc. "Let's hurry. Your people will grow anxious if left for long. We cannot allow them to disperse."

He walked away briskly and Crush had no problem following. Within the hour, the Ashen One led the orc king to a remote location where the orc survivors gathered. Arguing voices fell instantly to a hush when the specter of Lord Crush, with the pallor of those favored by Rallos Zek, broke into their ranks. The orcs then broke into excited jabbering.

Crush said, "Silence."

All of the orcs quieted at once, then packed tightly around Crush and fell to their knees. One whispered in astonishment, "Lord Crush, you have returned to us!"

In his best Crush-like ferocious swagger, Marrowsucker said, "I am Lord Crush no more. An emperor has failed to kill me, failed to destroy us, so I must be an emperor as well. Henceforth, I shall be Emperor Crush. Let all the Faydark whimper at the sound of my name!"

A deafening roar of approval swelled from the assembled orcs.

The new Emperor Crush continued, "And we shall rebuild our home on the site we have fled. Every orc, alive and dead, shall be part of our cause. Wood is the stuff of the elves. It is no fit home for an *orc*! We shall erect a terrible palace built of stone and bone. Our home shall live up to its name of Crushbone!"

The orcs pumped their fists and clanged their weapons together as they cheered again.

His lips flattened in the best approximation of a smile the terrible events of late allowed, the Ashen One moved away unnoticed. Everything here was in place as well as possible, and D'vinn would be welcomed by a descendant of Marrowsucker's some day long hence. But for now work awaited him in the court of Emperor Katta. General Seru would return a conquering hero yet again, and as before, he would throw his vast political weight against the inclusion of the dark elves in the Combine Empire. Their membership was something Aataltaal had worked hard to arrange, for it would be easier to gain entry to the dark-elf realm if the Teir'Dal were admitted *here*.

Clearly, Emperor Katta would seek the advice of the seldom-lucid, glaze-eyed ancient human called the Oracle. The Ashen One's eyes twinkled at the thought that this human even now conveniently remained too sick to see the emperor—until he, in a new guise, returned to the capital.

But first, the journey to his current home called for a detour past the now-cool embers of Shadow-Wood Keep. Some true ghosts could be put to rest, even if the oldest ghosts still wandered, unredeemed.

4

THE ORACLE OF THE LAKE

"I'VE NEVER BEEN CERTAIN," SAID THE HANDsome, middle-aged man, "whether you were named for the lake or if the lake was named for you." The man regarded his elderly companion with a critical eye, as if he might learn more by watching the old man than by listening. But the old man's face was indecipherable, inured to such scrutiny by having faced countless travelers seeking answers to often frivolous questions regarding their equally often frivolous lives.

At least the old man's present guest was the emperor of the most powerful empire on Norrath, the Combine Empire. Emperor Katta had risen from humble circumstances in the plains of far-off Tunaria where he forged first the humans there into a nation, and then with bold ideas and a grand vision, he seduced many of the other races of the world.

The Oracle understood what Katta himself did not—well, he understood many things the emperor could not, but among these was that the man was successful not in spite of being a human, but in some measure because of his race.

Sometimes regarded as the rats of the civilized races,

humans had earned disdain for their lack of focus. They lived everywhere. They worshipped nigh any god. They seemed selfish but only on their personal behalf, not in the name of their race or some god.

And Aataltaal, despite seeming to be human in this guise as the Oracle of the Lake, had to hide—among many other things—his own dislike of the human race.

So why should the other races of Norrath continue to dislike humans, when here was evidence of a man who represented the opposite of all the human faults? A man who brought humans together in a greater family and gave them focus?

Because of the one thing humans could not avert: death. Also like rats, humans lived such brief lives that scarcely anything that one man or one tribe or even the entire race accomplished could persist. And hence part of the reason why the dwarves, elves, gnomes, and others of Norrath ultimately accepted Katta and his Combine: they knew the man would pass and then, perhaps, they each expected to be the victor who could pick up the pieces of the empire.

Emperor Katta was still relatively young, and that time seemingly decades hence, but the Oracle thought he knew otherwise.

" 'Oracle Lake' predates my association with it, Emperor," said Aataltaal. "But its waters tell me that another shall come for whom it will be renamed."

Katta cocked his head with curiosity. He was a distinguished man. His black hair was cut short and the slightest hint of gray showed at the temples. His clothing of golden thread and short-haired furs set him well apart from any common man he might pass, but it was still short of regal. It suited him well, for Katta was proud— proud of his accomplishments—as well as humble, which showed in his authentic admiration of the other races of

Norrath for how they came together under the banner of the Combine Empire.

"Not for myself, I hope," said Katta. He'd consistently refused to have anything in Norrath named after him, saying he desired a legacy of deeds, not of places. The Oracle suspected that at some level the emperor understood how easily names could be changed, and how the passing of a name often signaled the passing relevancy of a legacy. Best not to set in stone what the tide of history shall soon wash away!

"Named for royalty, yes, but not you, Emperor. Not for a human king, but for an elven queen who shall be stronger, far stronger than I, in her powers of divination."

Katta chuckled, but without amusement, "Then I wish *she* were here to tell me of the future." Then he glanced quickly at the Oracle to make certain he'd not offended the old man.

Aataltaal was as unmoved as ever. As the Oracle of the Lake, he was a tall man, still over six feet despite his apparent advanced age, which was unknown exactly but looked to be eighty or more. The Oracle gave the sense of being much older, though, like a mountain—it was an aspect of himself that Aataltaal chose not to cloak in this guise, for it suited the Oracle's mystique, in fact, better than his own. Some even joked that he did not so much see the future as, having seen all of the past, he could simply guess at what would happen again. Sometimes, Aataltaal wondered if that truly was the secret of his divinatory powers. He well knew the past repeated itself in the future—and the present as well. Empires rose, empires fell.

Aataltaal liked this man Katta, though he was still just a human. And if time was a wheel that rotated with the passing of each generation, then the human wheel rolled all too quickly, until the cart it bore sped headlong and well out of control. The disguised elf worried that too many others were cargo in the cart of the Combine Empire.

Better the larger elven wheel that turned more slowly and covered more ground before the same dread points returned to earth.

"Oracle?" asked Katta with a touch of concern.

"Pardon me, Emperor, I am showing my age. You came seeking a vision for how your gathering, the Great Combine Summit, shall fare, yes? Never before have so many of the prominent races of Norrath gathered to contemplate their combined future."

Katta chuckled. " 'Contemplate'? I suspect 'conspire' is more appropriate."

"Why, because the dark elves have chosen to attend?"

Katta nodded and said, "That's part of it, of course. Even many of those who favored inviting the Teir'Dal suspect that they only agreed so that they could openly spy on the proceedings."

"And detractors?"

Katta drew himself up and gained a slight political air as he explained, "They argue that Teir'Dal attend for any number of ill reasons, including to assassinate me. But I never intended the Combine Empire as merely an alliance of the so-thought 'good' races of Norrath. In like-mindedness lies weakness. I believe the dark elves will not only provide balance of perspective, but I believe they and we, too, shall come to see our differences as not so vast. The gulf between their race and the others already within the Combine family can be bridged."

Aataltaal smiled to hear his own words coming from the emperor's mouth, in much the same argument he had presented a year ago when the planning for the

Great Summit began. Of course, Aataltaal could have used magic to attempt to sway Katta's decisions, but besides being too risky, it wasn't fair. None of his efforts had any legitimate purpose if he resorted to such base methods.

Even though he agreed with Katta, Aataltaal pressed, "Is this why you've delayed the Great Summit? You'll allow the Teir'Dal to set the schedule for the rest of the empire?"

Katta's lips thinned in frustration, "Yes. Oh, I know it's a great inconvenience to the members of the Combine, and only gives my detractors—or at least the detractors of my plan to include the dark elves—more fodder for their gossip and grousing. But I feel certain this occasion will truly determine the fate of the Combine Empire. If we must postpone in order to assure the attendance of the Teir'Dal, then we shall."

Aataltaal's heart was heavy. It was what he wanted as well, but where Katta acted out of optimism, Aataltaal had only a sense of foreboding. It was certainly no coincidence that the dark elves required a new date on the heels of Aataltaal managing to put Seru in the field and away from the event. But what he could not understand was how either side—the Teir'Dal or Seru—benefited. The human general opposed the dark elves' admittance to Combine, which was why Aataltaal wanted him elsewhere when that race attended the summit. Something he did not yet see connected these events. Perhaps a vision for Katta would hint at the answer.

Aataltaal inquired, "But the Teir'Dal worship the Prince of Hate. How can even the most noble institution survive an association with Innoruuk?"

Katta relaxed his political bearing and slightly grinned at the Oracle. "You're quite interested in this, I see."

The Oracle remained firm-lipped, stoic. "Understanding your rationale for the coming events may be key to understanding the visions I may momentarily gain."

The emperor said, "Well, I can only point out that the Combine Empire already thrives in spite of an association with that dark god. The Teir'Dal are not the only beings on Norrath to worship Innoruuk. He has humans among his followers as well, and I dare say some of his human worshippers are surely well-placed within the empire."

"Placed as high as general?"

Katta's eyes widened in surprise, but the Oracle did not retreat from the question. "If those words were spoken in the court—" growled the emperor.

"Which is precisely why I speak them only here, my lord, where we can talk as men and not shapers—or seers—of the future."

Katta's lips twitched and another retort seemed to be forming on his tongue, but he bit it back and fell silent for a moment. When he spoke again, it was quietly, as if they *were* in the court and might be overheard. "It's true that General Seru strongly opposes the invitation I've extended the Teir'Dal. To suppose he worships Innoruuk, though, is preposterous. The war god Rallos Zek, perhaps—don't all soldiers pay him some due? If he were allied with the Prince of Hate, then why would he stand in the way of the Summit?"

"Because it is the way of discord," said the Oracle. "Beware the two sides that play against the middle." He said this, though he knew it to be misdirection. The Oracle was surprised when the emperor vaguely grasped that fact as well.

"That sounds like the doublespeak of prophecy, Oracle." Katta smiled and gave a slight chuckle. And that set off what little talent the Oracle truly had for prophecy. The emperor's smile wavered and within a sun-faded flash in his mind's eye, the Oracle saw that grin turn to grimace.

The emperor knew this look of the Oracle's and fell silent, watching as the tall, old man turned slowly to look into the nearby waters. The ancient stepped closer to the lake, the embroidered white trim of his aqua-blue robe fluttering just above the surface.

Only the Oracle saw the images swimming in the water. Once upon a time, he thought his visions a gift of the goddess Tunare, but now he was uncertain whether the images were a gift or a hindrance, and perhaps more importantly, he doubted they came from Tunare at all. Whatever the source or value of the visions, the images in the water unfolded into a dreamlike sequence devoid of logic or obvious interpretation.

The source of the emperor's pained expression emerged soon enough, for momentarily a serpent slithered from the man's mouth. The creature's scales gleamed as if fashioned from shimmering emeralds, but they turned to aged, greenish bronze as the first portion of the snake's body looped once around the emperor's neck. Then, just as the serpent at last withdrew its tail from the emperor's mouth, the bronze transformed to natural scales.

It then again looped around the emperor's neck, but this time when its head reappeared, its mouth was wide, and unnaturally long fangs dripped with venom so acidic it burst into flame and smoke as it dripped. Around and around the emperor it wound, wrapping the man's face tight, like the wrappings of a mummy, and becoming far longer than it first seemed, until no part of Katta's flesh or hair remained visible.

Then the scale of the image grew so that the emperor's

entire body could be seen. The serpent grew thicker as well and stretched down Katta's back. It twisted between his legs and then ballooned to such a size that it became a serpentine mount and it slithered away with Katta upon it. Though the journey lasted but a moment, as in a dream the impression communicated a great distance. Across a sea the serpent traveled, until it slipped from under the emperor and shrunk again, though it remained at least man-sized.

Standing before him like a giant viper ready to strike, the serpent grew arms and gained a malevolent glimmer in its eyes that belied the danger of its still-dripping fangs. Suddenly, too, it was garbed. Heavy and elaborate gold jewelry decorated it, and fine silken clothing draped its upper torso. At this sight the Oracle gasped, an uncommon mid-vision reaction that made the real Katta nervous. It had been many long years since the Oracle beheld one of the treacherous race of shissar.

The Oracle's eyes never wavered from the image, though, and soon the shissar sprouted legs as well, and the regal garb it wore first became tattered and then fell away completely to reveal a creature more manlike-lizard than humanoid snake: an iksar instead of a shissar.

The lizard-man then emphatically pointed at the heavens, as if damning the gods for ills befallen its race. But when the iksar's arm began to dissolve into a gaseous form, the Oracle knew the sign here to be otherwise. The lizard-man's arm detached and transformed into a billowing snake formed of green smoke like the poisonous mist that the gods—or perhaps some other power unknown—used against transgressors.

The snake of green mist grew arms to again resemble a shissar and it floated high into the air above a nonplussed Emperor Katta. Just as the emperor, too, began to dissolve into smoke, the real world beyond the vision and beyond the Oracle's inner thoughts intervened.

The wind picked up slightly and whipped the Oracle's robe just enough so that its trim brushed the surface of the water. The faint spreading ripples broke the fragile barrier between the "is" and the "might be."

The old man turned to his emperor, absently dabbing a single bead of sweat upon his brow. He was left to wonder whether the gaseous emperor would also turn green? Did the gods plan to unleash the green mist again? Surely not against the Combine Empire? True, the Combine did not hold fast to the gods insofar as it did not officially hold any of them before another, but should that not please the gods? Should it not give their adolescent jealousies pause for respite? Did Tunare herself send the wind that disrupted his vision? Or did even noble Quellious, the ocean lord, stoop so low now? Or, least likely of all, did Innoruuk take an interest in the Oracle, in this shell of an aged human?

Katta's still-youthful face furrowed with worry. "I've never seen you react like this," he said, authentically concerned more for the Oracle's uniquely—though only very slightly—flustered state than anything the old man might communicate about the emperor's own fate.

The Oracle waved off Katta's attempt to steady him, and the emperor waited a moment for the old man to recover. "Is this why you would not see me for so many days?" Katta asked. "Because you anticipated a disturbing vision?"

The Oracle smiled. "No, Emperor. I rudely left you waiting because I am an old man." He motioned to the ground upon which he stood. "As I have demonstrated just now with my sign of weakness. No, I kept you waiting because I sleep now for days at a time. I can no longer see the future upon demand. It takes a toll on me, and between such occasions I am forced to rest. I regret that this sometimes causes me to sleep more than I am awake."

Katta nodded, his concern satisfied and so now overwhelmed by thoughts of himself, of his empire.

The Oracle saw this, and he said, "But one old man, even one who sees the future, is nothing compared to the Combine Empire."

"Nor is its emperor," Katta said sincerely.

The Oracle nodded, his feelings of fondness for the human reinforced yet again.

"Because I believe you, Emperor, I will not shield you from what I see."

Katta nodded. "Thank you. There have been times in the past when I could not tell whether you told me what you saw for the future, what you predicted for the future, or . . ." He paused, looking for a manner in which to express himself. "Or what for some reason you desired of the future. I have always imagined a desire for a future to be at odds with one who would reveal it to others, but no one is above a wish to somehow shape the events around us."

The Oracle's mien was expressionless.

Katta continued, "If you will merely recount, then I will set about the business of shaping."

"I do not know that these are so easily separated, Emperor. Regardless, I urge you to seek safety."

Katta's eyes closed to suspicious slits. "From the dark elves? Is this a ruse?"

"No. It is hard to imagine, but I believe them authentic in their desire to join the Combine, though you can count on their motives being less selfless than—or at best just as selfish as—those of other races that have joined you."

"Then from whom?" Katta exclaimed, looking into the distance as if considering a rogue's gallery of threats and assassins. Then he stopped short. "If the Teir'Dal are truly open to my invitation, then others must know this to be true as well."

The Oracle nodded, though Katta was not questioning but thinking aloud. The old man felt he owed this younger one a better truth, so he prompted, "Earlier we discussed you being in the middle of a game meant to sow discord, though in truth I am not certain if even all the parties on the extremities are fully cognizant of their roles."

"If not the dark elven side, then the other, eh?" whispered Katta, still thinking out loud more than conversing. Soon, his eyes narrowed again. "Then it must be . . ." He trailed off, sadly returning his gaze to the old man, who only nodded.

The Oracle's own machinations were at risk, but his plans would collapse more quickly with a dead Emperor Katta, so he suggested, "Would you consider canceling the Summit?"

There was no hesitation. The weary expression of an instant before shifted in a flash to the wild and fiery expression with which Katta cajoled his first alliances. "I will not bow to personal danger. Threats left to fester in darkness only grow stronger. Better to let them be aired now."

The Oracle nodded, but Katta had only paused, not stopped. The emperor continued, "And I will be frank with you: I sense something ripening within the Teir'Dal that the light of day may yet cause to bear fruit."

The Oracle could hardly believe his ears. His look of surprise was authentic, though its basis was other than that which Katta assumed.

"As you said, we are not in court, Oracle, and so

here I speak perhaps too freely, but . . . are you familiar with the myth that says the Teir'Dal were birthed ages ago by a high elven king and queen?"

"Yes, of course."

The emperor explained, "They were kidnapped by Innoruuk himself and taken to his Plane of Hate where he tortured them and formed them into the first of the dark elves. He then set them back upon Norrath and from them arose the dark elven race."

Again the Oracle nodded, still surprised at this turn of the conversation. "There is surely something of the truth in that description."

Katta, almost in a mystical trance of his own as he presented an idea clearly important to him, continued. "If it's even the slightest bit true, and I know many wise high elves who themselves believe it to be so, then does it not follow that within the Teir'Dal is something of the heart of a high elf? And if that is so, then perhaps the dark elves are not so far removed from the other races already a part of the Combine Empire as many of us imagine!

"Maybe," concluded the emperor, "an association, an alliance even, with the other races can undo some of the terrible damage Innoruuk inflicted."

The Oracle nodded. His face was again expressionless. It did not betray the hope that swelled in his breast.

5

The Empire of Katta

"IT IS ONLY RIGHT THAT THE FIRST OFFICIAL audience of this pavilion be granted to you, General." The high elf bowed slightly as he spoke, though the other man continued to march forward. "And as governor of these lands so honored to host the first Great Combine Summit, I welcome you."

The contrast between the lithe, pale-skinned, white-haired governor and the muscular, swarthy, scarred general could not have been more dramatic. Despite the kind words, when their eyes met it was like the clashing of swords. The governor stood in the one open doorway of the enormous double-doors that led to the descent into the amphitheater-like pavilion. With his skin so white it seemed heavy with makeup to a human eye, his ring-studded, uncalloused fingers, and his intricately decorated purple robe of silk, Governor Aataltaal was civilization incarnate.

On the other hand, General Seru was a barbarian at the gate. Just returned from his campaign against the orcs on the other side of the vast Greater Faydark Forest, the general attended the emperor immediately, without first pausing to refresh himself. The musky odor of the deep forest fought an invisible battle with the perfume that wafted off the governor. This confrontation caused a commotion, the kind of sensation Seru enjoyed creating. His dark armor exaggerated his size, for the banded plate mail featured enormous shoulder guards as decorative as they were impenetrable. Likewise oversized was the neck guard fixed to the top of the breastplate. It obscured the lower part of the general's face and often left his intense eyes alone to communicate.

"Yes, yes," said Seru impatiently. "You're welcome for my avenging your elven kin. Now go fluff your hair for the festivities."

He still gave no appearance of slowing or detouring and clearly expected to knock Aataltaal from the threshold. A half step from the anticipated impact, Seru jutted his shoulder out even further to ensure the contact. Quick as a cat, Aataltaal slipped out of the general's path. When the expected collision did not occur, Seru stumbled slightly, which caused Aataltaal to dryly remark, "Perhaps you should rest first, General. You seem tired."

Seru turned and faced the high elf. "You're as slippery in the corridors of power as you are upon the battlefield of politics, Governor. But I will not long be troubled by you."

"Just the admission I had hoped to hear," said Aataltaal, though more for effect alone than to disclose any sort of discovery. He looked squarely at the general, clearly not intimidated despite their apparent differences.

Seru hesitated a moment, perhaps wondering if he had indeed slipped an unintentional revelation, but he said, "Ever the politician, you create meaning where none exists. On the battlefield it is black and white." This he almost snarled, then added, "Your opponent strikes. You either defend, or you die."

Aataltaal smiled. He said lightly, "Ah, but what if

your opponent merely feints, watching for a reaction? Or an overreaction. Isn't that when your opponent truly wins the moment?"

General Seru glowered, his face darkening to challenge the pitch-black hue of his armor. "Would that this were a battlefield, elf!"

Though the newly constructed pavilion seemed to rumble with this threat, Aataltaal appeared undeterred. He even stepped toward Seru, though he did not raise his hands or move in any way as if to strike—or to defend. He said, "Beware your plots, General, or you may well have your wish."

Seru quivered as if on the verge of eruption. His dark face reddened. "Contemptible! I take to the battlefield avenging your brethren while you luxuriate in political platitudes and plush pillows, and this is the respect—the reception—I receive?"

"Very poetic, General. Perhaps you do have a career after soldiery."

Seru shook his head in disgust and turned on his heel. He adjusted his armor and then resumed his descent.

Aataltaal watched the general. The Combine Pavilion soon dwarfed even his impressive frame. The new structure was an amphitheater of sorts, set at the base of one of the rolling hills a league outside Felwithe, the capital city of the Koada'Dal, the elegant and graceful light-skinned elves who counted among their race many of the foremost masters of sorcery as well as swordplay, and who descended directly from the elves who battled the dragons for superiority upon Norrath. In fact, it was said that a few survived among the Koada'Dal who had lived in that long-ago time, which predated the so-called Lost Age that ended with the rise of the Combine Empire and the Age of Blood before that.

Emperor Katta sat at a great table on the stagelike platform at the head of the nearly one hundred curved rows of seats within the Combine Pavilion. A succession of messengers and advisors shuttled to and from the emperor as they arranged all the final details for this evening's opening ceremonies.

The Great Combine Summit promised to be an event without parallel in the annals of Norrath and, more important to Aataltaal, it was being staged for all the right reasons. He feared it would have all the wrong results, but as the governor of the Northern Reach and therefore of the presiding delegation—for the Koada'Dal had made a gift of the Combine Pavilion to Emperor Katta, and in recognition of the gesture he named this the site for the first summit—he had it within his power to take substantial measures to make certain all went well this evening. And the next, and the next, and the next.

Aataltaal sighed. It would be a difficult task, but the very best wizards would shield the emperor from sorcerous attacks, the priests most cherished by Tunare would extend their healing protections to him, and the mighty paladins of Mithaniel Marr, the Lightbringer, would lay down their lives to intercept physical threats to the emperor.

Even now a contingent of Koada'Dal flanked the emperor, fulfilling these roles. This shift had two magic workers—one male, one female—who stood at the edges of the platform. The male, a wizard, meditated to recover his strength, and the female, an enchanter, studied a large tome that floated in the air before her, but anyone with the least bit of magical talent—something Aataltaal possessed prodigiously—could see their spells at work upon the person of Katta. Every manner of arcane shield and protective incantation that could be extended to another by these masters of the arcane buffered Katta from danger.

Likewise, male and female clerics of Tunare stood ready. They were nearer the emperor and more alert—partly because the immediate application of their healing magic could mean the difference between life and death; but also because, unlike the wizards, the priests concerned themselves with matters of state and took this opportunity to glean more knowledge of current events in the royal house.

Three paladins, all male, stood within a few steps of the emperor's side. All these highly trained warriors were clearly poised for instantaneous response to any threat. A fourth paladin, a female whom Aataltaal had known since her childhood, and whom he had selected personally for this assignment, stood virtually in the same shoes as the emperor. Even so, the governor doubted Katta was very much aware of her at all. Lady Chastine moved quickly and cleanly to remain out of the emperor's line of sight whenever he turned his head. This allowed her a proximity that might seem claustrophobic for conversation, but despite Katta's initial reluctance, he had relented to Aataltaal's persistence. Of course, the high elf had the advantage of knowing what the Oracle told the emperor. A few subtle references to the foreseen danger meant Aataltaal could place guardians as he liked.

Governor Aataltaal knew that one of the emperor's main reservations about this phalanx of elven guards was that it seemed to put the high elves on a pedestal above the other races of the Combine Empire, an especially troublesome consideration in light of the expected attendance of the Teir'Dal of Neriak. The dark elves might be authentically angered by the move, or, just as likely, they could feign indignation in order to receive special treatment themselves.

However, Felwithe was the host, and high elves had a responsibility to protect their most treasured guest. Aataltaal argued that involving other races in the emperor's protection would not only be more difficult to manage than elves who had worked together in the past, but then *all* the races would want representation. And even if the Teir'Dal had not yet officially joined the Combine, they too might insist on participating. *That* created a potentially ruinous situation.

Aataltaal was turning away from the doorway at the top of the steps when he heard the name Rashalla and stepped back to investigate. Because his encounter with Seru had been more direct than he'd intended, he did not wish to continue to stir the general's wrath by lingering through this conversation with Katta, but the governor remained interested in the raven-woman. That Katta, who continued to surprise with a sometimes surreal subconscious awareness of things he did not knowingly grasp, would inquire after this woman now of all times made Aataltaal even more curious.

Below, General Seru dropped to one knee before Emperor Katta. His head was raised, though, to see the emperor on the stagelike platform where workers busily arranged final decorations, such as enormous vases of wildflowers from the fields between Felwithe and the Greater Faydark Forest.

Pleasantries had already been exchanged, and Aataltaal's sensitive ears caught the conversation as it moved more in the direction that intrigued him.

Katta said, "Where is this Rashalla who helped punish the orcs for their trespass? Or where does she abide? The empire owes her its thanks."

"My lord," replied General Seru, "Rashalla is but a mercenary and insofar as she's received the gold of the

Combine Empire, she has received thanks enough already."

Aataltaal choked back a snort of resentment. Thanked well indeed. He had checked, and her fee alone exceeded that of all of the officers of the campaign combined—Seru excepted. The woman certainly did not mind drawing attention. And so far there had been no backlash for her extravagant attitude or the brazen settlements Seru made with her—until now, perhaps.

Seru continued, "The ones upon whom you should bestow your thanks are the soldiers who are still marching for home."

Katta nodded. "I am glad you at least could return in time for the Summit. The empire should not be without its commander on such an occasion, though I understand your obligation is first to our borders and our member races who are threatened by cowardly ambush."

"My lord, our empire is now as secure as ever. So long as the Summit offers no surprises, then we may enter a period where we can dedicate our energy to making the center of the empire as strong as its borders."

With his sharp vision Aataltaal could see clearly the grimace that stole across Katta's face. To their credit, none of the bustling staff hesitated. Preparations continued even in the face of the disagreement between the two most powerful humans upon Norrath. And perhaps in this case "human" should be removed as a denominator.

"General Seru, I will not overlook the request or accusation—however you wish to describe it—implicit in your words. My intention remains unchanged. My invitation is still offered and still accepted. You feel that inclusion of the Teir'Dal will weaken the empire you desire to bolster; that we will become fractious; and that they plot to tear us down from within. Again I say, better the enemy you know than the one that remains unknown. And I do not discount the possibility that their darker impulses can be tamed."

By the time he finished speaking, Emperor Katta was standing, the final words of his oration delivered with a fist clenched before him. Now many of the workers in the amphitheater turned to watch; a few even dared to applaud.

But General Seru remained motionless, seemingly impassive. At last, he said only, "I shall not speak of it again."

But the emperor could not quite let it go so easily. "General, I achieved battlefield victories in my time upon the Plains of Karana, and you won political victories in order to receive appointments that advanced your position. Now we are the two heads of the Combine Empire. Just as I allow you near-sole command upon the battlefield, I expect the same for myself within the political arena."

Seru did not budge. His gaze did not waver from Katta. "Yes, Emperor."

Behind the emperor, Lady Chastine's eyes darted to the general and she smoothly stepped to Katta's side. No longer his shadow, she placed herself prominently beside him. Aataltaal watched her closely. Her body tensed and her eyes narrowed, and this elicited the same reaction in the emperor as well as the other three paladins, though none of these others was aware of exactly what was amiss.

After an instant, she relaxed and stepped to her customary position. Katta glanced at her as she moved from the periphery of his vision, but he rolled his head back to face Seru.

The emperor sighed. The weight of his melancholy filled the amphitheater. "Very well, General. Please get some rest and refreshment. We have four very long days ahead of us."

Seru rose, bowed slightly, and turned to depart. Aataltaal did the same, not wishing to encounter the general again, but he hesitated when Seru involuntarily grasped his stomach as if affected by a sudden pain. The general's stride did not slacken, however, and he did not draw attention to the possible injury. Few proud warriors would.

Something made Aataltaal uneasy about it, though, and he wondered if it was because he, too, felt a slight cramping in his stomach.

He left immediately for the Hall of Truth. The next shift of paladins would have to start early, because Aataltaal needed to speak with Chastine.

"I COULD NOT BE CERTAIN, MY LORD GOVERNOR, so I decided to take measured steps in the emperor's defense." The Koada'Dal paladin was positively radiant despite her stressful hours as Emperor Katta's nearest line of defense. Lady Chastine was yet young by elf standards and while even older elves retained much of the gloss of youth—smooth, white skin; brilliant, sparkling eyes; and trim, athletic figures—she was both still young and exceptionally attractive even among elves. These facts, as well as her limitless dedication to the Lightbringer, made Lady Chastine literally shine—a faint glow seemed always to surround her.

An individual less perceptive than Aataltaal might be tempted to concentrate on these surface features and not be wary of her martial prowess. In this most illogical way, her beauty made her an even better warrior, though she had skill enough with the blade that she did not require this tactical advantage, and of course it would mean little to those unmoved by her appearance, such as the Teir'Dal. Aataltaal knew that much for certain, for he'd participated in her training, and which was why he chose her for the delicate assignment of shadowing Emperor Katta. Besides, Aataltaal knew that even coarse humans found her beautiful, and so it was far easier to convince Katta to have a guardian such as Chastine by his side.

"I thought at first that he was making an arcane gesture of some kind, but then it was clear that he simply clenched his hand in pain, and he clutched at his side."

Aataltaal nodded and said, "Yes, I noted that he seemed troubled when he arose." He thought on his own discomfort that had followed, too, and asked, "And you? Did you feel any sort of pain in your stomach?"

It seemed to her a strange question and so it gave the paladin slight pause, but her face remained relaxed and nonjudgmental. "No, lord Governor."

"Just a coincidence, then?"

"My lord Governor?"

"Nothing, Chastine. Thank you for your explanation. I believe you acted appropriately. Please rest for a few hours and then resume your assignment."

Lady Chastine smiled. "I can return now, lord Governor."

"I'm sure you could, but rest. I fear you will need it." Aataltaal rubbed his own stomach, though the slight feeling of indigestion had already passed.

6

THE PARADE OF NORRATH

ONLY HOURS BEFORE THE SCHEDULED OPEN-
ing ceremonies of the Great Combine Summit, the
final member delegation arrived: the dwarves of the
Butcherblock Mountains. The reason for their tardiness
became clear as soon as their delegation pulled within
sight: their wagons were formed of solid stone. The
wagon train stretched only nine-long, but the thunder-
ing of the massive vehicles could be heard from leagues
away, and Governor Aataltaal joined the citizens attracted by the curious noise.

Not merely crude constructions of roughly hewn
stone, each wagon appeared to be an individual, sculpted
masterpiece. Typical of dwarven ornamentation, the deco-
ration included a vast array of gemstones. All mined
from the deep holes the dwarves dug near their underground homes, the gems were as masterfully carved as
the wagons themselves.

Each wagon was patterned after motifs central to one
of the member races of the Combine Empire, and they
rolled into view in the order these races accepted the
Articles of the Great Combine, which signaled their entry to the empire. First came three wagons of the races

of men: the human wagon, with sculpted images of a timeline of the Combine Empire itself and the landscape of the plains in the center of Tunaria where Katta was born; the Erudite wagon, with aquatic motifs of dolphins, clamshells, and seahorses befitting the island nation, and slender, graceful architecture like that of this tall, dark-skinned race of men; and the Northmen wagon, fashioned in an astonishing reproduction of the harsh glacial topography where this sturdy race eked a living, and featuring a single heroically scaled central sculpture of a lone Northman wrestling an enormous polar bear.

Next was a wagon for the halflings, beings that looked like plump men but only half their size. They hailed from Rivervale, a small valley just east of the Plains of Karana that birthed Tsaph Katta and the Combine Empire. The panels of the halfling wagon bore great sculpted reliefs portraying an endless pageant of foodstuffs, from grains and vegetables to bottles of rum and fruit pies.

By this time, a crowd had gathered to view the parade, and a cheer went up among a small cluster of halflings. Food and relaxation lay at the heart of this sometimes-comical race, and they did not at all mind that others knew it.

Next came the wagon for the dwarves of Kaladim themselves. Aataltaal thought it likely the dwarves had studiously ensured that their own wagon appeared to be the least grand of them all, but nevertheless, upon closer inspection, it presented a marvel of craftsmanship. The entire wagon was a rolling scale-model of what could well be the city of Kaladim itself. It appeared plain because the exterior was nothing but a sculpture of the mountain under which Kaladim nestled.

Though the terrain of the Butcherblock Mountains was stark and majestic to behold, in miniature it offered little revelation to the viewer. But to peer within the model! Cutaways at strategic points allowed a view of the innards of the mountain city. These view holes were covered with thin sheets of virtually transparent mica and they revealed a city in miniature, like a wooden ship in a bottle, though far more grand, for the "bottle" was a twelve-foot-tall "mountain." Even the mineshafts stretching beneath the city were detailed, and here, too, fabulous craftsmanship was displayed. Small prospectors examined impossibly small yet multifaceted gemstones that glittered brightly, and natural-seeming veins of gold, silver, and more gems cut across the surface of the model in geodelike striations.

Gasps of awe shuddered through the ever-growing auidence as the next wagon became visible. Dedicated to the hosts of the Great Combine Summit, the high elves who followed the dwarves in acceptance of the Articles, this display was a stunning gemstone sphere. The globe was at least eight feet across, formed by a patchwork of oddly shaped pieces of different sorts of transparent to semitransparent minerals and gems. This gave the globe the alluring impression of being mirrorlike at some facets and translucent at others, so that the great sphere alternately reflected and absorbed light. Aataltaal thought he recognized a veiled reference to the Koada'Dal, who were indeed a noble and highly regarded race, but one with a definite capacity to look down upon the other races as a parent might a child. The polychromatic display was especially dazzling as the sun of Norrath—the great eye of Sol—fell below the tips of the broadroot trees that stretched for miles and miles westward as the Greater Faydark Forest.

Next to adopt the Articles of the Great Combine, upon the same occasion as and so only moments after the Koada'Dal, were the wood elves of Kelethin—and formerly of Shadow-Wood Keep as well. The Feir'Dal dwelt throughout the Greater Faydark, but the treetop city of Kelethin was their capital and by far most-populated city. Where the Koada'Dal embraced architecture and art and a refined sense of interaction with the world of Norrath, the Feir'Dal remained entirely at one with nature and their most-beloved goddess, Tunare.

Though the base of the wood elves' wagon was stone like all the others, it seemed the most organic. Somehow, the master dwarven carvers created a stonework that appeared to have grown, rather than being fashioned by the earthly pressures of the Underfoot. The sculpted wagon, though solid stone, seemed to writhe and wriggle like the mass of tangled vines it resembled. Sprouting proudly from this mass of granite vegetation grew a dozen scale models of the great broadroot trees of the forest. Each tree was fashioned from a different gem or mineral, from amber to jade, though all were generally dark and so the "forest" was not a garish patchwork, but rather a nearly uniform whole, like the Feir'Dal's association with nature.

The most recent member race to officially adopt the Articles of the Great Combine was the gnomes of Ak'Anon, the capital city located some eight hundred miles to the south on this same continent of Faydwer. The dwarven crafters had meticulously avoided any sense of hodgepodge randomness where the natural landscape of the Feir'Dal was concerned, but they let loose all that repressed randomness on the gnomish wagon. Clearly the least orthodox among dwarven craftsman had found a home working on the eccentric gnomish sculpture.

The gnomes worked a kind of magic they called technology that utilized elements more mechanical than arcane. Windmills and steam from the great vents of their nearby Steamfont Mountains powered the contraptions of gnomish master tinkerers. Both of those sources of power were put to use here. Though it appeared decidedly unartful, a large windmill dominated the center of this display. When it turned, it powered not only a great vice but also a shovel that dipped into a container and extracted crystals to deposit within the vice. In a process surely abetted by magic in a manner not wholly consistent with gnomish ideals, the vice crushed the crystals, and the evidently magical energy released by this process was propelled through the thick core of the blocklike wagon until it emerged as a burst of steam that in turn drove the great windmill to continue to spin. This perpetual-motion machine, based on principles of magic and technology both, clearly delighted the crowd. Each time the vice compressed, there came a burst of light, followed by the roaring gush of steam. Already, gnomes were arguing over the merits of the contraption, and anything that set the gnomes to pestering one another instead of the other races would surely be heralded as a success.

Finally came a wagon for the Teir'Dal of Neriak, even though they'd yet to officially join the Combine Empire. This inclusion was a grand gesture on the part of the dwarves. And the work of art they created on behalf of the dark race was perhaps the greatest masterpiece of all. Completely unlike the works for the other races, the tribute to the Teir'Dal was an enormous work of abstract art.

At the sight of it, the crowd—from the chortling halflings to the bragging Northmen to the arguing gnomes—fell silent, gazing upon something the likes of which none of them had ever imagined, let alone seen.

An enormous frame easily ten-foot square was fixed atop the rolling wagon, which in this case was unadorned though still carved from stone. Thin wires zigzagged from side to side across the frame and gorgeously polished gemstones of striking color were affixed to the wires so it appeared as something akin to a great abacus. Rubies of the richest red, sapphires of brilliant blue, amethyst of deepest purple, peridots of shining green, and more glittered across the weblike confines of the frame.

Around the entire perimeter of the frame hung tiny crystal lanterns. Whatever the fuel within them, they burned strong and bright, and the crystals were oriented so that the light emitted from each lantern shone on one of the smooth gemstones. The light collided with each gem so directly that it penetrated even the semiopaque stones like the amethyst. The light that in turn blossomed from the opposite side of the gem had the full luster and color of the gem itself, and the manner in which these beams crisscrossed and intersected created a brilliant display the likes of which were rumored to exist within only Neriak itself.

As the dark elves themselves had not yet arrived, Aataltaal imagined he was the only one who could appreciate what a truly stunning facsimile that piece was to the incredible displays of light that existed within the dark elven city. It had been years since he'd insinuated himself among the dark elves, but he recalled similar masterpieces among the plethora of gaudy neon displays within that city.

Along with the enthusiastic clapping of all those assembled, Aataltaal solemnly applauded the dwarven parade. As the wagons moved on toward the Pavilion and the ovation slowly subsided, the high elf reflected for a moment on the true gift of that display: it allowed him for a moment to forget the past and the danger of the impending future and concentrate on the glories of the races of Norrath.

Of course, no empire could persist indefinitely. Even though the Combine was not the most powerful empire of all—Aataltaal believed that status still had to be reserved for the elven empire centered in Takish-Hiz that had been brought down only by direct assault of the gods Innoruuk and Solusek Ro—no other empire or even temporary alliance involved more of the prominent races of Norrath than did Katta's. And this in the lifetime of a single human! Truly, some of this species were rarified individuals.

The ancient kedge were not part of the Combine, but they had largely withdrawn from the surface world except for the occasional madness-induced raid. The dark elves had not yet joined, of course, but Aataltaal believed everything was in place so that would happen. He did not have the same cause to manipulate events and leaders to entice the other so-thought "evil" races to join, but once the Teir'Dal did so, would Katta not pursue the ogres and trolls, goblins and kobolds? And then eventually some of the less populous races, like the aviaks and centaurs that lived so near Katta's birthplace in the Plains of Karana?

Aataltaal had been so consumed by his plans and how current events needed to be steered in order to realize them that he had failed to stop, take a breath, and contemplate the immensity of the events happening here, and what exactly they could mean to those whose daily lives they would impact. This dwarven parade helped crystallize the potential of the next four days.

He recalled his astonished thought of a moment ago: all in the lifetime of one man, Katta. The test of the Combine Empire would be how and if it could carry on, following the eventual death of Tsaph Katta, especially considering he and Empress Lcea Katta had not yet produced an heir.

More than that, it would be the test of the human race itself.

The cheers for the dwarves rose in the distance behind Aataltaal as the wagons reached the far side of the Combine Pavilion. The high elf looked down the road in the direction from which the dwarven parade had come. The Teir'Dal had not yet arrived; they were cutting it close. Ceremonies would begin within the hour.

Emperor Katta had made the journey as easy as possible for the dark elves. With their permission, he'd constructed one of the giant teleportation spires within the Nektulos Forest, the gloomy, mist-shrouded woods that surrounded the only commonly known entrance to underground Neriak, the capital of the dark elves. At least it was the capital as far as most of Norrath realized. More dark elves were located deeper in the earth, close to the Underfoot region that was controlled by the god Bristlebane. But Aataltaal had failed centuries ago in his battle in the ancient city of Narthex'Hiz located there. Its ruler was a lich now, and Aataltaal had decided to focus his attention on Neriak. That's why the entrance at Crushbone was so important. Even so, an entrance to Narthex'Hiz also remained, also hidden because of measures undertaken by Aataltaal in the past. A great bay on eastern Tunaria now controlled by pirates served to conceal this route. Few noticed, let alone questioned Aataltaal's protection of this place as he quietly nudged expeditions to Tunaria toward other ports.

The teleportation spire near Neriak resembled the dozen others sprinkled across Norrath by the Combine Empire. These spires allowed instantaneous teleportation for individuals who possessed the knowledge of the appropriate spells—spells only shared with wizards of races who'd signed the Articles of the Great Combine, of course, and such arcane knowledge had played a pivotal role in convincing the Teir'Dal to entertain the idea of membership.

Even so, they'd not been granted that knowledge yet, so human wizards would teleport the Teir'Dal delegation. This magic required an enormous act of faith on the part of the dark elves, a step into the unknown, for what guarantee did they have that they would appear safely in the Greater Faydark Forest?

Shortly before the dwarves had arrived, Aataltaal received word by messenger that the teleportation was under way. That's why even as the crowd disappeared to follow the dwarves, the high elf remained within sight of the road from Felwithe. He'd purposefully instructed the high elves to leave their posts between the Pavilion and teleportation spire. Likewise, none accompanied him. He wanted to greet these guests to Koada'Dal land, but he felt he ought to be distinctly disadvantaged to their superior numbers.

He continued to wait patiently.

Some time later, trumpets sounded from the Combine Pavilion announcing the impending Summit; the delegations of the member races would soon file in. As the host governor, Aataltaal should be speaking soon, but his assistants understood the situation and would communicate it to the emperor, who would surely agree that this task took precedence.

Then he knew the Teir'Dal drew near.

He knew it because the forest fell silent. He knew it because his sensitive ears detected the soft steps of the elven-trained horses that pulled the carriages, as well as the slight creak of the carriage wheels. But mostly, he knew it because Koada'Dal and Teir'Dal were like day and night, water and fire, light and shadow—opposites that were nevertheless connected and reliant upon one another for definition—and so Aataltaal could *sense* them. He could *feel* them, like a prickling on his skin.

Of course, that wasn't the whole truth, but even Aataltaal didn't comprehend the biochemistry of his reaction, for it was impossible to know the basis of the alchemy that bound him to his "brothers." Perhaps such was known only to the Prince of Hate himself.

Did all of his kind—his *true* kind—have this reaction? Regrettably, he could not confide in them, and they had no interest in doing likewise. In the past the sensation served as a warning that had saved his life, and while now the moment of truth was not so dangerous, he was alerted to prepare for the events that might define his life.

And maybe even redeem it.

In a moment the Koada'Dal carriage rounded the last bend from the forest. Despite the few hours of the journey to become comfortable with their load, the horses were still skittish, and the driver worked hard to keep them under control and from causing embarrassment.

The driver immediately saw Aataltaal and drove the horses in his direction. As they drew near, Aataltaal could almost feel an aura of inky blackness emanating from within the carriage. It struck him as a strong odor might—noticeable yet invisible.

As the horses glided to a stop, a sharply dressed Koada'Dal riding on the rear of the carriage hopped down and extended some steps folded beneath the vehicle. Then he slowly opened the door and with a slight nod spoke to the dark interior, "My lord delegates, we have arrived."

Aataltaal's nostrils wanted to flare, but he stifled even that slightest reaction. Already, there was a problem. Why did the elf refer to the occupants only as "lords"?

Among elves in general, and perhaps especially among the Teir'Dal, where the king and queen were almost literally at each other's throats in an ongoing competition, females were held in equal regard.

As shadowy figures within the carriage stirred, Aataltaal considered this circumstance. Perhaps it was a political comment to express only grudging acceptance of the Combine Empire's invitation. Or perhaps it was a direct rebuke from the Teir'Dal queen. The king had first swayed to this idea, and so perhaps all these delegates were his, and he sent all males so he might stand out as the "true" leader among the Teir'Dal. But if that was how it would be seen, then the queen would never have allowed it.

Unless . . .

And then the first delegate lightly stepped down from the carriage. He was a young dark elf and he kept his face averted from the dying light of the sun, which conveniently gave him the excuse to ignore Aataltaal. Though dressed in sumptuous attire of black silk with hems and cuffs of plush red velvet, this Teir'Dal was a simple page. Once out, he reached back within to the foot of the carriage and withdrew a canelike implement. It was an enormous umbrella of exquisitely treated leather dyed deep black and dangling beads of gold, which he unfolded and held over the carriage door. Aataltaal knew at a glance what most others fortunately would not: the leather of the umbrella was tanned halfling skin.

Two middle-aged Teir'Dal emerged next. Each solemnly nodded to Aataltaal when they reached the ground, but neither spoke. The high elf understood it was not their province to do so. They were merely advisors, though decidedly more impressive than the page. They wore great robes of silk and velvet, with thick bands of golden thread woven at each seam, and the rich

black gemstones known as jacinth inlaid in the velvet
cuffs that drooped over the ministers' hands.

Then the leader of the Teir'Dal delegation emerged.
Unlike the others, who gave Aataltaal as little attention
as possible, this male dark elf made eye contact with the
Koada'Dal governor at the first possible instant. His eyes
were as opaque as the jacinth his ministers wore and they
contrasted with his impossible black skin only by their
luster. They sparkled with a shining polish equaled by
the enormous black diamond he wore on a slender platinum necklace of outstanding craftsmanship. A great mane
of hair as white as Aataltaal's own was fashioned in rigid
twin pleats shaped like scythe blades that seemed to extend from, as well as hang down, both shoulders.

Despite all this, the delegate's clothing was his most
striking characteristic. At first pass it seemed a more ele-
gantly cut version of the page's shirt and breeches, but
in an instant, Aataltaal recognized what only the most
discerning and knowledgeable observer could possibly
know: where the others' clothing was only black silk,
the delegate wore iridescent dragon hide. There were
still red decorations, but it was not velvet. Instead, narrow bands of oblong pieces of ruby formed the trim.
And where golden thread highlighted the other cos-
tumes, platinum bands to match his necklace provided a
striking final touch.

Obviously, this was enchanted armor, but so tasteful
in character that it was possible to wear it to functions
such as this.

Aataltaal recognized a purposeful posturing on the part
of the delegate, that he would wear clothing that could
easily be mistaken for something far less than its true
quality. Only those whom the Teir'Dal cared to impress
would recognize the worth of the garb, and both the
delegate and the governor realized that fact.

Aataltaal nodded slightly in greeting when the delegate finally stepped to the ground.

The high elf said, "Greetings, Lord Nazzu V'leal. Welcome to the Combine Pavilion, site of the first Summit of the Great Combine." This Teir'Dal was well known to Aataltaal, as were virtually all the high-ranking members of that society. But this one he knew in particular. The Koada'Dal had found himself at odds with this dark elf no matter the disguises that might win the confidences of others. Not that Lord Nazzu could know this, but by some canny sense, the Teir'Dal always recognized an enemy.

The Teir'Dal sniffed lightly at the air as if *something* offended him. Then his glittering eyes dulled as he regarded the Koada'Dal for an instant. "Thank you for your gracious welcome, Governor, as well as for the fine transport." He flicked a few fingers in the general direction of the carriage.

Aataltaal said, "I regret that our conversation should remain brief. The Summit convenes and your business is there. Allow me to show you the way. If you have baggage or possessions . . ." Aataltaal trailed off in a natural way that would allow any civilized correspondent to fill in the details. But Lord Nazzu's expression did not change, nor did he make any move whatsoever.

So Aataltaal concluded, "Then perhaps your page can oversee the comportment of these items while you and your ministers accompany me?" He half-turned and began to edge toward the Pavilion, clearly inviting the Teir'Dal ambassador to follow.

Lord Nazzu did not answer, nor did he budge. His same blank, though hardly expressionless, gaze remained. Then he abruptly snapped his fingers and he and the ministers stepped toward Aataltaal.

The Koada'Dal slowed so that Lord Nazzu might

gain him and walk beside him to the Pavilion, but the Teir'Dal evidently did not desire that, for they all three hesitated. Instead of allowing them the pleasure of creating a scene, Aataltaal simply resumed a normal pace and, more as a servant than a host, led the dark elf delegation.

In the dark elven tongue, Lord Nazzu hissed to his ministers, "Watch your step lest, like his precious horses, this Koada'Dal beast drops shit."

Shiny white teeth grinned through three pairs of purple-black lips as those who accompanied the ambassador pandered to his quip.

Aataltaal ignored the crude remark, though he, too, smiled. He realized the Teir'Dal surely knew he must understand something of their language. But since that had not been publicly established, the dark elves used the language barrier as poor yet sufficient camouflage to lodge the offhand insult. Which was fine, for the best secret was Aataltaal's own. What allowed him to almost smile was what Lord Nazzu himself had little chance of knowing: that Aataltaal had mastered much of the Teir'Dal's secret vocabulary in that cruel degenerate's very own home. So Aataltaal understood *everything* the ambassador said, even that which might escape the page's comprehension.

7

THE SERPENTS OF INNORUUK

DELAILITH HAD LITTLE TIME TO PRETTY HER-self for the Summit, but primping certainly held no fascination for her anyway, so as soon as she was able, she proceeded to the impressive Combine Pavilion. No seating remained, and even the platforms at the tops of the tiered rows of benches were crowded with peoples of various races standing together. Despite the conditions, as a unit commander in the most recent battle to defend the interests of the empire, Delailith encountered only nominal difficulty securing entrance.

She easily pressed her way through the throng, as many individuals seemed more determined just to be present for the historic event than to have any true interest in the proceedings. For Delailith the Summit represented something more: the culmination of the Combine Empire. And despite the casual attitude of many here, this gathering of races embodied all that the Combine hoped to be. Here it was, finally on display for the world to see that the Combine Empire wasn't just an illusion of papers and promises.

Admittedly, that's all she had thought of it when word first came to her. She had been a mercenary at the time, employed mainly by the dwarves of Kaladim to negotiate with the pirates who plied the waters of the Ocean of Tears between Tunaria and Faydwer. Trade was minimal then, because the humans did not possess a port along the east coast of Tunaria—partly because pirates controlled all the best harbors—but there was a trickle of profit to be had and a hardy few who sought it. Delailith made herself indispensable, for she was an uncommon combination of tact, prowess, and honesty. Even the pirates came to give her grudging respect, particularly after they kidnapped her from one dwarven vessel they keel-hauled, and she managed to escape the first night on a rowboat with the supplies required to repair the dwarven boat.

Delailith and the dwarves first heard of Tsaph Katta from the halflings with whom they also traded. Soon enough, groups of humans from central Tunaria frequented the coast more and more, and trade became more regular and more profitable. Katta needed ore from the dwarves, who in turn sought mainly foodstuffs and furs.

Eventually, Katta himself greeted one of the dwarven trade ships. That's when Delailith had first seen him, and she was instantly impressed. He seemed clearly an enlightened individual, not simply a warlord who rallied the human tribes with persuasive rhetoric and bloody swords, as some rumors had described. As the human among the dwarves, Delailith made introductions and then listened as Katta begged the dwarves to please deliver some papers to their king in Kaladim. He explained that these were the Articles by which he intended to found a vast cooperative, best described as an empire— an alliance that would eventually unite all the major races of Norrath.

Barely able to contain their mirth at the time, the dwarves made light of this idea on the voyage home while they washed their beards in ale suds. The message was indeed delivered, but the dwarves were not interested in the thoughts of a man in the center of a continent an ocean away.

They soon would be.

From there to here, the progress was inexorable. Delailith was surprised it had come to pass in so short a time and amazed that these other races ultimately accepted the idea.

And she was utterly astonished when the dark elven delegation entered. They'd actually come.

It all seemed like an enormous hoax being played on the gullible, "young" race of humans. But none could doubt the authority—the authenticity—of the Combine Empire now. Teir'Dal and Koada'Dal—or for that matter Teir'Dal and *any* other race—would no sooner unite behind a farce than they would throw open their cities to one another. And yet here the Koada'Dal did almost that. The Pavilion was nominally neutral territory, under the direct jurisdiction of the Combine Empire, but it stood directly in the shadow of Felwithe.

Host or not, the Koada'Dal who showed the Teir'Dal to the floor of the amphitheater was briskly snubbed by the dark elves. As soon as the path to their table was clear, two robed delegates brushed past the high elf, who then stepped aside so the evident leader of the group could pass unimpeded. Delailith recognized the high elf in question as Governor Aataltaal, who had a good reputation among both the rank and file and the elite of the Combine Empire even though he remained somewhat unapproachable. Or at least unlocateable . . . About a year ago, Delailith had failed for many days in a simple errand to deliver a message to the high elf. Politely delayed by his assistants, Delailith persisted, and eventually the Koada'Dal personally accepted the message from her.

He was an intriguing character in a great building now full of them.

Emperor Katta certainly ranked in that cast of characters, as did his wife, Empress Lcea. Near the conclusion of his opening remarks, he paused to welcome the Teir'Dal, but his words made it plain that he did not find it in the slightest bit remarkable that they would come—no more noteworthy or important than the attendance of any of the other races assembled. Equivalency was at the heart of the empire. And confidence in his course and his calling was the hallmark of Katta.

The acoustics in the Combine Pavilion were superb, and even though a continuous buzzing rose from the crowd as spectators gaped at the delegates and proposed and countered various theories in a thousand private conversations, Delailith could nevertheless plainly hear the emperor speak. And so, too, she heard his closing words.

Little did she or anyone at that moment realize that they would be his last.

"And so we have achieved this threshold of greatness—the entry to a grander and more glorious Norrath than ever before. With the blessings of our gods and with the hopes of our people, let us begin our work of shaping a future that will benefit all, as it benefits one."

Massive applause erupted.

As the emperor stepped away from the podium with a female Koada'Dal paladin shadowing his every move, out of nowhere appeared Governor Aataltaal, as if he'd been the master of ceremonies all along.

"Noteworthy words from a man who is as much a

man—as much a member of the community of Norrath—as he is our emperor," Aataltaal said.

More applause rang out before Aataltaal continued. "Let me now call upon another architect of this great dream of Combine to speak to us. General Seru has been the hand by which the empire has done much of its work. When your people are threatened by forces that have shunned the call to join us, then it will be General Seru who responds to your need.

"The Combine Empire seeks peace, but it is abundantly capable of responding to threats that will not respect our peace. General, please." The high elf nodded to Seru and gestured to the podium.

Seru rose. He did not seem cheered by the introduction or the enthusiastic reception, and his countenance remained dark, grim. Slowly he strode to the podium. As rudely as the Teir'Dal, he brushed past the governor, though Delailith suspected she was among the few who noted it. The general adjusted the clothing at his waist and then stepped forward to speak.

Before he spoke his first words, Delailith felt a discomfort deep in her stomach. Perhaps her dislike of this man was more extreme than she knew.

Seru said, "People of Combine, I am before you tonight to communicate my legacy to this empire."

Delailith wanted to concentrate, to allow Seru the opportunity to explain himself, but her discomfort turned to nausea, and that quickly to pain. This was something more than an emotional reaction. She did not wish to miss these proceedings, but Delailith could not remain here. She turned to work her way out of the crowd, but that's when she realized *everyone* clutched his or her stomach as well.

Nearby, a gnarled old dwarf loosed a terrifying belch. It might have earned a chuckle from those nearby, if not for the slender Feir'Dal matron only a few strides from the dwarf who suddenly vomited.

If Seru was still speaking, Delailith could not hear him. Groans, moans, and pained gasps rattled and rasped throughout the Combine Pavilion. Delailith remained silent, but each exhalation was a chore, and her stomach stormed with indigestion worse even than anything she had ever encountered shipboard.

On the verge of disgorging as well, Delailith whirled back to look at the floor of the Pavilion. The crowd roiled like an angry sea. As she felt phlegm forcing its way up her throat, Delailith concentrated, forced it down. First she looked at the Teir'Dal. They, too, suffered—one of the robed ministers fell upon his hands and knees, coughing up black bile. Then she spun to look at Seru, a wild, accusatory glare in her eyes. But he clutched the podium, his body wracked by the same pains.

What was the source, then, of this vile magic?

In the last, desperate moment before she became paralyzed by what happened next, Delailith knew. Out of the corner of her eye, she saw it. Though his face was gray with the pallor of death, a great smile cracked Seru's face.

HIS STOMACH HAD NOT FELT THIS BAD SINCE HIS days among the trolls spent cheerily eating their swamp-slop so he could gain their confidence. Sometimes their stews weren't cooked enough to kill the tapeworms, and the churning of his stomach now felt like the wriggling of those creatures in his gut and throat.

But Aataltaal ignored his own discomfort for the moment. He remained alert and wary, but it seemed no one appeared to take advantage of everyone's relative incapacitation. Whoever had poisoned the food or drink of the Combine Pavilion had apparently executed the plan perfectly: everyone was affected. The delegates of all the races—the Teir'Dal included—doubled over in pain. Worse now than the possibility that the dark elves sought to kill the Combine's elite, was that the Teir'Dal could claim the Summit was nothing but an attempt to slay the elite of the races of Norrath, most especially their own!

In a flash, Aataltaal realized that yet another of his plans to redeem the dark elven race had failed. Whether this time his plan was an accidental casualty to someone else's efforts, or whether the dissolution of his plan was the entire point of this episode did not really matter.

Now, the only thing left was survival: his, the Combine Empire's, the emperor's. Somehow, perhaps by virtue of his oracular proclivities, he sensed that not all three of those targets would be safe, come the end of this day.

Aataltaal looked across the stage. Emperor Katta, on the floor on his hands and knees, tried to reach out to his wife, Lcea, but he shuddered, and black ichor dripped from the corner of his mouth. Lcea curled on the floor of the platform, balled tight like a fetus and gripping her stomach. The high elf stood and moved toward the royal couple, but he abruptly stopped in his tracks with the sensation that his entire innards had indeed just twisted. He thought again of the vile meals in the Innothule Swamp—it felt as if an enormous tapeworm convulsed in his belly.

As he sank to his knees, Aataltaal saw one individual who was unaffected. His mind first recoiled at the incredible suspicion that she was somehow responsible. How could that be possible? Aataltaal had witnessed many terrible betrayals over the centuries, but this one was simply too far-fetched to contemplate further. Lady Chastine had her hand on the emperor's back and tried to soothe him.

Aataltaal overheard Lady Chastine whisper to the emperor, "Your wife is fine, though like you distressed. Lie still, my lord, help will be here forthwith."

Chastine, alone of the thousands within the Combine Pavilion, seemed unaffected. Aataltaal wondered how this could be? Even her composure, her years of training, had not prepared her for a circumstance like this. Where all the others in the Combine Pavilion writhed in pain, only Lady Chastine did not. What could it mean?

Whatever the cause or explanation, the elf-maid's expression of concern and pity surely absolved her in the minds of any others who sought a culprit. And perhaps whatever miracle preserved her would see the emperor through this day. So long as even one able-bodied guardian remained, the emperor would be safe.

It must be the stuff of nightmare for a paladin sworn to protect: tides of people in pain and distress, and no foe against whom to protect them!

Oh, but there was such a villain.

Even as his stomach did backflips and Aataltaal reeled at the implication of this attack, the Koada'Dal divined the identity of the villain: Seru!

The general, nearly paralyzed by the poison that was eating everyone from the inside, found the strength to remain standing at the podium. Between spitting gobs of bloody phlegm, General Seru laughed, and the acoustics of the amphitheater ensured that his glee carried to every corner of the place.

"Priests of Marr!" Aataltaal called to both of the nearby Koada'Dal clerics. But it was little use. One was in such distress that he did not even look at the governor. The other, though, turned her head to Aataltaal after a moment.

"Attend the emperor!" Aataltaal managed to choke, though his throat filled with phlegm.

The high-elf priestess staggered toward the emperor.

"My lady," said Lady Chastine, who took the cleric's hand and assisted her gently to the ground beside Emperor Katta. Even with the help, the priestess slumped beside Katta for a moment before she steeled herself to her pains and knelt more perfectly beside the human.

She began to pray, "Mother of . . . All . . . guard— guar—" But it was too much. She whimpered with pain. Tears streamed down her face, and she fought for the concentration she needed to complete the spell that might revive the emperor.

The priestess of Tunare looked helplessly back at Aataltaal, who growled in frustration. If he could but manage a spell, then even though he could not cleanse her body, he might clear her mind enough to complete her prayer.

Then it happened.

The "poison" that affected them all was revealed. It happened just as in the Oracle's vision, and Aataltaal couldn't believe it. Those visions—his visions!—were supposed to be metaphorical, subject to interpretation, with true meaning revealed only after much analysis or contemplation.

He never imagined that the metaphor for the future that he had seen in his vision would come to pass so unaltered in reality. Were his visions stronger? Or did his vision make its direct relevance clear in some way, and he was simply a fool not to have interpreted it well?

Perhaps because she'd been so active, the cleric of

Tunare was the first to be fully afflicted—at least of those on the stage, for Aataltaal sensed this same scene unfolding everywhere around him. First something slender darted out of her mouth. Out, in, out—a tongue, but not her own. Slender and fast and forked at the end—a serpent's tongue! Then the Koada'Dal whimpered in pain, and a trickle of thick, vomitous phlegm leaked from the sides of her mouth.

Then something more emerged from her mouth. The cleric's face went white with fear and, clearly against her will, her mouth widened, forced open by a serpent that wriggled within her. Pitch-black and shiny, the serpent thrust its head out of her mouth. The priestess fainted, slamming her temple against the floor of the stage. She rolled over unconscious, and the beast slipped easily forth—the muscles of its host no longer impeding its progress. Fully five feet long, the snake raised its head. Small black eyes glared at the pandemonium and then, as if drawn to him, turned inexorably toward Emperor Katta.

He was prone now, like Lcea, who still lay a few feet away. He reached a hand toward the queen, but she did not see it, or else was too pained to reciprocate even that feeble exertion. Lcea shuddered then, and a gag reflex lifted her head, neck, and torso off the floor. Her face contorted, and when she fell limply down again, she rolled to the side so that her back was to Katta.

"A Serpent of Hate!" Aataltaal shouted. He'd not taken his eyes off the fiend that slipped from the cleric's mouth. His voice was slurred, though, for the thickness in his stomach that had felt like a tapeworm was a serpent working its way up his esophagus. He could not manage much volume, especially compared to the chorus of groans from all around.

Even so, Lady Chastine did not need to hear the

beast's name. Its appearance was malevolent enough, and its means of arrival perfidious enough, that she needed no additional cause to smite it. Her sword flashed. The serpent twitched to escape the blade's path, but the paladin was too fast. Two halves of the serpent soon flopped on the floor like a pair of fish out of water.

And then suddenly three others swarmed forward. Whether by pure bad fortune or driven by the foul magic that created them, these black serpents slithered straight for the emperor. Lady Chastine was on her feet then. She intercepted the three snakes, deftly slashing two and then skewering the third.

Meanwhile, however, a fourth one approached unseen. A wracking cough from Lcea signaled that her throat was clear, but Lady Chastine did not make that connection. The serpent that emerged from the empress slithered around her body and coiled there while the paladin attacked the other serpents. Then, when she relaxed for just an instant, it struck. Though the paladin herself was a viable target, the serpent streaked direct for the emperor. Prone as he was, even his magical protections offered little defense, and so the venomous strike caught Katta clean on the neck.

A half-breath later, Lady Chastine's lightning-fast sword stroke split the serpent in two.

"The poi—" Aataltaal began, but he was unable to finish. It felt as if his internal organs were being pulled out of his mouth, and he collapsed in pain, barely able to move and certainly unable to speak. Whatever magic he might have offered in the emperor's defense or to attack Seru was now impossible to perform.

Dimly, he felt a pressure against the inside of his teeth as he lay struggling to breathe through his nose. Time slowed and the moment elongated as Aataltaal's thoughts cleared and he watched Chastine. Though the miracles that paladins could perform paled in comparison to those of true priests, the paladins did possess magical powers. Among them was a blessing that, while unable to completely cleanse a body of serious poisons, could at least stave off the effects for a time, or weaken the poison.

Still effectively immobilizd, ever a half-heartbeat ahead of intense pain, Aataltaal watched as the paladin cast her spell. Her beatific face lifted toward the heavens so Tunare might see the faithful servant who invoked her will in the name of the emperor. Instantly, a green aura blossomed around Chastine's hands. It shone with the bright and fresh green of a new stalk in the spring, and despite himself, despite Tunare's abandonment of him, Aataltaal found himself mesmerized by that green. In it he saw the sylvan forests that once surrounded the great city of Takish-Hiz. The life it represented gave him hope, even as death coiled within him. It nurtured him even though those vast woodlands were now deserted and desert.

It did not remain with him for long.

In order to relieve his pain, Aataltaal unconsciously opened his mouth, allowing the black beast to slither forth. He felt it poke from his mouth and he heard a snake's hiss issue as from his own throat. All the while he had little control over his body, which involuntarily gave form to hatred he'd know in his life. That he should be afflicted like all the rabble here demeaned him, made him feel sullied. Only pure Lady Chastine did not sink to know Hate. He could only imagine the fear suffered by the vast majority of those within the Combine Pavilion—those not accustomed to this level of pain and this degree of nefarious magic.

Even in his condition, Aataltaal kept his mind detached from the horror of the events. Not in a thousand years had he been so helpless as now. He remained level-headed and clear-thinking, and to help himself through the duress, he kept his eyes focused on the glow of Lady Chastine's hands, even as it faded. He watched intently as the faintest ember of green lingered.

Her magic seemed to work a bit, though, as Katta's body quivered and he released a great moan. He floated on the border between life and death.

But the emperor's suffering attracted other attention as well. General Seru spun at the sound. His hands gripped the podium, his mouth still wide from his laughter, and his eyes gleamed with a sort of madness. And dangling six inches out of his mouth was the general's own serpent of Hate. Its head bobbed from side to side as if a snakecharmer beguiled it. The vile serpent's sleepy gaze seemed casual beneath the general's wild-eyed, intense stare.

In an uncanny display of will—or madness—General Seru clamped tight his jaws. His teeth bit into the serpent, which shocked to wakefulness and thrashed madly, its eyes almost turning inside out as the general bit through the snake, but Seru seemed not to notice. He just stared viciously at the likewise shuddering body of Emperor Katta.

With hate in his eyes—with Hate in his eyes—Seru swallowed the wriggling reptile that lined his throat. Blood sprayed from the serpent's gnawed neck and out the general's mouth to run in rivulets down his chin and neck. The man persisted, unwilling to let loose of his Hate, swallowing it so he might feed on it yet some more.

Suddenly it was clear to Aataltaal. General Seru had given himself up to Innoruuk. He had surrendered himself to his Hate and even now rebottled it when he might have set it free. What was it that Emperor Katta had said to the Oracle?

The Teir'Dal are not the only beings on Norrath to worship Innoruuk. He has humans among his followers as well, and I dare say some of his human worshippers are surely well placed within the empire.

It had all been right in front of him: the vision of what was to come, the instrument by which it would be delivered, and the architect of the treachery! The Prince of Hate had struck at the heart of the great Combine Empire through one of its own.

Though bloody-mouthed Seru was still for a moment, silenced by the combination of dread and desire that inflamed him, the stage burst into motion. First one, then two, and then suddenly from every direction, venomous black serpents streaked toward the prone body of Emperor Katta. The product of Hate from everyone who had hated—and that included everyone within the Combine Pavilion, except for the virtuous Lady Chastine— the Serpents of Innoruuk innately knew their mission: poison Katta.

The emperor's paladin guardian regained her feet in a flash. She split the first serpent in two, pinned the next two to the floor with her flashing blades, and even barred the flood that followed with her flurry of attacks.

General Seru's gaze moved from the emperor to the valiant paladin who so deftly defended him. Seru's expression was the most harrowing that Aataltaal had seen in ages. The general convulsed, his face turning pale. Gasping for air, he bent over. Dry heaves shook his body at first, but momentarily a vast messy explosion spilled from his mouth, and the snake's carcass flopped to the ground. It did not matter that Seru had now expelled the thing—the magic lay in the metaphor. His Hate was not likewise disgorged.

Aataltaal attempted to pull himself up as well. Lady Chastine was occupied with the wrong enemy! Even as she slashed at countless serpents that slithered headlong toward the emperor, she ignored the true snake in the grass. Worst of all, Aataltaal could not warn her.

The high elf reached to his mouth and grasped the half-extruded, wriggling snake. He steeled himself and with a flashing motion he whipped the remainder of the serpent from his throat. The beast's scales raked and the violent friction burned him, but Aataltaal was free of the thing. He did not release the serpent, but instead dashed it upon the floor, crushing its head before it could arch back to bite his hand.

Still shaken from the ordeal, with a body that felt more gelatinous than muscular, Aataltaal leapt to his feet and rushed toward Katta. Too late.

Chastine was on her knees, a dagger deep in her back, between her shoulder blades. She twisted around and faced her treacherous assailant, but she could not counterattack. Somehow, miraculously, she did find the strength to defend.

General Seru thrust his sword at the prone emperor, but the Koada'Dal paladin acted at precisely the right moment, with just enough strength to bring her own blade to bear and parry the general's. Seru spewed vitriol in frustration and attacked again, but with the same result.

"Elf whore!" he shouted.

Then Seru looked up. Aataltaal hurtled toward him. The high elf carried only a ceremonial rapier, but it was a magically indestructible blade, which meant even Seru's larger longsword could not shatter it. The Koada'Dal's sword-stroke was a blur, but Seru disentangled his sword from the paladin's and now it was he who parried.

Then the general laughed, and Aataltaal instantly saw why. An insurmountable wave of black serpents spilled toward the stage from everywhere throughout the pavilion. The magic had run its course and now all the serpents slithered free, leaving behind heaps and rows of prone, confused, and grievously injured former hosts. Aataltaal slashed at one snake and before he could turn to battle Seru, he had to strike at another.

Haltingly at first, as if unsure he'd really won, Seru took a step backward. When Aataltaal unleashed a sequence of attacks like lightning unbottled, and still serpents spilled past him, Seru grinned. No laughter required this time, he turned and fled.

Aataltaal spared an instant he truly did not have in order to reveal a small dagger from a sheath hidden in his sleeve. With one flick it was in his hand. With another it sailed toward Seru's back. The general sought to escape the scene of his treachery, and though the slender weapon had little chance of slaying Seru outright, it might delay him long enough for the Koada'Dal and others to respond and apprehend him.

But it was not to be.

End over end the weapon hurtled toward Seru, but at the last possible moment it was plucked out of the air! A streaking black shape intercepted it, and after dispatching a trio of snakes, Aataltaal saw that it was a raven. The dagger gripped in its feet, the trained bird wheeled and climbed before diving out of sight below the walls of the amphitheater.

And though the other paladins now came to Aataltaal's aid, the Koada'Dal could not fend off all the serpents. Aataltaal considered various applications of his magical powers: offensive spells might injure Emperor

Katta, and new defensive spells could not fortify Katta while he was unconscious.

Then he knew what he needed to attempt—one spell that might provide a brief reprieve.

"Prepare to bear the emperor to safety," Aataltaal shouted to the paladins who assisted him.

In the frenzy of warding off the scores of serpents, the high elves could not directly acknowledge him, but they uttered their readiness.

With a fluid stroke, Aataltaal sheathed his rapier, but his arms continued to move. They whirled repetitively, hypnotically, and as they moved, they wove a spell of magic. Aataltaal drew upon the magical power within himself—his mana—and expressed it through the languid, rhythmic, mesmerizing motion of his arms. Fortunately, he could attune his spell so that only nearby foes were affected, or else the Koada'Dal defenders would be subjected to the powerful sorcery. In fact, this spell required such intense concentration and involvement from the enchanter who cast it that there was always the possibility that Aataltaal might be hypnotized by his own enchantment.

Unfortunately, in this instance, he was. So thoroughly did he give himself to the spell that it ensnared him—the lazy motion of his arms and the enchantment of the magic itself affected him like a narcotic, like a hundred draughts of ale.

But overall, the spell succeeded. A score or more of snakes that closed on the prone body of Emperor Katta suddenly pulled up short. They lifted their heads high into the air and, as if lulled by a snake charmer's flute, they swayed, caught somewhere between wakefulness and sleep. The high elf's spell completely mesmerized them, and this gave the Koada'Dal defenders a moment to marshal their forces and gather their wits.

For an instant, the high elves looked to the governor for guidance, but he rocked slowly from side to side in an eerie mimic of the swaying snakes. So while two of the paladins slashed at the stunned serpents, the third paladin grasped Katta's unconscious frame and hefted him over his shoulder.

Unfortunately, Aataltaal's hypnotic spell was not fool-proof. If a victim of the spell was disturbed, then the magical paralysis dissolved. So, when the paladin who bore Emperor Katta brushed against one of the serpents, that snake, freed of the magic, instantly struck. As an obstacle between it and its ultimate victim, the paladin was the target of its first bewildered attack. Unaware of the danger, the paladin presented an easy mark. Fangs well-oiled with viscous poison sank into the elf's centuries-old flesh—and the flesh withered at the poison's touch. As he crumpled from the effects of the poison, the paladin did the only thing that in that split-second seemed useful—he hurled the emperor's body as far to the rear of the stage area as possible.

Then he collapsed. Despite the best efforts of the Koada'Dal, the serpents overwhelmed the defenders and slithered over every inch of the downed paladin's body. They no doubt sought the emperor, but meanwhile bit the paladin relentlessly. However, this brief respite offered them their only hope. One of the Koada'Dal wizards, barely recovered from the release of his own serpent of Hate, gathered his wits and strength, and though he stumbled, he managed to stagger to the emperor's side.

Then, no doubt guided by some foul magic, the serpents sensed their target and streaked toward the emperor. However, the Koada'Dal wizard did not panic. He was centuries old and had faced many threatening circumstances under the tutelage of his elven masters. That he was the last hope of the Emperor of the Combine

Empire was a thought he did not allow to register. He began his spell, but even as the first glowing lights appeared in the shape of shimmering ribbons unfurling all around him, the wizard knew he would never complete his spell in time.

But the other wizard responded as well, delivering his incantation more quickly and following with a flurry of movements that looked as if he were tying an invisible string into a complicated knot. In this way he wove his innate magical energy to create a rainstorm of fire. Lava dripped as if from a cloudburst directly atop the lead serpents, incinerating them instantly. Snakes not directly struck by the streaming fire drove headlong into it, even while it continued to fall.

But there were simply too many of the serpents—it was a rude commentary on the brotherhood sought here that so much should be created by Hate. When the fiery spell concluded, the snakes pushed on toward the emperor, even though it meant clambering over the charred corpses of their kin.

However, those few seconds of the burning blockage bought enough time for the first Koada'Dal wizard to complete his teleportation spell. The light that streamed around him and the emperor suddenly expanded, also whirling around the nearest priest of Tunare. The light flared brightly, leaving luminescent trails on the retinas of all the onlookers, and suddenly seemed to materialize. With the foremost serpents only feet away from the still body of Emperor Katta, the three high elves disappeared. The ribbons of solid light seemed to shatter at that instant, and as the pieces fell they transformed to light again, leaving streaks in the air before fading away entirely as they struck the ground.

Unfortunately, the teleportation spell could only take the emperor further away from Felwithe, because all the spires constructed to receive wizards and their cargo were located outside urban areas. This was because the integrity of the spires was not entirely trusted, due partly to the magic involved and partly to the slightly unstable personality of the creator of the process: the geomancer Grieg. So fear of the possible misuse of teleportation as a means for invasion had prompted the placement of the spires in at least slightly remote areas. But no matter to which Combine Spire the wizard's spell bore the emperor, the serpents of Innoruuk would trouble him no more this day.

An instant later, Aataltaal shook off the effects of his own dangerous spell—dangerous because it too often left him in that defenseless condition. But he soon learned from the paladins that his had been the key first step to extricating the emperor, though it meant the death of one of their comrades.

Without the emperor to seek, the serpents seemed lost. As hate that has no target leads only to pure destruction, the serpents now turned on any nearby foe. In many cases, this meant another serpent, and several of them flopped and flailed in balls of dark flesh as they sought to destroy one another.

The cleanup of the others was quick. Paladins, wizards, and even a handful of other, sufficiently recovered guests, soon struck down the remaining serpents.

Without a moment's hesitation, Aataltaal drew the paladins to him and said, "Find General Seru. He is a traitor and must be stopped at all cost. Apprehension is preferred, but if he resists . . ." He trailed off, nodding to them to communicate his meaning.

Rubbing her throat, Empress Lcea hurried to Aataltaal. She was a slight woman, almost as slender as a Feir'Dal and claimed to be nearly their equal as an archer. Typically, the force of her personality and the degree of her zeal overwhelmed any impression of her size, but now she seemed as hurt and confused as the rest of those within the Pavilion.

"What of my husband, Aataltaal?" she pleaded.

Aataltaal took her hands in his. "Empress, he is in grave condition, but I promise you, he is alive. Whatever yet lives can thrive. I will go to him now and—"

"I must come as well!" Lcea blurted.

"I think that unwise." Aataltaal gently loosed her hands and pushed them back toward her as if gently refusing a gift, but in fact delicately disengaging from her. "There is turmoil here that you must soothe, if your husband's empire has any chance to survive Seru's treachery."

Then Aataltaal dashed away from her. He grabbed the remaining wizard and another cleric by the wrists and tugged them quickly away from the confused and milling crowd. "Begin your spell, Veris," Aataltaal said to the wizard. "Gerren went to the Faydark Spire, I am certain, so take us there as well."

Then the governor looked around quickly. In the event of trouble, he needed extra swords. Though it was unlikely anyone but Seru himself could duel past Aataltaal to the emperor, it never hurt to have a few expendables around who could delay a pursuing enemy.

"You two!" Aataltaal shouted to the nearest humans, a man and a woman, both armed with swords smeared thick with serpent guts. "Hurry to me, now. Quickly!"

As with the spell of moments before, ribbons of light expanded around the high elves. The humans responded immediately and dashed within the bands of light just an instant before they flashed brightly. When the light fell again in streaks, the three Koada'Dal and two humans were gone.

IT WAS A FIRST FOR DELAILITH—HER FIRST TIME
teleporting. The experience left her dizzy and confused,
especially on top of her terrible nausea and the pain in
her stomach and throat, ripped raw by the loathsome
snake. To be standing one moment in the chaos of the
Combine Pavilion and the next in the quiet shadow of
the Faydark Spire was too much for her. She sank to the
ground and clutched her head.

It was the same for her human companion—a soldier
she did not know—but the Koada'Dal went on as if
nothing out of the ordinary had occurred, as if between
steps it was not strange to have traveled a dozen leagues.

She looked up, trying to resolve this dizziness, but it
didn't help. In fact, her vertigo increased when she saw
the point far above her head where the two great stone
arches that formed the Faydark Spires crossed. Her gaze
followed one side of an arch back to the ground. The
arch thickened near its base, and the solidity of that sight
helped settle Delailith.

When her head felt clear a moment later, Delailith
understood the Koada'Dal's drive. The unconscious Emperor Katta was here as well. The high elf governor
Aataltaal motioned for everyone to step back from the
emperor. A dozen Koada'Dal clustered nearby, including
the wizard who brought them; another wizard whom
Delailith remembered seeing on the stage, too; two priests;
and a handful of guards. These latter must have been
elves stationed at the spires.

The governor moved everyone but the clerics away
from the motionless emperor. They quickly knelt beside
him and began spellcasting. The spot sung with the energy of magic as they crafted spell after spell. Each one

had a miraculous effect, like white light that surrounded the emperor's body, or golden beams that shone upon his face, but by the lack of movement on the emperor's part and the longer and longer faces of the priests, Delailith determined that while the spells looked marvelous, they generated few results.

His teeth gritted in frustration, Aataltal stepped away from the group. Delailith stood and approached him as the governor spoke to the wizard who had transported them here. She overhead Aataltaal say, "Go now, Veris. *Gate* back to Felwithe and return immediately with both a high priest of Tunare . . . and a gnomish necromancer."

Veris visibly paled at the second request.

"Yes, yes, you heard me. We have no time for scruples, not when it might be the only way to preserve Katta. Find Agado among the delegates from Ak'Anon. Speak with him privately, so it is not revealed in front of the other gnomes, and request his immediate assistance. He will at first deny this 'rumor,' but he will not fail to bring his secret talents to bear on the emperor."

Hesitantly at first, but then more surely, Veris agreed. He glanced briefly at Delailith as he stepped away from the others. He nodded slightly at the human and then began his spell. To Delailith's eye it looked similar to the other teleportation spell, but the effect was smaller, and it took far less time to cast. Within seconds, the wizard vanished.

Delailith shook her head. How strange it must be to take such awesome acts of power as casually as did these ancient elves.

"You. Woman!"

Delailith turned and saw that Governor Aataltaal addressed her. "M'lord?" She jogged over to him.

"Go to that building—" He pointed to indicate a small building made of the same stone as the spire, situated at the base of one of the four legs. "—and gather some skins of water and some fruit. The priests need something to revive their energy so they might continue their spells."

He turned away before she could respond, and Delailith flushed briefly with indignation. The Koada'Dal were much respected by the other races of Norrath, but they earned resentment for the way they looked down upon all others, even their woodland cousins the Feir'Dal. Delailith felt like a child sent on a simple errand, rather than a warrior who had fought to defend the Combine Empire. But her emperor needed help, Tsaph Katta, the man she first encountered years ago on the eastern coast of Tunaria, so she did not tarry. She hurried for fruit and water.

Delailith saw Katta's face as she sprinted past the prone human. She was no priestess or death-wizard, but years of battlefield experience allowed her to recognize a dead man—and Katta was as close to dead as one could get. Aataltaal's promise to Lcea notwithstanding, Delailith felt her stomach sink.

Now—this very instant—was likely the end of the Combine Empire.

8

THE OCEAN OF TEARS

THE LAST ARMADA OF THE COMBINE EMPIRE
ever to sail the seas of Norrath hastened westward on
the glimmering trails of the setting sun. That fiery eye
of the Burning Prince, the great fire-lord Solusek Ro,
glared at the remnants of the once-proud navy and prepared to pass his watch to the goddess Luclin, Maiden of
Shadows, whose own orb would soon become visible in
the night. One eye shutting, the other opening, and so
much forgotten in that moment, so much learned through
blood and despair and loss that would perforce come to
mortal minds only when those tragedies were relived.
Again and again.

Aataltaal stood braced at the prow of the flagship,
one foot atop the guard railing, the wind—for, thank
Karana, there *was* a wind—billowing his ebony hair in
streamers. Ebony hair, for he wore the guise of his friend,
the fallen emperor. The Koada'Dal sighed. Forever poised
between light and dark, Aataltaal did not overlook the
significance of the moment. He'd faced similar times before. Indeed, it was his curse to ever be at the epicenter
of such times. Fate decreed his place was in the shifting
light. Unfortunately, ruin always followed—day always

turned to night. All that was fair and light could only hope to escape and persevere for another day, another night, another era.

He wondered at the thoughts of Solusek Ro as his brilliant orb sank away to the west. Surely the baleful eye of the Burning Prince pierced Aataltaal's masquerade? But the gods were as prone to error as men, and that knowledge always reminded Aataltaal not to trust in his own judgment as often and to the degree he usually felt compelled. It might be folly for mortals to wonder at the thoughts of the gods, but Aataltaal well knew that the creators of all the races of Norrath played with the toys they had set loose upon the world a millennia ago and that they were mindful—and worse, prideful—of all that occurred. They were not so secure in their celestial positions that they ignored the plights of mortals. Instead, they moved energetically, strategically to diminish that which opposed them, and to fortify that which would strengthen them. He wished to think the earth-mother Tunare above this fray, but though in some way and despite all good reason he still loved her, he knew in his heart that she played these games as well.

Aataltaal looked to his heart for guidance, though it wept blood for the countless times it had been broken. How would the gods react when mortals made the leap beyond the confines of Norrath? Would the Maiden of Shadows be the only one concerned? For Grieg had promised an escape from this wretched, god-cursed sphere . . .

Aataltaal himself had considered departure, from this recent setback so devastating. It was so much easier to destroy than create. Years of patiently finagling events and personalities so the pieces could come together . . . all blasted apart by Seru's dark ritual. Seru did it for himself, but Aataltaal harbored no illusions as to why Innoruuk was involved, why the Prince of Hate would give that mortal such power: it was because of him, and Innoruuk's fear that Hate's prized children would even in that symbolic way rejoin the Koada'Dal from whom they were descended.

But Aataltaal would simply try again. New pieces in his millennia-long game awaited him on the distant shore to which they sailed. Besides, the Koada'Dal found that he could not abandon these humans.

Aataltaal knew that nothing so pure as the world he sought could possibly coexist with life, but there were ancient blights that commanded his service even as current events such as the fate of these humans demanded his attention.

A voice broke Aataltaal's reverie. "Governor?"

Aataltaal turned briskly, the crow's feet at the corner of his eyes clenching. He sharply reminded the sailor, "Who knows where the Eyes of Seru lurk?" Then he planted his feet firmly on the deck, straightening regal clothing stiffened into wrinkles by hours of sea spray as he watched the setting of a sun he could not for centuries ever seem to catch. Clearly an experienced sailor, he carried himself easily on the rolling vessel. No longer apparently an elf, he was darkly handsome and boyish despite the crinkles that suggested middle age, with hair shorn short, though now slightly overgrown and so at odds with the most popular styles of court. Most of all, he stood calm and composed—despite the circumstances, despite his hissed correction to the sailor, he seemed in control. His steady gaze took in all that the sailor's body language communicated, and his awareness seemed to spread almost supernaturally beyond the sailor to encompass all that his meditations on the ocean and setting sun would seem to have ignored. This demeanor of unflappable confidence made the sailor uncomfortable, likely because, though contrary to his personal taste and ways of leadership, Aataltaal played the part a bit too strongly—as an emperor, not a governor, ought.

The sailor gulped noisily and came to an attention more appropriate before the ruler of the once all-powerful Combine Empire. Aataltaal stood comfortably in this setting of mast and sails, and the gloom folded around him, like a dark cloud of ill omen.

The sailor was Hersis, first mate of the *Wolf of Faydark*, the armada's flagship. Like virtually all aboard the vessels, he was human, for humans, of all the constituent races of the Combine Empire, took most readily to the sea. And like virtually all aboard the ships, Hersis was weary, too tired to do anything but survive. "Survival is all I ask of you," Aataltaal had said when the armada launched from the northern coast of Faydwer. As Aataltaal regarded Hersis, he wondered if it had been too much to ask.

Hersis shifted uneasily in the silence.

"Go on, sailor," Aataltaal prodded, adjusting his billowing dark blue cloak so that it did not obstruct his view—or the view of any who might watch from a distance.

"My lord," said Hersis, "it's the Hand of Seru. They've been at our backs for some hours now, we think."

Aataltaal sighed. "Why was I not informed? My meditations here are of no real importance."

Hersis paled. "They were cunning, m'lord. They sailed at angles behind us so we would mistake their distant masts as any of the dozens of islands we've passed near."

"I see." Aataltaal then strode past the sailor, but as he passed, he gently gripped the man's shoulder and gave a reassuring squeeze. It reminded Hersis that Aataltaal did not relish his role, although Bristlebane himself must have blessed the ruse, so naturally did Aataltaal succeed.

As the emperor of the Combine Empire marched to the stern of the *Wolf of Faydark*, the darkening eye of Solusek Ro blinked below the surface of the Ocean of Tears, and night fell across the waters. Aataltaal looked heavenward and spied the moon that, like the goddess who supposedly dwelled there, was called Luclin. Could Seru's eyes see so far? Aataltaal wished *he* could. To what would the geomancer Grieg lead the bulk of the Combine Empire?

Whatever Seru could see, Aataltaal was bound and determined that he see Emperor Tsaph Katta alive and well, not only on Norrath, but just within his reach, in full flight across the great ocean.

"Hail, my lord Emperor," a sailor at the stern said as Aataltaal approached. The sailor stepped out of Aataltaal's path, yet thrust a hand into that space. It clutched a device of evident gnomish manufacture, for it looked awkward and inelegant, yet he handled it with care and respect, for it was a valuable contraption.

Even in the fading light, Aataltaal's keen sight could unaided make out the distant boats, so he brushed aside the offered gnomish telescope. The sailor retreated an additional two steps.

"There are six of them?" Aataltaal asked.

The thin sailor shivered and withdrew the telescope into the folds of his cloak, which he wrapped more tightly around himself. "No, m'lord. I believe there are nine. Three in the aft of their formation try to hide in the silhouettes of the fore vessels."

"We're outnumbered then." There was no surprise or concern in Aataltaal's voice. The plain statement seemed to set the sailor at ease, though he continued to shudder. Aataltaal's reaction made it seem as if he was prepared for this and almost as if he'd wished it to be so.

In fact, that was the truth.

He continued matter-of-factly: "More vessels here means fewer on the heels of our comrades."

The sailor knew Aataltaal spoke of those who escaped—hopefully escaped—to Kunark, where Grieg would complete promising work that he swore would bear fruit.

His voice still emotionless, Aataltaal said, "You spent too long above. You overstayed your shift by an hour. Go below for some warmth and rest."

Plainly astonished that the apparent emperor commanded such knowledge of the details of the watch, the sailor sputtered a reply instead of instantly obeying. "I felt there might be boats behind us, and I wanted to remain until I was certain."

Aataltaal chided him, "But all I ask—"

"I know, Gov—I mean, m'lord, 'survival.' But I just had to know before I left my watch."

Aataltaal nodded and said, "Go below deck and warm yourself."

Nevertheless, the sailor hesitated after only a few steps and muttered something that he quickly cut off, something that was unintelligible regardless. The cloak was pulled so tightly around him that it was difficult to make out that he was a young man, perhaps only sixteen.

Aataltaal's eyes flashed steel when he turned to face the sailor, but once he faced the bow and away from pursuing vessels, his features slightly softened. "Yes, what is it, Delson?"

The sailor stopped, surprised yet again, this time to be recognized and remembered. The emperor raised an eyebrow, coaxing an answer to his question, and Delson found his voice again. "It's what we wanted, right, m'lord?"

Aataltaal chuckled at that truth. He suggested, "To be chased?"

Delson nodded.

The emperor added, "Mainly, to be found. Now, we can only hope that the chase lasts for many days, and that their fleet is even larger than nine."

Delson shivered, not from the cold that had seeped into his bones over the long, hard hours of watch, but instead at the thought of those black sails behind them drawing closer.

"Go. I have work now, sailor," Aataltaal said to the boy as he turned again to face the east. This time, Delson left.

Aataltaal leaned against the rail along the stern. The light had almost completely failed and night's grip turned the whitecap-speckled blue sea wine-dark. Just a slight roll of foam from the flagship's rudder betrayed that the boat moved forward. Still, Aataltaal could see the darker spots—specklike in their insignificance—high in the air some distance away, circling like angry gnats above the coin-sized blotches of the pursuing vessels. He recognized the ravens of Rashalla, perhaps even including the one that had saved Seru from injury when Aataltaal had hurled his dirk. The Koada'Dal worried that the presence of the ravens meant Seru himself might not lead the pursuit, and that this task had been trusted to Rashalla. But at the same time he knew the woman was no sea captain, and so someone else surely had charge. Hopefully, that was General Seru.

Aataltaal also knew that, though the ravens were incapable of prolonged flight and so would not yet pose a direct threat to the *Wolf of Faydark* or her sisters, they did possess an uncanny eyesight, stronger by far than his own, and likely more used to piercing the gloom of night. Essentially, he knew that if he could note them even as pinpricks against the darkening sky, that they could see him entirely.

Which is exactly what Aataltaal wanted.

So, Aataltaal acted. Feigning anxiety and worry, allowing expressions of fatigue and concern to play across his face, the high elf governor of the Sixth District of the Combine Empire put on a show of all that a human emperor might do in this position: all that Emperor Tsaph Katta might do if he had not in fact been teleported with the remnants of his empire by the geomancer Grieg to the distant continent of Kunark, practically into the lap of the treacherous shissar, the race of snakemen who so long ago plied their lies to the Koada'Dal of Takish-Hiz— and whom Aataltaal had seen in his prophetic vision.

Yes, thought Aataltaal, let them chase us and no matter the wills of the gods, the assassinating traitor himself, Seru, will be aboard one of those nine vessels.

BELOWDECKS, AATALTAAL RECLINED IN HIS sparsely furnished and hastily arranged captain's cabin. Now, though, the true Aataltaal reclined, or at least as true a version as those aboard this vessel and the others of this last Combine fleet knew. Which is to say that Aataltaal, Governor of the Northern Reach, was a high elf again.

The scavenged chair was uncomfortable, but at least he sat in his own form again. Here below deck he wore a simple gown of the same nearly transparent purple as his eyes, and beneath that a pair of billow-legged pants afforded him complete comfort as well as freedom of movement. The high elf stretched his lithe limbs in an effort to shake the last of the human-form lethargy from them. The spell that allowed the transformation might be commonly called an "illusion," but in truth it wrought a true transformation, from the color of his blood right through to his beating heart, and Aataltaal imagined that the phantom sensations he experienced for a time after he returned to this form must be akin to those felt by an amputee.

Of course, no matter his form, Aataltaal's primary weapons—his intellect and his memories—remained his own. Like many elves, he was of indeterminate age, but even among the elves he was an enigma. Though apparently nearly middle-aged now, with the white of his hair and the purple of his eyes not nearly as brilliant as even a hundred years ago, he was younger-seeming by far than any elves considered his contemporaries, including King Tearis Thex himself. And his mind was just as agile, as if he were truly the age he seemed. Centuries of intrigue, decades spent in other forms and sometimes undercover, and his own millennia-long ambitions—always, always *that*—kept him sharp.

Because of this and an infallible memory that was legend even among the greatest of the bards, who themselves claimed to know more stories than the library of Erud could contain, Aataltaal was the obvious choice for this current role, one he alone could perform with the scarce preparation allotted. Hasty plans concocted to divert Seru from Felwithe—where the high elves smuggled Tsaph Katta after the poisoning at the first Great Combine Summit—put Aataltaal and his crews of volunteers on their present course.

These volunteers had given up their chance to see the dream of Combine continue on Luclin, where Grieg hoped to land the real emperor and the other refugees before the temporary retreat in Kunark was discovered.

But the volunteers were in the main humans, and Tunaria was their homeland. Aataltaal and his fellow Koada'Dal in Felwithe all understood that the humans, with their penchant for rabbitlike procreation, would soon overcome any deficit in population they might at first possess in comparison to the other races of Tunaria.

More quickly than any of the other races of the Combine Empire, the humans would rebuild what they'd just lost. For though all the races of Norrath suffered an irrevocable loss when the Combine Empire crumbled, it was the humans who perhaps suffered most of all. The other races, from the dwarves of Kaladim, the wood elves of Kelethin, the gnomes of Ak'Anon, the high elves of Felwithe, and even the final guests to the Great Summit—the guests that whetted the venomous ire of Seru and his supporters, the dark races such as the Teir'Dal of Neriak—all had ancient, established civilizations, with all the attendant codes and customs on which they might rely; but the humans truly lost everything. The work of two generations of men died when Katta fell to the poison, while the other races lost but a portion of one. The loss might be the most painful and regretted of a dwarven, elven, or gnomish lifetime, but for a human it was a grandfather's legacy ruined. This was true for all men, Erudites and Northmen and the original stock now just called human.

Of course, it was nearly the same for the halflings, who were the first to join the Combine Empire after those three nations of men. But Aataltaal, so laden with melancholy by a life early gone awry and spent forever chasing redemption, or at least solutions, found the halflings the most inscrutable of all races. Their jolly humor and pleasant country manners surely camouflaged sorrows as deep and dark as any other's, but they seemed to shrug it off and carry on; and the high elf could not but imagine them doing the same now.

Besides, the halflings had not invested too heavily in the Combine Empire. They'd joined quickly because Katta lived so near to them in central Tunaria, and that's where they remained: they still held their homelands in the vales of the Misty Thicket. On the other hand, humans had nothing but the emptied region from which the empire arose, the place known as the Plains of Karana because of the violent storms the thunder god unleashed upon that land.

And so Aataltaal found himself a leader of humans. Though the Combine Empire was shattered, if Tsaph Katta somehow miraculously survived—despite a poison that Seru knew resisted all manner of magic that the emperor's allies would employ—then he would flee to Tunaria, in the company of humans, for Tsaph hailed from Katta Grove in the heart of the plains. And this, too, Seru knew.

Now the scent of blood, from direly wounded prey struggling back to its figurative burrow, would arouse the predatory side so dominant in Seru. Or so Aataltaal proposed, in tandem with the ruse of his illusion. Many others doubted that aspect of the plan especially, for why stir Seru's suspicions of a trick or trap with the unlikely apparent recovery of the emperor himself? Yet Aataltaal convinced them. The Koada'Dal hoped the emperor's apparent recovery would sow dissent among the enemies. Ones such as Rashalla and Seru were allies of convenience, not friends with identical deeply held convictions.

Above all, Aataltaal considered himself fortunate to have this opportunity to play out multiple ruses. For in addition to the trickery surrounding the health of

Emperor Katta, this entire mission also created a cover story for the Koada'Dal's return to the small, pirate-infested port city of Weille.

And this ruse of flight wove an illusion of an entirely different sort as well. Those such as Seru who opposed Aataltaal feared his intellect and of course his wizardry, but the high elf allowed those qualities to lull his foes and overshadow what he personally considered his greatest virtue: a rare ability with the sword. "Once in a generation" they would say of his skill if he were a human, but as an elf who benefited from the experiences of living countless human generations, Aataltaal was beyond even that categorization.

Of course, there were two others. Two lost, like the rest.

No one had witnessed this rare ability—truly seen it unleashed—for many, many years. The high elf leaned forward and rubbed his knotted brow. His arm braced at the elbow on the empty desk, and his fingers massaged his forehead as Aataltaal concentrated. He nodded gently to himself as he closed his eyes and bowed his head over the desk. Many years had passed since his escape from the Underfoot, and his skill had not been called upon in earnest since then. He hoped that Seru himself would be the privileged one to witness his swordsmanship again.

Beyond the high elf's control, his eyes closed, his expression relaxed, and his head began to sag toward the inviting repose of the tabletop. Though sleep was nearly full upon him, a stray thought fluttered in the back of Aataltaal's mind. Undoubtedly he was very fatigued, after weeks of little sleep and now several days with scarcely any—but he was not one to submit to sleep except when he consciously deemed it time for such deep rest. Which meant—

In a flash that caused the folds of his gown to crack from the whiplash motion, Aataltaal drew his slender rapier and effortlessly pierced the wooden cabin wall. The sword's point met no further resistance as it extended six inches into the corridor beyond, and so with uncanny precision that did not widen the hole, the high elf withdrew the sword along the identical path and he plunged it through the wall again. This time he drew blood.

"By the Oceanlord!" came a gurgled oath from the corridor beyond Aataltaal's cabin. The voice sounded odd—someone in pain, yes, but more than that, the quality of the voice was garbled, like a great sucking of air from a tongueless man. Which was pretty close to the truth.

The high elf relaxed at once. He inspected the tip of his sword and saw a swathe of bluish ichor upon it. He waved his hand over the length of the blade and, with a twinkling of light, the blood vanished.

"Can you do this wound as well?" asked the manlike amphibian who opened the door.

Aataltaal looked up from the rapier and greeted his guest with a mischievous smile. "You think that is beyond my means, Menthes?"

Pressing a finger to the puncture wound to stop the bleeding, the kedge said with mock surprise, "Well, I've always been delighted that there's at least something you've yet to master."

"New times call for new methods, my friend."

Aataltaal muttered a few words in a guttural tongue and the tips of his fingers shone with dull light.

Menthes twisted his head fully ninety degrees and watched closely with one of his big eyes. "Was that orcish?" he asked.

Aataltaal nodded. "All part of a role I played recently. Healing magic was part of my disguise . . ."

As his voice trailed off, the Koada'Dal lightly touched the kedge's wound. The glowing fingers flared and then the light died down, then out. In the candlelight of the small room, Aataltaal inspected his work and nodded. Menthes rolled his arm at the shoulder and nodded as well.

"The sleeping? Your idea of a test?" Aataltaal asked.

"Yes. And you nearly failed, I think. If we'd been below water, you'd have succumbed and been my air-breathing slave." Menthes laughed at this with a rasping inhalation that sounded more like a man struggling to draw breath than one gladly expelling it.

Ignoring the jest, the high elf waved the other into the small cabin and said, "Close the door, my friend."

Despite being clearly out of his element—namely, not submerged in water—the kedge was resplendent. His green scaly skin glittered like emeralds. He wore a sort of loincloth, one that sagged a bit here on ship, without water's buoyancy to help keep it aloft. On his upper body he wore a matching dull-gray leathery vest, likely of shark hide. A strap sewn onto the shoulder of the vest provided anchor for a small bag that hung like a backpack behind Menthes. Something bulged within the sack. Completing the kedge's simple outfit was a shell-tipped harpoon. The weapon was so beautiful and delicate that many would disregard it as ornamental, but Aataltaal knew the spiral shell that served as the harpoon's tip was not only honed to a razor's edge but also possessed a magically enhanced hardness like that of steel.

Like most kedge, Menthes was sleek, cut slim to dart through the crush of deep water. In fact, he was nearly as slender as Aataltaal. Only a disconcerting triangularity to his limbs that first tapered and then blossomed at both hand and foot into enormous webbed apparatus gave him the illusion of more size.

Though a bit unsteady as he walked, Menthes strode with an admirable athletic grace that spoke of great power. Still, an unwary enemy unused to the kedge would take little note of this, for he would be entirely distracted by the kedge's head, which was more like froglok than the various permutations of vaguely elflike form possessed by many other races, such as humans and dwarves. In fact, given the bizarre appearances of some fish dredged from the deepest waters of the ocean, sailors joked that the kedge were a deep-water froglok. Their rounded heads were topped with a cranial fin, but dominated by a pair of bulbous, side-facing eyes. Without the refraction of water to make their eyes work appropriately, kedge on land all exhibited the tendency to turn their heads slightly and stare sideway in order to gaze what to a man would be straight-ahead.

When Menthes spoke, the vast orifice of his mouth opened to split his head nearly exactly in the middle, top to bottom, and also almost halfway around its circumference. Aataltaal recalled some of the earliest audiences with kedge who visited the elves of the ancient and now ruined Takish-Hiz, and could not help but smirk at the thought of how, when the kedge first spoke, many elves of less dependable constitution fainted weak-kneed to the throne-room floor.

Menthes noticed the grin and again spoke, this time feigning injury at the high elf's lack of concern, "Oh, oh, I see. It pleases you to see me hurt thus . . ."

Aataltaal deadpanned, "I apologize for wounding you through the wall of my ship when you sought to ensorcel me, but I have undone that damage."

But the kedge had not stopped speaking, and so

continued, ". . . and thus . . . and thus . . . and thus." Each time he pointed to a new wound, these three on his shoulder, his neck, and beside his cranial fin.

The wounds did not appear serious and Aataltaal did not overreact. "Those, too, appear fresh, my friend. What mishap recently befell you?"

"Your pursuers assailed me, Aataltaal. Or I imagine them to be such, for the chances that they follow your same path across an ocean so vast, and that you have not spotted them and so slowed to accommodate them overtaking you, are small indeed."

The high elf squinted as he inspected the wounds more closely. In a second he said, "The ravens of Rashalla?"

"That's the truth," said Menthes. "A small gaggle of them silently dive-bombed me while I thought myself watching unseen near the boats. The sharp-eyed beasts spied me, though, and their damned wings cut a few fleshy flaps for me 'ere I sunk like stone. This one—" The kedge paused to indicate the cut on the top of its head. "—dove too low and so followed me down."

Aataltaal's eyes gleamed. "Did—?"

"Yes," Menthes croaked, laboring to speak. His throat was drying out from so much time spent out of water. He grimaced and added, "I brought it with me."

The high elf smiled and motioned to the small table where he'd been seated a moment before. A glass and a bottle of wine rested along its edge. Menthes nodded and Aataltaal poured a full glass. Meanwhile, Menthes untied the sharkskin bag from the strap of his vest and withdrew a surprisingly dry bird from within it.

That drew a quizzical look from Aataltaal, though the elf eyed the bag and not the bird.

Menthes chuckled, again with little inhalations that sounded like hiccups. "I know what you're thinking. Yes, it's the same bag. It keeps what's to be wet, wet, and that meant to be dry, dry."

The kedge tossed the raven onto the table where it flopped, not yet stiffened in death. Aataltaal handed the glass of wine to the kedge and examined the corpse. With a thumb and forefinger he unfolded one of its wings. It appeared to be a normal raven, except the tips of the wings were armed with spurs of dark bone that shone in the low light. The bird's head, too, was different, slightly larger—though the cause was not only of biology. The reason was clear when Aataltaal rolled the bird over and revealed a sort of third eye atop its forehead—not a true eye, but a large replica fashioned from a black pearl and seemingly fused to the bird's skull.

Aataltaal nodded. "I thought I saw a flock of Rashalla's birds from our stern." He touched the razor-edged wings again, then the black pearl, running his finger over it, as if checking for imperfections. Evidently satisfied, he returned his attention to the kedge and said, "And you? What did you see, Menthes?"

The two remained standing and Aataltaal did not offer his friend a seat, though another chair was available. Kedge were uncomfortable when seated.

Menthes leaned his slender spear in a corner of the room and dropped the now-empty bag onto the floor beside it. Then he turned back to the high elf and said, "Ten boats to your six, Aat."

Aataltaal disliked this diminutive of his name, but he allowed it without reproach from friends when he knew that they in turn knew he did not care for it. It was the kind of small matter not worth the bother in a centuries-long life.

Besides, something else entirely demanded the high elf's attention. "Ten ships? One of my best pairs of eyes reported only nine."

"Perhaps there are only nine," Menthes allowed.

Aataltaal did not appreciate or expect this kind of reporting, and his glower communicated as much to the kedge.

"I know, I know," the kedge slobbered, waving a great, finned hand in the elf's direction. "I, too, *saw* only nine, but I swear . . ." His voice trailed off.

Aataltaal prodded, "Yes?"

"Well, it sounds far-fetched, but I believe there was a tenth boat, a tenth *invisible* boat." Weary with his own disbelief, the kedge waddled penguinlike to the other chair and uncharacteristically sat in it.

Aataltaal resumed his own seat.

"Invisible?"

"I think so, yes."

Putting aside the unlikelihood of such a thing existing at all, Aataltaal pressed the matter: "Why do you suspect as much? Was there another wake? Did you hear voices, such as shouted commands? What?"

Though to an earth-walker, a kedge's large eyes always appeared surprised or cowed, Menthes truly did seem at least embarrassed as he admitted, "I think I ran into it."

Aataltaal could not completely stifle a chuckle. "*That* must have been a surprise."

Menthes' discomfort turned to wounded pride, and he sat straighter and refused to answer the comment.

Serious again, Aataltaal asked, "So, the *ship* found *you*, but did the occupants of the vessel detect you? Or for that matter, can you be certain that this invisible object—if even a boat at all—has a crew? Or could it be something else entirely, cloaked by magic and perhaps towed by one of the other nine boats?"

Menthes shook his head. "No, I'm certain it's a boat. It's because I was concentrating so much on making just that determination that those razor-wings were able to surprise me."

"Speaking of which . . ."

The kedge waved off the concern. "No, I will be fine. Fortunately, at the last moment I realized the difference between the fluttering of wings and of a sail. Otherwise, the first bird might have sliced my artery." Menthes demonstrated with a slash of his hand across the side of his neck.

The kedge continued, "But before that attack I convinced myself of what I'm telling you. I felt the texture of a wooden hull and smelled the stink of unwashed men."

Aataltaal nodded, "But it seems likely you were detected if the ravens attacked you so promptly."

The kedge agreed and said, "That, or they were simply on reconnaissance anyway and attacked when they spotted me. Who knows what they were able to report back to this Rashalla, or," he added ominously, "to others who might command them."

Aataltaal frowned as if the words gave life to his thoughts as well. "What do you suspect?" Aataltaal asked.

Menthes shrugged but said, "I suppose I find it unlikely that a craft as fantastic as an invisible boat would carry any but Seru himself."

Aataltaal stood and smoothed the pleats in his silk gown. "Or someone he entrusts with an important mission." He pushed his chair away from the small desk and looked at the dead raven. "Let's see what secrets this bird might share."

The kedge stood as well and stepped back. He said, "So, you're not only a healer, but you are a necromancer now as well?"

The high elf looked very little like the popular conceit of a dark elf mortician in black and red as he stretched the stiffening bird. The pale white of his hands stood in stark contrast to the raven's jet-black feathers. Once he had the bird arranged so that it lay flat on its back with its head centered and facing the ceiling of the cabin, Aataltaal replied, "Knowledge of the deathly arts is unpalatable, and for many years I considered it antithetical to the cause for which I have struggled. But as I said before, times change. The practice of this sorcery can be extremely useful, and this has proven an interesting exercise even if nothing comes of it. I failed previously to divine any information from these ravens or their gems, but while in Felwithe I unearthed a process that I expect will be successful."

Then the Koada'Dal gazed hard into the divergent eyes of the kedge in order to make this point clear. "But mainly, necromancy is required of me now. Required of my methods and for my goals that I am able to move in the circles where necromantic ability is commonplace and expected. At least that is the next role for which I am preparing."

Menthes retreated a step. The high elf's voice held more than mere emphasis. The kedge had heard it before from this elf, but seldom from any other being: the clarion call of "purpose." There was no doubt that Aataltaal was driven, and driven deeply, passionately; and the kedge wondered to himself what bounds the high elf might place on himself in pursuit of his ends. Menthes gave no voice to such thoughts, though, but did press the Koada'Dal. "You stand upon the deck as the emperor. Belowdecks you are a necromancer. Where or who is Aataltaal? Do you yourself know where that line is drawn? What of you then is real, my friend, and what is artifice?"

The shadow that seemed to hover over the high elf and give gravitas to his words subsided, and Aataltaal said, with cheer in such dissonance with the earlier warning that it seemed eerie to the kedge, "My friendship for you is real, Menthes."

The kedge nodded silently, unsure how to respond.

Aataltaal continued, the warmth still in his voice, smoothing over the awkwardness of Menthes' feelings and thoughts, "That you can count on."

The kedge tried to keep the mood light. "Either that or you're afraid to rouse me lest I'll revert to the bestial state in which you first found me."

Aataltaal's fingers worked at the black pearl embedded in the raven's skull, and he did not look up at the kedge as he said, "You continue to give yourself too little credit for that time, Menthes. I worked no magic then to spare you or to save myself. Your battle was an inner one that you both fought and won. I trusted my sense of you then . . ." Aataltaal hesitated a moment as he screwed the black pearl left then right in an attempt to loosen it.

With an audible *pop!* the gemstone came free, as did a spray of blood as the pearl trailed the raven's brainstem behind it. Other chunky bits of flesh oozed onto the bird's carcass, and Aataltaal plucked the soft tissues from the smooth black surface and flicked them irreverently back upon the bird's corpse.

With a flourish, he presented the gem to Menthes, then concluded, ". . . as I trusted you to find me, wherever I might be in the Ocean of Tears, and no matter what force pursued me."

With a grin, Aataltaal added, "Though I did not expect you to find me so soon."

Menthes snorted, the rumble like that of a walrus. "Clearly, my sleep-deprived friend. Clearly."

Motioning to Menthes' bag, Aataltaal asked, "May I?"

"Everything comes clean in the ocean," said the

kedge, solemnly reciting an ancient kedge adage, though typically it referred more to lingering bad memories than magical bags.

Aataltaal just smiled faintly and retrieved the bag from the corner, where it sat beside the harpoon. Into it, he swept the carcass of the raven. Then he reached into the bag and plucked four long tail feathers. These he arranged on the table as if to indicate imaginary cardinal directions.

While the high elf worked, Menthes said, "Speaking of expecting people, I wonder what Solusek Ro thinks of this armada crossing back to Tunaria. The last refugees who were led across the Ocean of Tears by a Koada'Dal fled that continent because of the Burning One's wrath."

The statement hung awkwardly for a moment as Aataltaal pretended not to hear, though Menthes knew rather that the high elf simply did not wish to respond. Nevertheless, he continued, "I only wonder because he is surely not your ally still, and so that means he may send omen or aid to those who pursue you."

At that, Aataltaal looked up from his work and said, "Solusek Ro is not one to work through intermediaries, especially where I am concerned. More likely, if he knows who it is that returns, then he shall work against us directly."

"Would that I could offer the Oceanlord's hand in your defense," Menthes said. "I do not expect one such as I—created by my own people without regard for the eternal wishes of great Prexus—will ever hold sway in that regard."

Aataltaal shook his head. "It's no matter. Prexus would not defend me now, even if Phinigel Autropos himself blessed this voyage. I did what I could to mislead the burning eye as it set—for trust me in this, even a god can be deceived, just not for as long as we fools who stagger about the surface of Norrath or spelunk the depths of its oceans—so the die has been cast. We shall know when the sun rises this morning."

Then the high elf mentally calculated a point in the exact center of the prepared tableau and there delicately placed the black pearl. Though perfectly round, the gem did not roll or even wobble from the spot Aataltaal chose for it. It behaved as if it possessed an individual gravity that kept it perfectly positioned in the midst of the raven feathers.

"Now," said the elf, "let's look through a razor-wing's eyes."

With his hands extended palm down over the table, Aataltaal chanted ten ancient syllables. With the first, he felt the magic kindle. With the second, he took hold of the mana—the magical energy that was a part of him. With the third, he felt the mana begin to stir. At the fourth syllable, the Koada'Dal's mana undulated like a string suddenly pulled taut. With the fifth, he mentally took control of those mana waves at the instant they crested highest. At the sixth, he was committed. The spell could be stopped, but the mana would still have to flow—it would somehow find release. With the seventh, he grasped the mana and plied it as if it were a meta-physical dough, shaping it to his needs. With the eighth syllable, Aataltaal took hold of the mana and stretched it from his body like an ethereal pseudopod. With the ninth, he commanded the mana to flow into the black pearl. With the final syllable, he bound the mana within the gemstone, and a third eye opened to Aataltaal's mind . . .

9

THE FLIGHT OF THE NECROMANCER

EVEN AS THE DEATH-SIGHT CAME TO AATAL-taal, the third eye revealed only darkness. A long moment passed, with only the sense of motion.

Aataltaal sensed Menthes shift, and the elf opened his other two eyes and saw for a moment as two beings, though one had not reclaimed vision of the time before its death and so that sight remained dark.

The elf said, "You must remain very still, or leave the room." The tone allowed no discussion, certainly no argument.

Menthes protested, "But your sailors do not know me. If I—"

Suddenly, the third eye saw a crevice of light. Aataltaal's own two eyes bore hard upon Menthes for a split-second, and then they slowly closed.

As the light expanded in Aataltaal's mind, he sensed Menthes become as still as an eel preparing its ambush. Then the Koada'Dal was rocked by brilliant light, and all thoughts of the other—his true—world dispersed. It was as if a hermit of twenty years suddenly stepped from a cave, into a sunrise.

It was the barrier between life and death.

Water poured over him, for he witnessed these events as the bird itself. Sometimes, afterward, he would swear that he could more than just see what the deceased witnessed, but feel it as well, and he wondered if that, too, was an effect of the spell Rashalla wove upon this bird to trap him. Frothing waves spun in circles around him, but he rose fast, and out of the corner of his eye, Aataltaal saw the light of the moon Luclin refracting through the surface of the ocean.

Suddenly, he burst clear of the water. A jerk, and then he quickly flew backward, away from a face floating on the waves that soon became naught more than a black smudge as his motion flung him further away in his backward dive. Aataltaal knew the visage to be that of his kedge friend, and as Menthes had told the high elf, the kedge had been so distracted by his investigation that he did not sense the approach of the now-dead razor-wing raven.

From the point of view of the raven, it was a wonder that Menthes had survived the attack. Aataltaal was just barely aware of two wingmates, and the three of them retraced their dive as Aataltaal relived the bird's final moments, backward. Only the fact that the kedge's neck had been below water saved him. The water had blunted the attack of the slicing wing, deflecting it just enough.

With an eerily weightless sensation, Aataltaal hurtled up into the sky. Though the bird had concentrated on its target, this careful, silent dive now played in reverse allowed the high elf time to examine the bird's surroundings. He could concentrate his attention on even the smallest of details, so long as it entered the field of vision observed by the raven.

He saw the nine boats of the Combine traitors. For there were nine; Delson was correct. Three in the back stayed in the wakes of those before them, and all nine masts bore flags adorned with the black hand of the chief architect of the collapse of the Combine Empire, General Seru. Aataltaal gained an incredibly useful view of all of them as he flew backward clockwise from the tail of the fleet around the front and then back again along the northern length of the vessels. All the while the raven kept his mark in sight, although Aataltaal paid scant attention to Menthes.

At one point, Aataltaal realized that the three birds of his small flock had grown to become eight or even ten. He could not see them all, and the detail was not important enough to supplant other viewing opportunities. Then an instant later, two more birds rejoined the flock. Somehow, perhaps because they scouted on the arm of the flock that afforded the best view of the kedge intruder, Aataltaal knew these birds reversed their return to their mistress. Time flowing the other way would have them breaking formation and taking details of Menthes to Rashalla.

Only when he'd retraced a path that took him again to the back three ships, though, could Aataltaal gain a perspective on the mystery that clearly perplexed the kedge. Though the water was choppy, he could tell that the wake of the center of the three aft ships was being disrupted. With his aerial advantage, this phenomenon became clear to the elf. Floating on the surface of the water, the kedge must have struggled mightily indeed to decipher this oddity. But the wakes of the three ships stood out like the pale underbellies of Faydark slugs revealed from beneath stones in the foothills of the Butcherblock Mountains. The white lines of foaming water were as if drawn by Luclin's own hand upon the surface of the Ocean of Tears, for they scintillated from the light of her moon.

At least the northernmost and southernmost ones

did. In the center, *something* briefly broke this line before it reformed again over a hundred and twenty feet to the east. This meant the center wake stretched nearly twice as long as that of the other two. Without the report of the kedge, Aataltaal would hesitate to admit the only reasonable theory—if indeed an invisible vessel was within the bounds of reason.

Did Seru have so much might at his disposal that he could expend it so recklessly?

Aataltaal knew that Seru must think he was "winning" in a battle against the remnants of the Combine Empire and Emperor Katta, and so he would see such wastefulness as pressing an advantage, but the high elf suspected Seru had not thought beyond the moment of his victory. Indeed, what would he have won?

But such musings were hard to keep steady in his mind, for his eyes scanned everywhere within the vision of the raven. Swiftly, then, the raven reversed an initial ascent and, to Aataltaal's perspective, "landed" on the railing from whence it first took flight in preparation to attack Menthes. Of course, it "landed" facing the waters of the Ocean of Tears, and the beating of wings momentarily blocked Aataltaal's sight.

When the razor-sharp ebony feathers no longer occluded Aataltaal's line of sight, he realized that the raven perched on a boat that he had not previously seen. Nine boats still sailed in the peripheral left of the raven's vision, although Aataltaal could only see them through what appeared to be a fog so gray-tinged that it seemed a thundercloud.

Surely, this fog embodied whatever magic hid this tenth vessel, the command ship. The raven acted naturally, though, so neither the magic nor the invisibility effect made the animal skittish. Perhaps the bird was itself ensorcelled or mayhap simply well trained.

A few sideways hops and then a one hundred-and-eighty-degree spin, and the raven's perspective turned suddenly toward the interior of the vessel. Before him stood the dreaded Rashalla, mistress of the ravens. This view of the witch was the best Aataltaal had ever been afforded, and he took a moment to study her. A scrawny woman almost birdlike herself, Rashalla was a human, built with an elf's stature but little of an elf's evident grace. Yet she possessed a strange charisma, an animal magnetism of sorts, that must be what allowed her remarkable control over these birds, for they were typically wild, very wild, and it was unknown for them to respond to the commands of any falconer as they did Rashalla.

The woman flicked her hands, drawing them toward her body twice, and though the scene looked bizarre in reverse, especially because the woman was already a comical sight, Aataltaal understood the gestures as dismissive ones. She ordered her ravens to take flight.

A black shawl draped her frail frame, over which her long, stringy dark hair dangled. Her eyes sparkled as the birds danced in a line along the rail—presumably her final instructions to her murder of crows—and as her gaze glanced past Aataltaal's own she almost seemed to tarry a moment. It was probably just a trick of her animal magic that made her seem to single out each and every one of her "pets"; still, it made Aataltaal's spine tingle, and the Koada'Dal trusted that sensation.

Somehow Rashalla knew this specific bird's destiny as a portal for these visions, and that meant that Aataltaal could easily be walking into a trap. Perhaps he'd already been ensnared? Hypnotized through the eyes of the bird? Mayhap some subliminal message was imparted and would only reveal itself in a crucial moment in the dark days, weeks, or even years ahead.

The high elf let his focus blur for a moment, which served to slightly detach him from the other reality into which he peered. Thankfully, he was able to do so. He paused for a moment; should he risk going on? No doubt this mission was important. The diversion of Seru so that Lord Katta might escape and perhaps be revived was a crucial point as yet unresolved in the saga of Norrath, not just for now, but for what might happen a thousand years from now, even after Grieg went mad—

The high elf shook himself from that line of thinking. The future of those visions was ever uncertain, but what *was* certain was his last millennia of effort. This moment in history paled in comparison to his greater goals, and he could not allow himself to be compromised by Rashalla's or Seru's magic.

But he knew these events all interconnected somehow. After all, did this voyage of flight not provide the perfect cover for his return to Weille?

Deciding to risk going on, Aataltaal once again absorbed the scenes as seen by the razor-winged raven. Now, the bird watched as Rashalla walked backward, away from the flock and into a large cabin near the stern. Then she was gone, but the door did not close behind her. The raven began to prance and turn until suddenly it was flying—backward—again. By sighting along the line of the bird before it, Aataltaal knew instantly that it had flown from the same cabin from whence Rashalla— reversing the timeline of these past events—would momentarily emerge. Still, the high elf did not worry, for all the other ravens appeared to be on the same flight; it was not his odd bird alone that went that way.

The raven fluttered its way to one of many bird stands throughout the room. He could see perhaps two-dozen razor-wings, and, guessing by the size of the cabin, many more perched out of view. In the center of the room stood Rashalla. Her lips pursed with the twitter she must have sounded to signal the birds to leave the chamber. Before that she calmed the birds with what must have been cooing, for Aataltaal watched as her eyes partly closed and she rocked her head from side to side while her half-open mouth revealed a tongue pressed to the roof of her mouth. She was calming the birds, but from what?

The reason became clear a moment later. After a space of several seconds during which the birds seemed on edge and many flapped their wings in agitation, a far door opened. Rather, it closed, and the one who had been in the room the moment before, startling the birds, "returned."

More surely than the black hand emblazoned on the padded shoulders of his tunic, the man's erect posture instantly told Aataltaal who he was. His hair was still cropped short despite the rigors of the past weeks, and so black it appeared greasy. Aataltaal steeled himself as General Seru pivoted so that he now faced the raven's eye that was the Koada'Dal's vantage. The dark-complected man made a powerful, waving gesture with his arms and appeared to shout something to Rashalla. In that instant, Aataltaal saw that hint of wildness in Seru's eyes that always scared his opponents. Known as a man of absolute self-control, Seru nevertheless had a way of showing that beneath his fortified demeanor, he was a madman capable of nearly any act. This was itself an act, and a good one, for countless opponents quaked at the prospect of facing the man in the political arena, let alone a true arena where Seru had often amply demonstrated his physical talents.

The instant "before" the general's gesture, the birds became calm again, as did Seru himself. Aataltaal studied him closely for a moment. The general did not appear tired or stressed or in any way affected by recent events. He appeared healthy and, as always, tigerlike, dangerous, especially dressed as he was now in black leather pants and tunic instead of the heavier armor that he favored in battle.

Seru turned to Rashalla so that Aataltaal could not see his mouth to read his lips when Seru spoke. Then, in a terrible replay of the attention that Rashalla granted the single bird—Aataltaal's bird—Seru came toward the high elf's perspective until he stood directly before the living incarnation of the raven that now lay dead before Aataltaal. Seru was so near and his attention so pointedly directed at Aataltaal's bird that there could be no possibility—as there *might* have been with Rashalla— that it was a coincidence or Aataltaal's imagination. Seru *was* singling out this one bird, and despite himself, despite the vast distance that yet separated the general's vessels from his own, Aataltaal flinched.

Seru smiled. Always unnerving, the smile—both grim and deeply, almost cocksure confident—was ghastly when seen in reverse. Then, the general spoke.

With the ease possible only after centuries of mastering a dozen tongues and serving in a thousand guises in hundreds of covert missions, Aataltaal read Seru's lips. Of course, the last word came first now, and the mouthings of each word were backward as well, but the high elf instantly deciphered each word as Seru spoke it.

Seru said, "Tunaria of shore eastern the onto wash to corpse your allow I if only but, homeland your reach *shall* you, m'lord, yes. Destruction your complete to— five your to ships eight my—numbers superior my of use make then and leisure my at you overtake shall I so and, yours than faster are ships my for, complete to fail cannot I duty a is it. Spell Rashalla's by undone left job simple the complete personally to come I know you if—

think I, surprise no and—lost nothing is there so and, advantage my press shall I that well know you. Otherwise feel to seem all advisors my though—think I, directly so you with communicating in harm no is there. Katta lord my, hello."

When Seru finished, or rather before he ever began, he stood posed before the raven whose perspective Aataltaal commandeered. Then a set, determined expression gave way to a sarcastically cheering smile so near the raven's face that Aataltaal wondered why the bird did not peck the general's eye.

Then, suddenly, darkness.

The complete occlusion persisted for many moments. Patiently, Aataltaal bore it. Five minutes, then ten, which was enough. The elf relaxed his grip on the black pearl, and the third eye—the connection between him and the last mortal sights of the dead razor-wing raven—dispersed. The Koada'Dal did not doubt that the bird would have remained hooded for another dozen hours or more. Aataltaal did not have the time to spare, especially given the revelations he had perceived. If necessary, he could return to the bird later.

But for now, Aataltaal had questions. Foremost was this: how could Seru have known not only that a bird would be captured and its memory replayed by means of this not-widely known magic, but that *this* bird would be the one so captured?

If Seru had revelations of the fate of this bird, then how had the general managed to overlook the fact that it was not truly Lord Katta he pursued?

And what of his revelation that it was Rashalla's spell that birthed the serpents of Hate?

Finally . . . *eight* ships?

10

THE WOLF OF FAYDARK

THE ROSY-FINGERED DAWN STRETCHED WIDE across the expanse of the Ocean of Tears. The breeze had blown strong all night and seemed to pick up at the break of morning, and sailors, as if harnessing the heat of the sun to spur their boats onward, adjusted the sails just as the pink of the earliest morning sky grew more vibrant and luminous, tinting the very foam that tipped the ocean's waves.

Nevertheless, the sailors did not go about their duties without worried glances, for the unexpected, the unexplained, seemed to surround them. Behind them, the fleet of Seru's warships had drawn nearer throughout the night. The vessels were easily seen now not just with the naked eye, but also by sailors on deck without the benefit of a crow's nest vantage to extend their gazes farther toward the darker horizon to the west.

One big sailor wiped a brow already beaded from the morning sun and said, "They're massing to attack. No doubt." Nestor was among the few volunteers who actually knew the ways of the sea and had true sailing experience. As such, even though he was not a natural leader, he'd assumed a sort of sergeant's role for the duration of the voyage.

Though robust nearly to obese, Nestor stepped lightly around the coils of rope he tied off as they completed adjustments to the sails. Though they'd seen him perform this dance often over the course of the past several days, Nestor's friends still marveled at the man. Ashore, he resembled a beached whale, and usually a liquored one at that. Clumsy and always a threat to any woman's dinnerware, Nestor was transformed aboard this vessel, the *Condor*. The rolling waves that rocked the boats forced the gaggle of landlubbers among them to take small and sometimes sudden steps to maintain their balance, but Nestor seemed to roll with the sways as if his generous belly was part of the sea itself.

Or maybe the true hint to the transformation was simply that his breath did not smell of ale. He was still the same Nestor, still loud and generous, but now he seemed serious. His features were intent, focused, as if he was steeled to face a threat from which he'd been hiding.

"How far off are they?" asked Troy, the handsomest man among them—and by far the best dressed. Even after the flight brought about by the collapsing empire and the hasty preparations for this volunteer duty, Troy's clothing was clean and neat. Though the blue ribbons on the shoulders of his vest were undone, and one of them obviously shorn, his ruffled shirt was not soiled, and his leggings were still a deep burgundy as unfaded as on the day they were new. "I still can't tell distances very well at sea. There's nothing to judge against."

One of the other men nudged Troy in the ribs and verbally jabbed as well, "You just mean you have trouble gauging distances farther than from you to the nearest elven tart."

Troy certainly fancied the ladies, and elven maidens especially, but none of these men had ever known one in that private way. Still, since Troy generally had any human woman he courted stealing to a bedchamber, taunts like this were the only way to discredit him.

Nestor pivoted so that he could completely regard the pursuing fleet. "What you're really asking is how long until they catch us, eh?"

Troy nodded.

Nestor rubbed his jaw with a large hand and then regarded his friends, and the others nearby as well. "At their current rate, they'll probably have us by the end of the day. But the damned thing is that they could go faster if they wanted. They're working their sails a bit, but not like us. We're nearly full tilt, like a horse galloping, while they're just prancing along."

The assembled men grumbled at the news, but Troy appealed most directly, "But why?"

Nestor shrugged, and the silence gripped the men.

Then Delailith, a stern woman and the unlikely companion of Troy and Nestor, said grimly, "To frighten us." She slapped her leather wristbands as if to demonstrate that Seru's efforts were futile.

Another momentary silence was broken when one of the others exclaimed, "*That's* what frightens me!" He was a thin man named Cadmus. None of the others knew him very well, but he told funny if improbable stories that entertained them all, and that earned him a place among them.

Now as Cadmus pointed, the men followed the sudden gesture of his rail-thin arm and they all received a start. The *Condor* was starboard and slightly aft the flagship, the *Wolf of Faydark*, almost near enough to shout, and so plenty close enough to see those on board. The sailors watched in astonishment as the emperor emerged a step ahead of as alien a being as they ever saw walk among men.

Nestor chuckled and, with a thick forefinger, pushed closed Troy's literally gaping mouth. Nestor asked, "None of you ever seen a kedge before?"

Never a part of the Combine Empire—and for an empire that intended to embrace even the dark elves, the exclusion of this race spoke volumes of the state of the kedge race and their place in the politics of the surface world—the kedge were widely regarded with suspicion. Especially one such as now spoke quietly with the emperor.

Cadmus again exclaimed, "But that one's an abomination!" Mutant kedge were widely believed to have been created for the sole purpose of enslaving the surface world. These abominations were the result of terrible deep-sea experiments rivaled in their cruelty only by the Teir'Dal of Neriak.

Troy spat in the direction of the kedge; his spittle, though, caught by the wind, whipped down onto Delailith's boot. The two exchanged glances, but as usual Delailith was stoic, and the matter passed without even a joke.

Then Troy said, "It's because of those monsters that we're all—" He spread his arms and gestured to encompass not just those nearby but everyone on this boat and within the entire fleet. "—in this predicament."

Delailith shook her head. "How so?" she asked, her tone doubtful.

Troy insisted, "The kedge brought down the Combine Empire!"

Without having ever taken her eyes off Troy, Delailith said without inflection, "Unsubstantiated rumors. And unlikely, regardless."

Normally, comments from Delailith brought conversations to an end because she spoke little, and when she did, others respected her opinion. But Troy was too excited, and he was unlikely to be calmed so long as Cadmus kept muttering oaths under his breath.

Troy said, "Sure, Seru moved to stop the dark elves from joining the Combine, but plenty—and I mean *lots* of plenty, Delailith—of people say he didn't really mind the dark elves at all, but feared it was the first step toward admitting the kedge! By Marr! If Seru learns that we've got kedge on our ships, then he'll really want to get us."

Nestor laughed. "As opposed to just chopping us up, it's worse if he chops us into tiny pieces? Besides, better the kedge than the Teir'Dal, if you ask me," grumbled Nestor.

"You're crazy," shouted Troy.

Several of the men shushed him for that. The emperor and the kedge were concentrating on their own conversation, but none of the sailors wanted to draw their attention with raised voices.

But upon hearing Nestor's suggestion, Cadmus calmed down. "Well, Nestor might be right."

Everyone sensed a story from this man who said he aimed to become a bard, and they were happy for him to ply his trade. Nestor first looked to the sails, but then he, too, gave his attention to Cadmus.

Cadmus recited, "It is said that the kedge abominations were not meant for war, but instead for the very survival of the kedge race. You see, the kedge cannot breed like the races of the surface world."

The bard exaggerated a sly wink to his companions and continued, "To be sure, the kedge bring youngsters into the world by the same mechanical means as we land-walkers do, but they have a slight hitch in their process: no new kedge can be born until an elder kedge perishes. Their population is always stable. Such was the blessing of Quellious, she who created the kedge upon Norrath. In this way, these people would never over-populate the waters and require more territory, as we on the surface have overrun the lands and do battle between the races for the ownership of new territory, where more and more people might be born."

As Cadmus settled into his story, the motions of his slender limbs seemed ruled less by the nervousness of before. Instead, they swayed and darted to emphasize his tale. His comrades were hypnotized not only by the story, but the snake-charm arms as well, and for a time they forgot that one of the horrors of this tale rode a ship but a few boat-lengths away. Even Nestor forewent his habitual checks of the sails. All except Delailith, who though listening to the telling, also kept an eye on the surroundings.

Cadmus continued, "But in time, the kedge grew envious of the prosperity of land-walkers and wished they, too, might create a mightier civilization. If the kedge failed, say the wise men, then it is because they have not heeded the blessing of Quellious. The kedge experi-mented exhaustively, but eventually they succeeded in creating more of their kind—ones who lived even with-out the soul of a departed kedge available to claim the body as a new home.

"Unfortunately, it soon became clear that these new kedge perhaps possessed no soul at all. For the most part, they were barbarians, bent on plunder and destruc-tion, and they waded ashore even far inland up rivers and demolished many a land-walker settlement. These were . . . abominations."

Cadmus paused for effect, especially because he noted that the kedge no longer stood in the company of the emperor, and at his last word, to a man the sailors looked that way. Finding the emperor standing alone, some moved uneasily toward the railing and scanned the white-tipped waves.

The bard drew them back in, saying, "The true kedge themselves seek to destroy these abominations, which they call hybrids, and they have largely succeeded. Some, though, still swim the oceans. Some still seek the blood of land-walkers."

Troy was the first to glance again at the waters and Cadmus concluded, "And some—well, it is said that some can be trusted." The bard trailed off unsteadily, the spell of the story broken by this unfavorable ending.

Troy squealed, "By the blood of Innoruuk, what's the point of that? I'm sure some dark elves can be trusted as well."

Cadmus looked nervous again and defended, "Well, I'm not a true bard yet! I just knew this story about the kedge, and thought it might relate in some way."

Nestor rubbed his mouth with his mitt of a left hand. Staring into a space above the men's heads, from whence he evidently snatched a thought, he said, "Maybe the point is that the Teir'Dal are *all* abominations in the same manner as these *few* kedge."

Troy was unconvinced. "How do you figure that?"

Cadmus jumped in, taking the lifeline offered by the large sailor, "Yes, yes, that's it."

Troy's frown remained, but he turned now to Cadmus for explanation.

The bard said, "Your ill-advised oath holds the answer, Troy."

Troy rubbed his fingers through his long blond hair and massaged his scalp for a moment, in an attempt to knead forth the answer.

Delailith provided it. "Innoruuk."

The young man's eyes remained glazed, but Cadmus said, "Just as the God of Hate crafted the Teir'Dal from the Koada'Dal, so, too, were the abominations created from kedge."

Troy grunted. "Just makes them all bad, doesn't it?"

Cadmus said, "Well, you said the kedge were worse—"

"Oh, whatever," said Troy. "Abomination . . . dark elf . . . whatever."

Nestor stepped close to Troy and slung an arm around the more handsome man's shoulder, his big fingers tugging at the undone blue ribbon on Troy's vest. The big man said, "I think the point is that kedge try to atone for their errors, while the Teir'Dal revel in theirs."

Troy wilted under the pressure of Nestor's arm and the argument, but only for a moment. With new vigor he said, "Then why was the emperor inviting the dark elves into the Combine? That's really what caused all this trouble, isn't it? It's why we're running for our lives, or at least running for the emperor's life?"

Nestor remained at Troy's side and said, "Whoa, whoa, friend. Seru is our enemy, not anyone or anything else, at least right now. He's the one who did this. Just because the emperor invited the Teir'Dal to attend the Summit does not mean they were to be included. And even if they *were* invited to join the Combine, then I don't know about you, but I trust the judgment of guys like *that* more than I do blowhards like us."

With the arm that was not embracing and supposedly calming Troy, Nestor gestured toward the boat where Aataltaal still stood alone. All the men fell silent at the thought, for the figure did seem weighed with responsibilities and wisdom that none of them, even clear-eyed Delailith, could comprehend, let alone match. The wind lashed the faux-emperor's cloak and framed his bowed head with whipping hair.

Even the least poetic among them felt the loss of the scene: the emperor gazing back at departed shores and into the face of his enemies. Cadmus, of course, was inspired most of all and his gentle voice sang:

> *"Look away, O king,*
> *Look away to the east.*
> *Look ahead, O king,*
> *For you sail toward the beast.*
> *Catch the wind, O king,*
> *Your enemy draws near.*
> *Catch the wind, O king,*
> *On the trail of elven tear."*

Nestor let go of Troy and clapped Cadmus on the back. "By the gods, you'll be a true bard before we make shore, little man!"

Cadmus flushed, but when everyone else joined in, the laughter became infectious, and Cadmus joined them, too. Only ever-stoic Delailith resisted the merriment, and so only she noticed when Aataltaal turned to regard the sailors. He nodded at Delailith and smiled in recognition . . . and something more, too, then stepped back within the confines of the flagship's cabins.

Then Delailith laughed as well, for in the emperor's smile she thought she saw a plan. Perhaps the presence of a kedge abomination would incite General Seru to a careless rage. Or to wariness, for fear a kedge army was poised beneath the waters, a fear that would keep Seru's sailors on edge even if the general himself overlooked it. The fog of war created by those clashing emotions would surely work to the advantage of these remnants of the Combine Empire.

AFTER A LONG, SLEEPLESS NIGHT SPENT COGI-
tating on the mysteries revealed by the last sights of the
razor-wing raven, Aataltaal had embraced the morning
wind. For the space of a split-second, the bracing air
whisked his worries away, and if he gained that much reprieve every nonce, then Aataltaal felt rewarded.

As usual, the respite was short-lived, lasting only for
the instant Aataltaal's eyes remained closed. Not one to
live his life blindly, the high elf could not stand for them
to be long shut, so when he opened them and saw again
the Ocean of Tears streaming behind him, he recalled a
morning centuries ago when he stood much as now.

This ocean—the Ocean of Tears—was fancifully said
to be formed from the tears of the elves who fled, those
long years ago. That flight led to the division of the elven race into the Feir'Dal and the Koada'Dal and the
rise of new elven nations. The result? A generally peace-
ful interior region on the continent of Faydwer, where
the Combine Empire could take root and become a
truly global construct. Aataltaal wondered how many
more empires he would see fall in his lifetime. Did his
flight westward mean Tunaria would be the home of the
next great empire? The Combine Empire was birthed
there, but it bore its juiciest fruit in Faydwer.

Aataltaal shook the ghosts from his thoughts. Yes, a
legion of ghosts counseled his every action, but even for
plans measured in centuries, the details of each moment
mattered the most. Aataltaal took this for granted now
and was still seduced into thinking it was self-evident,
but prolonged periods dwelling among the shorter-lived
races reminded him that this truth remained a mystery to
most. Humans were always in such a hurry, furiously
burning brightly for the entirety of their short lives, so

that they seldom paid close enough attention to the moment. Even the long-lived races—elves and dwarves—stubbornly resisted admitting this truth. They believed that the sweep of the years would carry them inexorably to the end they desired and that the "little steps" between the "here" and the "there" would resolve themselves, just as dripping water eventually cuts through stone. These ancient brothers of his overlooked the need to daily haul the water.

Aataltaal had decided centuries ago to burn as bright as a man for as long as an elf. Excellence in categories beyond count was his compensation—and that now included necromancy. The failure of most elves to do the same explained why in a short lifetime a human could learn to master the sword equally as well as a millennia-old elven swordsman.

This meant a nearly daily accounting of all the pieces upon which Aataltaal might someday draw. It meant taking nothing for granted and packing a human's passion for achievement into each of the many lives Aataltaal lived, rather than stretching it thinly over the course of one bored existence.

And it meant that the pieces so painstakingly put into play long ago in the Teir'Dal fortress at Weille had finally become valuable again. On the heels of the crushing defeat inflicted upon him in the tunnels now commanded by the lich king, Aataltaal had taken stock of his sparse advantages and preserved them for play even without the benefit of the grandiose plan he now pursued.

The next grandiose plan. Aataltaal's enemies had defeated one effort in the darkness below Weille, but they did not realize how many of those pieces were still in play. In fact, he did not even know for certain if they realized that *he* was still in play. Until recently, he did not know if *she* was. But Opal Darkbriar's location was difficult to guess. She had the incredible advantage of working from the shadows. Keeping secrets cloaked in darkness and choking all investigations into them had always been her modus operandi, and there was no likelihood she would reveal herself in the process.

"You're thinking about her, aren't you?" said Menthes as he stood in the doorway between the hold and the deck of the ship.

Aataltaal grinned despite himself and said, "Did the kedge experiments make you a mind reader as well?"

Menthes rasped what the high elf took to be a chuckle, but the fish-man's gills were too dried out to make his usually sucking chortle.

"But yes, I was." The Koada'Dal glanced at the trailing ships.

Menthes stepped fully into the morning light. The sun was now a complete circle above the surface of the ocean and in its strong, morning light, Menthes glittered like a man-sized, iridescent gem.

The kedge said, "I wonder more whether she knows where you are."

Aataltaal said, "I have to assume that she does, and I have to count on her moving against me when I am at my absolute weakest."

"Like now?"

But Aataltaal went on as if he did not hear the question. "The trick will be to force her hand. To give her a seeming opportunity to defeat me when in fact I am not as weak as she imagines."

Then turning to face his friend, Aataltaal said, "But no, because though this mission is important, it's just a ruse that can be given up at any time, even if it means the lives of these humans. I have no ultimate stake in the charade as emperor, though I take it seriously, of course."

Menthes grunted. "I think you protest too much.

If this mission matters so little, then why did you not sleep last night? I have never known you to undertake anything lightly, especially when lives are at stake, and especially when those lives amount to the destiny of an entire race."

Menthes stepped near the edge of the deck, into the spray of the water, and regarded the human. "You never take half-measures, and your ambitions are never half-sized are they, Aat——?"

With a quick, two-fingered motion, Aataltaal interrupted the kedge. Menthes stood perplexed for a split-second and then imperceptibly nodded. He said, "Emperor."

The high elf smiled slightly.

"Besides, even your farewells have strategic purposes."

"Noticed that, did you?"

Menthes wiped the sea spray along the length of his arms, moistening his skin. "I think my skin has bounced enough sunlight back at Seru's ships that his navigators might wonder if Sol's eye turned green this past night."

Aataltaal chuckled wryly. "Did you leave the bird?" he asked, nodding at Menthes' bag.

"Yes, consider it a gift," he answered with a shudder. "So, anyway, the pirate's name is Danaan. He's only about a score strong, so I don't think he'd pose a problem regardless, but he's one of the many who owe me their lives." Something silicon-white flashed between Menthes' fingers, and he handed the coin-sized sand dollar to Aataltaal. It was polished smooth on the bottom, while the top was marked with a glyph.

Menthes shrugged and said, "I don't know. Some secret cutthroat word for 'friend,' I think."

Aataltaal chuckled. "You are a wonder, Menthes. Thank you for keeping an eye on this small port."

"It's no matter. By owing me a life-debt, Danaan in turn owes you."

Menthes stepped close to Aataltaal as if to hug him, but he thought better of it. Instead he lowered to a knee and bowed his head.

"That had best have been only for the show, Menthes."

"Mostly." Then, stepping to the deckrail, the kedge looked back. "And there are only eight boats now."

Aataltaal nodded and said, "You are in fine form this morning. No wonder I can rely on you."

Menthes frowned. "I thought you hadn't noticed."

"No, I just did not want to stay your departure any longer. You have other business, I know."

Pointing to the polished seashell, Menthes said, "Don't lose that." Then he launched himself off the railing, tucked his body, and slipped without trace into the churning waters behind the *Wolf of Faydark*.

Aataltaal pushed the sand dollar into a pouch and counted Seru's vessels: only eight, not that he had doubted Menthes' tally. In truth, he had *not* noticed this fact; but it was also true that he did not want to delay the kedge, and so had made little of the revelation. Aataltaal knew that many sailors were watching and that they would be concerned about the presence of a kedge. It was best that Menthes be on his way.

In any event, something else to the east riveted Aataltaal, probably the reason he'd not noted the number of ships. Well in front of Seru's armada, black dots sprinkled the sky. At the moment, they resembled little more than pepper spice blown into the air, but already the specks grew more distinct. Flocks of razor-wing ravens were incoming, and they established the timetable for Seru's attack.

11

THE SPELLS OF AATALTAAL

"**O**F COURSE I SEE THEM," NESTOR SAID.

"It's like midnight at noon!" Troy cried.

Nestor ignored the jabbering man and continued his work aboard the *Condor*. The winds were gusting, so the sails had to be constantly adjusted both to maintain speed and to keep the various vessels of the armada in close contact. If one stalled now, then it would be like an old deer caught out from the herd. Seru's boats would likely pounce upon it before the Combine armada could turn into the wind and recover it.

The eight pursuing vessels and the vast, dark maelstrom of ravens that hung over and wheeled about the boats were that close.

Troy continued to sputter indecipherable nonsense. Finally irritated with the display of cowardice, Nestor said, "I've watched them gather for the past two hours while you did what? Slept off your late breakfast?"

"I was sick," Troy protested. "Must we eat fish for every meal?"

"We *are* at sea, Troy."

The two men were not alone on deck, and they

acted out a scene similar to that between many others aboard the armada. Even children, though largely confined belowdecks where they were less apt to cause mischief, were now shepherded on deck in small groups chaperoned by their parents to see the awesome sight of a sky black with hundreds—perhaps thousands—of birds. This mind-boggling display left many men and women needing reassurance.

Fortunately, others as unruffled as Nestor could lend that comfort. The big man had watched through the past hours as dots of black in the morning sky grew larger—and as Seru's vessels grew closer as well. About an hour ago, the swirling morass of black could be distinguished as an enormous flock, and within the past few moments the flock noticeably disengaged itself from Seru's boats, which also closed in upon the Combine fleet.

The pursuing fleet surged forward, as even the land-lubbers could see.

Troy said, "They're going faster now, aren't they? A lot faster than us."

Nestor attempted to play it off as nothing and went about his work. "Yes," he said.

And indeed, Troy fell silent for a moment. The sweep of the flock was hypnotic, even beautiful, and that, even more than Nestor's calm, soothed Troy. But female beauty was the only kind that truly dazzled Troy for long. He swore, "By Xegony, they're creepy."

Nestor hissed, "Don't call upon the Mistress of Air unless you really need her. She's capricious, Troy, and if she takes notice of us mortals at all, she's as liable to send terrible winds that wreck our fleets as she is to punish those who created such monstrous creatures as those ravens."

"Rashalla."

"Aye, the raven lady."

"How long until they catch us?"

"Only an hour if they stay their speed."

Troy whistled. "I better go get some lunch then, as it might be some time before dinner."

Nestor laughed at his friend. Troy's pluck survived the ominous ravens, and the whalelike sailor hoped all the others doubters would discard their worry as easily.

As Troy wandered away, Nestor called to him, "Take that group of children with you. They've seen enough."

"I'm a dad now?"

Nestor grinned a toothy smile, "Ha! You're probably a father twenty times over! But no, just take their mind off things . . . for an hour, anyway." He paused, thinking, and then suggested, "Tell them the story of how you learned where that newlywed hid her diamond ring at night."

"What, and tell them I'm a thief?"

Nestor motioned Troy toward a group of older boys. "I think you stole more than her ring that night."

Troy laughed. He turned and walked toward the teenagers who gawked at the dizzying spectacle to the east.

Soon enough, Troy disappeared belowdecks, already the new best friend and idol of the youngsters, and Nestor heard the cry from the flagship's lookout, "Land ho!"

The cry echoed from a half dozen other lookouts, and Nestor again wondered why, by all the gods of Norrath, the fleet steered so near the only island this could possibly be: Dinosaur Isle. The man glanced helplessly at the stairs to the lower deck where Troy regaled his coterie with tales of courtship. Nestor wished someone could comfort *him*.

———

BACK IN HIS QUARTERS, AATALTAAL'S MEDITA-
tion slipped to light sleep, slipped to deep sleep, slipped
to dreams. Some devotees of the dark goddess Terris
Thule, the Dream Scorcher of Nightmares, suggested
that dreams revealed a person's other lives, if he'd made
different choices. When he first heard that theory, Aataltaal wondered if that meant there was another him somewhere throughout the planes of existence who dreamed
his own life.

It was not a comforting thought, because Aataltaal
could not imagine such dreams being anything but nightmares.

Much like the current visions that afflicted him.

Dark and wraithlike, a gaunt caricature of himself,
Aataltaal wandered a barren landscape lit dully as if by
shaded moonlight. Not exactly a desert, it was a land on
the verge of being beaten into submission. The noise of
his footsteps across gravel not yet turned to sand echoed
loudly. At the periphery of his vision, the elf could see
vegetation: the tall scrub grass of a prairie. There was a
stillness that implied the infinite, as if this state of things
had been under way for a long time. This made what
happened next seem sudden, even though the dream itself was perhaps only moments old. Inky black shadows
rushed from the ground like quick-growing stalks. But
they were not inanimate; they were the silhouettes of
emaciated humanoid figures, and each bore a dagger,
dripping with thick poison, in a hand that flashed hypnotically. As quickly as they appeared, they leaned in
upon Aataltaal and their slender figures melded to become a black wall that blotted out the pale light . . .

Aataltaal shook himself to consciousness. He'd not
intended to sleep, but it was just as well that he had. He
seldom required sleep, so long as he meditated for an
hour or so each day, but recent events had kept him off

balance and off schedule, and this deep slumber sharpened his mind as even his magic could not, even if it *did* open his subconscious to all manner of ill tidings from the gods.

He did not trust dreams as he did his oracular visions, but he felt something prophetic in this one. Perhaps in the dried and wasted landscape, he saw something of the fertile lands that once surrounded Takish-Hiz, before the hateful glare of Solusek Ro burnt them. And in the shades that overwhelmed him, wasn't there something of the dire shape of the Teir'Dal who dwelt not far north of the plains that surrounded the now-ancient city of Weille?

He wondered if the gods could read the thoughts of mortals. Perhaps dreams were the transmission of thoughts to the gods, and the mortal who delivered the message was merely a spectator to a translated version of his mind that he could not decipher.

He suspected the gods would read his if they could.

Sleep could accomplish some feats his magic could not, but there was a far greater host of blessings that his magic could bestow. The sighting of land that extricated him from his dream meant that the time had come to prepare.

Aataltaal opened the top drawer of the small bureau in a corner of the room. The loose contents rattled together and the high elf scanned the interior. He deftly selected a handful of items, then he turned and spread them out on the table. As he did, Aataltaal glanced near the door to reassure himself that the dead raven was still there. It was, and it glistened as if freshly dead.

Aataltaal then looked over his assembled items: a few translucent green gems, and nearly a dozen toy daggers. The gems were beautifully faceted and polished, obviously valuable, but Aataltaal casually, indelicately plucked

one from the table. Without inspecting the peridot gemstone further, he brandished his arms as if preparing to
strike a blow against an unseen opponent. The sudden,
almost violent gesture softened, though, as his arms began to wave through the space of the small room. Slowly
at first, his arms picked up speed until soon they flashed
and twisted as if the high elf were some dire spider intent upon wrapping troublesome prey. But Aataltaal
did not spin silken thread, instead he spun magic. Soon,
green strands blossomed from the peridot and these
wound around the elf's body until the thin filaments coalesced into a second skin that glowed with the same
translucent sheen as the original gem itself. Aataltaal's
"web" was in fact a protective magical barrier woven
over his entire body.

Next, Aataltaal selected three of the daggers. They
appeared to be toys, yet very lifelike ones, for their
points were needle-sharp, though the edges were dull.
With a deft and practiced motion, Aataltaal fanned the
three tiny daggers in his hand so that one lay between
each of his fingers from index to pinky. Like a presti-
digitator seeking to delight a crowd, the elf whirled his
hand with a flourish and then spread his fingers wide.
No daggers clattered to the floor or table, though, for
they'd disappeared.

Instead, two objects hovered a few paces behind and
to the side of the Koada'Dal. A longsword waved hypnotically back and forth as if wielded by an invisible man
forever seeking an *en guard*; and a thick and nondescript
shield hovered motionless beside it. Taken together with
the sword, the shield seemed to be held by the same unseen warrior.

The high elf enchanter took little notice of the animation, other than a brief appraising eye as if to gauge
the relative might of the invisible warrior. His main

concern was that the presence of the guardian would reveal his identity, or at least raise the possibility that "Katta" was indeed an imposter even if his own identity remained unknown. However, though these animations were typically beyond the complete control of those who summoned them, some could be commanded to guard another, and so perhaps Seru would believe that this was such a one. Besides, the traitor general wasn't going to turn back now. If nothing else, it would break the morale of his crews.

Content, Aataltaal returned his attention to the table, where three more gems and five more of the small daggers waited. He stepped to the bureau and plucked one more dagger from within the drawer, and these nine items he then dropped into a coin purse at his waist.

Aataltaal heard the echoing footfalls of the scores of people on the boat as they took their positions. The ceiling, floor, and walls of this small cabin all reverberated with the motion. Despite the urgency communicated by the movement, Aataltaal did not hurry. He knew there was plenty of time. Seru had failed to overtake his armada prior to sighting the island, and while Aataltaal's plan might yet fail, he would achieve the island and at least have an opportunity to succeed.

Of course, Seru had no reason to try to stop "Katta" before the Combine fleet rounded Dinosaur Isle. Hundreds of leagues of the Ocean of Tears still lay between this island and the ancient port city of Weille. Seru could play cat and mouse for days, and he probably would.

The general's propensity for breaking the morale of his foes before he broke the foes themselves was well known. Much lauded when he had been an ally, this characteristic lately seemed to reflect a very dark streak in the man's character. Aataltaal assumed that was what he attempted now, although he realized that Seru might simply be waiting for Rashalla's flock to assemble in order to launch his attack.

It didn't matter; his own plan was in motion, and fate would let him play the hand. Quickly, Aataltaal made the remainder of his preparations. The *rune* spell created partly with the peridot would make him nearly invulnerable for a time, but he also needed to erect his personal defensive spell, *shield of the magi*. It was an exhausting spell to cast, but unlike the *rune* spell, it persisted—he would not need to cast it again until the coming battle concluded. Nor did the spell require any outside agent to augment the magic, though Aataltaal wished it could be the other way around, and that the shorter-term spell could go without the fortifying component. It was counterintuitive, but then that was the logic of magic and why not everyone could master it.

Aataltaal centered his thoughts in the pit of his stomach. His body followed his mind and turned inward as well, concentrating its vital force in the core of his being. Soon, he felt fat with mana—there was no other way to describe it. The sensation lasted a fraction of a second, for as soon as the mana gathered, it exploded, radiating from his center and racing to the tips of his extremities, from which burst strobe-fast flares that pulsed a dozen beats before subsiding.

As a spellcaster, Aataltaal could ill-afford the encumbrance of armor, and so, like other mages, he relied on the spell in place of armor. It had the fortunate side effect of protecting him somewhat from magic as well.

Next, Aataltaal needed to help his body recover the mana he had expended for these spells and more that would come. While difficult to define to those who could not sense and manipulate it, mana *was* quantifiable—at least, in the sense that it was a store that could be depleted. Aataltaal's ability to cast magic was finite over any period of time. Even the smallest, simplest spell, if cast a thousand times, would leave him incapable of further magic until rest, sleep, or—best of all—meditation replenished his energy.

Fortunately, a spell known to only a few could speed this process. Much sought by those without the knowledge to cast it, as well as those whose method of magic would never allow them the ability to manage it, the spell was a staple of Aataltaal's arsenal. Like the *rune* spell, its effect would pass sooner than many others, but the degree to which it augmented his recovery was worth the mana expended for the spell itself.

He cast it now. Hands high beside his ears and palms inward, Aataltaal spoke the appropriate enchantments. Beads of light like morning dew appeared on his hands. Indeed, the light seemed to have the attractive properties of water, for as the beads grew and were proximate with one another, they promptly bonded into a larger whole. This process steadily continued until orbs of golden light surrounded both his hands, which Aataltaal then clenched into fists. With that motion the orbs grew until both encompassed a portion of his head when, like the smaller beads, they, too, combined to form a sphere of light that encased his skull.

The light then shattered like glass and disappeared. A different light shone from Aataltaal's eye then, for those windows to his soul stretched deeper and attuned him to the flow of energy that bound the planet itself. Tapped into that flow, the elf felt his magic returning.

Finally, he cast a spell to enhance his physical awareness in the same way the prior one augmented his spirit. It boosted both the speed and quality of his thought. That made him a better spellcaster, for there was a degree of perfection in the use of mana, and in general, more clever individuals could use their powers for longer. No one knew whether this was a matter of using the same amount of mana more effectively or a simple correlation between intellect and magical energy.

For this spell, Aataltaal raised his hands as before, but the effect was more dramatic. Instead of growing orbs of energy that enhanced him, now livewire rifts of lightning crackled first from fingertip to fingertip on the same hand, and then these bolts fired across the distance from left hand to right and back again, seemingly passing each time through the elf's very head. No evidence of harm appeared, though, and Aataltaal did not flinch. In a few seconds, the crackling subsided, and Aataltaal's mind, already working at an unbelievably high level, now pursued a hundred tangents at once instead of merely scores.

The high elf sighed. He seldom felt overwhelmed, but so much was in progress. His ancient plans were in a rare period of flux, and they demanded his attention, which he could give once he arrived at Weille, but he felt a growing responsibility for these humans as well. He didn't doubt the abilities of that race, for he'd witnessed them firsthand—after all it was a human who pursued him and a human whom he impersonated, so clearly the race had insinuated itself in the primary events of Norrath—but they seemed to need someone to take charge.

Or perhaps that's just the sense he got because, whenever he spoke to them, he looked like their dying human emperor, Katta. But he thought not, for even in private the humans were attentive and responsive.

For his own part, he'd spent so many years as a loner—or at least alone in his thoughts and plans, even when part of a community seemed to suit and adopt him—that he checked his own perceptions to rule out wishful thinking. The centuries wore at him, and at times had worn him out so that he had to disappear completely to refresh himself. That was helpful in the long run, for even his brethren elves did not comprehend his true age, but there had never truly been a choice in the matter.

His greatest fear was that the humans would become like pets to him. Just as a human's dog would never live long or richly enough to absorb and then clarify its experiences into the kind of wisdom a human could achieve, so was a human's life to Aataltaal's. The Koada'Dal felt this gulf of acumen made him seem inhuman to these people, but he remained simply inhuman. He decided that astuteness was the hallmark of the human race and was why his great fear would go unrealized. Humans learned more than mere tricks, of course, but they also seemed to grasp things beyond their actual experience. How else to explain, for instance, the great number of human monks, and the handful of such enlightened individuals of all the other races, elves included? True, elven wisdom found its best home in the grove, in those who became druids, but still, the difference was amazingly absolute.

Aataltaal nearly laughed aloud at the folly of his daydreaming. The spells that sharpened the acuity of his mind seemed sometimes to displace common sense. If his centuries-old mind had any flaws, he realized, one was that it sometimes blotted out the ordinary in search of mysteries buried in the sediment of memory. Simple deduction told him what was happening on deck, where the clatter of feet had stilled. In a final instant of reflection, Aataltaal imagined he felt the humans' collective breath still as well.

Likely, they had spotted an allizewsaur.

Suddenly, Aataltaal had a thought regarding his plan. Perhaps he'd chosen the wrong target? He returned to the bureau and opened the bottom drawer. It was filled with airtight bottles. Quickly fingering over a few, he alighted on a larger one and withdrew it. He twisted the lid and extracted several pieces of flimsy black leather. He peeled apart the bat wings. They looked as unsullied as if from a freshly slain animal. He rolled one a bit and replaced it in the bottle, which he in turn returned to the drawer. He tucked the other three membranes into another waist-pouch.

Quickly, he scooped up the corpse of the razor-wing raven and hurried into the hall. Three men stood outside patiently awaiting him. Two were slightly startled, and the third's face went as white as a fresh canvas sail when Aataltaal's hovering guardian floated out of the room behind him. The Koada'Dal had virtually no control over the construct beyond the simple rules instilled in it by the magic that created it, but to set the men at ease, he gestured toward the floating sword and shield, and it—they—stopped. The sword and shield still wavered, but they pivoted around a constant central spot. The animated guardian had achieved the proximity to Aataltaal that it required, so it would have stopped anyway; but the high elf found that this illusion of his control set others at ease.

It worked, although one of the two less worried men acted as if Aataltaal had forgotten something else. He said, "M'lord?" It sounded more like a reminder than a question.

Aataltaal smiled and said, "Of course." One more spell. The high elf closed his eyes and summoned a mental image of his friend. Then he began to raise his right hand, but as the limp corpse of a bird drooped from that hand, Aataltaal thought better of it and raised his left. This he held over his head and pantomimed the act of sprinkling dust on his head.

As the imaginary dust settled on his body, Aataltaal transformed from head to toe into the semblance of Emperor Katta.

The third man, the ship's cook, lit up with a stupid grin as he watched. It made him look even more out of place, for the other two men wore officer's uniforms and did not appear surprised in the slightest. The cook couldn't help but mutter, "Amazing. I've never seen anything so amazing."

Aataltaal looked at him and said, "Thank you, Crystos. You require . . . ?"

Crystos started, as if awaking, and offered Aataltaal a plate of food: two pieces of still-aromatic bread, a length of dried meat, and a small handful of assorted dried fruits. Aataltaal scooped up all of these and turned to his officers.

Then, after Crystos had taken a few paces away, Aataltaal turned around and said, "Also, some fish corpses, please, Crystos."

A glimpse of confusion dashed across the cook's face and Crystos glanced at the dead bird Aataltaal held, but he said, "Of course, m'lord."

Then to the officers, Aataltaal asked, "We're prepared?"

The two men exchanged glances, but both nodded.

The disguised elf cocked his head slightly and looked at them appraisingly.

They exchanged glances again, but Avers, the man who'd given the illusion reminder, said, "M'lord, it's enormous."

"The allizewsaur?"

"Yes, m'lord."

The other officer added, "M'lord, are we not inviting disaster by sailing so close?"

Aataltaal looked at them squarely. "You believe we should turn and fight?"

Simultaneously, "No, m'lord."

"That we can outrun Seru?"

They gave the same response.

Aataltaal said, "Very well then, let's proceed."

As the faux-emperor strode toward the stairs to the deck—his vigilant, animated guard trailing a few paces behind—he said over his shoulder to them, "How big? It's been centuries since I last saw him."

THE BREEZE REMAINED STRONG, BUT ANTICIPA-tion hung in the air, and with prebattle tension to heighten awareness, time seemed to move in the slow motion of a deathstroke.

Aboard the *Condor*, preparations were complete. As soon as Dinosaur Isle came into sight, Captain Elderath assembled the sailors and heads of families. This island was the initial destination, he said. The "emperor's" strategy might seem dangerous, but the captains of all the vessels supported this course of action. Yes, it had been the plan ever since departure, but only if they were pursued by an obviously superior force.

The groans and mutters at that point made it painfully clear the captain had chosen his words poorly.

Nestor told Troy, "It's because he's speaking to civilians. He's trying to explain gently, but he's really just explaining too much."

A "larger" force, the captain corrected.

Except that's when the truly larger force loomed high upon the horizon: a beast. An allizewsaur.

Troy—and many others, though a variety of gods were chosen—said, "Marr preserve us."

The allizewsaur stood atop the highest rise on an island now fully bared to the approaching armada. It appeared to be a smallish island, for instead of continuing to reveal itself as the Combine fleet approached—its inlets or jutting peninsulas—it simply rounded out of sight. The island was both exaggerated and diminished by the size of the immense bipedal lizard that surmounted it.

The creature known as the allizewsaur was mottled green and resembled a colossal iguana. Twin ridges of thick plates ran the length of its back and continued to the tip of its tail. The trees on the hillock seemed large and fully formed, yet their spiny, leafless tops did not reach the monster's belly.

And though the wind blew at their backs and could not possibly carry the scent of a huge beast to them, the people aboard the *Condor* imagined they smelled the pungent odor of the great reptile. From atop its isle, the allizewsaur seemed to them a god of the Ocean of Tears, and they fools for nearing its throne.

The captain attempted to reestablish order, but the din drowned out any complex communication. So Eldrath simply shouted, "To your posts, sailors. Others, belowdecks. Now!"

Half of the crowd, the sailors, immediately heeded the order. Their abrupt movement left the passengers—the fathers and mothers and elder siblings of youngsters huddled below—suddenly exposed. The sense of vulnerability silenced them as well, and though a few men thought to remain behind and question Captain Eldrath further—he rebuffed these attempts by turning his back to the crowd and speaking with a lieutenant—the crowd thinned and soon dispersed completely.

As Nestor and Troy moved away, Cadmus joined

them. The bard said, "They say the beast is in reality a god."

Troy groaned. "Fabulous. That's *just* what I wanted to hear, Cadmus!"

Nestor said, "Come now. Settle down. You know that kind of talk is fanciful nonsense."

"Nonsense? Look at that thing."

They couldn't stop themselves. All three men turned their heads to gaze at the awesome creature. Despite the throng of boats that approached it, the allizewsaur took little notice. As they watched, it turned and wandered down the far side, though it took long moments before its enormous bulk was completely obscured by the terrain.

Nestor groaned. Then to Cadmus he said, "Let's hear it, bard."

Cadmus drew himself up and recited, "An age ago a race of serpent people called the shissar ruled much of Norrath. Though little known these days, the shissar were great wizards, warriors, and engineers; and thousands of beings from all other races served as their slaves."

The bard continued rattling off the information as if he saw it written in front of him.

"When the warlord, Rallos Zek, sought to conquer the Planes of Power in the War of the Gods, the shissar sided with Rallos Zek, for in their hubris they thought themselves equal enough to the gods to battle among them. Masters of instantaneous transportation, the shissar did manage to create entry to some of the planes, though it mattered little. The warlord was defeated and the races he fathered—the giants, ogres, and trolls among them— were cursed with the stupidity that confounds them even to this day."

Troy quipped, "Maybe old Zek cursed Seru as well."

Cadmus ignored the interruption and continued, "The shissar, too, were cursed, their intellect crushed, and their elegant form reduced to that of the barbaric lizard men who today wander the swamps and bogs of Norrath.

"Among the shissar was a chosen of Cazic-Thule, the god to whom the shissar truly paid homage. This one was called Allize Ssrateh, and he was known as the Herald of Fear for his devotion to the god of fear. The curse of the gods expunged the herald's mind, but the intervention of Cazic-Thule caused Allize Ssrateh's form to achieve gigantic proportions. He became the allizewsaur.

"But the gods had not finished. In his new form, the Herald of Fear posed great danger, so the gods flung the allizewsaur into the Ocean of Tears, where it could not disturb the races of Norrath. However, it's said that the mind of Allize Ssrateh is in truth undiminished and with his ancient knowledge and vast strength, he has done what the shissar dared to imagine: become a god."

Troy's mouth agape, he stared dumfounded at Cadmus. After a silence that was awkward only for Troy and only because he was so obviously nonplussed by this information, the man managed, "By the gods, how do you learn that? That's amazing, Cadmus."

Cadmus beamed. "Thank you!"

"And frightening as the grave," said Nestor. The big man looked pale; he seemed unhealthy for the first time since returning to sea. He stepped over to a large barrel of water and splashed some on his face.

Troy and Cadmus took no notice of his distress. Any of Troy's concerns had washed away in the rousing tale, and the young man focused more on the adventure than the danger. Meanwhile, the bard basked in the battery of compliments Troy bestowed and eagerly gave himself up to Troy's enthusiasm. Deep in conversation, they stepped away from Nestor to the ship's railing, where they could best view the island and watch for another glimpse of the allizewsaur.

Fortunately, sharp-eyed Delailith was both unmoved by the story and unconcerned with Nestor's comfort. As always, the woman patiently observed the events around her and so she alone realized the ship was under attack. She reached cross-armed in front of her body and drew two long daggers. They slipped silently from sheaths kept relentlessly well-oiled and clean despite the sea air and the salt water.

Armed with a pair of daggers, Delailith casually flipped the one in her left hand a half-turn so that she held it by the tip, while her right hand still held firm to the pommel of the other weapon.

As she stepped toward Troy and Nestor, Troy shook his head in disbelief at the bard and said, "So they all just changed into lizard men?"

There, she saw it. The slight scratching along the hull of the ship led her to the correct spot. Two talons of a long-fingered hand slid over the railing and dug into the wood to support whatever beast carefully stalked the two men.

The wrinkled flesh of the hand was algae-blue, and a delicate webbing stretched between the two visible digits.

12

THE GOD OF THE ISLE

AATALTAAL AGAIN COUNTED THE TRAITOR'S boats. He did not draw a breath of fresh air before he counted the eight vessels.

"Where in the name of the Three is that ninth ship?" he wondered aloud.

Avers, the more obsequious of the lieutenants, explained, "Our lookouts reported last night that its mast broke in the gusting winds and it fell behind the other eight. It's not been seen since."

The other lieutenant, Orleax, a former paladin who still bore himself with much of the honor and dignity of that breed, said, "A rotten fate to be stranded at sea, even if they are fools who follow Seru."

Aataltaal nodded. "Agreed, but why didn't one of the other vessels—or several of them—slow to take those sailors aboard?"

Avers said, "M'lord, they would have fallen well behind us."

Orleax added, "Perhaps they feared we would turn to fight if the odds were more even, in the event some boats continued and others slowed."

The disguised Koada'Dal shook his head. "Then the

entire fleet could have stopped. They are much faster than we are."

Both lieutenants remained silent. Avers seemed unconcerned, though Orleax, like Aataltaal, looked worried and unconvinced.

Aataltaal *knew* something was amiss. How did Seru know in advance that one of the ships would be fouled and only eight would remain to engage the Combine fleet? Perhaps the same divination that allowed him knowledge of the fate of the raven Aataltaal employed in his scrying?

The elf let the matter go. He should rely on these men more by revealing more of his thoughts, but there were too many details, and he remained uncertain what information would be useful to the humans. For his part, Avers had little use except in battle, where his bravado inspired the men. It was for battle that Aataltaal wished to preserve his concentration. Orleax was an astute human, but Aataltaal doubted the man could conclude anything not already considered. Arrogance could be a weakness, this much he recognized, but Aataltaal believed his decision pragmatic, rather than egotistical.

He looked across the foam-flecked blue waters of the Ocean of Tears at the stretch of verdant island, and a touch wistfully said, "Let's see this allizewsaur." He did not add the "again."

Avers eagerly provided some details. He said, "We spotted it from a distance, shortly after the island itself was detected."

Aataltaal nodded in silent acknowledgment. He walked from the stern of the *Wolf of Faydark* to the prow and made no further comments. The two lieutenants and his invisible armed guardian trailed in a bunch close behind.

That didn't slow Avers' tongue though. He continued, "We knew immediately it was a truly enormous beast. To see it from so far away . . ."

Avers trailed off in an effort to invite comments, but he was not rewarded. Undaunted, he added, "But it disappeared behind the island's central plateau and has stayed out of sight for some time."

Aataltaal said, "Well, don't look now."

Avers had been glancing alternately at the deck and at Aataltaal while they walked and he talked. When he looked up, he stopped in his tracks. The allizewsaur again stood atop the great rise in the middle of Dinosaur Isle. Sunlight scintillated across its scaly hide, and for an instant the beast turned toward the fast-approaching armada and seemed to observe them.

Avers gasped.

"And imagine," said Aataltaal. "That's the female. She's about the size of the male when I saw him last. Hopefully, he's grown up a bit more as well. Within the hour, he's going to need every ounce."

Avers' jaw remained dropped for an instant longer, but he recovered his composure when the "emperor" turned to him. Before Aataltaal spoke another word, Avers nodded to him and said in a steady voice, "I will make certain the team is assembled." Avers bustled away, but Aataltaal put a hand up, and Avers stopped. "I'm sorry," the lieutenant said, and stepped back to the "emperor."

"No, you are right, it's time for the team, but I want only three of them, not all ten. The fleetest three."

Puzzled, Avers involuntarily looked sideways at the water that surrounded them. "Fleetest?"

Aataltaal nodded; and to his credit the lieutenant questioned no further. Avers hurried away. Then to Orleax, the "emperor" said, "Prepare to make the maneuver around the island. But I want the formation of the armada adjusted slightly. I'm sorry for the late notice, but I fear our earlier plans have been compromised."

"Spies? Surely not, m'lord."

"Indeed not. I believe the enemy has gained intelligence through magic—through the scrying of the future, to be precise—and we can only hope to combat that brand of knowledge by making last-minute adjustments that perhaps the magic did not predict.

"In any event, I want this flagship in the center of the formation, not at the front." Aataltaal sighed and looked up into space for a moment. Orleax waited patiently. A moment later, Aataltaal said, "I cannot tell you why, lieutenant, so call it a hunch. We're in for a surprise—a boat that will appear out of nowhere." The "emperor" paused for moment, but Orleax remained attentive. He only nodded slightly to fill the brief silence.

Aataltaal continued, "It makes the most sense that this invisible ship will position itself to target this flagship, so I want a close-packed formation that will not allow it to sail unseen to our side.

"The most forward vessel should be one without families aboard. I leave the other details to you."

Orleax pondered for a moment, but he seemed unmoved by the strange tidings. "With your leave I will make those changes to our alignment. And may I inform the crews to expect to see a great deal of magic?"

Aataltaal said, "They will, so you may."

When Orleax stepped away, Aataltaal immediately turned to Crystos, the lanky ship's cook who had come to stand silently a half dozen paces away. A sailor stood near him to make certain he did not approach Aataltaal without the "emperor's" permission.

"Come, Crystos."

The cook smiled and picked up a basket at his feet. Even in the salt air, the odor of fish was unmistakable. Crystos said, "M'lord, you requested corpses, so I brought the least fresh of the fish from our stores. If you require otherwise . . ."

Aataltaal shook his head. "This will be fine, Crystos. Now, see to securing the kitchen. The ship will be maneuvering hard in less than an hour."

Crystos smiled. "Just keep us above the water, my lord." He knelt and set the basket before Aataltaal, though he kept a wary eye on the sword and shield that hovered nearby.

Aataltaal smiled back. He nodded slightly as in answer to an internal question and said, "Let's see if this magic still works, shall we?"

"What do you mean, my lord?" Crystos asked.

Aataltaal stooped and selected a random fish from the basket. He grasped it roughly with two hands and wrenched at the flesh. He did not tear the skin, but nevertheless, when he was done, his hands were covered with fish scales. He dropped the fish and it fell into the basket.

Crystos was plainly perplexed, and this expression turned more to surprise when Aataltaal began to incant an enchantment. He made slight swimming motions with his hands as strange words tumbled from his lips. After a few seconds, Aataltaal's scale-covered hands glowed mother-of-pearl. After another phrase, the sheen became even more translucent and his hands almost shone blue.

"Don't be afraid," he told the cook when the incantation ended. Aataltaal stepped toward Crystos and extended his hands toward the man's weathered face. Crystos flinched just a little, but when he looked into Aataltaal's calm eyes he, too, was calmed.

The "emperor" placed his hands on opposite sides of Crystos' neck, and immediately the bluish aura expanded to encompass that flesh. Crystos shivered, but did not seem pained.

When the glowing light faded an instant later, Aataltaal withdrew a step and inspected his work. "It seems a success."

Crystos stood stiffly, awaiting something momentous, but he was startled only after he sighed in relief. He threw his hands to his neck and felt. The realization came instantaneously, for the man had handled similar organs for two decades. "Gills!" he exclaimed. He removed his hands, and his flesh folded back together so that the new gills were barely visible as a thin line on his skin.

Aataltaal said, "Just in case it gets wet down there."

Crystos laughed. The sound whooshed in and out both his mouth and the new gills. The sucking sound of that laughter reminded Aataltaal of Menthes, but the cook had no such fond memory and the sound alarmed him. He stopped suddenly, but a last bubble of air popped from one gill, like a final, uncontrollable giggle. That caused him to laugh again.

"I knew you would wear them well, Crystos."

"They really work?"

"Absolutely."

Aataltaal looked past Crystos, over the man's shoulder. Avers approached with two men and a woman.

"Now, off you go, sailor."

Crystos gently touched his throat again, rolled his eyes with astonishment, and then bowed to Aataltaal before he departed.

Aataltaal looked again at the approaching trio of recruits, then back at his hands. A number of fish scales still covered his rough, human hands. Of course, the scales were not the commodity he should preserve. His mana reserves—that was the most valuable resource right now, the potential difference between not only buying Emperor Katta the time he required, but also reaching land safely with these boatloads of humans. Faydwer was for the older races now; it was up to Aataltaal to get the humans to the continent that could be their own. So why had he spent precious mana on a spell for the ship's cook?

Initially he cursed himself for the exuberance that led to his oversight, but then he bit his tongue. Could it be he liked the man? Aataltaal nodded grudgingly to himself. That was it, of course. He'd come to care about many of these people. Even Avers.

Before the lieutenant could speak, Aataltaal began his spell again. Soon, his hands glowed blue like the crystal waters of the lakes within the elven capitol of Felwithe, and he touched them to his own neck. He felt his flesh part like the seam between pieces of silk. Cool air brushed his insides in a strange but, for him, not unfamiliar way.

He looked at his hands. All of the scales were consumed.

Then he raised his eyes to Avers and the assembled volunteers. Avers looked slightly disgusted, the shorter, balding man and the blond woman seemed worried that Aataltaal was injured, while the last fellow, tall and grim-faced, did not look at much of anything. His gaze was straight ahead and steady on the horizon.

Aataltaal stooped for another fish, and as he massaged the carcass, he spoke to the humans. He said, "The first spell is purely for safety. Hopefully, you won't even get wet."

Then he cast the spell three times in succession. Once the three had the power to breathe underwater, Aataltaal withdrew the bat wings from his pouch. "Yes, more animal pieces. It's not just in children's stories that they play a part in magic."

He shifted two of the wings into his right hand and held the third in his left. This he held toward the tall, expressionless man. Aataltaal fluttered the wing in front of the man's chest and began an incantation. Avers and the other two sailors winced, for some of the noises Aataltaal created werc unearthly, like the high-pitched notes that bards achieved when they strove to shatter glass. There was no musical quality to the sounds Aataltaal emitted, but they certainly possessed magic.

The bat wing Aataltaal brandished began to disintegrate. The tissue curled as if affected by a great heat, but when these pieces fell away from the mass of the wing, they transformed into purple-black motes that swirled in a great cloud. This effect quickly swept along the length of the wing until hundreds of tiny dark lights whirled around Aataltaal's hand and forearm. The enchanter then swept his hand in the direction of the man who was as yet unmoved and evidently unimpressed. The motes fell upon him and cascaded down his long torso and legs. They wormed their way beneath his feet, and then they did the miraculous—they lifted him into the air!

This caught the dour man completely off guard and a look of surprise washed across his face. He threw out his arms to maintain his balance, but there was no need. He remained perfectly upright, only now he hovered several inches above the deck of the ship. The man regained control, but now looked down at the deck as he slowly bobbed up and down above it.

Aataltaal said, "That is the primary magic you require. It's called levitation, and it will allow you to run across the surface of the ocean and deposit this on the island." The "emperor" withdrew the corpse of the raven Menthes had delivered the night before.

He handed it to the levitating man, who accepted it

without comment, though he was plainly becoming less and less comfortable with all these odd events.

Then Aataltaal cast the spell of levitation on the shorter man and the woman. All three hovered in place and remained fixed in relation to their spot on the deck of the ship. So even as the boat moved, they moved correspondingly.

Aataltaal explained, "Aqua-goblins that worship the great allizewsaurs as gods live on this island as well. I require you to slip onto the shore, slay one or more of these goblins, making certain no witnesses survive, deposit this raven's corpse alongside a dead goblin, and then escape the island. Return to any of our boats that you can reach. I will see you and know that the fact you return at all means you succeeded."

He paused and then said, "You must be successful. Any questions?"

All three volunteers shook their heads.

"Then hurry. Our fleet will soon assemble into a new formation that will put you farther from the island. May your god smile upon you."

The "emperor" stepped away and Avers had a final word with the threesome. Then the lieutenant led them starboard where, to the astonishment of a number of sailors, they leapt over the rail and into the water. Except, of course, they did not sink into the water. Instead, they hovered above it, just as they had the deck of the ship. The boat quickly left them behind as they became accustomed to their strange new ability. Jogging slowly, the woman was the first to turn toward shore. The men caught up to her and then all three sprinted together, dashing across the waves.

Aataltaal looked back at his pursuers, eight sleek vessels with a vast cloud of birds swooping and wheeling above them. Soon those birds would be set loose upon the sailors and sails of the Combine Armada. The only thing that could stop them would be an allizewsaur itself.

DELAILITH STEPPED CLOSER TO THE DECK RAIL, and then paused, almost crouching, ready to pounce just as the creature beyond prepared its ambush. Her first instinct was to warn the others, but if this was a lone, silent assassin, then Delailith did not want it to flee at her alarm and then be free to attack again later, perhaps even on another boat, when it would not be detected. No, better to lure it in now and be done with it. Besides, she had confidence in her expertise.

Cadmus laughed at some joke of Troy's. When the bard's laughter rang out, Delailith saw the fingers tense. She sprang instantly between the men.

Troy yelped, "Hey—"

Cadmus couldn't manage even that, because Delailith elbowed them both in the chest to knock them out of range of the attack. The bard gasped for breath.

Delailith continued her fluid intervention and opened her left hand briefly so the blade fell through her grasp. She caught it, so now she clutched it by the pommel but blade-down. Then she drove the point of the dagger through the blue hand and firmly into the wood beneath it.

A bestial howl caused both Troy and Cadmus to scream in shock. The beast hauled itself onto the deck with one great, swooping motion—an act that required amazing physical strength. Because the action exceeded the capabilities of any man, it took Delailith by surprise.

The creature was humanoid, but blue-green and long-armed. Nearly hairless, it wore only a piece of sharkskin strapped around its middle. Now the creature snarled in rage and pain, and used Delailith's momentary confusion as diversion to wrest the dagger from its pinned hand.

It spun then, hissing, a slender tongue waggling through its scowling mouth. Its forehead sloped back and the tips of its large, pointed ears stretched above the height of its bald head.

"It's a goblin!" Troy shouted. "Except for its color, anyway."

"An aqua-goblin," Nestor said as he hurried to Delailith's back, his earlier discomfort forgotten in the excitement of the outburst.

The goblin crouched and extended its taloned hands threateningly toward the four humans.

Cadmus said, "Delailith, you saved us. Thank the gods, you saved our lives."

Delailith stepped back a pace from the goblin. She sheathed her remaining dagger and from matching scabbards she withdrew a pair of slightly curved shortswords. Ignoring the compliment, she said, "Get ready, there are two others."

At that, the goblin with the bloodied hand spat and seemed to curse at her. Simultaneously, two more goblins flung themselves from the hull of the ship onto the deck. One of them tucked and rolled so that when it came to its feet, it was fifteen feet from the rail and close to Troy, who stood between it and the open seas.

The third goblin, the burliest and deepest blue of the three, hurled itself directly at Delailith. Had it chosen any three of the men as a target, it might have claimed a victim. But Delailith, already prepared, crossed her shortswords at their midpoint to fend off the creature. When the goblin fell onto the blades, she whipped aside the right, outermost blade. A great slit of red opened across the goblin's stomach, chest, and arm, as the creature deflected off the woman and, off balance, onto the deck with a terrific smash.

Delailith warned, "They understand our common tongue."

Nestor translated, "So 'be wary what you say,' is what she means."

The goblin near Troy paid scant attention to its comrade's fate and lunged at the man with an outstretched claw. The monster's apelike long arm made it difficult to judge the speed of the attack, but Troy, so used to dodging the drunken punches of jilted lovers, evaded the blow.

Troy made a show of faking this way and that as the goblin gathered itself for another strike. "Glad you can follow my words, Chuckles. Half my combat techniques would be worthless if I couldn't taunt you! You keep swinging like that and the only thing you'll hit me with is spittle."

Meanwhile, thinking itself perhaps momentarily forgotten, the first goblin rushed Cadmus. The bard was indeed paying closer attention to Troy's predicament than his own, and the goblin snagged him by his collar and trousers and amazingly hefted him right off his feet. The goblin turned toward the railing and reared back to hurl the bard into the ocean, but its wounded hand collapsed, and the goblin lost its grip. The other hand clung tight to the bard's pants, but as Cadmus fell to the deck, the pants ripped and nearly set him free.

Troy jeered, "Keep your pants on, Cadmus. He's a handsome shade of green, but make him show he loves you first."

"You know," Cadmus began as he log-rolled across the deck, "goblins were also cursed after the War of the Gods for"—he continued as he pulled his trousers completely off—"also siding with Rallos Zek."

With that he rolled to his feet and brandished his tattered pants like a whip, cracking it in the face of the goblin who scrambled after him. The first snap startled the goblin a bit, but then it realized no real harm could be dealt this way, so it rushed again.

This time, Cadmus' attack tangled the pants over one pointed ear of the goblin, and as the goblin nearly grappled him, the bard tossed the other end as well onto the creature's head. Completely blind for an instant, the goblin staggered and missed the ducking bard. Cadmus stretched out a foot and tripped the goblin. It hit the deck as hard as its fellow had a few seconds before.

That goblin regained its feet, attempting to get inside Delailith's guard. Her deftly circling blades kept it at bay, until it tried a different stratagem that displayed more cunning than its harsh, savage face suggested it possessed. It crouched and then leaped toadlike straight up. Its arms came down like battering rams and with the weight of its body, too, the goblin smashed one deck plank—the one on which Delailith stood. The force of the blow seesawed the plank up right beneath Delailith, and it smashed into her knee and then between her legs, sending her tumbling backward, one sword skittering from a hand as she clutched her leg.

Meanwhile, the goblin facing Troy backed off, strangely patient where a moment before it had attacked as ravenously as if on the edge of starvation.

Troy blathered blithely on, "Oh, now you see you're in over your head, eh?"

The goblin curled its lips and ground its incisors together. Then, most frightening of anything it had done yet, the goblin slowly shook its head. "Fool," it said in the common tongue.

And Troy looked around and saw why. He saw why he and his friends would truly have to fight their way out of this, why he could not just hold out until more crew came to their aid. Aqua-goblins overran the *Condor*. He and his companions were well forward on the boat, and so one good look aft revealed dozens of goblins scrambling over the sides of the ship. Troy saw some sailors down and more falling. He did not see goblins in any condition but exultant.

"They're everywhere!" he shouted. "Nestor, for god's sake, put your oath aside!"

Nestor stood strangely apart from the peril the other three faced: one goblin bore down on Delailith, another ripped Cadmus' pants from its face and strode toward the defenseless bard, and the first chortled at Troy.

"I . . ." Nestor muttered.

The burly goblin leapt into the air again, this time angling to land upon Delailith. Her body was twisted, and her injured knee kept her from positioning herself for a strike with the sword she still wielded, so the goblin hit her. Delailith's face contorted but she did not scream when the goblin landed on her arm. The crack might have been the deck, her arm, or probably both.

"Nestor!" Troy called again, but the large man stood still, his face whitewashed with panic and indecision. Troy dashed to Delailith's assistance, but the first goblin intercepted him.

"Don't forget me, cocky human," it said. It raked him across the chest and tricep with a sweep of its fearsome talons. Troy retreated, glancing imploringly at Nestor.

It was enough. Whatever inner demon manhandled Nestor while ashore, he had come slowly to grips with it throughout the ocean voyage, and now he could face it. "Unhand her, you beast!" Nestor roared. He pumped his two thick arms out from his side and then thrust his meaty fists forward in the direction of the goblin that stood on Delailith's weapon arm. In unison with this motion, a great swell of fire erupted from the thin air and engulfed the goblin. The heat forced Delailith to lie flat on the deck or be singed as well.

The goblin shrieked in pain with such volume and vigor that the assault ship-wide slowed to a crawl for a moment as the goblins everywhere wondered what grievous attack incited the reaction. The creature shrieked and thrashed as its flesh sizzled, and abruptly it was silent, falling over, dead before it hit the deck, but still flickering with flames.

"Alright!" Troy whooped as he ducked a followup attack. He dove forward toward the weapon Delailith dropped, but with his fingers inches from grasping it, he was yanked back. The goblin had his foot and reeled him in, painfully ripping the flesh of his leg as it went hand over hand up the length of Troy's limb.

Delailith struggled to get to her feet and ready her weapon, for it was now a race. Could she attack the beast before Troy fell completely into its clutches?

Meanwhile, Nestor continued his attack. Cadmus still backed away from the gangly goblin that threatened him. The ample wizard gestured at the goblin, and the creature's anticipatory smile melted as it stopped dead in its tracks. Clearly, this was not by choice, for it looked at its feet and even used both hands in an attempt to pull one foot free of the deck. It was no use—the goblin was rooted to the spot.

And then, now safely out of range of the goblin, Cadmus broke into song. His voice rang with the danger of the moment while another bar seemed to also be a call to action. He groped the air as the passion in his voice found translation through his body. He sang a patriot's tune, the Combine Anthem, and through a subtle magic it invigorated his friends, enabling them to a greater-than-human celerity.

Just enough speed. The first goblin clawed the final stretch of Troy's torso and then grasped the man by the chin, while the deadly claws of the other hand prepared to shred his throat.

But it never happened. Implored by the rousing music and somehow overcoming a knee bent wrongfully crooked, Delailith gained her feet and she let her final sword fly. While the sword was not the best projectile because of its slight curve, the maneuver, practiced countless times, was this time accomplished expertly. The sword punched into the goblin's chest. Without even a death rattle, the goblin collapsed.

Delailith looked at Nestor. "A wizard?"

Nestor nodded vaguely but insincerely, as if he scarcely believed it himself.

Troy shushed the warrior. "This is one time you *should* remain quiet." He then whirled to Cadmus and said, "As for you! Well, you've some magic in that voice, don't you? I didn't know you were a *true* bard. I thought you just meant the tavern-variety kind."

Cadmus almost blushed. "I've still so much to learn."

"Nonsense, that song of yours saved my life. Suddenly I felt like I could sprint across the boat in nothing flat, but of course, I wasn't going anywhere."

"But it was—"

Troy shook his head. "No, no. No good thanking her. She knows I know she knows . . . and all that, and *I* know she'd rather not hear about it."

"This human is never quiet." The gutteral voice sounded disgusted.

But Troy did fall silent. He turned and looked at the immobile goblin. "Excuse me, slimy? You've got a problem with my mouth?"

The goblin growled at Troy and muttered something in its own tongue.

"Well?"

The goblin smiled. "No, human. *They* do."

The goblin nodded to a place behind Troy. The man wished he did not have to turn around, but he knew he'd better.

"Oh, we are dead," he said when he saw a group of a half dozen more aqua-goblins less than twenty paces away and closing.

Grimacing, Delailith limped to her second sword and retrieved it. She alternately tightened and loosened her grip, testing the strength in her bruised arm. Satisfied, she stepped to Troy's side and faced the goblins.

"May I have that?" Troy asked her, gesturing.

"Take it," she said.

Troy reached to her waist and withdrew the lone dagger. He wriggled the toe of his soft boot beneath the pommel of the other dagger where it lay on the deck. He flicked it into the air and caught it gracefully. "Yuck," he said, though, when droplets of goblin ichor sprayed from the blade and onto his face.

Nestor moved behind the pair and nearly eclipsed them both with his bulk. Further back yet, Cadmus again began the Combine anthem, and the threesome's blood ran hot.

Troy said, "We're still dead."

And then the goblins closed.

INSTINCTIVELY, AATALTAAL BRACED HIS FEET wider than his shoulders to maintain his balance as the ship turned. The maneuvers were not casual ones. Orleax did not want invisible vessels breaking the ranks of the other ships while the curtain was being drawn around the flagship, so the ships moved as lithely as possible through the choppy waters.

While Orleax commanded the movements of the boats, Aataltaal concentrated on the three humans. They'd nearly reached the shore. No allizewsaur was in view, so Aataltaal did not feel anxious. These humans could handle themselves against the aqua-goblins, but if one of the great lizards spotted them, then they and their mission would be forfeit. The humans' levitation magic allowed them to outrun a swimming goblin, but not a wading allizewsaur.

In the end, there was little to worry about. With his amazing eyesight, Aataltaal watched the action unfold. A pair of aqua-goblins hid behind a large fern at the base of a wide, squat palm tree, watching the humans approach. The dour human male noticed them both, though, and the three humans drew their swords and charged.

Already a bit awkward on land, the goblins had no hope of outrunning the floating humans, and to their credit the goblins determined this quickly, for they prepared to fight. Both men were slightly injured in the struggle, but while they harried and met the goblins' power, the woman slew both creatures. The humans then dragged the goblins into plain view near the edge of the beach and placed the dead raven between them.

Unfortunately, they were seen. A group of foraging aqua-goblins rounded a small rise at the base of the island's large central hill. First, of course, they saw the two fleets stretched across the waters. Then, as Aataltaal watched, one cried out and pointed to the trio of humans at the edge of the water. The humans heard the cry as well and stopped. They turned and saw that the group of goblins consisted of five of the creatures. After a brief discussion, they made a decision to fight. They again drew their weapons and charged.

The attack was brought up short, though, when one of the five enemies retrieved an object slung on his back—a conch horn. Its blast carried from shore to the Combine armada and likely across the entirety of Dinosaur Isle.

Just then, Orleax rushed over and said, "M'lord, one of the ships, the *Condor*, is not responding to the maneuver instructions. It appears they are unable because . . . they've been boarded."

"Already?"

"M'lord, the aqua-goblins were aboard the *Condor* before the island's horn sounded."

"Show me."

Orleax hustled toward the stern of the boat and Aataltaal followed, though he watched the humans on shore as he walked. The Koada'Dal's animated sword and shield floated dutifully behind as well.

On the isle, the three humans retreated. Another dozen aqua-goblins responded to the conch horn almost immediately and advanced with the first five toward the intruders.

The humans dashed back toward the water and, with their levitation magic still functioning, they fairly flew across the surface. That did not last long either. One of the goblins stepped to the fore and began an incantation. He was obviously a shaman, for he wore an elaborate outfit of colorful polished shells that set him apart from the others. He concluded his spell and pointed a crooked finger at the three humans. Instantly, the blond woman was swallowed by the hungry water.

The men paused, confused. Then a taloned hand reached from the water and grabbed the ankles of the shorter of the men. The other, humorless one looked down into the depths of the Ocean of Tears and then did not tarry. He ran.

Still following Orleax, Aataltaal wanted to reach across the water and choke the coward. But he misjudged.

206 • STEWART WIECK

With only a split-second to decide, the man chose bravely. He gave the Combine armada its best chance for success—he ran toward Seru's fleet.

"See, m'lord?" said Orleax quietly, as his eyes, too, followed the man's sprint across the water.

Aataltaal spared a glance for the other two lost sailors. Swimming goblins now held the smaller man by both ankles and a third goblin clambered upon him.

Of the woman, there was no sign. Doubtless, the swarming aqua-goblins killed her under the surface. Though she could breathe the water because of Aataltaal's first spell, she could not match their dolphinlike swimming prowess.

Then Aataltaal turned his attention to the matter of more of his charges in distress. Orleax indicated the boat, the *Condor*, and Aataltaal saw that it was overrun with aqua-goblins. Blood spilled on the deck, and while some of it was goblin, the situation looked grim for the humans that remained.

The high elf quickly accounted for the rest of the armada. He looked closely with his fine elven vision, but he saw no indications of a similar strike against any of the other ships.

"An attack like this in advance of the horn call must mean this is a war or hunting party that's acting on its own," said Aataltaal.

Orleax said, "Whatever the case, m'lord, the *Condor* can't make the maneuvers we require."

"Then fall in behind it."

"M'lord?"

Aataltaal repeated, "I said make our formation behind that ship. Those aboard her who can jump might conceivably be pulled safely onto our trailing vessels. Have sailors with lines at the ready on all the ships. And give some room between her and us, so we don't just run these people over."

"But our route? The unmanned ship will lead us off course in the sweep past the isle."

Aataltaal shook his head, sighed, and said, "Stay behind her as long as possible, but then pull off when you must to continue."

As Orleax hurried away, Aataltaal looked again at Dinosaur Isle. The Combine armada had pulled as near to the shore as he planned, and so he could clearly view the action there.

The goblin shaman who stripped the woman of the levitation spell seemed to rank high among these goblins. He stood now at the site of the two goblins slain by the sailors. He crouched, inspecting the dead. Then he stood, the razor-winged raven dangling from his hand. As Aataltaal watched, the shaman's gaze immediately lifted and went to the ships behind the Combine armada. And then they lifted to gaze above Seru's fleet, at the wheeling black mass of ravens. He then dashed the raven to the ground and shouted angrily at the nearby aqua-goblins, one of whom bore the horn that sounded earlier.

This goblin raised the horn again, and instead of merely another blow, a two-noted rumble issued, the first a short and high accent note, the second very low and sustained for a full three-second count.

Suddenly, the hills and forest swarmed with aqua-goblins, who rushed the beach in droves. In every imaginable shade of green and blue, they created an undulating tapestry that in moments obscured the beach. Arrayed against the thunderous tide, the goblins advanced on the ocean, smashing against the waves as against opposing armies. The goblins overpowered the surf, slipping into the water where their strength seemed to suddenly become grace.

The aqua-goblins dove into the water and, in a great synchronized parabolic swoop, they rose to the surface some forty feet from land. Then they dove into the deeper water and entirely disappeared from view.

As he factored all these swirling events, Aataltaal managed a grim smile. His plan might work yet, because the resounding horn also drew the attention of an allizewsaur—the male allizewsaur.

13

THE HAND OF SERU

"**A**T LEAST I LIVED TO SEE YOU CAST MAGIC again, big man." Troy flashed a winning smile at Nestor, but the large sailor did not hear, or at least did not react. He was deep in thought, but also looking around, casting hopefully for a solution.

The rogue shrugged. Gripping one dagger overhand and the other underhand, he crouched at Delailith's side. "Parry high," he said.

Delailith nodded.

The blood of all three raced from exertion and adrenaline and at least partly from fear, too, but also because the bard Cadmus continued his song. He lyrically hummed the notes of the Combine anthem—the magic lay in the delivery of the song, not the words themselves.

Troy swore his arms quivered with anticipation. He'd never felt so fast, so unavoidable. He recognized the feeling as foolish overconfidence wrought by the speed imparted by the bard's song, but he'd rather go down thinking he was going to win than actually have to admit his defeat and certain death before even a blow was struck.

Meanwhile, the *Condor* rocked side to side more than

normal, but the steady wind and tight sails kept her generally on her prior course.

The aqua-goblins facing the group of four friends numbered seven. All bore bloodied weapons and several dripped blood from their maws as well. The humans allowed them to close. No sense being the ones off balance, especially when fighting aboard a boat that seemed to have no one at the rudder.

Perhaps one of these goblins had killed the helmsman . . .

The goblins grunted back and forth, and the one held fast behind the humans joined the conversation.

"Don't tell them all our secrets, slimy," said Troy. "We could have killed you, you know!"

From behind the rogue, the goblin parsed through the words in the common tongue, "I will snack on your toes."

Troy rolled his eyes.

The goblins closed to within ten feet. Then they lost their coolheadedness, as two of them suddenly charged, one each at Delailith and Troy.

Troy saw Delailith subtly shift her weight, preparing to favor her wounded knee. One goblin bore a trident and the other a slender rapierlike sword. Two thrusting weapons, so Delailith's defense was one-dimensional even if two-pronged. With savage cries, the goblins attacked.

With speed born of training and bardic magic, Delailith's outstretched twin swords whirled down and then across her body and up, knocking the rapier over Troy's ducking head and the trident over her shoulder.

Unfortunately, she brushed the rogue, upsetting Troy's own cobra-quick strike. Forced lower, he could not reach the vitals of either goblin. One dagger punched into the belly of the rapier-wielding attacker, when he'd intended to puncture its heart, and the other slashed the groin and gut of the trident-wielder, though he'd aimed for the creature's femoral artery.

Nevertheless, both goblins staggered back. Delailith's swords continued to sweep in circular blurs and each caught an attacker's arm, but the hasty step of retreat saved the goblins from severe harm.

The five goblins behind laughed at the failed attack, until a larger, sapphire-blue goblin stalked up behind them all and shouted a litany of harsh exclamations.

"Now you are in trouble, human," said the immobilized goblin. "Sacron will feast himself on you."

"Fabulous," Troy muttered. "Does that mean he gets my toes?"

The eighth aqua-goblin was clearly a commander, perhaps *the* commander. He wore armor fashioned from a single gigantic bivalve. Both portions of the monstrous clamshell were tied together by sinew; one half protected his chest, the other his back. It looked at first glance as if the huge clam had swallowed all but the aqua-goblin's legs, but in reality, the shell had been altered with some skill to fit the warrior. Divots and scratches across the face of the chest shell indicated that, as armor, the piece served its purpose.

The goblin also towered a full head taller than his fellows. And if his brilliant sapphire skin and glistening shell armor did not cause him to stand out enough, then the actual sapphires that adorned a platinum circlet, and a thick golden bracer told of his status.

Sacron hissed again at the goblin warriors. The two wounded ones fell back another step, and then all seven reformed ranks and advanced.

"Nestor?" begged Troy.

"Farewell, my friend," said Nestor.

"What? That's not—" Then Troy held his tongue when he realized Nestor had not finished speaking.

"—and live with pride," Nestor completed, the middle part of the statement inaudible over Troy's protest.

Then Nestor turned to face the open sea. He held his right index finger aloft and chanted as he swept his left in two complete circles around it. His finger glowed red hot, but his face showed no pain as he harnessed magical energy.

Nestor extended his arm and pointed, not at the goblins, but toward open water. A fiery bolt shot from his finger and with a searing hiss blistered across the distance between the *Condor* and the *Wolf of Faydark*.

Mindful of these events from the corner of his eye, Troy could not believe what was happening. Nestor had shot a bolt of magical fire at the former governor of the Combine Empire—who commanded the armada!

THE TITANIC MALE ALLIZEWSAUR STRADDLED the top of the island's dominant rise as if this one peak were the summit of the world. The beast looked across the waves at the wooden-hulled gnats that darted around its throne and seemed not even to see them. Its gaze swept on until it lighted on the beach where frenzied goblins still hurled themselves into the smashing turf.

It shook its enormous neck and then threw back its head. Its roar caused the island to tremble.

The monster impressed Aataltaal. Its awesome size made it easy to anthropomorphize it and imagine it truly rallying its goblin troops. More likely, thought the elf, the proximity of all the ships disturbed it, and the noise and activity aroused its hunger. Aataltaal was glad he was not among the goblins on the beach—for that was the nearest source of food.

The goblin shaman seemed to realize this as well and

he motioned for the aqua-goblins to fan out across the beach and not gather so centrally.

So much was happening, and though it was too much—for instance, the aqua-goblin attack on one of his armada's own vessels—Aataltaal was grateful. Better too much than too little. The only chance to shake Seru's pursuit was now, in this maelstrom of chaotic events.

The human's sprint to Seru's fleet was nearly complete. So thick were the waters behind him with aqua-goblins that some of the monsters even skittered across the surface, their smooth bodies slashing through the whitecaps as if they were streamlined dolphins.

This did not go unnoticed by the commanders aboard Seru's boats, or perhaps even by Seru himself. The Combine human fell, shot down, his body riddled with countless arrows and bolts from the traitor's archers. He was dead in an instant, and with his death, the levitation magic faded, so that his body sank unceremoniously into the water.

Aataltaal closed his eyes for an instant, a pause in his practically immortal life to honor the courage of one not so long-lived.

When Aataltaal opened his eyes, he wondered for a flash what he'd missed. The razor-wing ravens previously wheeling chaotically about Seru's fleet suddenly moved in rhythmic waves. Their diving and soaring became coordinated motion, the massive flock now twisting as one.

Aataltaal understood the agitation of their controller. In the close quarters of the shipboard combat near commencing, the ravens would serve little purpose. Most thought they were present to shred the sails of the Combine Armada and harry the sailors on the decks before Seru's forces boarded, but Aataltaal suspected otherwise.

He anticipated an ancient spell that might make the ravens a much more direct and catastrophic threat.

But Aataltaal watched with great interest, for it appeared that Rashalla had in mind a different purpose. A pattern gradually formed in the flock of birds, and Aataltaal nodded his head admiringly as the shape he expected became evident. Impressive magic, this went well beyond the mere animal control for which Rashalla was renowned. It was work in the league of the world's greatest practitioners of the arcane.

The movements that first synchronized the birds came to literally combine the birds into a single entity. One portion of the flock lost their individual identities and merged to become a wing of a new great bird. Others melted together to form its body; others its beak, its legs, its talons. Suddenly the swirling motion resolved, like a blurry vision now seen clearly. There were no longer thousands of ravens, but one single gargantuan one.

The bird dwarfed any single ship and could surely snap masts with ease. The Combine Armada would be at the mercy of such a creature, which is why Aataltaal felt this route past the Isle of the God would be pivotal to the fleet's chances.

But now the bird had another matter to attend: the aqua-goblins. With thunderous wing strokes, the giant razor-wing raven descended to the water. Its vast taloned claws skimmed the surface of the water and scooped up dozens of the beasts. Blood-curdling screams came from those unfortunates, but the noise did not persist—no more than did the goblins themselves. The bird flexed its claws and the goblins were instantly dismembered, the fractions of their bodies dropping into the ocean like raindrops in a puddle.

With a few gale-force strokes of its wings, the bird darted to Dinosaur Isle and without hesitation it savagely smote the ranks of goblins arrayed there. Already spreading at the shaman's behest, the goblins now scattered, their lines broken so that the ones already at sea and even now scrambling up the sides of Seru's ships were isolated. These goblins were still a great threat, but there would be no reinforcements.

Aataltaal knew what was bound to occur next, but even so he gasped in astonishment. The scale of the beasts that now contested the suddenly diminutive-seeming island awed him, though he had witnessed the gods themselves and viewed celestial events that shaped the history of Norrath.

The male allizewsaur did not charge down the island's summit to attack the bird—it *leapt*. Though he was concentrating on the attacking bird, from the corner of his eye Aataltaal caught what seemed to be a falling mountain as the great lizard vaulted from the peak of the central hill directly onto the giant razor-wing raven.

The collision rattled the very air, and lizard and bird crashed from the air into the shallows at the edge of the beach. The allizewsaur righted itself first, and a flick of its tail sent twenty-foot waves in a semicircular arc behind it.

Aataltaal could scarcely believe this good fortune. He'd hoped at least to lure the aqua-goblins into attacking Seru's fleet, and a single brave man had made that possible. Now magic that potentially rivaled his own was set not against the Combine armada, but against the god of Dinosaur Isle.

And then a blistering heat erupted at Aataltaal's side. The elf's magic shield and protective web of spells deflected all but the sensation of the attack's heat, but he was surprised—which usually proved deadly in battles between masters of the arcane. He cursed his own inattention and whirled around to the source of the attack. As he did, he noted his magically animated defender already in motion. It flung itself over the side of the *Wolf of Faydark* and swept across the surface of the water in single-minded and relentless pursuit of his attacker. That could be good, for the animation would harass Aataltaal's foes, or unfortunate, for the attack might have been a diversion solely intended to relieve him of his guardian. Either way, Aataltaal had no say. The animation reacted by rules of magic, not force of logic or by his specific command.

But what Aataltaal saw surprised him. The attack came from the vessel of his own fleet that was overrun by aqua-goblins. More than that, it had not come from a goblin. Instead, the assailant was a human, a sailor who evidently possessed reasonable command of a wizard's might and whose comrades were outnumbered by a host of goblins.

Aataltaal shook his head with sadness. Those humans needed no additional foe, particularly not one as powerful as that which careened across the ocean in unthinking pursuit of the human who dared attack it or its master.

But the human nodded at Aataltaal. Though now wary of other mischief, the elf found himself more interested in this contest than the titanic one playing out on the island behind him.

TROY GAPED IN ASTONISHMENT. THEN HE SHOUTED, "Nestor! Have you lost your mind?"

Nestor paid no attention. Instead, he carefully tracked the passage of the enchanted animation across the rippling water between the boats. He said, "Keep your guard up."

"What's happened?" asked Delailith.

Tory said, "The magic's gone to his head and addled his thoughts. Nestor completely misfired a spell, and he's acting as if it was on purpose."

Delailith said, "Then it was."

"You don't see what I see, battle maid," Troy grumbled.

Delailith glared at him.

Troy said, "I know, don't call you that. Take heart, because it's probably the last time I will."

Sacron growled something, and the immobilized goblin behind the humans answered. Then the sapphire-studded aqua-goblin shoved the backs of two of his soldiers and the seven-strong squad of aqua-goblins advanced methodically. Three with shorter weapons—the one with a rapier and two others with sticks crudely studded with shark teeth—moved to the fore and readied their weapons in defense. Two with tridents and a third with a spear formed a second rank and prepared to attack.

Then Nestor said something unintelligible.

"What?" Troy asked. "See, he has lost his mind."

Delailith swung her swords wide and batted aside a shark-tooth stick. Then she grunted, "Gnomish."

"Oh."

Troy noticed Delailith edge slightly away from him, which opened both of them to more attacks than if they held their position. He began to delicately bring this to her attention, but then Nestor yelled. The demonic howl was a surprise even amidst the chaos of the battle that swirled ever nearer on the deck of the ship.

Then suddenly Nestor clawed his way between Troy and Delailith. The warrioress seemed prepared and rolled with the shove, maintaining her balance. The move caught

Troy unaware, though, and the combination of Nestor's strength and girth bowled him over. Troy toppled and even lost his grip on one of the daggers. It skittered across the deck, and as Troy fell he watched with almost comic interest as one of the goblins gaped at the dagger spinning between its feet and did not notice the looming human until Troy was on top of him.

Nestor broke through the ranks of his comrades and then shouted again. The throaty cry, loud enough to gain the attention of a tavern full of drunks, momentarily shocked the goblins who had been set to the task of a steady advance and proper execution.

Their hesitation gave Nestor the slim opening he sought. Weaponless, the big man burst into their ranks. The arrayed weapons all struck him. Two prongs of one trident bit into him, one of them wedged deeply into his side. It seemed to work to the man's purpose, though, for he grappled at all the goblins, seemingly intent on dragging them down with him—the goblin who wielded the trident first among them.

When Troy recovered from the bull rush, he saw Nestor at the bottom of a great tangle of mostly green and blue limbs. His thick human legs stuck out unceremoniously, and the deck was slick with his gushing blood.

And then a fast-moving metallic shadow whizzed past Troy, and the rogue threw himself onto the deck again, this time in self-preservation. He realized Cadmus' song had ended, as indeed the bard, overwhelmed by the sudden events, stumbled over his tune and sputtered into silence.

The goblins were as surprised as any. The rapier-wielding one had managed to retain his footing; now, when he saw a foe rushing him, he quickly intercepted it with a lunge.

Aataltaal's animated warrior was scarcely delayed by the feeble attack. Without breaking its "stride," the disembodied warrior brought its shield to bear. The rapier snapped against it. Its own sword then flashed, striking the goblin's head cleanly from its shoulders with no more than a swish. It continued its motion into a circular spin and thrust its sword straight down into the pile of goblins. It struck with uncanny accuracy. Despite the jumbled goblins, the sword bit deeply into the back of Nestor's right thigh, just below his buttocks.

An aqua-goblin who beheld his beheaded cohort screamed at the same time Nestor howled in pain. That goblin raised its spear and struck at the animated sword and shield. The sword spun into a quick semicircular parry that deftly lifted the spear from the goblin's hands and sent it sailing into the blue water.

The goblin leapt back, but the hovering warrior was not slowed by the jumble of fallen bodies and it elongated into a lunge. The sword punched through the goblin's breastbone. Shattered ribs ground and grated as the goblin shuddered while still impaled. That wriggling further entangled its body on the sword, even as the goblin madly attempted to extricate the weapon. Remorselessly, the point of the sword rummaged about through the goblin's internal organs, and soon the creature was dead weight draped from its tip.

Meanwhile, Delailith engaged one of the stick-wielding goblins and harried it, leaving it unable to attack prone Nestor. The big wizard yelped again as another goblin's weapon struck him, but he shrugged it off just as he sloughed off the goblins themselves. One that had formerly held a trident was pressed flat upon the deck under Nestor's large frame.

Another was hypnotized by the death-dealing animation, and this allowed Nestor to grab it by the loincloth and sling it toward Aataltaal's defender. The goblin extended his tooth-studded weapon at the animation. For an instant the floating sword tangled hopelessly in the goblin corpse, which gave the other goblin courage. He swung his stick. The poor blow was handily parried by a shield that whooshed to the spot. Unable to disengage its weapon from the other corpse, the sword simply lifted into striking position and thrust. First this caused dead goblin to bludgeon living goblin, but the sword slid the rest of the way through the corpse and then suddenly, smartly, into the other foe.

Lubricated by fresh-spilled blood, the sword slid neatly from both.

Delailith feinted and stabbed past the guard of her opponent and then, despite her wounded knee, sprang to Nestor's side. Her booted foot crashed down on the wrist of the prone goblin now readying an upward thrust at the wizard. Before the goblin could roll from beneath her, Delailith slashed across its face with her curved sword and then gashed its chest with her other weapon.

The remaining goblin tried to crawl from the fray, but Troy sighted and then hurled his remaining dagger. It punched into the goblin's throat, and the creature dropped to the deck too quickly even to register its own death.

With the whirling death-machine on his heels, Nestor charged Sacron, who with barely a flicker of motion had watched the scene play out. At the last instant, Sacron's scimitar leapt from his pearl-studded belt and the weapon smashed into Nestor's temple with a dull crunch. The big man's legs buckled, and he collapsed to the deck.

Troy braced for the aqua-goblin commander to meet the animated warrior, but instead, Sacron lowered his weapon. Troy nearly burst into a cheer for the imminent death blow.

It never fell.

Spinning madly ever since Nestor flung his fiery bolt, the animation became suddenly docile and lowered its weapon as well. For a moment, Troy wondered if the thing belonged to Sacron.

But then, without warning, the ship exploded into a shower of wooden fragments and all the humans and goblins erupted into the air.

IT BECAME DIFFICULT TO OBSERVE THE ACTION aboard the *Condor*. The *Wolf of Faydark* faded aft of the contested boat, and Orleax maneuvered the fleet into position behind the nearly unmanned vessel.

But Aataltaal watched intently, knowing he witnessed an act of unbelievable heroism. The human absolutely understood what he was doing. He knew the response his firebolt attack against Aataltaal would incite. The creator of such an animated warrior could seldom command it, but could rely upon it to protect him because of the simple rule of its existence: unto its destruction it would ceaselessly attack any being that intended to harm either its creator or itself.

The wizard had intentionally triggered this response with his firebolt, then sought to lure the animation within range of foolish goblins that might attack it as well and hence seal their own doom. Of course, the wizard understood that his own life was forfeit in such a scenario.

Unless . . . unless Aataltaal could dispel his guardian at the crucial moment, using the only command the animation would heed: self-destruction. So the disguised emperor watched not only with curiosity and respect for the ingenious human, but also for the precise moment he might dismiss his creation—the split-second between when it may have served its purpose and when its purpose would become killing the wizard.

The human wizard lured the animation into a mass of goblins by crashing headlong into them. In the confusion, the wizard stood and charged the evident leader of the aqua-goblin war party, a sapphire-hued warrior who seemed to Aataltaal to possess a calmness in battle that marked him as the leader, moreso even than did his accoutrements.

The goblins fell like game pieces before the comparably invincible animated sword. Their livewire combat reflexes caused them to strike at it, and in turn, it cut them down, even as it continued to pursue the wizard. The woman—whom he knew among the humans—reacted with impressive levelheadedness and took advantage of the chaos to kill more of the enemy. It meant that the split-second Aataltaal awaited would come sooner.

To maintain sight of the melee as the *Wolf of Faydark* fell behind the *Condor*, Aataltaal walked toward the prow of the ship. He noted other Combine ships closing into a loose circle around his vessel, but his attention was elsewhere.

The sword and shield bore down on the large wizard, and Aataltaal hesitated, opting to give the man one chance to somehow entice the goblin war chief to make the same mistake as its underlings. But it wasn't to be. The blue-skinned warrior almost offhandedly slew the wizard. Then, with the threatening animation hovering in front of him, the goblin wisely withheld its attack.

Aataltaal wanted to shout a warning, for an immobilized goblin behind the humans crept free and took its first sneaky steps toward one slender man who remained behind his fighting comrades. But the beast's attempt would prove useless.

Because suddenly, inexplicably, the *Condor* shattered.

It was as if the ship plowed into a cliff and ground instantly to a stop. The stern of the vessel collapsed accordionlike toward the prow. Where the force was too great, wooden planks sprayed outward across the surface of the ocean. The great central mast did not break, but it ripped and careened forward like a mighty Faydwer oak tumbling in a millennial thunderstorm. Humans and goblins were lifted from the deck like children's toys, their faces washed with surprise and their limbs spinning madly for a balance impossible to achieve.

Of the combatants Aataltaal watched—the friends of the wizard—the elf caught barely a glance. Their drama was tertiary now to the tragedy that was itself secondary to the mystery.

Nevertheless, Aataltaal saw the woman and two men flung high and over the front of the boat. The wizard's limp corpse was even lifted from the deck, so great was the force that demolished the ship. Among the living, the goblin leader fared best of all. His spinning motion was quickly controlled, and he executed a midair pirouette during which he sheathed his sword and somersaulted in order to slip into the water hands—then head—first. Aataltaal's animated defender was the least affected. It, too, was thrown upward, but it arrested its own motion and floated down amidst the *Condor*'s disintegrating hull. Before it reached the surface of the water, it already rapidly returned toward Aataltaal's side.

Aataltaal cast about to find the source of the attack. His first thought was the giant razor-wing raven, but that behemoth still struggled with the allizewsaur. The aqua-goblins on the shore peppered the bird with javelins and arrows, but its massive talons ripped enormous gashes in the lizard's hide. The allizewsaur was also missing the digits of its left hand, which Aataltaal guessed it had used to grab at the bird's wing. The razor-sharp forward surface of the wing must have dismembered those fingers. The lizard's other hand, though, clutched the bird's pinion feathers, and it wrestled to down the bird.

The elf looked back. Had Seru's fleet closed so quickly? No, it was in complete disarray. Goblins swarmed at least three of the ships and those not infested were swinging in wide arcs to avoid the water where the goblins had appeared.

Aataltaal whipped his head forward again. He suddenly realized what had happened. His own ship was turning hard to avoid crashing into the rear of the *Condor*, but the real danger they must avoid was one they could not even see: an invisible ship.

In the same flash, the rest of the mystery came clear. There were two invisible ships. The *Condor* had plowed into one.

Where was the other?

14

THE CRASH OF THE CONDOR

SOARING THROUGH THE AIR, THE HUMANS were short of options. Troy was weaponless, but knew survival now would depend on wits, not blades. Cadmus possessed no breath for song, while Delailith briefly wondered if her wounded knee would withstand the rigors of swimming. For the moment, their only option was to protect themselves as well as possible. This instinct for self-preservation gracefully allowed them for the moment to overlook the fact that they were likely doomed. A crash at sea at the beginning of a naval engagement did not offer high odds for preservation.

Delailith's eyes, though open as narrowly as a sleeping snake's to protect her from the splintered wood that ricocheted everywhere, remained firmly pointed toward Nestor's body. She'd not write off his life until she witnessed firsthand his lack of breath. The wizard had saved all their lives, and even if his bravery bought them only moments more so they might live to be tossed into the frigid, foam-flecked ocean, she owed him every effort she could muster.

Only Delailith, watching the spinning world through slits of eyes, realized that their vessel must have collided with another. Could it have been the goblin's plan to scuttle the ship? In her mind's eye, though, Delailith replayed the crash and saw Sacron's surprise, too, so she knew he wasn't responsible.

Then: impact. Unfortunately, they did not carry far enough to clear the second vessel, so the humans crashed though its crumbling deck and, with a boatload of the *Condor*'s wood, smashed into the water-filled hull. Cadmus cried out in shock when his body hit the cold water. Troy grunted in pain as a jagged deck plank dug into his side. Both men howled in frustration when they saw the sail above them lose its wind and sag. Simultaneously, they bit back their protests in surprise when they saw the black hand on the sail.

Delailith pushed all this out of her mind. Even as she hit the water, she craned her neck in the direction where Nestor's limp body slapped whalelike into the ocean. She redoubled her effort when she saw Nestor's body react to the cold water with a convulsion, though she knew it might have been only the force of the entry that made him appear to move.

The wizard sank quickly, and she dove after him, her efforts confounded by thousands of pounds of wood and all manner of shipboard junk like clothing and food that swirled in a great morass. She pushed through it and caught a brief glimpse of the sinking body. She lunged ahead, arm outstretched through the detritus, clutching at the space where she imaged he would be. She snagged fabric and clamped her hand tight upon it. She pulled and the weight resisted. Delailith used her free hand to swat aside debris that pummeled her and obscured her vision. Her breath running out, Delailith finally saw her catch: a pair of trousers caught in the lid of a large chest.

Pained, she slowly released it. As it plunged deeper, she imagined it to be Nestor, and it may as well have been, for her hope of rescuing the wizard sank as well.

And then, as her body sucked the last pockets of oxygen from her lungs, Delailith saw something moving upward. Her eyes felt as if they were bulging and she wondered if the movement was a trick of her exhaustion or the water, but she didn't have time to second-guess, so she surged after it. If it was Nestor struggling for the surface, then he would be in more desperate straits than she.

Darkness crept over the periphery of her vision as she struggled through another tangle of debris. Little did she know that the collapsed sail above was responsible for much of the darkness. It now lay across the surface of the ocean, and Troy and Cadmus both battled to extricate themselves from its adhesive weight. The water-slicked canvas grappled with their skin and made it difficult to break free and find the edge.

Delailith's legs went numb and she knew she had reached the very edge of consciousness. Then she saw the movement again, and amazingly she recognized Nestor, but he was too far away. She reached a hand gamely in the wizard's direction, but while her willpower could overcome physical obstacles, it could not overcome an absolute limitation.

Her last confused impression was of Nestor's still-limp body rapidly moving toward her, as if by magic. That vision ricocheted in her mind's eye as she turned upward, her lungs on fire. She swept at the water with her arms and she tried to kick, but her legs felt like dead weight.

Halfway back to the surface she realized she did not know if she was going the right way, for it seemed dark in the direction she thought was "above" her. She eked a few precious seconds of alertness by expelling her breath. The tiny bubbles that emerged bobbed out and then shot up. Despite the darkness, she was right, and she forged on.

Until she encountered the canvas sail. It may as well have been the surface of an icy lake, for water tension sealed it tight to the top of the water, and while at another time she might possess the strength to shift it or the wits to slash it, Delailith was spent.

The warrior pressed her lips to it and tried to draw breath through it, but the rough fabric was too thick. Every fiber inside her body was engulfed by an inferno of pain. Unable to resist her body's yearning any longer, Delailith gulped for the air beyond the barrier of cloth, but only cold, salty water rushed into her mouth. She felt it choke her throat and spread throughout her insides. The sudden icy inhalation extinguished the fire within her, but the sense of smothering intensified.

Suddenly, Nestor was beside her, and she thought she felt his grip enfold her waist. With a speed so unimaginable that it must be magic, Delailith whipped through the water, inches from the surface but unable to escape the spread of the sail.

As if in a dream, Delailith felt separated from herself for this second. Her mind and body, time-honed to function in unison, were suddenly at odds. She pressed herself to hold still, to hold her breath, to simply hold it together, but she knew that her body bucked wildly in Nestor's grip, and the spreading cold told her that she sucked in more water.

Then there was light! Glorious rays of the sun struck her face. Blinded by the scintillating aura, she nevertheless realized she'd been pushed partly free of the ocean's embrace. She wheezed for air, but water still filled her throat. She heard Troy cursing and Cadmus exclaiming bewilderment while hands grappled her.

A weight pressed on her belly and she was defenseless, completely unable to move or respond. Then she heard herself coughing, then sputtering and then . . . air. She breathed deeply, dimly aware that she was alive.

Her thoughts fell over themselves and she was in a turmoil to answer a dozen questions, but other than the rising and falling of her breast, she was unable to move. So she lay there, recovering, listening.

"Thank Xev's fortune! He's alive," Troy cheered.

A strange voice, a woman's, said, "Aye, barely. Let me see to him."

"And how are you, Delailith?" whispered Cadmus, close to Delailith's ear.

Delailith managed a nod and tried to rise or turn to see the other woman whose voice she heard, but she could not.

"Ssshhhh. Lie still," Cadmus said. He placed his hands on her shoulders and held her down, though it required virtually no effort on his part.

Delailith choked again, and a final fountain of water sprayed from her. The breath that followed was the first that seemed to fill her water-burned lungs, and she felt some strength return.

"Unbelievable!" exclaimed Troy. "How did you hold your breath so long, Delailith? You were down there for an age."

Delailith croaked, "Nestor?"

"He'll live," said the other woman. "But he's going to have a headache for a week, I think."

Burning with curiosity, Delailith finally managed to roll over. She saw that all of them were afloat on a chunk of deck. Whether from the *Condor* or Seru's vessel, she didn't know, nor did she care.

The other woman knelt beside Nestor, between Delailith and the wizard. Troy was on the far side, and he flashed Delailith a relieved, almost triumphant smile that made her feel fortunate indeed. The warrior could not see Cadmus, but knew he was on her other side.

The young woman turned to Delailith. She was short but muscular and attractive—clearly a soldier and not a sailor, and certainly a volunteer for their mission and not a family member accompanying it. Her straight blond hair was shoulder-length and unbraided. She wore a leather tunic that by the oil stains seemed to usually be an underlayer for a breastplate now missing. Her features were sharp and her eyes at once alert, compassionate, and discerning.

Delailith liked her immediately. She felt the woman could be trusted. The warrior looked back at Troy, who gazed admiringly at the young woman, while she was unaware of his rakish inspection. Delailith grinned. Troy clearly liked the woman, too.

Then Delailith looked at Nestor. He lay pale and motionless. Even his chest and stomach seemed still, as if there was no breath.

"You're certain he's alive?" Delailith asked.

The other woman turned back to Nestor, and it was Troy who answered. "Yes, Evanis cast a spell upon him as soon as we had him out of the water, and Nestor opened his eyes for a second before he blacked out again."

Evanis turned back to Delailith. "His breath is shallow, but he's fine." Then she put her hands on Delailith's shoulders and pressed her back down. Delailith did not resist.

Evanis said, "I think you could use some of the same."

The slim woman lifted her hands and clasped them

before her. As she chanted a few words, of which Delailith could only make out the name "Tunare," Evanis pulled her hands apart until only the tips of her index fingers touched. Then she pulled them apart, and in that instant, each fingertip lit with a sparkling green light, as if the fingers were candles. Evanis then pressed her fingertips to Delailith, one on her stomach and the other upon the warrior's throat.

Instantly, Delailith bloomed with vitality. Energy surged into her limbs, and the pain that had still throbbed inside her torso subsided.

"You are a ranger." It was a statement, not a question.

Still, Evanis answered, "Yes."

Cadmus reached across Delailith, pointing. He said, "You should consider yourself as well." The bard gestured at two places where Evanis' tunic was pierced. One spot was slashed and a several-inch-long wound beneath was evident, while in the other spot there were two large punctures, both holes tinged red about the edges.

"I'm fine. I should save my energy in case your friends require more assistance."

Still on her back, allowing the energy to flush through her completely, Delailith asked, "By what magic did you rescue us?"

Evanis smiled warmly, the sunlight spilling through her blond hair as she turned to indicate the water.

She said, "It was indeed magic that made him my friend, but only Tunare's blessing placed him near me in my time of need—and entirely his own selfless effort that saved the three of us."

Delailith sat up, this time without pain. She regarded the water, where a dolphin's head poked up near the end of the wooden platform upon which they all drifted.

The animal greeted her glance with a friendly head bob and an openmouthed, chattering call.

Despite herself, Delailith laughed.

THE WRECK OF THE *CONDOR* WAS CATASTROPHIC. When the debris-filled sky cleared, Aataltaal saw that virtually nothing remained intact. He gripped the deck-rail tightly, for his own vessel made extreme maneuvers to avoid the larger flotsam, as well as clusters of survivors pulling themselves onto any piece of wood they could grab.

Fortunately the aqua-goblins seemed to have fled. Aataltaal guessed that the unexpected cataclysm had scared them off, at least for now.

As the *Wolf of Faydark* righted itself and the elven enchanter no longer felt as if he might spill overboard, Aataltaal released his hold and took a seat on the deck. He withdrew a slim volume from a large pocket in his navy blue cloak and unerringly selected the proper page and opened the book. Runic letters and arcane diagrams covered the page, and the merest glance imprinted the spell therein elaborated upon Aataltaal's mind—a necessary step prior to actually casting a spell. Any magic-worker's mind could only contain the patterns and demands of a handful of spells at a time. Of course, Aataltaal could command more spells than most, certainly more than a novice spellcaster, but even he faced certain limitations. To push too hard at these near-absolute boundaries was usually a recipe for spell failure, something that a spell-caster could ill afford, especially under duress.

Aataltaal returned his book to the pocket and stood. The boat still rocked from the hard turns in the choppy sea, but with feet braced, the elf could complete his spell. He pressed his palm flat against his face to cover both eyes. Then he spoke an arcane phrase and spread his fingers. This revealed that his eyes were closed, and when he opened them, sparks seemed to leap from them and flash between the spread fingers.

This spell was relatively simple, and one that—given his knowledge of Seru's fleet—Aataltaal should have earlier used to augment himself. It allowed him to see objects and beings invisible to ordinary sight. He'd decided it seemed pointless to cast it on himself alone, for what were the chances he'd have the proper vantage at just the right moment to spy an invisible boat? And though the spell did not require a large portion of his magical energy, casting the spell on dozens of individuals would quickly deplete him of power best reserved for when the enemy struck.

He'd certainly not expected to be engaged by an invisible vessel before the entirety of Seru's fleet attacked.

Still, these rationalizations paled in the face of scores of humans spread across hundreds of feet of the Ocean of Tears. In the guise of a human himself, Aataltaal felt an even greater connection to those unfortunates, and so he was not merely acting his role when, with spontaneous anger, he glared back at Seru's fleet.

And not a moment too soon! For when Aataltaal's gaze cast back along the length of his fleet to Seru's vessels beyond, he spied the second invisible boat, a single boat-length behind the Combine armada's trailing boat, *The Bountiful*. Ten boat-lengths from the *Wolf of Faydark* and invisible to normal sight, this deadly vessel prepared to inflict grievous harm. The crew aboard *The Bountiful*, momentarily concerned with avoiding the wreckage of the *Condor*, was completely out of position and unprepared to respond to what occurred next.

Seru's vessel closed with *The Bountiful* and a wall of invisible archers dipped the tips of their pitch-laden arrows into pots of red-hot coals. The arrows instantly burst aflame, and in unison the bows discharged their fiery cargo. Most of the arrows arched to *The Bountiful*'s taut sails, though a handful aimed at different areas of the deck, and others spitefully targeted individual sailors in position to respond to the fires.

In an instant, the great ship was effectively disabled. The arrows touched off fires across the sails and throughout the length of the vessel. Even from this distance, Aataltaal heard the cries of alarm and panic and he watched as the boat immediately swerved out of control, nearly plowing over a handful of humans clustered atop a large piece of wooden deck.

Those aboard *The Bountiful* were shocked to see a boat appear as if from nowhere beside them, which is what occurred the moment the attack launched. Whatever the source of the magic that cloaked the boat, at least the general rules of the arcane that limited such magic still held firm. One of these incontrovertible rules of magic caused invisible objects to reappear the moment they interacted directly with a visible object. No variation of this spell was yet able to overcome this limitation.

Nevertheless, the wave of arrows constituted just one dimension of the attack. A lone figure at the very prow of Seru's vessel, one dressed in ornate black armor, raised a mailed hand and pointed a finger in the direction of the next nearest Combine ship, a ship rechristened *The Beast* by the sailors who prepared it for this voyage. Shards of magical fire leapt from that finger and exploded into the side of *The Beast*. The magical attack was so prolific that this one man generated a volley of fire bolts equivalent to all the ranks of archers that fired upon *The Bountiful*. The targeted area of the hull blackened and burst into flame, and as the attack concentrated on the spot for another second, a huge piece of the hull blew out completely. Unfortunately, the portion so affected was at the waterline, and *The Beast* hungrily swallowed ocean water into its hold.

The perpetrator of this attack was none other than Seru himself—either that or a man who could perfectly mimic the ex-general's arrogant posture and haughty body language. Despite being at sea, the man wore his famous battle armor, midnight-black banded plate mail with enormous shoulder guards and an oversized neck guard like a horizontal half-moon that ran across the front top of the breastplate. This guard obscured much of his lower face, but thereby afforded him enough protection that he required only an open-faced helmet to protect the remainder of his head.

Worse yet, the boat disappeared again from normal sight the instant Seru's fiery attack subsided. Whatever extended this cloaking effect over the entire boat—itself an unheard-of modification to such spells—reset itself quickly.

Aataltaal considered magically attacking Seru, but from this distance it would be difficult, with anything but a direct hit unlikely to do more than injure the general. The man wielded awesome power, that much Aataltaal had always known; but only since Seru unleashed the serpents of Hate did the elf truly believe that the human must have made pacts with forces far older than himself in order to gain even greater power. That he could cloak two enormous ships from sight proved a degree of might almost impossible for a human to develop and command within such a short lifetime. Or perhaps the spell of invisibility was Rashalla's work. Surely she was the man's connection to other powers.

No, Aataltaal would withhold a retaliatory attack for the moment. No sense showing his hand before a more favorable situation presented itself. Or a more dire one, if it came to that.

With magically enhanced vision that allowed him alone to chart its progress, the elf watched as the invisible boat adjusted its course to intercept the next Combine ship in its path. The elf cursed, then hurried to find Orleax. At least this ship's captain should see what the shattered Combine armada faced. At least this ship would make landfall at Weille!

Orleax huddled in harried consultation with a handful of subordinates when Aataltaal found him. The elf overheard pleas expressed on the part of the survivors currently stranded in the ocean, and fears that they would soon fall victim to returning aqua-goblins. Another human advised the complete opposite: use the carnage of the battle to escape and hopefully lure Seru farther afield, prolonging his pursuit by days or even weeks, to buy the emperor more time. Aataltaal was glad Orleax had at least one unsentimental advisor, but the elf was also heartened to hear this proposal vigorously denounced by all the others present.

When Aataltaal stepped toward the group, they all fell silent. Only the man who pushed for flight kept his chin up, and while Aataltaal disagreed with that decision, he appreciated the man's conviction. Who knew, perhaps everyone but he *was* being too sentimental.

Aataltaal said, "I am charmed to find my commanders arguing philosophy when an invisible dreadnought is hacking our fleet to pieces." His voice was earnest, but the trace of a smile revealed the elf was not actually leveling accusations.

"My lord, we're formulating the basis of our response. If that is philosophy, then so is any battlefield stratagem," Orleax said.

They'd not understood, except for the one man who disagreed with the others, who now appeared clearly amused at Orleax's overreaction. Aataltaal broadened his smile to ease the tension and communicate his light-heartedness.

"Oh, I see," Orleax said with some confusion.

"No matter, lieutenant," Aataltaal said. "Your issue was a weighty one. We must recover the survivors, of course."

"Of course!" Orleax spoke, but everyone nodded agreement, including the dissenter.

"Your name, sailor?" Aataltaal asked that man.

"Agathos, m'lord."

The elf nodded, pleased that the man did not attempt to explain or rationalize the position he'd taken on the matter of the water-borne survivors.

Aataltaal looked from man to man and explained, "The enemy ship can cloak itself with a spell of invisibility except whenever it or those aboard it launch an attack. There were two such ships, but one is destroyed—the one strategically abandoned in the middle of our course, specifically to cause a collision like the one that occurred."

Agathos said, "And this vessel was to have been in the front!"

Orleax paled at the thought.

"Exactly," Aataltaal said. "Fortune allowed us to avoid that event."

Orleax claimed, "No, m'lord, your decision saved us. You said to fall in behind the *Condor*."

Aataltaal overlooked the remark. Humans often preferred the providence of good luck to good planning, which is where he thought to steer the sentiments of this discussion, despite Orleax's proper placement of insight.

Besides, considering the next phase of his plan, Aataltaal himself would welcome a little luck in the looming battle with an invisible boat.

15

THE AMBUSH OF THE TRAITOR

IN THE LONG MINUTES THAT PASSED IN SILENCE as everyone contemplated the next move—or faced up to the likelihood of their death at sea—Troy, Delailith, Cadmus, and Evanis watched the end of the titanic struggle on Dinosaur Isle. The allizewsaur and the giant raven battled to awesome mutual annihilation. Despite countless wounds that the giant bird inflicted upon it, the mighty lizard would not relinquish its hold. Painfully, slowly, it reeled in the raven until the feathered body was within range. Then the allizewsaur lunged, its great mouth flung wide to reveal incisors the length of a man's arm. The teeth ripped into the side of the bird, and though it did not kill it outright, the terrible blow surely meant the bird's inevitable destruction.

For its part, the giant, razor-winged raven managed one final attack. Though mortally wounded, the enormous bird brought one razor-sharp wing to bear on the allizewsaur. The stroke hacked a wound along the entire length of the lizard, gashing its flesh from midtorso to neck and striking deep enough to bare rib and even organs, some of which spilled from the hole.

The goblins scrambling upon the beach, like so many ants in comparison to the battling behemoths, loosed a mighty cheer at this exchange. They surged toward the giants' melee as the allizewsaur sagged to the ground and, still clutching the raven, dragged the bird down with it.

"I don't get it," Troy said. "I thought the lizard was their god? They're applauding its death?"

Cadmus said, "At best it's a tyrant god."

Delailith shook her head. "That's not the reason," she said. "The aqua-goblins are hunters first and fore-most. Watch."

Suddenly, though, the bird disintegrated. The great feathered mass broke apart and fell like black rain upon the bloodied body of the allizewsaur. A few pieces of the raven drifted up into the air, and soon everyone saw that they were ordinary birds again—a handful of the original razor-wings that combined to form the larger bird. In all, fewer than a score survived, and they fled out to sea in seemingly random directions.

The aqua-goblins were taken aback by this, but only for a moment. The shell-studded shaman raised his hands and shouted something the humans could not hear. The roar that rose from the goblins afterward carried to them on their drifting platform, though, and they watched the goblins surge forward again.

The allizewsaur lay on its side, writhing in agony. With each spasm more of its innards flung out of its body, more mounds of gelantinous viscera oozed onto the sandy beach. And after each shuddering roll, the beast weakened. Before its motion ceased entirely, some few, foolhardy goblins clambered upon it, though most sought purchase on the organs that trailed from its side.

Even from a distance at sea, the humans could see the goblins devouring these oversized morsels. Their nearly naked bodies embraced quivering chunks of flesh larger than themselves, and they fed upon it.

"By the gods," Troy exclaimed. "That is revolting!"

"Like many primitive hunters, they probably believe that by feeding upon the organs of the creature, they will gain some of its strength," Evanis said.

Troy's face paled, but he managed a dashing smile in Evanis' direction.

However, the allizewsaur did not accept this quietly. When it saw the little creatures clambering upon and around it, the lizard's energy returned. It bucked and rolled, blindly but powerfully. Scores of goblins were crushed, some were pierced by the allizewsaur's fangs, and the rest hastily retreated.

This time, the goblins did not advance again until the allizewsaur fell still. Even then, their first steps were cut short when a deep-blue-colored goblin that glittered with gems emerged from the ocean.

"Sacron!" Troy gasped.

The large goblin roared at the others on the beach, and they fell back. Behind Sacron came the remnants of his war party, many of them badly injured. The powerful aqua-goblin evidently demanded first tribute for himself and his troops. The other goblins, including the shaman, held back even as Sacron mounted the dead allizewsaur.

The brilliantly blue goblin looked like a wart on the hide of the massive allizewsaur, but the image the war chieftain wanted was one that would surely reside in the memories of aqua-goblins for ages. As Sacron traversed the length of the allizewsaur, it was wracked by its final shudders and lay dead. Sacron, astride the lizard's corpse, truly seemed triumphant at the moment. The goblins cheered loudly, but the humans adrift in the Ocean of Tears were simply grateful for anything that distracted the goblins for a time.

The distraction would continue, and even escalate, for the female allizewsaur, drawn by the scent of bountiful blood, cleared a rise and strode toward her dead mate.

"The blue goblin will get his due now," Troy said, the blood-thirst of revenge evident in his voice.

But Sacron held his ground. He watched the female carefully as she approached, but he did not budge from his position atop the fallen male allizewsaur. The other goblins, including those who came ashore with Sacron, carefully retreated. They did so slowly, knowing that any sudden movement might provoke the goddess who walked so near to them.

But the female allizewsaur ignored the goblins. With every step she took, she sniffed in the direction of the male lizard. Her huge nostrils flared, and she moved warily, but without overt hesitation.

When finally she reached the corpse of the male, she regarded it first and then, finally, Sacron. The aqua-goblin did not stir. Barely did he even breathe. The gaze of the female lizard then moved past Sacron, and she stooped so her nose brushed the gigantic scaled body before her. In a flash, her maw opened, and she sucked a mouthful of enormous intestines. The pipelike organs shuddered like giant slugs as the female drew them into her mouth. Likewise, Sacron fed. He lanced hunks of severed flesh with a trident and ripped the raw meat with his teeth from the weapon. The female took no notice of this activity, and so Sacron fell full upon the meal and shared it with the goddess of his people, none of whom dared approach even a single step.

"I guess he's the goblin king now," Troy amended.

Evanis said, "Let us hope they all have the opportunity to feast on the dead lizard. Maybe they will forget us for a time."

The humans looked around and saw others pulling

themselves out of the water onto pieces of the wreckage. Troy glanced at Evanis and said, "Not that I am complaining—"

Cadmus, who possessed a bit more tact under pressure, interrupted, "Considering that you saved our friends Nestor and Delailith." The bard eyed Troy, who'd fallen uncharacteristically silent in the face of this reminder.

Nodding, the rogue continued, "—but where exactly did you come from? You're not one of those water elves. I mean, you seem to be human like us, but here you come riding a dolphin?"

Evanis chuckled. "I'm as lucky to be alive as you, friends. I was one of three volunteers who just a short time ago ran over to that island." She motioned in the direction of the feeding frenzy. "The elf-emperor who commands our mission sent me and two others to plant some evidence to mislead the goblins into attacking the ships that pursue us. We did so, but we were discovered 'ere we could escape."

"Ran?" asked Troy, incredulously.

Evanis' smile was disarming, completely natural, and utterly beguiling. Her face brightened with relief, and the others could not help but share in her sense of satisfaction. She brushed back a lock of blond hair that fell across her face and, though clearly weary, she seemed invigorated. Her cheer was infectious, and the others suddenly felt better despite their predicament.

"Yes, ran," she laughed. "The elf enchanted all three of us with a pair of magical effects. The aqua-goblin shaman dispelled the one that let me run on water, though, and I thought I was doomed when I fell into the ocean with nothing but goblins closing in on me from every angle."

"The dolphin saved you?" guessed Troy.

"Absolutely, with a little encouragement. My magic is humble compared to that of many, including no doubt your friend Nestor's, but I lived among the rangers of the Faydark for my adolescent years and they taught me something of befriending animals. Fortunately, it works as well with a sea creature as with a squirrel."

"Astounding," Troy overenthusiastically proclaimed.

"Can your pet save us again?" asked Delailith.

Evanis looked questioningly at Delailith.

The warrior gestured back in the direction from which they'd come. All of the humans raised their eyes in that direction, and all their eyes widened. *The Bountiful*, its huge sails bursting into flame before their eyes, lurched suddenly out of control, bearing down upon them as smoke trailed from the ship's blazing canvas to the deck of an enemy vessel festooned with archers.

Mortified because it should be *his* reflexes that awed everyone, Troy watched flat-footed as the two women seized the initiative. Delailith leapt to her feet, cat-quick, balancing as the fragment of wooden deck sloshed from side to side. She crouched next to Nestor, her arms twisting and struggling beneath his bulk, ready to heave the unconscious man into the water and out of harm's way.

Meanwhile, Evanis slid instantly into the water. Troy was shocked at her flight, but before he could conclude whether or not to follow her, the ranger resurfaced beside their makeshift raft and started pushing it ever so slightly toward Dinosaur Isle and thereby fractions of a deckspan away from the midline of *The Bountiful*. As she pushed, she chattered like a hoarse dog at the water, and after a moment's confusion, Troy understood that she somehow spoke to the dolphin, for suddenly it rose up beside Evanis, its bottlenose braced on the wooden raft and its tail thrashing furiously in the water.

Troy and Cadmus watched in mounting horror as a great gout of flame blasted from the enemy boat and exploded into another Combine vessel. Before they could be certain of the result of that attack, *The Bountiful* was upon them. Troy remained tense even when he sensed Delailith relax, for the larger boat came *that* close to demolishing them.

Her hair matted to her forehead and salt water dripping from her brow so she kept her eyes almost closed, Evanis grinned and said, "Yes!"

Delailith nodded, but then her eyes narrowed, a reaction that Troy recognized as a prelude to trouble.

"What now?" he demanded.

"It's gone. Seru's boat disappeared."

The others looked up. Here *The Bountiful* careened out of control, the winds ripping at the burning sails, and there *The Beast* swallowed water through a gaping hole in its hull, but *nowhere* could they see the enemy boat.

"By the gods," said Cadmus. "No wonder it so easily dispatched our boats. We never saw it coming."

"Could it be what downed us?" Troy asked.

"I don't think so," Delailith said.

Evanis said, "It wasn't. I saw your wreck, and I couldn't explain it until now because you seemed to suddenly upend and fly to pieces. But you must have struck an invisible boat—like that one."

Cadmus craned his neck around, scanning every direction. "There could be more of them anywhere!"

Evanis pulled herself out of the water. Troy offered a hand, but she was mostly aboard before then, and she just smiled at him. The rogue gave her a serious-faced nod, as if he were a respectable man and they not a couple stranded in the middle of a great ocean. Nevertheless, he noted her slim, athletic build and, deep in his prehistoric

brain, contemplated prolonged abandonment on a remote island—though one not controlled by human-
eating goblins.

Unable to imagine the foolishness the man pondered,
the ranger gave him a quizzical look, and then looked all
around as well.

The dolphin chattered at her and Evanis nodded and
patted its head.

"He says there are no other such boats. There were
two, and now there's but the one."

Cadmus moaned. "One such boat is all that's required
to decimate our entire fleet. Our mission is doomed and
our lives forfeit."

Regaining some of his wits, Troy said, "You'd best
begin composing our dirge, then, friend."

Delailith said, "How does the dolphin know there
were two?"

Evanis looked at the warrior and then at the blank
expressions of everyone else. "That's a good question."
She turned to the dolphin.

"I love this part," Troy said.

As Evanis gibbered and jabbered back and forth with
the dolphin, Troy said, "I like this lady."

Cadmus laughed. "We know."

When Evanis turned back to them, Troy and Cadmus wore conspiratorial smiles. Delailith grinned and
shook her head at her friends' nonsense.

"What?" asked Evanis, oblivious to the cause.

"No matter, Evanis," said Delailith. "Just that we'd
like to officially welcome you to our group, if you'd care
to join us."

Troy nodded repeatedly and Cadmus laughed again.

"We're a crew within a crew," Delailith explained.
"Although there remain some mysteries among us—"

She glanced in Nestor's direction. "—we count ourselves as one."

"Absolutely," the ranger said. "You seem like a steady bunch." She smiled at Troy, which caused him to cease his fawning nods.

"Lesson number one," said Delailith. "Don't feed the animals."

Troy mock-glared at the warrior.

Evanis said, "Anyway, I can't explain because I don't understand exactly what the dolphin means, but he can somehow see the invisible boats, even though he cannot literally 'see' them. Something about how he can sense its shape and location by making sounds. Regardless, that's how he knew there were two. And now just the one."

Delailith looked thoughtfully in the direction the invisible boat last sailed. She said, "So, could he lead us to it?"

Evanis grinned. "That's a really good idea!"

THE FIVE HUMANS AND ONE DISGUISED ELF stood in a chamber next to the captain's cabin, and Aataltaal spoke to the three magic-wielders who stood ready to depart. "You will be the eyes for your ships— the only individual aboard capable of seeing Seru's ship while it maneuvers to attack. You have your instructions, but let me add that you should release your compatriot from his or her duty. It's admirable that the men of the other two boats went down with them or remain to assist the survivors among whom they remain, but I require every possible pinch of magical energy at my disposal here."

The three spellcasters—two men and a woman—

nodded solemnly and began their spells almost simultaneously. One of the men, a slender, bookish fellow, was just a split-second ahead of the others, and also just a bit more adept in his casting, so that while they appeared as if they should be synchronized, in truth the thin man outpaced them. His fingertips lit with golden light a heartbeat before the others, and they had only begun to trace a doorway in the air when his was nearly half complete. His glowing digits left a trail that formed a portal of sorts, and the instant the lines drawn in the air by his two hands intersected, he physically stepped through the gate. In a flash he was gone, and before the retinal shock dissipated, the other two disappeared as well.

Aataltaal glanced briefly at Ilzathor, one of the two wizards who remained. "Await the first arrival and then join me on the deck." To the other man, the elf said, "Remain for the other two, then come up as well."

The elven enchanter paused to renew the magic of his own illusion as well as a handful of other spells, and then hurried above deck, where he sought Orleax.

"Don't stare," Aataltaal admonished.

Orleax calmly moved his fixed gaze from a seemingly empty spot off the *Wolf of Faydark*'s starboard side. As naturally as possible he turned to face Aataltaal. "Curses, Emperor, but it's hard to remember all of these misdirections."

Aataltaal nodded.

"Calling you by the correct name, pretending to be unable to see an invisible ship that's threatening another of our ships . . ." Orleax sighed in frustration.

Aataltaal had anticipated that reaction when his spell allowed Orleax to see the invisible ship, but not to engage it. He also knew Orleax would have resisted his newest plan if the elf had simply presented it to the human. But now, after stewing in his own ineffectiveness for nearly a quarter-hour, the human would be ready.

Aataltaal said, "Then you may relax. In a moment we will turn back as if to collect survivors from the other wrecks, but we will in actuality be laying an ambush for General Seru."

Orleax grinned, and the steely glint in his eyes at the thought of dishing out some punishment instead of merely sustaining it told Aataltaal that he'd made the best decisions to guarantee the man's complete support.

The elf said, "Simply await my word. I require at least two additional spellcasters."

They did not wait long. Ilzathor, the wizard charged with delivering the first returning spellcaster, arrived moments later and introduced Altan, from *The Guardian*. The latter said, "Thank y—" but Aataltaal interrupted him with a look of disapproval.

"There's no time for that now. Immediately meditate to prepare your most offensive battery of spells."

The wizards looked at one another, but both soon withdrew their spellbooks to imprint that magic in their minds' eyes.

As they did so, Aataltaal retrieved two brilliant peridots from his pocket. "Continue your work," he said. "I am going to cast a protective spell on each of you." Then he did so, drawing filaments of energy from the peridots as before that he wove into a protective second skin that encased each of the men. Ilzathor, more accustomed to the powerful spells of Aataltaal, still exhaled sharply at the rush of power, but his concentration held. Altan, however, shuddered when the green energy laced onto his body, and he looked up from his book. Aataltaal set the last strand in place and nodded to the wizard. "Complete your preparations and join me at the prow."

Aataltaal stepped away, but hesitated. He turned back to Altan and cast another spell upon him. Glittering magic twinkled around the man's eyes.

He also examined his own protections. The runic magic had nearly expired, for such effects could persist only so long, given the materials and magical power applied to the effort. But neither would he require the magic much longer, so he left his own protections unaltered.

"Ilzathor, explain the rules regarding the magic sight. I'll expect you both within a few minutes."

As Aataltaal strode to the front of the ship, he followed his own rules. That is, he noted the location of Seru's ship as he swept his gaze across the horizon, but he did not linger on the invisible boat, for fear that a sharp-eyed lookout on board would realize him capable of seeing it. That would be disastrous to the plan.

By his earlier command, the boat began to turn as the "emperor" walked this way. When Aataltaal reached the prow, the boat was headed back the way it had come, and the two other Combine ships followed suit, falling into position behind the *Wolf of Faydark*—just as the wizards had instructed the ships' captains.

In the guise of emperor, Aataltaal was here presumably to oversee the recovery of any survivors. In actuality, he planned to ambush Seru. When the two human wizards arrived, he explained as much to them, including that he required them to strike the first blow. Unsurprisingly, they blanched at the idea of leading an attack against the powerful man, but of course they both agreed.

Aataltaal outlined his intentions. "Seru's certain to be wary of an attack, and I think will be almost surprised to not be targeted, so we'll play to his suspicion, but only with your best attack." The elf chose his words carefully.

"Not that your power is inconsequential, but his defenses will be far stronger."

The two men nodded and then at Aataltaal's direction they waited patiently while pointedly not watching as the invisible boat, to the port side of the stern, drew nearer. As the Combine armada adjusted its course, Seru's ship did the same, evidently passing on tackling the nearby *Guardian* in lieu of the *Wolf of Faydark*, where the emperor himself stood prominently at the prow.

Just as Aataltaal hoped.

16

THE REVENGE OF THE CASTAWAYS

"**W**E CAN'T LEAVE NESTOR!" TROY ARGUED.
Delailith nodded.

"I want to stop the arrogant bastard, too, but even if we had the means of chasing him, then we'd be forced to leave Nestor defenseless."

Delailith nodded again.

"Damn it, Delailith, argue with me!" Troy growled. He wanted to get in the woman's face, but he knew that would get a rise out of her—the wrong kind, a dangerous kind. "You're supposed to convince me that it's necessary. Or that Nestor will be okay. Or that . . . by the gods, I don't know what. But something other than rotting on this driftwood within an orc's fart of an island swarming with goblins devouring their god!"

Flatly, Delailith said, "Even if Evanis' dolphin can locate the boat again, we have no means of propulsion."

"I know, I know. But you're the tactical brains, right? I thought you'd have three backup plans."

Evanis, finished checking on Nestor again, scooted close to Troy and Delailith. Cadmus sat nearby as well, but absorbed in his own thoughts.

"There's just no way one dolphin can effectively drag

this entire raft," the ranger said. "Maybe I could round up more of them, but they've probably been scared a good distance from the island because of the goblins and the boats. By the time I could get them, Seru would be beyond even a team of dolphins."

Softly at first, but then with growing excitement, Cadmus said, "What if we could get within bow range? I bet you're skilled with the bow, Evanis. Aren't all rangers? Anyway, tie a rope to our raft, the other end to an arrow that's shot into the general's boat, and then we could pull ourselves across the distance and not have to leave Nestor behind."

Troy groaned. "I think you have an arrow up your butt, Cadmus. If we could . . ." The rogue trailed off when Cadmus raised his arm and pointed. All three of the others looked, almost comically, following the line of his arm and then looking into the distance.

"I *will* be damned," Troy muttered.

"I'm counting myself luckier and luckier," Evanis said, grinning.

Cadmus continued to point at the crates and debris floating all around. "There are parts of a couple smashed boats here. Surely there are some weapons?"

Delailith interrupted the excitement. "The *Wolf* is turning back toward us. Could they have decided to re-trieve survivors while Seru's fleet is still plagued by gob-lins?"

Troy shook his head sadly and said, "I guess they don't know about the invisible boat! Well, maybe this maneuver will bring Seru toward us as well. Evanis, have that dolphin be on the lookout. Now find a bow and ar-rows!"

All the humans scoured the wreckage with their eyes and it took little time to find a cluster of boxes of weap-ons floating nearby. Cases of swords labored to poke a corner above the water, but several cartons of various sorts of arrows bobbed weightlessly, one spilling its contents in a trail of steel-tipped rods that stretched back to the main body of the *Bountiful*'s wreckage.

Excited, the ranger cheered, "Definitely lucky." Spontaneously she hugged Troy.

A dumb grin washed across his face and he said, "Agreed." And he hugged her back, but with feeling, which surprised the woman.

A voice droned, "Lucky? Lucky would be if we were still on the boat and could walk down the steps and find all these things organized for easy taking."

"Nestor!" Cadmus shouted.

Troy moved quickly to see his friend, too—though after initially drawing back from Evanis, he hesitated, looking into her crystal blue eyes and losing himself for a fraction of a second, to which she was entirely oblivious, before he snapped to himself again and joined Cadmus at his friend's side.

"Your timing, as always, could stand improvement," said the rogue, clapping his hands to the big man's shoulder.

While the men bantered, Evanis leapt back into the water. Her dive cut the surface cleanly and her dolphin companion followed instantly. A moment later, she was back, two bows, a crossbow, and a tangled coil of rope in hand. These she tossed onto the raft and then helped steer a bobbing crate to the side of the makeshift vessel. The dolphin nosed the crate forward and when it was near, Delailith grasped it and hefted it aboard. The warrior then gave Evanis a hand up, the ranger's clothes again plastered to her body, revealing the outlines of an athletic figure.

Evanis saw the three men looking at her and innocently she said, "What?"

The men smiled conspiratorially and Delailith half-closed her eyes and shook her head.

Nestor clapped Troy and Cadmus and said, "Some fish you caught while I was sleeping!"

Not comprehending, Evanis chuckled. "A dolphin's not really a fish—it births live young, like people."

Troy grinned. "I bet it does. I just bet it does."

Nestor rubbed his head and glanced at his body through the rips and holes in his clothing. He found very few wounds where wounds should be. Then he said, "I am amazed to wake up. To whom do I owe thanks?"

"Yourself," said Delailith.

"That's true," Cadmus said. "We'd all be at the bottom of the ocean with goblin points in our bodies, if not for your courage and sacrifice."

Troy shook a finger at Nestor. "And don't let it happen again." He eyed Nestor with a friendly menace, then added, "But it was the ladies who rescued you. Delailith must have chased your sinking body to the floor of the ocean. And this is Evanis—she's a ranger." He said it proudly, as if he were somehow responsible. "She and her dolphin brought both of you back from the deep."

Nestor stood and, though the raft wobbled from his shifting bulk, he ably stepped to the women and shook their hands. "Thank you."

Delailith kicked the rope in the direction of the men. "Enough chitchat and ogling. Make yourselves useful and unknot that." She glared at the men, and Nestor at least looked a bit guilty, while Cadmus flushed with embarrassment, but Troy continued to watch Evanis. Delailith shook her head again. Still, she readily acknowledged that Evanis did possess a rare, magnetic sex appeal, a sylvan allure that drew attention. She was natural and carefree, yet poised and confident.

Then Delailith turned and worked open the lid of the crate, while Evanis inspected the bows.

"Yes," the ranger said. "This one will do fine." She double-checked the crossbow's mechanism and then nocked a bolt that Delailith handed her. The weapon was large and impressive, but in the ranger's hands it did not seem unwieldy. Evanis was clearly practiced in its use. She turned sideways and readied the bow, then aimed and mock-fired in the direction of the *Wolf of Faydark*. She nodded to the others. "So, where do I shoot?"

No one said a thing.

"We're not out of danger yet," Delailith said, turning back to Nestor. "An invisible boat of Seru's has now effectively destroyed three of our ships. I'm not certain what has the *Wolf* turning back this way."

Nestor said, "I believe we can count on our faux-emperor having a plan."

As the *Wolf of Faydark* approached, the castaways hastily completed their preparations, which involved Nestor creating a small fire cupped in his hand, and Cadmus and Troy quickly working to pass the water-logged rope near it in order to dry it. Evanis warned that the wet rope would be too heavy for even a crossbow bolt to carry.

By the time the Combine flagship approached, the companions were ready and hoping for an opportunity. They saw the "emperor" standing at the prow of the ship, with two wizards in robes nearby, presumably to "protect" him, though they knew the elf's personal power far outstripped that of those men.

Nestor stretched out on his stomach. The additional rest was welcome, but mainly he reposed so that his bulk could obscure the neatly coiled rope.

Just in case Seru was watching, Troy and Cadmus acted the part of castaways. That is, they stood and waved their arms dramatically at the *Wolf of Faydark*,

though they hoped the flagship would sail past them—
and likewise hopefully Seru's ship as well. Other survivors
dotted the ocean, but mostly they had drifted farther from
the *Wolf.*

Evanis sat near the edge of the raft, gripping the
loaded crossbow out of sight, and prepared to communicate with the dolphin, which swam underwater, scanning
in its special way for Seru's boat.

Delailith eased back into the water. Troy and Cadmus argued against her return, considering her near-
drowning a short time ago, but they could not dispute
the fact that she was the strongest of them all. Also the
most determined, which meant that one didn't stand in
her way for long.

Suddenly, Nestor asked, "Why doesn't this invisible
boat leave a wake behind it? Have any of you been looking for that?"

"Who can tell, with all this choppy water?" said Delailith, as a wave thrust her against the side of the raft.

Evanis patted the water and in an instant her dolphin
rose up beside her. "He can," she said with a grin.

The dolphin chattered.

"The invisible boat is coming, too," Evanis said ex-
citedly. She shushed the dolphin and looked at the *Wolf
of Faydark.* She saw the "emperor" at its prow and she
wondered if he'd note her survival. Likely not, she assumed, for the elf had a hundred matters to attend at the
moment. But then the emperor paused for a moment,
and Evanis could see that he inspected her group. She
thought she saw him slightly nod at her and perhaps
Delailith as well, but it must have been her imagination. Then he moved away from the rail, and when he
did, both wizards beside him glanced in the same direction. She realized they could somehow see the invisible
boat and then she knew they had a plan. But plans can

fail, just as their own could. Better to carry through with theirs and hope that one or the other was successful. Hopefully both!

The hesitation of that moment left the others on edge. After a heartbeat of silence, Troy gasped, "It's coming? How do you know?"

Evanis grinned. "The dolphin, silly."

Delailith bobbed a bit as another swell swept past their makeshift craft. Shaking salt spray out of her eyes, she said, "Well, if Seru is near to us, then let's get to it."

Suddenly, the *Wolf of Faydark* sheeted some sails and it swung away from the raft, turning inside of it so it would pass on the side of the raft nearest the island.

A few sailors on board the flagship cheered the raft as they passed, and Troy shouted back.

"The emperor is drawing Seru's boat toward us," Evanis said.

Troy stopped his waving for a moment and looked down at her. "Um, how do you know that?"

"Just a feeling I have. I think he recognized me just now."

Troy smiled.

Cadmus stopped waving as well and groaned. "Great, now there's two of you who go with your gut instinct. Dangerous. Very dangerous."

The dolphin chattered again.

"Get ready," said the ranger.

Nestor propped his head up to speak, but also to remove himself from the coil of rope that would soon be shot. He looked at the water on the far side of the *Wolf of Faydark*, which was passing nearby at that moment.

The dolphin chattered.

"Swim, Delailith. Hard toward the island."

The warrior dove below the raft and reappeared on

the southern side. Then she kicked hard underwater and the raft began to shift, drifting slowly toward Dinosaur Isle.

Evanis licked her fingertip and then held it aloft, checking the wind.

"Good luck," said Troy.

Evanis nodded, then said, "On my mark, everyone."

In a flash, the dolphin disappeared, diving deep into the water.

Cadmus jumped in surprise, though he knew it was coming. The raft wobbled a bit from the motion.

"Steady," Evanis said.

They could all hear Delailith grunting in exertion as she worked to calm the raft.

Then, about thirty yards distant, the dolphin emerged from the water. It seemed the animal covered the distance in a heartbeat. It slowed, presumably keeping pace with an invisible ship right in front of it.

Then the dolphin turned, following a path parallel to that of the *Wolf of Faydark* from a moment before.

Cadmus said, "Um . . . when—"

"Steady!" Evanis insisted.

When the dolphin doubled its initial separation from the raft, Evanis said, "Now." She lifted the bow and Nestor rolled off the coiled rope. The ranger raised herself to one knee, checked that the rope tied to the bolt was not tangled with her arm, aimed high, and let the crossbow bolt fly.

There was a whumping sound as the rope spun from its pile and flew after the bolt, like a line being drawn across the sky. Then the dolphin dove, and the arrow suddenly stopped in midair directly above and just beyond where the dolphin had been.

"All right," Troy cheered quietly.

"Unbelievable," said Nestor.

Unable to see from the far side of the raft, Delailith asked, "Did it work?"

"Yes!" Troy screamed. "Now get on, hurry!"

Delailith hauled herself partly up the raft and watched as the final coils of rope disappeared. Troy grabbed her wrist, and with her other hand Delailith grasped a hole in the old ship's deck.

"Hold on!" Evanis warned. And then the raft bucked like a wild horse. Delailith strained to keep herself on board, her feet dragging in the water as the raft began to scoot across the surface of the Ocean of Tears.

A second later she was safely with the others as the raft bounced over the water. They all stared wonderingly at the taut rope, connected to an arrow that for all the world seemed to be flying through the air and pulling them all. Fortunately, the arrow struck the boat high enough that the leading edge of the raft was held aloft, and so did not threaten to drag into the water and dump its passengers.

Troy said, "I wonder if they see what we've done?"

"One way to find out, smart guy." Evanis laughed and slapped his back. "Get going."

Troy grimaced, but stood and exhaled three times rapidly to prepare himself. Then he grasped the rope and walked his hands out as far as he could reach. The first ten feet of line barely cleared the water, and so as Troy hung from the rope, the water rushed over him. "Brrr!" He shivered. But he crossed his feet at the ankles to get a grip and then he hauled himself hand over hand toward the ship.

Evanis took up a longbow, then reached into the crate and withdrew an arrow that she held gently against the string of the bow. For now, there was nothing at which to aim, but that could change at any moment.

She prepared for that eventuality by reaching into her leather pants. She withdrew a small feather from an in-seam pocket. Evanis held it close to her lips and whispered a series of incantations. Then she blew gently on the feather, around which a dull glow appeared. As the ranger blew harder, the intensity of the glow increased. In two seconds it glowed brilliantly lit. Evanis brushed the feather bearing her mana against her right eye, and the eye changed suddenly. It was no longer blue, to match the cold water of the Ocean of Tears, nor was it apparently a human eye at all! The golden orb was that of a bird of prey, and the ranger turned its piercing gaze toward the rope that held her new friend, and beyond it to the space occupied by an unseen enemy. If that enemy should but twitch, her hawk's eye would notice, and the vision it imparted would help her arrows find their truest marks.

Meanwhile, Troy faced hard going, but he had soon pulled to three body lengths away. Then Delailith's weight eased onto the rope, too, pulling it even farther into the water, but she was strong and overcame the current, soon working herself far enough along that she cleared the ocean.

Within moments, Troy, Delailith, and then Cadmus all inched their way along the length of rope.

Evanis carefully watched the space beyond where her arrow seemed to hang unsupported in midair. She waited for any movement, any sign of an attack to which she could respond, ready to track the trajectory of any arrow that might suddenly materialize and threaten one of her new comrades.

Instead, a crackling explosion sounded, and pyro-technics lit the empty space above the rope-strung arrow. Then came a responding attack, an awesome response from Seru's ship, which as the ranger looked on suddenly appeared as if from nowhere, but right in the spot where she knew it to be. She saw that along the length of the ship not a single assassin prepared to attack her friends.

No, not a single one: more like a half dozen. The archers poised at the rail, all with bows strung and loaded. The attacks seemed to have surprised them, and the explosions distracted them momentarily.

That was all the time Evanis required. She pulled her own bowstring taut and let an arrow fly.

THE BLOND-HAIRED WOMAN WAS AN AMAZING human indeed. There she was, alive. Despite the aqua-goblin shaman's attack, despite plunging into the ocean at the mercy of a horde of wrathful goblin warriors, she lived—yet another amazing testament to human perseverance.

Aataltaal nearly laughed aloud when he recognized that she'd joined the wizard who had played cat and mouse with the animated weapons that still guarded him. All the man's companions crowded onto the makeshift raft with him, including the woman Delailith, who continued to demonstrate her usefulness, so the wizard's gambit paid off. Aataltaal saw these humans from a distance, surely before they could discern his own indentity at the prow of the *Wolf of Faydark*. Evidently they were planning something. The body language of the two men waving for rescue wasn't natural. They were acting.

Then he saw the dolphin.

The flagship drew closer as Aataltaal struggled to divine the humans' intentions. Ultimately, his sharp elven eyes provided the clues. He saw the crossbow, the bolt, the rope attached to it. His own experience ages ago in the guise of a dolphin came back to him, and he realized that despite the invisibility that cloaked Seru's ship, the dolphin could "see" it.

Close enough that the humans could see him now, the "emperor" nodded to his subjects. He wished he could embrace them and commend their courage, but they all had deadly threats to overcome and leagues of open sea to traverse before Weille—and before any such celebration.

Aataltaal issued commands he imagined would give the humans the opportunity they sought—which was not rescue. His commands maneuvered the ship past them.

As the *Wolf of Faydark* rounded the humans' raft, he looked back at them. Natural enough a reaction, and a gesture that allowed him to assess the position of Seru's boat without being obvious. Seru was nearly upon them and with no sign he imagined his position compromised, for no hesitancy slowed his advance.

The enchanter hid a smile when Seru's ship passed the humans and he watched their plan unfold. He'd guessed correctly, and they'd managed to pull it off, at least this initial stage. Now, if they could actually get on board . . .

Unfortunately, he saw that the humans were climbing into danger. There was little chance their tether would go unnoticed, and regrettably it did not. Seru dispatched a group of archers to attend to the meddlesome threat. The tyrant just flicked a finger in the direction of the raft, as if those humans were little more than insects to be squashed.

It was slightly too soon to show his hand, but Aataltaal refused to let the humans' bravery be snuffed out.

"Slow down and bring her about toward those survivors," Aataltaal shouted. He indicated not Delailith and the wizard and their friends, but other humans in a

264 • STEWART WIECK

large cluster of debris who clung tenaciously to scraps of wooden planking.

To the wizards, Aataltaal said, "Get ready." He saw they were prepared, but unsure. "Be brave. You will survive this day."

As the *Wolf of Faydark* sheeted the sails and slowed, Seru's vessel quickly overtook them. This change of events caused the archers to pause, but they prepared their bows and began to gauge shots at the pesky humans.

"Now."

Altan and Ilzathor stepped boldly to the deck rail and began their spells. Less potent magic often took less time to dispense, and so it took only a few heartbeats before they launched the attack. Suddenly, a gout of flame burst with a roar in the vicinity of Seru.

With a great rush of air like a thunderclap that sent sparks flying in every direction, the fire fizzled instantly into smoke, but a second later, freezing winds appeared in a swirling mass above the man and poured jagged ice upon him.

As Aataltaal expected, these attacks had little effect. After the briefest pause of surprise, General Seru shrugged and the magical attacks dissipated into nothingness. What little fire and ice actually contacted him through his magical defenses was deflected by his gleaming black armor. But it was enough. Aataltaal needed only the tiniest spark or snowflake to land. Any such contact would subdue the general's little-known but awesome defense: it negated the first attack that landed against Seru in any engagement. Such was the greatest power of that armor and the reason why more than one assassin had failed.

Energy seemed to leap from the man's dark eyes, and he shook a mailed fist at the *Wolf of Faydark*. An instant later, the general's ship materialized from thin air, for Seru launched an attack. The fist that railed in a gesture of defiance suddenly glowed with the light of coalesced mana. The energy leapt in the form of a fiery orb from the man's hand and exploded toward Ilzathor. In midflight, the orange-red bead blossomed. It expanded into whirling discs of fire that slashed like swords, but burned with intense heat. In a flash, they converged on the young human wizard. The arcane skin Aataltaal had placed on the wizard flared with a bright light as its power attempted to fend off the inferno that cut at Ilzathor. The wizard screamed, and the odor of sizzling flesh bloomed from the man and he collapsed. Then the fire was gone, and Ilzathor groaned from the terrible pain.

At least he lived. Aataltaal refused to be made a liar.

Nevertheless, the elf grimaced with concern. Seru had not cast an actual spell. Aataltaal looked across the gulf to Seru, the man's grin a swath of white above the oversized jet-black neckguard.

No, his power was an innate gift, and that could come only from the gods—or from a very small handful of mortals. It was the confirmation the high elf sought, and it revealed the truth of all the recent plotting. It was not simply directed against the Combine Empire, but against himself as well—perhaps primarily against him.

Such were the machinations of the Teir'Dal.

ONE ARROW. TWO. EVEN A THIRD BY THE TIME the archers regained their wits. All these arrows trembled in the throats of three dead men. Only the lack of a quiver limited Evanis' attack. She could hold three arrows at a time and still effectively handle her bow. She reached her left hand toward the crate of arrows and snatched three more. By the time she could reset, the archers aboard Seru's ship responded.

One fired at Troy, in the forefront of those scrambling along the rope that bridged the raft to the boat, and the other two concentrated their fire on Evanis. One of those shots thunked into the side of the crate near the ranger's hand as she reached within, while the other struck her in the right thigh.

Evanis exclaimed in pain, but she knew her new comrades relied on her now, for they were defenseless. "Help me, wizard. The others are in danger."

A shot whizzed past Troy. The rogue yelled, "Whoa! Evanis, help!"

The ranger nocked an arrow and fired. The archers were wise to the attack now, though, and presented a more difficult target. The missile sailed past one archer's head, perhaps grazing his ear, but doing little to discourage him. Evanis followed with a second against the same foe, and that arrow turned the man's eye to slush as it plunged into his skull.

The other two quickly ducked behind the deckrail.

"Where?" Nestor complained.

"Toward the prow. They'll go for reinforcements. We cannot allow them to make it." Evanis turned to him briefly to emphasize the need.

The wizard stood straight, his sailor legs keeping him balanced as the fast-moving raft bounded atop the ocean. When he saw the ranger's eye, he smiled, nodding.

He said, "Then they shall not."

Nestor's tongue skipped daintily over a tussle of arcane words, and at the conclusion, he thrust his arms before him, slowly widening them at the elbow as if to encompass an oversized ball within them. Soon his arms formed a loop—though notably misshapen on the side against his body where a large belly interrupted the smooth lines of his arms—and then harmless traces of lightning flashed across that space. The bolts of energy became more numerous until, in a flash, so many fired at once that they seemed to create a disc of solid energy. At this, Nestor pulled his arms away and stepped back. The disc remained, hovering in place. Then, at the center on both top and bottom, the disc bulged. The flat circle ballooned into the silhouette of a sphere with outlines of electricity. The energy transformed to flesh until the floating orb appeared to be a giant eyeball hanging in space.

Nestor closed his left eye and then motioned with his head toward Seru's boat. The great eye, at least three feet in diameter now, shot over the water, levitating above the lapping waves.

"Get two arrows ready, dear. From what I've seen, that's all you'll require."

A few heartbeats later, the eye reached the side of the boat and turned at a sharp angle to fly along its length toward the prow.

Her voice a bit uneasy—unsure of the wizard's command of his creation—Evanis said, "About that far."

Nestor allowed the eye to sail another fifteen feet, then it turned on a coin as before and shot straight up into the air. Once it reached the height of the deckrail, the eye looped over it and spun so that its vast pupil glared back toward the stern.

Nestor, his left eye still closed, said, "There they are. Get ready."

The grotesque eye sank out of sight behind the railing, but not before Evanis saw it begin in the direction of the crouched archers. Nestor chuckled, amused with the sight of two bewildered archers threatened by a vast eye that hurtled toward them.

When the archers stood to run toward the stern, Evanis dropped them with an arrow each to the throats.

"It's safe now. Hurry!" Nestor shouted to the other three.

Troy said something in return, but the distance and continuing magical attacks launched back and forth between the two great ships drowned him out.

"Okay, climb!" Nestor shouted back.

"What did he say?" Evanis asked.

Nestor smiled. "No idea and I cannot make a giant ear to know better," he joked. "But I'll bet it was a wisecrack that we didn't need to hear just now."

Evanis grinned and nodded. She grabbed three more arrows and trained her hawk eye on the ship again.

17

THE SECRET OF DARKBRIAR

AATALTAAL DID NOT WASTE A SECOND.
Thoughts of the origin of Seru's power ran parallel
in his mind to the incantations required to properly
weave mana for his own effect. The invulnerability that
Seru's armor conferred had been used up, and so the
Koada'Dal did not pull any punches—he went for the
knockout blow.

In the back of Aataltaal's mind ran the thought
that—more than merely winning Katta's protectors the
time to transport him to safety, and more than simply
seeing these humans safely to Tunaria—one chance remained to salvage the Combine Empire. Seru's death
upon the water of the Ocean of Tears might convince
those in league with him to capitulate. If Katta could
then be revived, the empire might be saved as well.

Throughout these heartbeats of time passing, Aataltaal
cast his spell—not an overt one, but psychic in nature.
Meanwhile, Seru's own attacks battered at the "emperor."
Seru's ship was visible now. He had lost the advantage of
surprise, so the traitor ordered his crew to swing closer.
Already, banks of archers readied pitch-covered arrows.

Cries of alarm rang across the decks of the *Wolf of Faydark*.

Meanwhile, Seru loosed another fiery blast. This one demolished Altan, who shrieked and collapsed as the gout of flame swept across his body. As Aataltaal surmised, at this point Seru wanted Katta alive. His assassination failed, so now the empire would entirely become his only with Katta as his hostage.

Aataltaal's face—Katta's face, though the high elf still wore it—turned gray and then dark like a Teir'Dal's as he focused his inner demons and the terror of nightmares into his little-known spell. The spell was an ancient variation of an already powerful spell, but this version was known only by those of, or descended from, the elves of Takish-Hiz.

As another second passed, the emperor's dark pallor bubbled from his skin and gained form as a sort of gaseous cloud. Sparks flared within it and laced the cloud with traces of lightning. Then these bolts gathered the darkness; and a discharge of energy, shot full of black and purple sparks, streaked from Aataltaal toward General Seru.

The blast struck the human full in the chest. Seru's face was almost comical as he beheld not the bolt that pummeled him, but instead the source of the attack. Katta did not possess such powers!

Then the bolt spread crackling across the surface of every inch of Seru's black armor. The general's hair stood on end, and then with a great discharge the bolt exploded, hurling Seru backward. Like a metal-clad rag doll, he flopped upon the deck of the flagship and lay still.

Aataltaal's concentration fixed on the general and he began the spell that would exterminate the human, but out of the corners of his eyes he could see that already this affected Seru's crew. The archers, the sailors, the officers—all of them stood, shocked at their motionless commander.

The Koada'Dal knew Seru wasn't dead, but the stunning effect of being wracked by the chaotic visions carried by that spell made it look so. And in those precious seconds when Seru was defenseless, the *coup de grâce* would land!

MORE USED TO CLIMBING, OR AT LEAST HANGing precariously, because of training in his shady past, Troy outpaced both Delailith and Cadmus in the rope climb to Seru's boat. Of course, the threat of more arrows—like the one that had whistled past his ear when the boat appeared out of nowhere—enhanced his speed, but the rogue soon realized that Evanis, a marvelous archer, and Nestor, the ex-wizard turned wizard again and seemingly without a hiccup in the execution of his spells, suppressed that threat.

As the rogue neared the boat, he studied Evanis' crossbow bolt with a greater regard than he watched for more enemies. The shaft bore a tremendous weight, especially now that Troy worked his way to within a body-length of it. However, Evanis had promised it would hold if she could hit the ship with a solid shot. Troy had watched as she had notched the arrowhead, barbing it so that once in the wood, it would be less likely to pull out. Troy had been doubtful, but it seemed the ranger knew her stuff as well as Delailith knew her swords, and he knew the ways of the shadows.

He was relieved to have another companion in whom he could place his confidence.

Troy arrived at the arrow and, not wishing to hang directly on it for fear of breaking it, he reached past to the grooves between the planks of the ship's side. His fingers, nimble enough to lift coins from the pockets or purses of men who might otherwise have refused to buy the rogue a drink, were also exceptionally strong, able to bear his entire weight with as few as three fingers total. Since he found a home for all four on just one hand, the transition from the rope to the ship was not a problem. He swung over, steadied himself, cupped the fingers of his other hand into the boat, and then found purchase with his toes.

Finally he glanced back at Evanis and Nestor. The big man motioned him on, so Troy scrambled up the side and over the deckrail, flipping onto the deck in a fighting stance in case he was immediately threatened. Not only did he seem safe for the moment, but no attack seemed forthcoming at all.

Troy heard shouting men and the banging of their feet, but he saw precious few of them, except four dead archers about ten paces away. It was a stroke of luck that their bodies lay crumpled between the ship rail and a bank of wooden storage chests. Without looking around again, Troy hustled to the bodies. He pulled an arm and a dangling leg completely behind the cover of the chests. Next, he looked inside the chests and, in the second one, he found what he desired: rope.

By the time he anchored the rope around the handle of a storage chest and looked overboard with it in hand, Delailith dangled near the arrow, clearly uncertain how to proceed, but waiting patiently and quietly for Troy. He got her attention and tossed her the rope. She caught it on the first attempt and, after a nod from Troy, she released the first line and swung. Her legs splashed into the water, and while that made it difficult to hold on, it also slowed her momentum and she stopped on the backswing. Hand over hand, the warrior hauled herself up.

When a figure clad in a tunic bearing the black fist of Seru reached a hand over the side to assist her, Delailith whipped out her sword and nearly beheaded the man. Frowning at Troy for this deception, Delailith sheathed her weapon and heaved herself onto the deck.

"Stay down," she cautioned. "Seru and Aataltaal are hurling some major force around."

Troy stayed low, pulling off the uniform of one of the archers; as she watched, Troy expertly completed the job. "I'd rather be undressing a pretty princess," he said with a grin.

Delailith crouched next to him, careful to remain out of view of the enemy. "You're incorrigible."

Troy said, "But it'll do me good to watch you put these on." He dumped the clothes at her feet. "They won't fit over your others," he added with a smile.

The woman did not dignify the comments with a response, and honestly could care less anyway. After all, the two had shared countless beds together—if only in bedrolls, and usually on uneven ground surrounded by many other people. Nevertheless, she knew that when in the field, the vicinity of her bedroll seemed a popular spot, especially among the younger recruits.

Despite herself, Delailith chuckled. Though Troy was a long-time friend and companion, and counted as an adult by most usual measures, he remained a child at heart, which is why—she knew herself well enough to admit it—she so enjoyed his company.

As she slipped from her worn and soaked clothing, Troy glanced over the rail of the ship to check on Cadmus, who had almost reached the ship. Troy glanced back playfully at Delailith. He caught an eyeful that would have kept new recruits quiet in their bedrolls for a handful of nights, but, from the corner of his eye, he also spotted a black blur flying low over the ocean. It passed out of sight too quickly for him to be sure just what he had seen. The rogue quickly looked all around. He scanned the surface of the water and, seeing nothing, looked everywhere skyward. Still nothing. He looked at Evanis, who was squinting into the distance over Troy's head, and just then dropped her gaze down to Troy. She pointed, and the rogue followed her finger.

A razor-winged raven. So, the blur was its flyby. Now it circled and prepared to swoop again. Troy looked down at Cadmus. The bard was close, but not close enough. If the rope were to be cut now, then the bard would go into the sea . . .

Troy looked again at Evanis. But she was no longer gazing up at him. She knew nothing but her bow, the raven, the space between.

The bird completed its turn and picked up speed as it dove toward the bard. Its flight flattened when it reached the water and, as it closed, it turned so its wings spread perpendicular to the ocean. It aimed for a point near Cadmus, but far enough away that the bard could not interfere.

Suddenly, a missile sped toward the bird. Faster than Troy's eye could follow, the bird subtly adjusted its flight and Evanis' arrow hurtled past. But somehow the ranger had known the first shot would miss its mark—either that, or she intended it—so directly on the heels of the first arrow flew a second. This one punched cleanly through the raven's breast, skewering it and sending it limply into the ocean.

The rogue prepared the secured rope to toss to Cadmus as he had to Delailith. Troy looked out at Evanis again, and his breath caught in his throat. The sun, poised to the west directly behind the ranger, at once silhouetted and highlighted her, bringing her beauty fully to bear, her delicate features as well as the sublime shape of her body. Gorgeous women usually stoked Troy's bravado, but this sight made him weak-kneed. He might have gone overboard if Delailith had not grabbed him by the scruff of the neck.

"Calm down, lover boy."

Troy cleared his throat, trying to reclaim his nonchalant mien, but achieving only a feeble acting job. That he didn't retaliate with witticism was itself telling. The rogue bent and retrieved the rope Delailith used to climb aboard and, ignoring the warrior, he swung it toward Cadmus.

Then, just as the bard reached for the swinging rope, his legs loosening on the rope bridge so he could shove free of it for the new purchase, everything—the entire world, the ship, the ocean, Cadmus, and Evanis, too— disappeared completely.

AATALTAAL THRUST A HAND TOWARD THE downed figure of Seru. He looked down at his clenching fingers and *squeezed* . . . hard, as if crushing an invisible stone. His fingers flared and lit with the outline of mana purified into red light. The elf looked up, and across the gulf between the ships, Seru's body twitched. Then it wriggled and finally it shook as if in the mouth of a hungry beast from the darkest wilds of Kunark.

General Seru had recovered from the nightmares that assaulted him, body and soul, but now he found himself in the grip of an invisible, strangling force. He clawed at his throat, but his mad efforts were thwarted by the neckguard of his own armor.

As the traitor struggled, Aataltaal prepared yet another spell. He thought the second would do the trick, but the man was too strong: more magic was required. And even as he cast a third spell, Aataltaal saw Seru stagger to his feet. Seru's head bent to the side, and his face creased with pain and frustration, but in his grimace rose hate and madness, too. Aataltaal's spell was choking the very life out of him, but not until he breathed his last would the general's determination wane.

The traitor raised his hands and instantly everyone aboard his flagship snapped to attention and resumed their business, including the archers, who raised their fire-laden bows.

But Aataltaal loosed his attack first. He drew once again upon the ancient magics of the elves of Takish-Hiz, and another bolt of dark violet lightning streaked toward Seru.

Midair, it evaporated.

"Innoruuk will feast upon your soul, Aataltaal!" came the shrill cry. The hag Rashalla lowered her arms, and the last trickle of the mana she spent to unweave Aataltaal's lightning dribbled to the deck of Seru's ship.

Aataltaal knew that voice, knew it from ages past, from encounters both intimate and deadly. Much about Rashalla, and about Seru's foul power, became clear to him in that awful moment, and Aataltaal found himself nodding in understanding and disgust.

"Not this day, Opal Darkbriar, nor upon any other!" Aataltaal retorted.

"Fool, you are revealed!" Rashalla laughed. His ancient nemesis waved her hand again, and the powerful magic she used to dispel Aataltaal's psychic attack seemed to melt his illusion as well. Just as the Elddar planned, he stood revealed as Governor Aataltaal. In the heat of battle, even Rashalla seemed convinced her magic was the cuase of the revelation.

Then Seru motioned with his hand and flaming arrows flew at the *Wolf of Faydark*. As with *The Bountiful*, they snagged the sails and lit the deck. Aataltaal realized then that by dismissing his illusion, Darkbriar thought to injure the resolve of the Combine fleet. Little did she comprehend that these people *knew* they did not follow Emperor Katta these past days: they led others away from him!

Then suddenly, the witch gestured and Seru's entire boat disappeared again. The last thing Aataltaal could see was Seru sinking to his knees, for strangely, even though his sight was attuned to the invisible world as well as the visible, the elf could no longer see the boat either.

CADMUS NEARLY LOST HIS HOLD ON THE ROPE IN that instant when a veil dropped over the world and he could see nothing. Then just after that space of time, probably infinitesimal but somehow infinitely long as well—the time it took Cadmus to realize he could see nothing at all—everything reappeared again.

Looking up, Cadmus saw Troy's face. Blank at first, recognition washed over the rogue's expression, and Cadmus realized that Troy, too, must have been blinded for a moment. Mainly, though, the bard was pleased to not be drinking ocean water. He dangled now from the new rope Troy had swung toward him. Cadmus could not have told how he'd managed to grab it and hold on in the space of his confusion, but here he was. Lest something even more bizarre threaten his safety, Cadmus quickly climbed the rope and flipped over the rail.

Just then, a series of crackling explosions sounded, as if lightning repeatedly struck the deck of the ship. However, no magical attack, and certainly no thunderstorm, was evident.

"One mystery at a time," Cadmus said, watching Troy

pivot his head in an effort to determine from whence the noise issued. "What happened just now?" Cadmus asked.

"Look," answered Delailith. She pointed to Nestor and Evanis, who both stood on their makeshift raft scanning the horizon and looking confused.

"The boat's invisible again!" Troy whispered urgently. He wanted to shout it, but he had the sense to keep his voice down.

"And it's about to mete out vengeance on our governor and his flagship," Cadmus said.

Troy and Delailith looked in that direction as well. They were close enough to the *Wolf of Faydark* to plainly make out her sailors, and even the "emperor" himself. Confused glances passed among the three again, for the "emperor" no longer wore the guise of beloved Katta. Now Aataltaal appeared as himself, meaning that the illusion behind their entire mission was pierced and the ruse revealed.

Nevertheless, Seru seemed fully intent on crushing Aataltaal and the *Wolf of Faydark*. While the sailors aboard the *Wolf* ran frantically in circles trying to come to terms with an invisible enemy, Seru's vessel slowly wheeled around the Combine ship.

Cadmus said, "I think he means to board the *Wolf*."

Delailith said, "Our objective has not changed. We boarded this boat because it was invisible, and now it is so again."

Troy nodded. "We need to kill whoever's magic is cloaking this boat. And we need to do it fast, because if Seru gets in position against the *Wolf*, then a whole lot of people are going to die. Not to mention the ones still in the water waiting for a rescue."

Cadmus motioned vaguely in the direction of the explosions of a moment before. "I think I know where to start." He then gathered the pile of clothing stripped off another of the archers and arranged it so he could quickly change.

Troy's smile gleamed with feral delight, but a hint of worry tugged at the corners of his lips. He glanced back over his shoulder, his concern for their comrades evident.

His clothes half swapped, Cadmus paused and put a hand on Troy's shoulder. He said, "Don't worry about them. You can't worry about them. The best way to help is to put this boat out of commission. Then the governor will do the same to Seru. I've heard stories about that elf. I've not believed them enough myself to tell them until now. As I climbed that rope, I saw some of the magic he hurled at General Seru and how it *hurt* him. If his swordplay stands up to the legend as well as his magic, then we've got a real chance to survive.

"Besides, that lady can take care of herself. She's got a year's supply of arrows in that crate. Plus, Nestor is practicing magic again. They'll be fine." Then the bard nudged Troy in the ribs and said, "Although there's always the chance he'll put the moves on her while they're stranded!"

Troy mock-glared at Cadmus, but he smiled, too, and nodded in the direction the bard had indicated. "Let's get started, then."

Delailith motioned the two men to her side, and all three humans crouched low behind the storage chests.

Delailith said, "Cadmus, your songs will help eventually, but they'll get us noticed, so you need to stay quiet until it's absolutely time to make our move."

The bard tightened the belt of his new tunic and nodded.

Troy put two fingers to his mouth and turned them, as if buttoning his lips, and then he crept from behind

cover and toward the doorway from which the explosive
noises had issued moments before.

Two paces into a wide-open expanse of deck between
the railing and the doorway, he froze. Many footsteps
plodding in unison like a martial full march sounded
from the deck on the other side of the raised platform
that housed the doorway. The sound came nearer, and
the rogue realized a small troop of soldiers would momentarily round the far corner to the side of the ship
and spy the three of them.

Delailith reacted first. She grabbed Cadmus by the
front of his shirt and dragged him forward. She stormed
into Troy and shoved him to, into, and through the
doorway. Without stopping, she barreled all the way
down the steps beyond the threshold, Troy stumbling in
front of her and Cadmus staggering behind. The rogue
recovered his composure halfway down the steps and
Delailith relented her pressure on him, but the bard still
seemed stunned, so her grip on him remained firm.

The footsteps above pounded beside the stairwell. If
the three had moved an instant less quickly, they would
now be in pitched combat. Instead, at the base of the
steps, Troy started down the hallway. It stretched ahead,
and their destination was obvious. Acrid smoke billowed
from beneath the closed door some twenty feet distant,
at the far end of the hall.

At the head of the group, the rogue was the first to
enter the smoky embrace of the wafting blackness. He
ground to a halt, a gag reflex causing him to dry heave.
He threw a hand up to stop the others, but Delailith
overruled him: they were still in view from the top of
the steps. She yanked Cadmus one final time and stepped
past Troy so they all stood out of sight.

Cadmus gagged as the smoke drifted around him. He
threw a hand to his mouth, as his stomach threatened to

rebel. Delailith wrinkled her nose, too, but the smell of burned flesh only made her more battle ready, for what kind of battlefield did not stink of charred bodies, if not from the attacks of wizards and magicians, then bodies burned in the aftermath of battle.

The warrior motioned for the men to steady themselves. She half-turned her head toward the stairway and listened as the soldiers above marched past the door. Then she examined the hallway: three doors, one each on the right and left sides, and one at the end. Delailith tapped Troy on the chest. A woeful expression clouded the rogue's face, but he nodded when the warrior waggled her fingers at both the side doors.

Troy stepped forward to the left door first. As he edged ahead of Delailith, the warrior slowly, silently drew her swords. The slender man waved a hand in front of his nose and mouth to clear the air, but nevertheless grimaced as he took a deep breath and pressed close to the wooden door. He locked to rigid stillness and, without inhalation to cloud his silence, he listened intently. He shook his head to no one in particular, though it was a signal to Delailith. Then he stepped to the other door and did the same. This time, though, his duty was paramount in his thoughts, and the foul air did not cause him noteworthy distress.

The rogue's pause at this door was longer and he raised a finger to his friends. The finger soon became two, which he shook slightly, then he tilted them to the horizontal and wobbled them.

Delailith relaxed her grip on Cadmus and looked him in the eye. She nodded and then motioned onward with her head. Then she crept to Troy and all three stepped gently past the doors, including the one to the right where two men slept.

Troy led the way to the end of the passageway. The

hall was now partly fogged by the black smoke that still trickled from beneath the door. Troy stood with his feet wide apart so they would not cast a shadow at the floor and he edged closer to listen as he had before.

Just then, another series of explosions resounded. Clearly the same sort as before, they seemed more dramatic this time for the humans' proximity; that, plus a human element, for beneath the crackling concussions came a man's muted cries.

"Innoruuk preserve me!" he whimpered.

A second series of crackling detonations erupted, and the man cried out again. His faith was willing, but his flesh was not. Faith and lightning won, for thick black smoke surged beneath the door and quickly enveloped Troy's feet. As it swirled to the rogue's waist and then higher still, Troy took a deep breath.

A choking voice inside the room beyond demanded, "Rashalla be damned. Open that door or we'll die of asphyxiation as surely as by this crystal!"

Troy threw an alarmed glance behind him, as still holding his breath, he dropped to his knees. Clad in the dark tunic of Seru's archers, the rogue virtually disappeared in the billowing, choking smoke.

When the door at the end of the hall began to swing open, Delailith stepped to the middle of the passageway, between Cadmus and the door. She crossed her swords and raised them high, much higher than practical for a battle posture.

More smoke poured out through the opening doorway, and a man stood revealed, clad in a fine silk robe of midnight black, decorated only by the clenched fist of Seru. The human recoiled before the crossed swords in the hallway. Reflexively, his eyes lifted up at them—just as Delailith and her rogue companion intended. As the man opened his mouth to cry out, Troy rose like a demon from the mist. One of his daggers plunged into the man's chest, while the other cut off the man's cry as it sliced across his neck. As if the move had been choreographed, Troy, too, crumpled to the ground when the dead man instantly collapsed; both the corpse and the rogue disappeared in the smoke.

Delailith marked his spot, leapt over the prone rogue, and fairly flew into the room. Most anyone else would have hesitated at the scene that greeted her, but Delailith was not prone to reflection in the heat of battle. This capacity for forthright action often earned her the seconds of precious advantage that marked the difference in a battle of otherwise equally prepared and skilled foes. She did not pause to consider the implications of the ring of wizards that stood in a semicircle around an enormous stone, one that seemed crystalline in structure yet shone with the gleam of darkest obsidian. Nor did she concern herself with the fact that there were five of these wizards. All that mattered was that, a moment before, there had been six. And after her blades swept a path, leaving smoke rolling in rings in their wake, there were but four.

Only then did she pause long enough to note two facts that did disturb her. First, two other wizards already lay dead, their corpses charred. Second, one of the remaining wizards—surely the leader of the group, for the sleeves of his black robe were banded with crimson embroidery—was a dark elf.

Even Delailith paused at that sight, for it was an association with dark elves that drove the wedge between Seru and the Combine Empire, and supposedly forced his move against Emperor Katta. Delailith's nostrils flared. She had little patience for politics in general, and less for deception. Regrettably, the two were ofttimes intertwined.

Unfortunately, even this infinitesimal delay removed Delailith's advantage of surprise. Her initiative was thwarted, and the wizards, with the notable exception of the dark elf himself, responded at once. The wizards all faced the central dark crystal, and ebony tendrils that stretched from that object and twisted around the waist of each wizard retracted, dissipating into the nothingness of the smoke that swirled throughout the room. Only the dark elf remained so entwined. The strain of assuming sole responsibility for the crystal's magic was clearly great, for the Teir'Dal grimaced and then hissed, "Quickly, you fools!"

Two of the wizards, one a heavyset woman with an unattractive, pear-shaped face, and the other a very short man of otherwise average build, extended their arms toward Delailith. The warrior recognized the spell they wove, as she'd been burned by it before, and she knew her chances lay not so much with her own skill, but by the hopeful lack of it on the part of the wizards. She threw herself forward into a roll, tucking her swords along her sides, in the direction of another of the wizards, the nearest, a crook-toothed, stringy-haired hag of a woman who unfortunately seemed to anticipate the attack.

As Delailith rolled, the arms of the two attacking wizards glowed yellow, then orange, and then flared to brilliant red before bolts of fire leapt from their fingertips. The woman's blast splashed into the wall and charred the wood, but the small man was more accurate—his fiery bolt flared across Delailith's back as she rolled. The magical energy burned through clothing and onto flesh. The threads of her tunic glowed red-hot for an instant after the attack, but Delailith fought through the pain and executed her attack. She regained her feet and thrust both swords toward the old woman. But even as the swords hurtled toward her, the wizard drew the darklight shadows toward her from every corner of the room and from the midst of the smoke. They wrapped and swirled around her before the attack landed, and by the time the swords reached the intended mark, the woman was gone, disgorged by the shadows ten feet away on the far side of the obsidian crystal.

"All at once now," said the small man, grinning wickedly behind beady little eyes that glared feverishly at Delailith. "Cut the bitch down."

Delailith found herself dangerously exposed. The three human wizards all stood on the opposite side of the enormous crystal, all casting another spell. The small man, so successful with a fiery bolt the first time, clearly prepared to cast that spell again.

Unused to battle, Cadmus reacted slowly to the situation, but fortunately he responded just in time. His soft hum was at first indistinguishable above the din of the wizards' chamber, but it grew quickly in volume. By the time he stepped into the room, Cadmus' voice sounded like a lion's roar, and before he unleashed the fury of his war cry, he roared louder still. A thunderous boom blared from his wide-open mouth, and the magic in his song amplified the vibrations of his voice into a force that could quite literally crack bones.

The sonic power he created rolled across the room in a great wave that could be marked by how the smoke was pushed aside. That wave of invisible force could therefore be seen rushing toward the fat woman as sparks of electricity danced on her fingertips. The instant it struck her, the piledriving power caused her flesh to shudder and then her entire frame snapped backward and she was flung like a doll into the wood-paneled wall.

The old woman who teleported away from Delailith's attack was sufficiently unnerved by the bard's attack that she faltered and her spell failed. The short man was unmoved, though, and his hand glowed red. Strange, then, that Delailith charged the old woman and did not change targets. The reason for her decision was plain a split-second later, though, when rising from the smoke-covered floor like a demon from a grave, Troy appeared behind the man. He thrust both his daggers into the man's back, one near the kidneys and the other near the base of the neck. The diminutive wizard's final fiery blast may as well have been his lifeforce flailing from his body, for when that spell discharged, so, too, did the life flee his body. The stream of fire gushed awkwardly into the ceiling, and the fire persisted briefly on the wood there, but the blast was not sustained enough to ignite the ship.

Again, when his victim died, Troy sank into the smoke with the corpse.

Unfortunately, in a bizarre parody of the rogue's disappearance, a corpse also rose from the shrouded floor.

18

THE HARBOR OF WEILLE

"**INNORRUK SHALL FEAST ON YOUR SOULS**," snarled the Teir'Dal. "Arise, minion, to protect me." At the necromancer's command, a fleshless skeleton emerged from an unseen resting place within the smoke at the dark elf's feet. As it stood, the skeleton seemed to unfold, the bones of its body clicking into alignment as if a moment before it had been nothing more than a pile of disconnected bones. The final click was the vertebrae in its neck snapping its head forward. Then a red light flared to life deep in the eye sockets of its human-shaped skull, and it positioned an arm in front of its chest. That hand held a curved sword not unlike Delailith's, though the skeleton's was a true scimitar, narrow at the pommel and widening along the length of the blade.

Even while this occurred, Delailith continued her charge. The old woman tried to cast the same spell that earlier allowed her to teleport to safety, but even that brief spell required too much time, for Delailith knew to expect it and did not pause. Instead of making certain of a killing blow, Delailith lashed out simply to injure the wizard. The result was a wound across the hag's belly and a spell left incomplete. The woman's jaw dropped, her peril instantly clear, and Delailith finished the job with a slashing blow that sent the sorceress' head tumbling into the mist.

The warrior immediately turned to charge the necromancer, but with a quick step, the skeleton interposed itself between Delailith and its dark elven master. The warrior struck instantly, but even without muscles to power its movement, the skeleton parried easily, the magic that created it lending it an agility as unearthly as the creature itself.

Meanwhile, the Teir'Dal glanced about for the annoying rogue. The majority of his concentration still focused on the great obsidian gem that hung in the center of the room, but he clearly did not wish to be an easy target for another of Troy's stealthy attacks.

The black tentacle that stretched forth, seemingly from the depths of the gem, and entwined the necromancer's waist began to shift in a strange manner. Already formed of the purest blackness, the tendril seemed to phase out of existence entirely and leave only a shadow of itself behind. As this happened, the black light of the gem began to pulse, and the dark elf cursed. He returned his complete attention to the gem and placed both his hands upon the tendril. The Teir'Dal spoke a few words and his mana flowed into the tentacle, along its length—which served to make it solid again—and finally to the obsidian itself, which stopped pulsing and instead again glowed with a steady, baleful light.

Clearly unsteady on her feet, the fat woman stood and threw her arms wide. She spoke words that sounded like cracking ice. In response, a blue disc appeared over Cadmus' head. The bard shivered, but instinctively knew better than to look up to where a wave of cold emanated. Instead, he threw himself backward down the passage—and just in time. A great blast of hoary frost fired downward from the magical disc. The blast encompassed the entire space Cadmus had occupied, but only a portion of it actually struck the bard. Even so, Cadmus yelped in pain, and his trailing left leg appeared to be shod entirely in a thick layer of ice. A similar block of ice stood in the bard's spot and partially blocked the entrance.

For his part, Troy slithered along the smoke-shrouded floor to a position behind the necromancer. When he saw the dark elf's stance tense, he recognized his opportunity. Without wasting a second, Troy struck, precisely on target. But it was not to be. Troy's dagger struck a magical shield that formed a second skin around the necromancer's body. The tip managed to penetrate and shatter the shield—barely—but instead of piercing the Teir'Dal's heart, it only scratched his skin.

To Troy's astonishment, the necromancer did not even turn to see his assailant. With a deft movement, he slipped the ebony tendril from his waist and flipped it in the rogue's direction. The unexpected attack was unavoidable. Troy dodged sideways in a blur that would have left most swordsmen flat-footed, but the tendril struck like a whip and wrapped around Troy's waist. The Teir'Dal made a waving motion and the tendril stretched, pushing Troy two arms' lengths away.

"Pitiful human," said the necromancer. He pushed back the hood of the embroidered robe and the shock of white hair atop his ink-black skin looked like a patch of the smoke that swirled below.

The villain made a clenching gesture and the tendril constricted, crushing the air from Troy's lungs.

"Just wait until it desires to feed. It devours only raw magic. Whether you run dry—" The dark elf gestured to one of the charred corpses barely visible through the smoke. "—or have nothing to offer it in the first place, then your fate is the same."

He then turned back to the battle. Troy had his other dagger ready to throw, and the rogue surely tried to raise his hand, but the tendril's embrace sapped him, body and soul. He lost his strength and his arm wilted to his side.

Meanwhile, the skeleton wildly launched attack after attack at Delailith, who at first parried the blows, but was then forced to retreat. The warrior seized a moment of reprieve when she managed to interpose the floating obsidian crystal between them. Seeing Troy's predicament from the corner of her eye, Delailith used the split-second to strike at the crystal, hoping to shatter it and destroy the tentacle that grasped her comrade, but when the first blow bounded off, leaving the gem unscathed, she did not waste her time trying again.

As the skeletal guardian maneuvered around the central gemstone, Delailith noted that the tentacle that bound Troy was fading out. That evidently meant it needed replenishment or . . . or what she wasn't certain, but Troy's situation looked dire. She guessed that this gem's power was what allowed Seru's entire boat and its occupants to remain invisible, and that if it did not receive the necessary magical energy, then life energy seemed to suffice as well. How that led to the deaths of the two wizards, Delailith could not know, for the dark elf and four other wizards remained, but she suspected it was the result of Teir'Dal perfidy.

Troy jerked upright in the clutches of the black tendril, and Delailith stepped toward him, but the skeleton intercepted her and its attacks forced her back again. Working hard to fend off the skeleton's furious assault,

Delailith shouted, "Cadmus, I need you now! The loud voice—use it again, but direct it at the gem!"

Talking and fighting at once proved to be too much in this case, and the skeleton's scimitar drew a red line across Delailith's forearm. Her grip nearly slipped, but as she parried with the other sword, she recovered in time to ward off further injury.

"Silence!" demanded the necromancer, and with a gesture he completed a spell that Delailith had not seen him begin. Currents of heat that distorted the very air blasted toward Delailith, and she gasped in agony.

"On fire!" she howled, though no flames were in evidence. But steam poured through the pores of her skin and out of her open mouth as well as her ears and nostrils. She was on fire inside—the necromancer's power affected the biology of the living as well as the dead. Delailith's very blood began to boil, and she managed just one more parry as she sank to her knees, near death and in agony.

Delailith did not witness what occurred next. Her skeletal opponent stepped up to deliver the death blow. Troy, too, was on the verge of dying. The tendril had faded so completely that it seemed no more than a shadow. With a shudder, Troy fell backward, his mouth open to the ceiling. Beams of purest black shot out of his mouth and from his fingertips as the tendril greedily sucked the rogue's life.

The Teir'Dal cackled in appreciation.

Then Cadmus poked his head past the block of ice that barred his entry and released a shrill shriek even more impressive than the one that had shredded the wizard. This time, the attack focused, as Delailith had instructed, on the obsidian gem. When the sonic waves struck the crystal, cracks appeared instantly.

292 · STEWART WIECK

"No!" howled the necromancer, choking back his merriment.

The bard's face turned red with the effort, but just as his breath trailed off for lack of air to expel, the hunk of obsidian shattered. The fragments exploded around the room, but more importantly, the ebony tentacle that gripped Troy disappeared to nothingness.

Even as he fell to the floor, the rogue recovered his senses. He launched the dagger that remained poised in his throwing hand, and it thudded into the base of the Teir'Dal's neck. The necromancer dropped like a fleshy sack, dead before he fell.

And as its master died, so, too, did the skeleton. Its sword was inches from thrusting into Delailith's breast when the bony animation disappeared. The sword clattered to the ground, and its rattling was the only accompaniment to the choking and gasping on the part of all three heroes.

Delailith shrugged this off and spun to face the final wizard. But the haridan lay dead. A great black tentacle stretched from a fragment of the obsidianlike crystal and wrapped around the wizard's arm. Clearly, the thing had struck out blindly in search of power, even as it was destroyed.

THE FIRES ON THE *WOLF OF FAYDARK* RAGED briefly, but an instant after Aataltaal's ancient foe Opal Darkbriar caused Seru's boat to fade from view, the elf assumed the form of an elemental creature made entirely of water. His guise as emperor was of no use now anyway, so as a water elemental he blasted gouts of seawater at the thickest fires on the deck and in the sails, while the sailors managed the smaller outbreaks.

Then, as he puzzled about how Darkbriar had managed to cloak the enemy ship from even his sight, he ordered a series of maneuvers to reorganize the remaining Combine ships. Seru's other boats had apparently repulsed the aqua-goblins—or else the creatures had retreated when news of the allizewsaur's death spread—and now Seru's ships gathered into an attack formation.

But before any attack could be launched, Seru's vessel reappeared just as suddenly as it had vanished. Heavy black smoke poured from the ship's hold; and Aataltaal recognized it as ethereal smoke. Only a spell of infernal power gone awry, or the destruction of an artifact of great evil, could create such.

Either way, Aataltaal would know shortly, for when he saw three humans dive off the side of Seru's ship, he ordered the *Wolf of Faydark* to speed to their rescue. Unbelievably, the humans had succeeded.

After that, the Combine ships waited an hour for an attack, then, when it did not come, they began to collect the other survivors, first of whom were the ranger Evanis and the wizard Nestor, who like their companions now safely aboard the *Wolf of Faydark* deserved high praise indeed.

Then, Aataltaal turned the Combine armada toward Weille. This time, the black-fisted flags did not pursue. Aataltaal watched Seru's flagship closely for any indication of the general's fate, but he suspected that the moment her spell artifact had been destroyed by the humans—the bard Cadmus told the very entertaining story to Aataltaal—Rashalla must have whisked herself and Seru to safety.

Assuming Seru lived, the Koada'Dal hoped those two would fall to fighting among themselves for a time. Unless Seru was too addled by Aataltaal's second spell, the general would surely have noted that, while he was surprised by Aataltaal's true identity, his cohort Opal Darkbriar was not.

OPAL DARKBRIAR CHURNED THROUGH THE WA-
ters of the Ocean of Tears, watching in disgust as the nearly broken ships that constituted the remains of the Combine armada staggered into the vast harbor outside of Weille.

Worse yet, the pirates there allowed it to happen. Here were boats laden with treasures and broken men, and the pirates did not lift a hand against them. She could not tell if the artifact that the cursed elf held aloft was magical or mundane, but the sight of the small white coin earned them free passage.

If she'd but known Aataltaal would dare to return to Weille or that he and his pitiful force would be welcomed like this, then Opal Darkbriar would have crushed the lot of them before now.

Or at least pulled enough strings in the court of Ne-riak to see that it happened, just as she'd delayed the ar-rival of Teir'Dal at the Great Combine Summit even though she could not cancel it entirely. Her standing in Neriak would be precarious for a time following this failure, but she knew she still possessed the confidence of her lord Innoruuk, and that was all that mattered. With that resource, she would soon be re-armed, and if the pirates of Weille would so easily bow down before the tattered Combine fleet, then Opal expected little resis-tance when she infiltrated the city through the many dark and nearly forgotten tunnels and tombs of the an-cient city upon which the pirates had built their hovels.

Of course, none of this—most especially her failure— would have come to pass if Seru had not given up the chase. Grievously injured as he was, his passion to seek out Emperor Katta—and surely naught but a corpse remained of that fool human!—unmanned the general. Opal had taunted him with his defeat at the hands of Aataltaal, but even that did not sway him, nor stay his wrath against her.

She'd no choice but to flee, and quickly. How Seru had gawked as she shifted from the crooked and creaking form of the human witch Rashalla into the incarnate fluid of a water elemental! In a flash she was an undetectable portion of the vast ocean, and beyond Seru's fury.

But also beyond hope of catching or stopping Aataltaal.

The most that Opal Darkbriar could manage now was to command a handful of her ravens to keep watch on the remains of the Combine fleet. The birds would find homes near the rocky harbor and continue to report to her while she licked her wounds and counted the days, months, or even years that might pass before she could strike again.

But in the life of an elf, what even were a few years? The passing of a thousand such had not dimmed her hatred of Aataltaal.

19

THE CITY OF FREEPORT

AS SHE PLUNGED HER SWORD INTO THE SOFT belly of the Deathfist orc, Delailith wondered if this could be what Aataltaal felt for humans: casual superiority with a hint of disdain and even revulsion. She wrestled her weapon free, and a trail of splattering ichor traced a path across the ground from victim to killer.

It wasn't far-fetched. She'd fought too many orcs these last years, and while she counted them as dangerous opponents, Delailith now respected little about them other than their tenacity. She could not shake her disdain for them as a lesser race, one savagely scrounging a meager existence in the shadow of the greater humans and their burgeoning settlements nearby.

No wonder Aataltaal and his Koada'Dal brethren looked down their noses at so many other races, including humans. Even though the governor was a charismatic and capable leader who certainly respected many of the humans with whom he had dealings—Delailith included—the woman nevertheless often detected in him a certain innate nonchalance about the fate of individual humans—the ones nameless to him, like a farmer who did not return from the fields, or one of the so-called wharf rats, parentless children who gathered at the free port formerly known as Weille, but now called Landing.

But to be fair, did the majority of humans them-selves generally give a damn for such people? The spirit of cooperation and aid lasted only as long as tragedies that enveloped the fortunate as well as the downtrodden.

She readied her weapon and fell back a step so as to draw shoulder-to-shoulder with the warriors who served on her patrol. These men all bore both sword and shield, while she forsook the shield in lieu of her practiced two-weapon style, though for now she wielded only one of her blades.

The orc rabble had grown bold enough to threaten settlements like Freefield that were near Landing itself. Delailith had come here at Aataltaal's direct command to report on their methods, their likely goals, and their chances for success.

What the woman warrior saw filled her as much with pity as loathing.

The Deathfist orcs counted as rabble compared even to the Crushbone orcs Delailith had fought a handful of years ago, back before the glorious Combine Empire collapsed because of General Seru's treachery. This breed of orc was slighter than their Crushbone cousins; they rarely achieved a height of six feet, and that meant De-lailith looked down upon virtually all of them. And their skin was only faintly green and so looked mottled or pale compared to the darker shades of the Crushbone orcs. The Deathfist looked like street dogs where Crush's Clan had resembled wolves.

Looking at them, Delailith could summon only the pity one would feel for a wounded, starving animal.

Except now she faced thirty of them, all brandishing weapons that in many cases they had looted from outlying human farms, from farmers too foolish—or too stubborn—to heed the advisories that Aataltaal's government issued for their protection.

Advice issued as if the humans were the high elf's children.

And if we are the children, thought Delailith, then these orcs are naught but our pets—or pests.

Her patrol of a dozen horsemen was outnumbered, and they had been outsmarted as well. Just as a human could trick an elf, likewise orc cunning could still trump a human's alertness. Thus it was that the dismounted horsemen found themselves ambushed within the yard of a pillaged farmhouse that seemed to have been abandoned for at least a day or two.

As the orcs slowly circled the soldiers of Landing, they gabbled back and forth in their native tongue. Delailith understood their language, but nothing of import passed among the orcs, so she would allow herself to appear ignorant until she heard something worth communicating to her patrol.

But still, their brutish language only reinforced her condescension. Surely this was how the human tongue sounded to elven ears weaned on the musical elven language.

Delailith didn't doubt it. Aataltaal worked hard to keep his feelings in check, but Delailith possessed a keen eye for understanding people. She'd even grown to mistrust Seru, in those weeks before the end.

She chuckled to herself, drawing sidelong glances from the other humans. She ignored them as she recalled that it had been while battling those Crushbone orcs that the seeds of her doubts for Seru had been born.

Delailith greatly respected Aataltaal, and like many

others who held him responsible for their lives and safe passage across the Ocean of Tears—all the while successfully gaining time so Emperor Katta could escape Seru's clutches—she almost revered him. But this one standout flaw of his left her unsure of his true motives.

Now, faced with representatives of a race that possessed civilization, culture, hopes, dreams, needs—in short everything that humans, especially those who arrived at Landing a few years ago, possessed—but so obviously fell short in comparison to their recently arrived foes, Delailith wondered whether she could hold the governor's derision against him.

In fact, didn't it make him even more commendable if he rose above that instinct, to act on behalf of the humans? Delailith doubted these orcs would ever be anything but an enemy to her, for in her lifetime at least they were unlikely to be swept completely aside. Given different circumstances, she doubted her ability to accept them as Aataltaal had his human friends.

The orcs growled some more among themselves. Two of them in particular, the ringleaders, had devised a strategy. Delailith was about to communicate to her soldiers—revealing her knowledge of orcish, if any orc in turn commanded the common tongue of humans— but one comment caused her to remain quiet for a few beats longer. One of those two orcs referred to the "commanders," with more emphasis than might refer to commanders in general, or so it seemed to Delailith. She got the impression that this battle was being inspected by these "commanders," and if there were more enemies near, Delailith needed to know how many and where, before they could spring a second surprise on her patrol.

Then the orcs taunted the humans in stock-phrases of poorly spoken common, drawing crude images of how the humans engaged their farm animals and even calling them "elf-slaves," which, given her earlier thoughts, made Delailith chuckle once more. This confused those nearest her again. A couple of men on the right flank grew edgy and seemed ready to unleash upon the orcs in response to these crude barbs.

"Steady," she whispered to her soldiers. "It's just what they want—to separate us, to break our formation. Then they'll pounce, and the chaos of *that* will favor them."

The same orcish leader, a half-head taller, twenty pounds heavier, and a shade of green darker than the others, kept his eyes on Delailith. He grinned, the gums on the gaps between his canines black and rotting, and said, "Kill them all, but leave the bitch alive. The half-breeds she'll birth will be larger than the lot of you put together!"

The orcs all guffawed at that.

Indignant, one of the soldiers began, "It said—"

"Silence in my ranks!" Delailith commanded. The soldier fell silent. Still, the secret was out.

"The humans understand Deathfist," one of the ring-leaders hissed in orcish. Many baleful eyes shifted to glare at both the young soldier and the woman who commanded the humans.

Even so, Delailith was both appreciative of the young man's chivalry and surprised to learn he knew orcish. He'd wisely bitten his tongue for a time, but the barbaric threat of capture and rape evidently overwhelmed his sensibilities. At the same time, Delailith didn't miss how he'd referred to the orc as an "it." Evidently, he shared her own ethnocentric estimation of these foes.

Now Delailith might never uncover the threat the "commanders" posed, but it was a moot point as the orcs, clearly seeing no more advantage to waiting, gripped their weapons and charged. The crude war cries rattled the air, but not the soldiers' nerves. Nor was Delailith distracted by any of it. Instead, she noted how the less vocal of the two orc leaders glanced nervously over his shoulder toward the upper rafters of the human-built barn that still stood largely undamaged on this land. Could this be the vantage of the "commanders"?

"Step and release!" shouted Delailith in Koada'Dal, the language she used for battlefield commands on her patrols. Some few orcs understood a smattering of the common tongue, but none yet displayed a glimmer of recognizing the language of the one-time masters of all this land.

In unison, her line of soldiers suddenly retreated two small, brisk steps. Then, instead of bracing their weapons for impact, they relaxed, remaining loose and ready to respond—a stratagem that required absolute confidence in a captain.

Executed at precisely the right moment, the sudden disengagement of their ranks left the orcs floundering instead of smashing into the line of soldiers as they expected. So the Deathfist orcs stumbled over one another, several losing their balance completely and sprawling into the scrubby grasses.

The humans reacted instantly because their relaxed postures allowed them that freedom. In an instant, every human sword was red with orc blood, while all the Deathfist weapons remained dry, which meant in that instant, the odds were very nearly equalized.

Again in high elvish, Delailith commanded, "Charge and hold!"

Usually she ordered the more cautious "Advance" at this stage, but these orcs so thoroughly blundered into the first formation that Delailith saw the opportunity to end the battle in a flash. The hold was an unusual addition, but none questioned her.

The humans cried their own battle oaths and vaulted forward even as a few of the orcs still struggled to recover their wits. Some Deathfist managed to defend and counterattack, but as their fellows fell, these few stalwarts were quickly outnumbered and cut down as well.

Delailith advanced toward the orc who'd eyed her as a concubine. Black lips quivered and his eyes went wild with fright. The woman warrior saw that he clearly wanted to retreat, but primal fear drove him forward—perhaps he feared reprisals from a commander. He wielded a wicked warhammer that he swung with some ability.

The first stroke whistled over Delailith as she ducked. The follow-up blow was delivered with enough skill that instead of again dodging and attacking to end the fight, Delailith was forced to parry. This clang of metal meant advantage orc, for his weapon far outweighed her sword and was swung with force. But the second sword on Delailith's hip was not merely for show. Though forced back a step, she twisted her parry to delay the orc's reset, while with her left hand she swiftly drew and struck with the other blade. The orc's eyes clouded in death while he looked mystified at the weapon tangled with his warhammer and surely wondered how the fatal blow could have been dealt.

Only four humans injured—and only lightly—and thirty ambushing orcs slain, but the soldiers did not cheer. They honored the "hold" command and stayed their celebration, awaiting another directive.

It came in an instant. Delailith said, "Lock down that building!" She pointed with both swords toward the barn. She'd never issued this command before in combat, and so shouted it in common for fear the men would forget the Koada'Dal words. But perhaps she need not have worried, for the command tapped the constant drilling the men had received, and so the soldiers executed it perfectly, each even recalling in which direction to circle the barn.

The soldiers sprinted, breaking ranks to surround the barn. Four men, each located approximately ninety degrees from the next around the perimeter of the barn, sheathed their swords and withdrew small arch-shaped talismans. These they brandished as if warding off some unseen evil in the sunset shadows that fell across the building.

Delailith approached cautiously, watching for any sign of motion from the barn. She concentrated on the upper level, but kept glancing at the great sliding door and two windows on the ground floor.

She was satisfied that they'd caught the unknown quarry. The talismans bore a remarkable resemblance to the great teleportation spires built for the Combine Empire by the geomancer Grieg—like the one where Delailith had fetched water for a striken Emperor Tsaph Katta. But where the larger spire was the terminus of roads between points that could be instantly traveled, these smaller shards instead kept all such doors closed. So long as these remained, the "commanders" within the barn could not magically transport themselves from the enclosed location.

The soldier to the right of each one who bore a spire shard broke rank and stepped to his comrade. These four held forth their shields to protect the shards and their bearers.

Delailith thought for a moment, then once again in Koada'Dal said, "Badger." The four soldiers not otherwise engaged at the cardinal points around the barn all cautiously approached the large sliding door at the barn's entrance. Like a badger that enters the tunnel of its prey, they were to methodically plumb the interior of the building.

Hopefully, the prey would flush and not fight.

JUST A HANDFUL OF YEARS SINCE THEIR LANDing here and already the remains of the Weille that the Teir'Dal race had commanded so long ago were largely covered or sloughed off into the sea. How they must now regret that they had not overrun and reclaimed this city in that great span of years when the pirates, lately under the command of Captain Danaan, roosted here!

But it was just as he hoped when, with Menthes' help, he had installed the pirates here, encouraging them to pester the Combine Empire. The dark elves surely saw those pirates as useful tools and so did not deem it necessary to oust them. And now a Koada'Dal had returned to these shores, with an army, and the city itself had become a free port for all the world: an *homage* to the unity Emperor Katta sought.

He couldn't restrain a chuckle. Someday, Aataltaal mused, that should be the city's name: Freeport.

"What's so funny, Aldred?"

The tousle-haired youth turned to those nearest him. Another wharf rat, a dark-complexioned boy named Gynok, was the one who'd spoken. Aldred liked the boy, but found something unreadable about him, and he was quickly falling in with the wrong crowd among the humans at the docks of Landing.

Aldred wondered how in the space of so few years things could already have grown so disorganized in this new city. Yes, boatloads of humans seeking relief and a place to call home still arrived every month from distant ports, and it was difficult to integrate them all, to find food, shelter, and succor for them all. But he wanted Landing to be a free port for men, so the humans came and found welcome.

He guessed some would always slip through the cracks, especially among a race that bred and spread so prolifically. But in Gynok's faltering steps, he could see the first signs of corruption that might lead to more ill in Tunaria than even what the dark elves of Neriak, so near to the north, could produce.

Aldred flashed a smile at Gynok and flipped his head so his long blond bangs did not hang over his eyes. He answered, "I was just thinking about how dumb we are to always be sitting here trying to catch fish with a string and a greasy lure, when we could travel out to Freefield or Nearfield and make a real living."

Gynok's faced scrunched up as if he'd eaten something sour. "Are you crazy?"

Those towns were partly intended to move this new human civilization in the right direction. The burgeoning population required food, and the sea could not provide all of it.

"Crazy? To get free land? And a place to live?"

Gynok shook his head, so far from being convinced that he didn't think it worth further discussion.

One of the older boys, within a year one way or the other of Aldred's apparent age, took up the conversation, though with a conspiratorial wink to Gynok. "Aldred, you dope, wise up. Why go out to the fields and spend your life farming and marry some fat old woman, when if we sit here long enough and maybe get a couple years older, we'll get to join Danaan's crew? Then we'll have money, adventure, and all the sweet ladies who want to spend the money and hear about the adventures!"

Aldred came here to learn precisely this kind of

thing. Danaan was supposed to steer clear of such recruitment, as part of the bargain that allowed the pirates to remain on the fringes of Landing, in many cases right below the city proper, in the vast subterranean tunnels of the old Teir'Dal city.

Aldred had hoped that the presence of a criminal underground from the very founding of Landing would dissuade other, less controllable ones from creating a foothold here. The deal for Danaan should have been perfect for the pirate: secret but official sanction to continue operations from a base in the protected harbor, in return for a promise not to spill their corruption onto the streets of Landing itself.

Any such agreement would naturally end following the death of Danaan—which meant it would not stand long because he was, after all, a human too—but it should still be in effect. That it seemed no longer to hold meant that Aldred had either miscalculated—a rare but not utterly impossible situation—or Danaan had been usurped in some fashion.

The man was not dead, for they'd spoken recently, but something else might have happened. Perhaps instead of assuming this guise of Aldred to keep the pulse of the city, he should have simply killed the pirate and become leader of both the city and its underground.

Aldred sighed.

"You *are* crazy," said the other boy, named Fenderin, "if *that* doesn't sound good to you." He shook his head, attached a piece of cloth soaked in drippings from somebody's last night's dinner, and tossed his line back in the water.

Aldred looked over his shoulder at the other nearby boys, looking at none of them in particular and so speaking to all of them.

"That's not the point. I'm talking about being your

own man. Join those cutthroats and you'll always be somebody's lackey. Maybe there aren't a lot of high times battling the soil instead of fighting the wind with a sail, but there's nothing so great about sitting on a dock fishing with garbage. And at least here and in the fields, you're your own boss.

"Plus," he added with a wink to lure Gynok back to his side, "there's always orcs to battle. It's not just farmers who get land in the fields, but those with a strong arm who can protect them."

Staring out over the swelling waters of the Ocean of Tears, then turning his gaze south of the docks to where the "secret" entrance to the pirates' lair was commonly known to be, Gynok sat silent for a moment. Then he said, "Yeah, that could work. I don't think I want to stay in this crummy port forever anyway, so maybe I should start by moving on a little bit."

"By Quellious, you both need a splash in the face," Fenderin said. At that, he tied his string to one of the stout posts of the dock, tipped forward, and fell like a dead man toward the cool waters below. At the last moment, though—so as not to scare the fish too far away, and also to prove to the others he was the best diver of the bunch—he turned the fall into a dive and sluiced with very little splash into the ocean.

This was why Aldred was among the wharf rats and not the leader of the pirates. Pirates going diving off the docks of Landing would draw attention; it would even lend credence to the fishmongers' tales of treasures buried in the bay.

No doubt some treasures waited underwater. After all, pirates had used this port for centuries. There were a number of wrecks below, and looters had salvaged only the most obvious valuables. Aldred knew as much, because he'd investigated many of the nooks and crannies of the decaying vessels and found amazing treasures, but hauling them to the surface would only attract the crowds he did not want.

What he *did* want was a spoke of wood, gilded in gold and set with a gem. When he heard of a bejeweled "wand" sighted in the harbor but lost to a clutching, youthful wharf rat's hand when the swell of the tide carried it beyond the boy's gasp of air, then Aldred had known his camouflaged place among the people of Landing was here among these orphaned boys and girls.

Besides, they had ears everywhere and served as conduit for all manner of rumors and fears.

Aldred tied his string as well. Then he backed up and made a run for the end of the dock. His last step was atop one of the posts, which allowed him to push high into the air. All the other kids loved to watch him do this, which he managed with a grace they never saw elsewhere in their dirty, humble existences. They did not suspect the twelve-year-old's ability was in truth the display of a being a millennium old.

With a balletic twist, Aldred seemed to suspend in the air for a beat, then he rolled and dropped like an arrow, soundlessly, wavelessly into the water.

Somewhere down here, he knew, waited part of Tarton's Wheel. The few spokes he'd found an age ago had been left in the safekeeping of the mostly collapsed tunnels of Weille that led to the lich-king's lair far beneath the land. These tunnels even the pirates did not approach, for the walls were unsteady to this day, vulnerable even to the tremble of a halfling's noiseless, patient footstep.

These tunnels he'd barely escaped, those many years ago. But he knew their secrets now, and his own most precious treasures lay hidden there.

But for now he would search for another of the ten

pieces. He knew one to be in the vicinity of Weille, which had been one major reason he had protected this harbor from his station as governor within the Combine Empire; but he had not realized it was in the harbor itself.

Now he circled back from the end of the dock and saw Fenderin kicking his way back to the surface, something in his hand, something small . . . a silver coin. Fenderin would not be seen fishing for the week as he savored the life such riches would bring.

At that thought, Aldred also kicked to the surface. His human lungs could not stand the exertion to which his mind wanted to put them. When his head popped above the water he heard the bragging above. Then he sank down again. Maybe a few extra eyes poking around the docks would not be such a bad idea, especially if he needed to leave soon. Better to go with the spoke in hand, even if it meant acquiring it more openly.

Also, he had an argument to win, and there was nothing as persuasive to humans, especially wharf rats like Gynok, as money.

Aldred kicked his way toward a barnacle-covered mound. He scratched his way around to the back of it and dug quickly into the sand, uncovering a small chest with one of the corners smashed in. A glint of silver shone within. Somehow one of these coins must have worked loose and rested on the harbor's floor until Fenderin found it. Aldred pulled out eight others, one each for the other five wharf rats and just enough of a majority for himself, so that he would not appear too generous.

Let them all eat well tonight—and maybe hear some tales to share with him next week.

If Aldred was still here to hear them next week.

———

WHILE THE FOUR SOLDIERS SLOWLY EDGED toward the large sliding door, Delailith carefully traced a path around the perimeter of the positions the other eight soldiers maintained. She gave close scrutiny to all four of the second-floor windows. At first glance each one seemed to be latched shut, but she thought she detected a flicker of movement from one, soon after she passed it. As it was a near-windless day, one of the stifling days in the arid terrain a bit too far removed from the more lush and fertile farmsteads nearer to Landing, the movement must have been man-made.

Or orc-made. Or perhaps something else.

"Badger, hold," Delailith shouted without looking back at those four soldiers who stopped a handful of paces shy of the sliding door.

The woman had a sudden taste of sour metal in her throat, a bit of nervous bile. Aataltaal had suspicions about the orcs, and for lack of evidence no one, including Delailith, put much merit in them. But now those suspicions were suddenly her own.

The lockdown was intended to strand "commanders" who might either themselves be orcish shamans or for ease of transport bear relics fashioned by the same, capable of simple teleportation spells.

But what if . . . ?

A barely audible murmur caught Delailith's attention, an oath, not the buzz of conversation.

"Turtle," she shouted reflexively. And just in time, too.

Each of the four pairs of soldiers spaced midway along each of the sides of the barn ducked and drew both their shields over themselves and Grieg's shard. The four individuals near the entrance of the barn likewise clustered and covered themselves with their shields.

Delailith stood poised, ready to react, swords in both

hands, watching both the second-floor shutters above the sliding door and the one to its right that she could also see. The shutters to the right flipped open and a lithe, shadowed shape flickered in smooth motion before the shutter was quickly drawn closed.

So fluid and quick was the motion that Delailith could not register what exactly the figure did, though a half-heartbeat later when a crossbow bolt exploded into splintered fragments about ten feet in front of her face, the woman knew the foe was an expert shot. Only her Captain's Charm had saved her. A gift from Aataltaal to all the unit captains, it was why Delailith did not seek cover at her own command. It only protected against two missiles before its magic required renewal, but typically, even if a foe persisted beyond one fruitless shot, he was seldom stubborn enough to try a third time.

Fortunately, there seemed to be only one crossbowman; if there'd been more, then the attack would have revealed it. As it was, a single crossbowman's best target was the enemy commander, or so the shot at Delailith seemed to make clear.

But this confirmed Aataltaal's suspicions: the Teir'Dal had a hand in the recent coordination of the Deathfist orcs. The slim, athletic silhouette could belong to few other races, and no race save perhaps a few dwarven experts had as much mastery with the crossbow as had the dark elves. And that was no dwarf in the barn!

If the dark elf thought it worth attempting a sniping shot, then it must also believe it had a good chance of escaping, otherwise why reveal its presence or the involvement of the Teir'Dal? In turn, that meant that others were likely inside, at least one of them potentially a wizard with knowledge of teleportation magic.

So the shards and the soldiers had to remain in place, and in danger. But this was a suddenly very important mission, an opportunity to capture a dark elf and give Aataltaal the proof he desired.

Retreating to the horses, Delailith shouted, "Badger, stampede." At that, the four soldiers near the barn's entrance slowly withdrew. When they moved, Delailith sprinted to her mount, suddenly afraid to leave those eight locked-down soldiers alone.

Delailith whistled to alert the horses, both so they'd be ready for her, and so she did not startle them. She untied her own and four others at random, then thought better of it and quickly slashed all the other reins with her sword. The horses whinnied a bit at that rough action, but they were well trained and generally held steady. Holding the five intact reins, Delailith mounted her own black-and-gray mare and punched it to a gallop. The reins she held tugged at the four others and soon all the horses bolted after her lead mare.

Her worries were borne out as she flew back toward the barn. The shutters opposite the one used by the crossbowman whipped open. Delailith could not see the figure because of her vantage, but she did see a robed arm reach from the building. A slender dark hand quivered snakelike from within the voluminous sleeve and with a flash that scarred Delailith's retina, the tip of the index finger lit brilliant red and shot that gleaming seed of smoke-trailing light at the soldiers who crouched turtlelike beneath their shields.

"Fire!" she shouted as she released the reins of the four horses and sharply veered her mare in the direction of the assaulted soldiers. The four other horses slowed to a canter and the eight trailing them did likewise, allowing the four "badger" soldiers each to grab the horse of his choice.

Delailith watched as the fiery seed of light shattered like glass upon the shield of one of the soldiers. Instantly, each of the tiny broken fragments blossomed into fire and the small area around the two soldiers roared into an inferno. Cries of terrible pain fluttered on the edges of the noise of the explosion itself.

Readying one of her swords, Delailith shouted, "Net!" Then she nudged her horse slightly so its momentum would be behind her attack and she launched her sword. It hurtled end over end at terrific speed and clipped the robed arm as it withdrew and the shutters clamped shut again.

A high-pitched, otherworldly shriek issued from the barn, and loud curses followed in a tongue so foreign that Delailith knew it must be Teir'Dal.

Delailith galloped along the broad side of the barn and turned left to loop back to the charred remains of the soldiers. To her right she saw the soldiers opposite the sliding door doing as instructed and moving in close to the barn. She completed the turn and, holding the saddle pommel tightly with her left hand, she flopped down along the right flank of the mare. The pounding hooves threw clouds of dust and clods of dirt into her eyes, but squinting she could see well enough. Perhaps too well, for as the mare bore down on the dead soldiers, Delailith could make out ivory-white bones shedding black, crisped flesh.

Fortunately, she was a tall woman, and her reach was commensurate. Amidst the tableau of black-and-white horror, she spied the shiny metal artifact of arches and grabbed it.

Evidently in the nick of time, for a moment later more curses sounded from within the barn. The pain of the wound her sword inflicted had given her just enough time to retrieve the artifact and complete the lockdown before the wizard recovered enough to try her spell of teleportation again.

Delailith rode close to the barn, slowed her mare to a half-gallop, and slid off the saddle while slapping the horse to continue on her way and perhaps disorient the dark elves as to their foe's actual location. She stumbled a bit and fell to the ground at this awkward dismount, but caught herself and suffered nothing but a few bruises. She stood and pressed her back against the barn and waited.

Three deep breaths as she recovered her wind before her earlier "stampede" command was implemented. She heard the barn door shatter and her now-mounted soldiers whooping as they plowed inside. At the noise, Delailith sprang back into action. She had to hold Grieg's device for it to function, so she clenched it in her teeth as she spun to face the barn. Two steps sideways and she reached the lower level window that, like those above, was shuttered.

With a booted toe she kicked the bottom of the shutter, forcing it inward a couple of inches and creating a toehold with just enough traction to launch herself higher, grabbing hold of the framework that ran around the barn at the height of the second level's floor. The ruckus created by the soldiers inside the barn gave Delailith confidence that she would be undetected, for she heard a horse whinny in pain and could hear the men shouting to one another, though she could not make out the exact words.

Her triceps strained and she pulled herself up. Delailith got her chin over the railing and, with the artifact still in her mouth as she breathed raggedly about its edges, she braced her chin there for additional support and she carefully let go with one hand. This she used snake-fast to pummel the shutter from which the wizard had attacked, then she again grabbed the frame just as her chin began to slip.

As she'd hoped, the shutter was not latched, so when she hit it, the casement shutter rebounded on its hinges and swung outward. A cacophony of noise blasted through the open portal, including that of the soldiers below, and a surprised exclamation voiced in Teir'Dal.

Delailith's arms burned with the effort of hanging like this. Even with her light armor, such suspension required a huge effort. But her reward came when a shadow passed near the portal; Delailith choked off her labored breaths and relaxed to motionlessness.

The shadow froze as well, and Delailith had the impression that one of the dark elves stood there, spying out the portal. Of course, all the elf could see was the pile of skeletons and ash produced by the wizard's spell, until reflexive curiosity got the better of the elf's caution, and the shadow shifted toward the center of the portal. At this movement, a soft whisper of preparatory incantation began as well, and Delailith realized it was the wizard.

The magical words trailed off as the wizard still saw nothing and then finally leaned out of the portal to look down. Delailith suddenly found herself face to face with a narrow-eyed menace. Mauve-skinned, the elf, like all the elven-kind, was beautiful. An intricately coiffed mane of white hair framed her delicately featured face, with silky-smooth skin, small intelligent-looking eyes, button nose, and pert, sensual lips. But this instant of placid beauty soured when the Teir'Dal saw Delailith, and the lovely features creased with wild madness and crazy-eyed malice. She screamed deafeningly and recoiled back into the barn—or tried to.

Too late, though. The human released one hand and shot it up, grabbing a handful of robe. Delailith heaved the dark elf out the open window.

The Teir'Dal's screams intensified as she fell, and she

clutched at Delailith's arm. Her strength sapped, Delailith lost her precarious hold and they tumbled down together.

Neither combatant could do anything more in the split-second that followed. The next thing Delailith registered was the dull crunch of her landing. Her forearm pounded into the wizard's stomach, for the Teir'Dal landed flat on her back with her head toward the outside wall of the barn, having almost completely flipped over during the fall.

A fountain of blood splashed from the wizard's mouth, and she groaned piteously, her eyes unfocused. Delailith grimaced. The arm she landed on was limp and felt heavy and on fire. She knew it was broken.

Likewise, looking down at the wizard, Delailith knew the dark elf's spine had broken upon impact. But the human could see the charred corpses of her two soldiers beyond the wizard's mostly still body, and any thought of mercy was washed away.

"I'll drag you broken and bleeding all the way to Landing, you dark elf witch," Delailith whispered hoarsely.

The wizard's torso and arms began to twitch. Her eyes went large and she hissed something in the dark elven tongue. Delailith could not understand the language, but the words were so broken and slurred that her inability mattered little. Aataltaal would have words with this woman.

It wasn't to be. With a whooshing of air, a crossbow bolt whipped past Delailith and plunged into the eye socket of the wizard. Without hesitation Delailith hit the ground and rolled toward the side of the barn.

Just in time, for the Teir'Dal crossbowman landed solidly at the spot she just vacated, then tucked into a roll. Even while he tumbled, the Teir'Dal reloaded his crossbow and he came to his feet facing Delailith.

He looked more assassin than archer. He wore black leather armor studded with dull yet still-purplish amethysts. Over his armor was a large cloak, the hood of which had fallen back during his descent and somersault. The elf himself looked like a personification of evil. Cruel mouth, cruel eyes, and large pointed ears that, because his head was shaved bald, looked at first glance like a demon's horns.

The Teir'Dal almost loosed the bolt at her, but he reconsidered and pivoted slightly to the right where a soldier appeared on horseback from the front of the barn. The soldier bore down on the dark elf, his mount throwing up great clods of dirt and grass as it accelerated to close with the demonic figure.

"Scramble!" Delailith yelled as loud as she could, hoping the locked-down soldiers around the barn would hear her.

One breath of patient hesitation and then the dark elf loosed his bolt. The soldier raised his shield to ward it off, but the bolt passed right through the wooden barrier and punctured the soldier's neck.

Delailith's eyes must have been wide with shock, for the dark elf glanced her way and cackled. Then as if the horse were his own and they'd practiced together countless times, the assassin nonchalantly stretched out a hand and, his hateful eyes fixed on Delailith, grabbed the saddle of the passing horse and flipped himself upon its back.

With this unfamiliar rider aboard, the horse tried to resist, but the dark elf took one of his crossbow bolts like a dagger and stabbed it into the horse's flank. At that, the horse careened across the savannah.

Two other mounted soldiers took off in pursuit. At the sound of pounding hoofs behind him, the dark elf then loaded another bolt and turned in his saddle, pointing the weapon behind him.

Wincing at the pain in her arm as she moved, Delailith shouted even louder than before, "Reform!" She would not lose another soldier to those magical bolts, though she wondered if, like her own charm that had limited use, the elf had but one or two such enchanted weapons and only hoped to scare off pursuit with the threat of more.

She also shouted with greater vigor partly so that the Koada'Dal word would ring clearly all the way to the dark elf's ears. She grinned with mock exaggeration in the direction of the dark elf and had to be satisfied when his own condescending smirk evaporated.

20

THE FURY OF THE THREE

THE INDUSTRY OF THE HUMANS WAS UNDENI-
able. Lean-tos quickly organized to become marked-
off plots where wooden buildings soon rose, only to be
replaced in some cases by piled stone or, more amazing
still, by quarried granite. Aataltaal found it hard to explain. Humans all around seemed to be in lines for hand-
outs, or searching for the means to slip a work detail, or
too old or too sick or too new to the city to have the
means to get along.

Yet the buildings continued to rise.

He smiled at the bustling streets. From his fourth-
story window, the highest point in the free port, he enjoyed watching the crowds. He caught himself then . . .
smiling. He seemed to indulge in such foolishness more
readily among these humans, which meant it might be
dangerous to remain among them too long. He never
before thought it possible to be distracted from his age-
old tasks, but now he would sometimes go hours at a time
overseeing the affairs of these people without dwelling
upon the horrors of his past.

Perhaps it was because, like each of them, he, too, was
different, one of the few who stood out as exceptional

among the merely excellent. After all, his was the race that defeated the dragons of old to claim Norrath for the bipedal races. There had only been three like him: the Three, prophesied never to fall in battle. Not never to fail—would that it had been so!—but instead simply never to fall.

The sounds of commerce and domesticity among the humans below faded from his thoughts as Aataltaal was drawn back many centuries to the abduction of the Koada'Dal king and queen.

Innoruuk had tricked them. Rather, he tricked their son. In some seductive guise, the Prince of Hate was on the verge of luring the young Koada'Dal prince through a portal directly to the Plane of Hate. Aataltaal never fully resolved to his satisfaction the truth of the vile god's goal, but he still suspected that events unfolded far better than Innoruuk had imagined possible, for King Naythox and Queen Chistianos presented themselves as substitutes for their son.

Why? Why both of them? Why didn't Naythox alone step forward? Aataltaal believed that Innoruuk would have leapt even at that opportunity. But both of them? In his mind's eye, Aataltaal could see Innoruuk nearly tripping over himself on the royal dais above which loomed the portal to Hate.

It was a deal the god could not decline.

And so he took the king and queen of the mightiest empire of Norrath to his home plane, where his power was near absolute. There, Innoruuk twisted, perverted, and tortured them, even remorselessly set them against one another so that they could become the embodiment of the hate that filled him—the hate he felt for Tunare, one of the three gods who had planted the seeds for many of the races of Norrath, without inviting Innoruuk to participate.

In the three hundred years that passed—centuries during which the Koada'Dal scrambled to uncover the secret of accessing the Plane of Hate, delving into every tome and tomb that even to them was half-forgotten—those brilliant beings, the shining examples of mortal life on Norrath, the Koada'Dal king and queen devolved into monsters, into the first Teir'Dal, the progenitors of most of the dark elves to follow.

Most.

A knock sounded at the door and Aataltaal shook off the cobwebs of the past.

"Yes. Enter," he said over his shoulder toward the door as he straightened himself and snapped his robe so it did not lie flat against his body, but instead spread voluminously about him.

So it began. He supposed it could seem like an ending, especially to the humans of Landing, but it would launch a bold new time for them.

"Delailith," said Aataltaal. "I've been expecting you."

The tall human woman smiled and shook her head as she stepped inside the spartan chamber. "Have you now?"

The warrior was still dusty from travel and her left arm hung in a sling obviously applied in the field and not yet addressed by the healers or priests of the city. Aataltaal liked the energy that pulsed around this woman. That she was a leader among humans none doubted, but the Koada'Dal sensed something more than that—a vitality that he knew meant she might serve him for some years to come. Perhaps even beyond her mortal years . . . but there was no call to scare her with that thought.

Still smiling a bit and with challenge in her voice, Delailith asked, "But, future-seeing elf, do you know what it is I bring you?"

Aataltaal shook his head slowly. "No," he admitted.

"But I know that I will find it very interesting and that it will lead to many things: a conversation that you, too, will find interesting, a circumstance that you may not find comforting, and perhaps a conclusion that will leave you questioning much of what has gone before."

Delailith's smile melted and she looked hard at the elf.

"No matter my efforts, you continue to trump me, Aataltaal."

"Exactly. I am glad you already begin to see my point."

Delailith hesitated another moment, and then chuckled. She turned back toward the open doorway to the hall beyond.

"Bring her in."

Two household guards entered, the first walking backward bearing the head of a stretcher. The slight figure on the palette was wrapped tightly, like a mummy, in the same field-dress bandages as Delailith's arm. She was plainly a woman, and she was clearly dead, for an arrow was planted in her eye.

"Ah, I see . . ." Aataltaal began, clearly prepared to say more, but first he motioned the guards from the room. At their hesitation, the Koada'Dal said, "Anywhere."

The guards placed their burden on the floor and briskly retreated from the room.

"Elisha Goldbloom. Or . . . Lady Defyr."

A slight hint of sadness tinged the elf's voice, but Delailith didn't catch that. The other surprise won her attention.

"You know this Teir'Dal?"

"Yes, I do. The reason will be clear soon enough."

"My patrol discovered her in the company— probably the command—of a band of orcs near Freefield. There was another dark elf as well, but he escaped."

Aataltaal looked up from the face of the dead Teir'Dal. "He?"

Delailith nodded. "Yes. This one was a wizard—though perhaps you knew that, too?—while the other was a warrior, a crossbowman."

"Ah, yes, Xerxis."

Delailith shrugged, clearly hoping the Koada'Dal would tell her more.

Aataltaal said, "The good news is you've brought the proof I need to convince the people of Landing of the danger that will march on them. The bad news is that the involvement of these particular Teir'Dal means another, very powerful sorceress is involved. Her name is Opal Darkbriar, but as you will learn about me as well, she has gone by many other names. You will know of her most recently as Rashalla."

"The witch who controlled the birds and pursued us with Seru?"

"Yes. I did not know where she went during these past few years, but I knew she plotted against Landing. Plotted against me."

Aataltaal looked resolutely at Delailith's face. "You see, young lady, you and others here may count me as a blessing for Landing, but many troubles from the past pursue me as well."

"It doesn't—" Delailith began, but Aataltaal cut her off with a raised hand.

"Thank you, but you may not be so quick to leap to my defense once I have shared more of this with you. Please attend to your wound and return here in an hour, and we shall talk some more."

Delailith did not move at first, but the Koada'Dal added, "One hour. In the meantime, I must have words with this lifeless enemy." He motioned at the corpse of Lady Defyr. "I assure you, it's something you'd rather not witness."

Delailith nodded and slowly left the chamber.

Aataltaal knelt beside the tightly wrapped body of the Teir'Dal wizard. He looked at her face for a long moment. Like a flashback, memories flared from one of their past times together. Despite many years of strict, sometimes obsessive cleansing, perhaps some trace of the exotic, intoxicating drugs did still reside in his body. Either way, his head swam for a moment with disorienting blurs of neon, spine-chilling cackles of pleasure, and the sense-shattering crack of the whip. It had been how Defyr made love. No, not love—copulated. Nothing among the Teir'Dal of Neriak could be called love. Fortunately, once was always enough for her, and she moved to the next partner. Unfortunately, Aataltaal had smitten the she-devil in two guises.

Well, three if he counted Takish-Hiz. But she'd been different then, as well. It still had not been love, but the pleasure at least had been shared.

The Koada'Dal slowly pulled the crossbow bolt from the wizard's eye. Dried from days on the road, the orb crackled and flaked at the extraction. Then the living elf drove the bolt into the corpse's other eye.

He'd rather she be unable to see him as they spoke. It would be easier for them both that way.

THE ORCS WERE MARCHING.

It didn't surprise anyone, though, because Aataltaal had warned them, and the people from the fields rushed ahead of the advancing orcs, though in some places mere hours separated them.

However, few others knew as much as Delailith did.

About Opal Darkbriar, a dark elf witch whose obsession to destroy Aataltaal now conveniently aligned with Neriak's need to crush the infant human civilization at Landing before it grew any stronger. About the Divine Rage, a perfidious organization that spread mischief and corruption from the tunnel under Landing where they'd either ousted or taken control of the pirates. About Weille, the dark elven city that used to stand where Landing did now, but was obliterated by Aataltaal himself when he led an exodus—the reverse of the ones the humans made scant years before—of ragtag elven survivors of Takish-Hiz to safety in Faydwer.

About Aataltaal himself, who admitted to Delailith some of the roles he'd played in recent years, including that of the orcish shaman she'd encountered within the walls of Crushbone.

She also knew something of the Koada'Dal's forthcoming plans, of the trap he was setting and how he was empowering Danaan and the pirates to fight back the Divine Rage shadowknights who invaded the tunnels below the city.

And of the rod he'd given to her. The rod of command, he called it, a device he never cared to use, but which would allow Delailith to keep the peace in Landing in the years immediately following the events of the long night ahead.

Aataltaal had promoted her to general for this battle. Humility begged her to decline, but she knew no other more capable, so she accepted. She only regretted that it kept her from the elf's side in these last hours before the battle, though those she trusted most would see to him. He'd set out the plans, but it was up to Delailith to execute them with a ragtag army of humans, bolstered by a few crews of seasoned warriors from the patrols like hers.

All this against an orcish army that numbered in the hundreds and was supported by dark-elven wiles, steel, and magic.

It would be on this night that the city of Landing would either live or die.

THE ONES WHO DIDN'T WARN HIM AGAINST BE-ing near the impending battle wondered why he would not engage directly. His magical powers, rumored to be vast, would surely serve the army of Landing well. These same doubters, and there were few, in the end were satisfied by his presence near the field of battle, where it seemed he could assist the humans wherever the orcs might break through.

"Nothing short of razing Landing will satisfy them," Aataltaal warned the assembled humans when he introduced Delailith as the people's general. "Orcs care nothing for the houses of men and would rather dwell here upon the heaps of rubble from the collapsed buildings."

Now surrounded by an assortment of pages, messengers, and other assistants on the periphery of the battle, Aataltaal appeared prepared to maintain central command of Landing's defense even while Delailith led the battle directly. Appearances could be deceiving, though, and Aataltaal had absolutely no plans to participate in any battle, except that which came to him.

Relinquishing command to the human woman was necessary, both to make himself accessible to assassination, but also to put a human face at the head of the human army. Aataltaal could not remain bound here. The humans were becoming too dear to him, and they too reliant upon him.

As dusk fell to darkness, in the distance Aataltaal could see the swaggering orcish horde. Among them rode the black-armored elves on nightmare stallions: the dark elf shadowknight commanders. Aataltaal wondered if there were any among those Teir'Dal whom he did not know. How many more would die tonight—some by his very hand—to add to the tally of those he failed to redeem?

He had made a different choice, but he knew where the power of the gods was concerned, free will was not a given, and these elves could not be held accountable for their actions—at least, not in his eyes.

Still, a line was drawn, and if his ancient kinsman passed it, then they would have to die so that he might continue his fight for the others. He wanted to lift his head to the heavens and say a prayer so that Tunare might bless the coming events, but he could not force a sound. Still, a woman spoke to him, for suddenly, a clear, steady, feminine voice called out from the darkness.

"So concerned with the future that you're not mindful of the present, Aataltaal?"

Aataltaal turned to the side, back toward Landing, and away from the oncoming orc army. Torches and lanterns that burned on the low walls around the still-mostly makeshift city silhouetted a host of figures so slender as to seem almost skeletal. In truth, there actually were some black-boned skeletons among this host, but they were not as ghastly as the dark-clad Teir'Dal outfitted in demon masks or blood-stained robes. And none was as ominous as the forward-most figure, a female elf actually shapely enough to be called buxom. Her seductive allure was not limited to her obvious femininity: her posture and the depth of her voice spoke of vast experience, and the leather-clad and -collared skeletons that escorted her on either side lent an air of empowerment that many Teir'Dal males ached to test.

The Koada'Dal recognized her. "Opal Darkbriar."

The servants that milled around Aataltaal scurried behind him, though two brave messengers remained a few paces before him.

Opal Darkbriar grinned, the brilliant white of her teeth shining between lips painted iridescent purple. "Quite a hovel you've made for yourself these past years, my old foe." She swept her hand toward Landing, like a hostess revealing dinner for a welcome guest.

Instantly, her seductive exterior evaporated, and the hateful heart of the Teir'Dal was revealed. She snarled, "I did not think you could sink so low to live not only like a beast, but among them as their master! You must dream at night, wishing that I'd slain you centuries ago so you would not endure so demeaning an existence."

"Hate sustains you still, Opal?" He looked at her sadly, though well aware of how those behind the woman slavered at the pull of her animal magnetism. "Yes, my time among the humans has made me weaker. The proof of it is that I am not hesitant to share that in front of them. But they have given me perspective as well. Glimpses into the struggles of the everyday not possible in the grandeur of ancient Takish-Hiz—"

Opal Darkbriar snarled at the name. She cleared her throat and spat blood upon the ground.

The Koada'Dal continued, "—or when I promised my life be given solely to the pursuit of redeeming the evil for which you and your monstrous lord Innoruuk stand."

"So many weak emotions in you. We remain baffled as to why Hate does not wipe them aside and find anchor in your soul." Opal Darkbriar shook her head with a look as much of astonishment as horror.

"Know you this, then, Opal Darkbriar. This time of reflection and discovery has granted me a moment of peace, a moment of clarity. The humans do have secrets even our ancient race has not tapped. There are wise men among them, monks, who have developed a sense of what they call 'no-mind.' It describes the sense of being in the center of a storm, where it is calm, and all about you is chaos, madness. This is something I have learned from them, and I have this sense now."

Opal Darkbriar cackled. "Oh, there is chaos aplenty here. Your human armies may cut down the orcs we hurl at your city, but you've left yourself unprepared." She gestured at one extremely obese man in the Koada'Dal's company by way of proof. "And without its head—you—this city will fall. If not this night, then one very, very soon."

"Not for a hundred years or more, I think," Aataltaal said calmly. Then, with a poisonous challenge growing in his voice, he added, "Not long really, but long enough for the flesh to rot from your bones."

The Teir'Dal screamed and flailed wildly. Without further warning, a swarm of crossbow bolts sprang from the dark elves behind Opal Darkbriar. All of them targeted Aataltaal. And they all found their mark, yet none pierced his flesh. Where each razor-sharp tip struck him, the Koada'Dal enchanter's skin flared with a spot of translucent green as his arcane second skin shielded him from harm.

Then, as the Teir'Dals' skeletons sprinted forward on creaking bones, the "pages" and "servants" who milled behind Aataltaal shed their plain, disguising robes. Almost to a person, the dozen humans with the Koada'Dal were revealed as wizards and priests in their ornate cloaks and robes bedecked with magically inscribed talismans, enchanted baubles, and arcane accoutrements.

One of the figures beside Aataltaal rushed forward, sweeping past the skeletons. As it ran through the ranks of the Teir'Dal, the illusion that cloaked it washed away to reveal an animate guardian of Aataltaal's. Its blades quickly slashed the flesh of the crossbowman unfortunate enough to have landed the first bolt on its master.

Opal Darkbriar's flailing frenzy ceased immediately. She no longer possessed so clear an advantage as to revel so soon. "A trap!" she shrieked.

The large man whom Opal previously mocked as proof of Aataltaal's unpreparedness stepped forward. "Now she's got the hang of things," Nestor laughed. He raised a thick-fingered hand and a blast of fire that roared past Aataltaal, toward a half dozen opponents, including Opal Darkbriar, but the blaze bent around her as if held in check by an invisible spherical barrier. Still, it engulfed several others, leaving one Teir'Dal smoking and Darkbriar's two skeletons lit by crimson flames.

Among the wizards were also Ilzathor and Altan, the same two who had stood by the Koada'Dal's side when he engaged Seru in the Ocean of Tears. As with Nestor and the others here, they'd benefited greatly from years of instruction at Aataltaal's feet; and a fierce desire to vanquish a dark threat to their new home fueled the mana that wrought their spells.

From the low walls where the Teir'Dal themselves emerged, a lone archer fired arrows with pinpoint accuracy into the ranks of the dark elves. The Teir'Dal doused themselves in shadow and traveled by secret tunnels, but Evanis' ranger skills allowed her to hide unnoticed in broad daylight. Nightfall only made it easier.

"Close with them, you *fools*," Opal Darkbriar raged as smoke that glowed red in the night seeped from her fingertips and drifted near to her mouth. She inhaled the magic and then loosed a feral scream that caused all of the humans nearby to clasp their ears.

"Oh, blast!" said Troy, one of the two men who stood in front of Aataltaal, and one of only two humans present who wielded steel. His sword wavered in his hand, unresponsive even as dark-elven shadowknights and black-boned skeletons bore down upon him. He turned and saw that even Aataltaal was staggered by the maddening noise. The Koada'Dal's rapier also hung loosely in his hand.

From the corner of his eyes, Troy could see Cadmus straining at the sound as well, except the bard's battle was not physical. Though his eyes were closed and he dropped his weapon, the bard's mouth was wide open. At first, Troy could hear—could sense—nothing but Darkbriar's insanity-inducing cacophony, but slowly an angelic murmur welled up against it. Just in time Cadmus' song rose to the fore, an aria of cleansing that overwhelmed Opal Darkbriar's untrained though magically empowered voice.

Still, the blades of three foes were on the verge of skewering Troy. Then, like magic, they were gone—but not by the arcane. Aataltaal's steel flashed like a serpent, and in three separate maneuvers that seemed like one blazing motion, the steel turned aside steel.

Troy gaped. He'd never witnessed anything like it.

"You forget yourself, Opal Darkbriar," Aataltaal hissed through his teeth. "Do you no longer believe the old prophecies?"

The Koada'Dal's rapier rattled then with the blades of the six foremost opponents, including two who threatened Cadmus. Aataltaal struck at seven blades, though, for with glancing blows he maneuvered Troy's sword to areas Aataltaal could not reach without overextending himself. Troy watched in fascination as his own sword leapt and whirled in a more skillful defense of himself than he could have mustered alone.

The foes before Troy were as unreal as the battle to which he was a spectator: three skeletons with thick, black bones to which hung tiny morsels of desiccated flesh. These creatures moved with an uncanny athletic grace that, if anything, outstripped the effort of their three dark elven shadowknight masters. These warriors, whose prowess was said to come partly through communion with the dead, wore black armor detailed with crimson leather. Their helmets looked like the skulls of the bone-men that fought beside them, and indeed the six together fought almost as one.

As if telling him to snap to, Aataltaal's next parry and redirection of Troy's sword set the man up for an incapacitating blow. Troy's instincts recovered and he lunged, skewering a chainmail-clad shadowknight between his belly and groin where a slight region was unarmored. When the dark elf slumped, the wall of steel the six together created faltered. In the briefest hesitation, Aataltaal's rapier whipped murderously and struck the Teir'Dal's head off. In the same instant, the skeleton that battled beside the dead shadowknight loosed a voiceless scream and fell into dust.

Behind this faltering forward force of skeletons and shadowknights, Opal Darkbriar staggered back a few paces. Her other forces pressed the attack of the wizards, as few of the Teir'Dal could circumvent Aataltaal's electric confrontation.

Aataltaal saw her inching back. "Oh, no, Opal Darkbriar. This time we see this through. Do not move!" He raised his hand and heat waves visible even in the low light of night washed over his Teir'Dal nemesis. Her face contorted in an effort to break the magic, but she failed, and so was swiftly and forcefully pulled to the ground, stuck there as if gravity had special hold over her.

However, loosing this magic opened the Koada'Dal to the attacks of the foes he'd previously stymied. While

EVERQUEST: OCEAN OF TEARS • 333

one skeleton struck mindless at Cadmus, the two remaining shadowknights and a skeleton nearest Aataltaal all smote him with their blades. The first two bounced off his protective magic, the flashes of wan green light illuminating the ghastly attackers. The third, though, was only partly stopped. The green light that flared did so weakly, and the shadowknight's sword left a bleeding gash on Aataltaal's neck where he had aimed a decapitating blow.

Aataltaal's eyes flashed with anger, and he pivoted to regard the Teir'Dal who wounded him. "Have you not fought at my side in ages past? I know your fighting style, Jeleb Ashray, even if I no longer recognize your countenance or the name you call yourself in the hell pits of Neriak! One million swords could not now stand between yourself and the dark god you have chosen to be your father, rather than still calling me brother.

"Go to him now," commanded the Koada'Dal. "Go remind Innoruuk that I will not stop until he undoes his foul work or until his demolished spirit has been vanquished and can no longer meddle in the affairs of Norrath."

With that, Aataltaal launched attacks the likes of which had not been seen since the days when the empire of Takish-Hiz subdued the last dragons of Norrath.

Upon the ground, scarcely able to move by dint of the magic fetters that weighed her down, Opal Darkbriar saw it all as well. The images burned into her mind's eye and there they would propagate countless acts of retribution.

Even Cadmus, witness to this awesome display, and who would in later years become a loremaster without peer, would never have the command of words as did this elf of his blade. He would recount the facts, but not as clearly as he would relate the myths. Such as how Aataltaal was one of "The Three"—the greatest of all Koada'Dal warriors, prophesied never to fall in battle. And how with Aataltaal's disappearance, the fate of all Three was unknown.

But Cadmus would never aim for more than a cursory description of how the mighty Koada'Dal hero waded through the assembled Teir'Dal host and cut them down, calling out to them as they fell, using the names of old that they might have forgotten or at least sought to hide. Sascha Rivermane. Palentir Embereyes. Daedus Waverider. And many, many more, until at the last all were dead.

All except Opal Darkbriar.

By the time Aataltaal turned to her, she'd already cast her last treacherous spell, her baleful gaze turned to Troy, who instead of fighting sought to aid the human wizards injured prior to Aataltaal's onslaught.

So, when the Koada'Dal stepped to Darkbriar, he did not suspect danger when Troy and the other survivors closed ranks behind him. Sweat, blood from a dozen minor wounds, and tears all wept from Aataltaal. Only his eyes echoed the emotion of his tears, though, for his face was still stoic, resolute.

He looked upon Opal Darkbriar and said, "Now, Felicia Morningsong, your part in this drama may finally conclude."

"How dare you call me by that name?"

Aataltaal did not respond; he flicked his rapier upright and then—

An arrow raced past his ear. The wooden shaft splintered as it struck steel and the Koada'Dal, alerted to a threat, whirled around, his rapier deflecting a strike at his heart delayed just enough by the wooden missile. His battle-rage welling again, Aataltaal struck back.

But his sword, too, was turned aside when another

arrow rattled against it. Aataltaal saw then that the assassin was a dull-eyed Troy.

"Whoa, what magic is this?" Nestor sprang forward, knocking a few others aside as he grappled Troy in a great bear hug.

Aataltaal looked back to Landing, from whence both arrows originated. Evanis stood there, another arrow already taut against her bow. She relaxed and nodded to the Koada'Dal.

Whatever her true goal, this drama granted Opal Darkbriar time enough to escape. When Aataltaal turned to her again, she'd managed to wriggle one hand to a medallion at her neck. Its mirrored surface clouded and the Teir'Dal laughed even as Aataltaal's sword plunged through her dark heart.

"Too late, Xanit K'Ven . . ." Darkbriar's voice trailed off toward the end because even as her flesh shuddered in its final throes of life, a ghostly double of the Teir'Dal witch separated from the body. Then, as if inhaled by the earth, she disappeared.

Troy's eyes regained the sparkle of sentience, and he looked around at the beleaguered humans. "Hey, what happened? What did I miss?"

Cadmus stepped forward to face Aataltaal. "That name? It's not like the ones you shouted as you killed the dark elves."

Aataltaal looked weary. With his toe he nudged the lifeless corpse of Opal Darkbriar. Then he looked at Cadmus. The eyes that always seemed so soulful, so reflective of the Koada'Dal's inner turmoil, were cold and dead, and Cadmus shuddered.

"Never repeat it," Aataltaal warned. "Ever. Nor write nor speak of what I will tell you now. If you do, if any of you do, then you shall have failed my trust, much as these Teir'Dal, whom I have slain."

He then turned to face the surviving humans. He nodded to each in turn, acknowledging the fact that they lived and, in so doing, that some had died. "I called my foes by their original names, the Koada'Dal names that they were given when they dwelled in Takish-Hiz, which once lay to the south in what is now desert. It is thus they were called before they, like I, sought to engage the god Innoruuk so that he might return to us our king and queen, whom he abducted. We failed."

Aataltaal looked past the humans for a moment, to the battle that raged with the orcs.

"In so doing, we were undone by the same foul magic that claimed our king and queen. They had become Teir'Dal, the first of that race. Their pure skin and innocent souls were befouled as they became the progenitors of the race that will forever threaten Landing. The others of us . . . we, too, were 'changed.' "

At that, Aataltaal waved a hand gently before him, and an illusion like so many others rippled across his features, transforming him into a dark elf. The crowd of humans could not help but gasp, for it was indeed a terrible transformation. Aataltaal now bore the icy mien of a Teir'Dal, and his eyes were still cold, distant. His skin was pitch-black, and shockingly white hair streamed to his shoulders.

"This is the person Opal Darkbriar named. Unfortunately, unlike all my guises that you have seen before now, such as that of Emperor Katta, this is my true self. Yes, even the Koada'Dal governor of the Combine Empire who first earned your trust and became ruler of Landing for a time was a disguise."

He looked again past them to the battlefield, this time focusing on something much nearer. But the assembled humans were too shocked to take note.

"Now I take my leave of you, as you humans must find your own way. I do not regret my charade, for I cannot, as I have done its like for ten times your lifetimes, but I find I do not have the heart to deceive you any longer."

He then walked toward them and they parted to let him through, a bit from fear and a bit from respect. And as they stepped aside, they saw Delailith upon her horse near to them all, where she overheard at least the last revelation.

She said, "My lord, one thing you did not tell me."

"Yes?" Aataltaal stopped between her and the others who were now all behind him.

"What was *your* first name?"

The Teir'Dal chuckled: an eerie sound, for some of the ringing joy of the Koada'Dal was replaced by the mirthless annoyance of a dark elf.

"I was called Aataltaal Nightbane."

Then he walked past her, sparing not a glimpse for Delailith nor any of the humans whom he departed.

NEAR HER, THE OTHER HUMANS IMMEDIATELY set to whispering among themselves. But Delailith watched the troubled dark elf carry his burdens away from her city. She no longer envied him his long life, his magical heritage, his vast wisdom. She no longer worried if she was anything more than a mote passing quickly through the elf's life.

"Aataltaal?" she called out. She was pale and nervous, her voice hesitant.

The other humans quickly quieted.

At first the Teir'Dal continued to walk, but then he stopped and turned.

Delailith said, "You say you are Teir'Dal, anathema to us—a dark elf who for many years gained our trust as a high elf."

Aataltaal nodded, accepting the indictment.

Delailith continued, her tone more certain now. "But what were you before? Before you tried to rescue those you loved in the land of the Prince of Hate?"

Aataltaal looked at her for a moment. And then a great load seemed rendered weightless when he said, "I was Koada'Dal."

Delailith smiled. "And so shall you always be to us."

EPILOGUE

THE KOADA'DAL OF INNORUUK

THE TALL, LITHE FIGURE RODE SILENTLY IN THE shadows at the edge of the orc army. He was dark-skinned, like the frightened, wounded orcs that lumbered from the battlefield, but there the similarities ended. Where the orcs were gnarled despite their relative youth, the elf was smooth as polished ebony and . . . far, far older.

Though it was midnight and though the landscape was devastated by battle, a bright light illuminated the area. Luclin shone in the sky, and the elf wondered if it was a sign that the Combine Empire, like the city still known as Landing behind him, was safe.

They had reached Luclin. That much he knew of those who traveled with Katta, though he'd heard nothing since their departure and had for a time feared them lost, trapped, or dead on the fickle goddess's orb.

His nightmare stallion was anxious to return home to the gated city of Neriak, but Aataltaal forced it to slow. Orcs complained as they rounded the steed, but not too loudly, lest the dark elven lord smite them for their audacity.

"Are you hurt?" hissed a plate mail–clad dark elven

vixen who galloped back to him. Her voice held the offer of succor, but also revulsion at his show of weakness.

"Guard your tongue, witch, else I add it to my trophies," Aataltaal snarled back.

The cleric of Innoruuk smiled and maneuvered her steed closer. With strong, delicate fingers she grasped his thigh and moved her hand higher. "I anticipate your visit to the temple to display your trophies." Then she kicked her own stallion and it hurtled back into the thick of retreating orcs, trampling one of them as she went.

Aataltaal shook his head. Was he really returning to such a life? Regrettably, it was the obvious next step.

As the army of orcs and dark elves left him farther behind, the elf dressed as a Teir'Dal necromancer looked back at the faint lights of Landing. Even with his miraculous eyesight, he was too far away to make out much detail, but shadows continually passed before the lanterns at the front gate, so the human army was filing back into the city.

Had he finally ended the cycle of empires brought to ruin? Not just Takish-Hiz, but more just within the past handful of years. Shadow-Keep. Even the Great Combine Empire itself.

But Takish-Hiz most of all.

No common element linked these civilizations except himself.

Aataltaal sighed. That wasn't true. He was the only recurring mortal component, but the gods that had looked down upon the Norrath of Takish-Hiz were the same that glared this eve in Luclin's sinister light.

In any event, it was too soon to say. For now, for a thousand years, for an entire age even, Landing might endure. However, Aataltaal judged things in a different time frame entirely. If Landing fell in five hundred years, was it any different than falling now? Did this seeming victory have any meaning whatsoever? Or did it merely stay the darkness a bit longer?

Was mortal life akin to nothing but running farther and farther downstream, erecting dam after dam against the onrushing flow of evil? What happened when the river came to an end? Or was there a blessed ocean awaiting—one not filled with tears of despair—and life only needed to persist until that journey reached completion?

Aataltaal still did not know the answers to such questions. Living throughout so much time should have afforded more perspective, when instead it just seemed to enmesh him in a larger, more complex tapestry.

The humans of Landing had become his friends, but now he abandoned them. He told himself it was for their own benefit, that he would only put them at risk, and that from afar he could do more to protect them, unseen, than if he were among them. He told himself that with him leading them, they would never grow into their own.

And grow they could. The Combine Empire proved as much, though it was here and gone in the blink of an eye, to his thinking. Still, within that span, dams were built that might staunch the flow of the gods, or even— with magic like Grieg's that allowed travel to Luclin's home; or Tarton's Wheel that he believed could grant him passage to the true home of the gods—reverse the course of the river itself.

Aataltaal looked around at the foothills of the Rolling Hills, and beyond to the dark embrace of Nektulos Forest. Content that no else would see, Aataltaal rode back to the thick of the savannah that surrounded Landing and led to the fields.

He reached to his neck, where a small pouch hung from a silver cord. Within it rested two acorns, one each from the trees at the sites of passed elven strongholds. He withdrew one at random, not really caring which. To prove it, he did not look at the acorn and he resisted the temptation to feel its surface with care. It came either from the Faydark where Shadow-Keep once stood or from the great forest of Takish-Hiz itself. If such was fate, then the humans of Landing deserved even the latter.

He dropped it to the ground and a stream of green glitter flared in its path. He heard the acorn bounce and roll to a stop and then his sensitive ears heard it burrow into the ground. It would require long, long years, but the oak that grew here would fall to no woodsman's axe, nor to any bolt of lightning. It would persist, and a forest begins with a single tree.

He looked at Landing, and solemnly said, "May you walk among trees."

He knew no better blessing.